Los Gusanos

A N O V E L

JOHN SAYLES

A hardcover edition of this book was published in 1991 by Harper-Collins Publishers.

LOS GUSANOS. Copyright © 1991 by John Sayles. All rights reserved. Printed in the United States of America. No part of this book may be used or reproduced in any manner whatsoever without written permission except in the case of brief quotations embodied in critical articles and reviews. For information address HarperCollins Publishers, Inc., 10 East 53rd Street, New York, NY 10022.

HarperCollins books may be purchased for educational, business, or sales promotional use. For information, please call or write: Special Markets Department, HarperCollins Publishers, Inc., 10 East 53rd Street, New York, NY 10022. Telephone: (212) 207-7528; Fax: (212) 207-7222.

First HarperPerennial edition published 1992.

Designed by Helene Berinsky

The Library of Congress has catalogued the hardcover edition as follows:
Sayles, John, 1950–
    Los gusanos : a novel / John Sayles. — 1st ed.
      p. cm.
    ISBN 0-06-016653-3 (cloth)
    I. Title.
    PS3569.A95G87 1991   90-55892
    813'.54—dc20

ISBN 0-06-092159-5 (pbk.)

92 93 94 95 96 NK/RRD 10 9 8 7 6 5 4 3 2 1

This novel is a work of fiction. Any references to historical events, real people (living or dead), and actual locales are used solely to lend the fiction its proper historical setting. All other names, characters, and incidents are fictitious, and any resemblance to actual persons or events is entirely coincidental.

MIAMI 1981

ONE

MARTA SITS BY the Virgin of Charity, waiting for the men to decide. She has never seen any of them, not that she knows of, although there are rumors. She thinks they are probably all men. Marta palms dust off the Virgin's head. She sits stiffly in a hard wooden chair across from San Francisco in his brown cassock, across from one of the Magi bearing incense, from San Cristóbal with the Infant hugging his neck. Another Virgin rises behind Marta, eyes to Heaven, her bare foot crushing a snake.

Señora Luque is in the rear of the shop, beyond the sunlight, with the African masks and santería idols. Marta hears her turning the statues this way and that, scolding them in a soft voice as if they had moved out of place overnight without her permission.

The waiting is like the waiting before Confession. Remembering her sins, preparing her words for Padre Martín. They'll let her in, she thinks. They'll accept her. She feels the same weight in her chest, the heavy black liquid she always carries into the confessional booth. They'll let her join, she prays.

Marta sits by the Virgen de Caridad, waiting. The Virgin's face is peaceful, there are roses in her hands. Behind Marta another Virgin spreads her arms in blessing, eyes to Heaven, her bare foot crushing a snake.

"Bueno. Y la muchacha?"
The faces of the men are shrouded behind cigar smoke.
"No la conozco."
"Her father is in the stroke ward. He was a good one."

"De la Pena?"

"Scipio. He was a good one."

"Her brother is that Blas. El droguero. Who went to Tampa."

"Somebody should cut his fucking throat."

They sit on food crates pushed into a half circle. Rufo stands behind. In a month, he hopes, maybe two, he'll be sitting with them.

"Qué sabe de nosotros?"

"Only what she's heard. The ones who come to Señora Luque's have only heard the rumors."

"What can she do for us?"

One of the men makes a noise.

"Nothing we can't do for ourselves."

Rufo wonders if he should speak. He wonders which of them pulled the trigger on the boy that morning. They had decided on it the last time they met, but no date had been mentioned, no one picked for the hit. There were decisions that weren't made at the meetings.

"Qué vamos a hacer con ella?"

"Ignore her. She'll fade away."

"Y si no? If she does something on her own?"

"We can't stop a patriot."

One of the men laughs.

Rufo feels sick. The storage room is hot. There are plastic bags of bean sprouts against one wall, and one of them has burst with slick, rotting sprouts that spill out onto the floor. There are bunches of green plátanos with tiny flies whizzing above them and fresh yuca and over everything a heavy blanket of cigar smoke. Above them the big industrial dishwasher moans and rattles the floor. Rufo takes a deep breath.

"I knew her in high school," he says. "She was a quiet one. The nuns thought she might have the calling."

It is hard to see the eyes of the men through the smoke.

"Qué vamos a hacer con ella?" says one of them, yawning.

The boy was shot on West Flagler, just above the high school, on the route Señora Luque walked to her shop every morning. The ambulance had gotten there first. Two men in white sat on the stretcher on the sidewalk, smoking, waiting for the police. Another in white searched the little patch of grass in front of a travel agency for something, a blue plastic bag in his hand. Tiny lizards hopped away from his feet as he searched. The boy was spread out belly to the sidewalk in a puddle of what had come out of him. They had folded a sheet and placed it so it covered only his head. Señora Luque wished they had covered the rest of him. She didn't like the way his feet turned out at right angles to his knees like a ballet dancers. She had crossed herself and walked on the other side of Flagler to the shop.

Señora Luque wishes the girl would go away.

"Señorita," she calls, indicating the clock on the wall, "son las once."

"That's okay," says the girl. "I'll wait."

A customer comes in for a Bleeding Heart of Christ medallion. The customer is full of news about the boy on the sidewalk. Señora Luque doesn't mention that she saw him that morning. Politics are dangerous.

"They took credit for it already," says the girl waiting in the chair as the customer leaves. "The Omega 7. Lo escuché en la radio."

Señora Luque goes back behind the register, pretending not to hear. César would never let her have a radio in the shop and now she doesn't keep one out of respect. She sits. It is nice to have the register back out of the sun. No one will steal a blessed object, you can lie down in the back if you want and listen for the bell. Señora Luque wipes the dust from a statue of a huge hand with a bleeding wound in the palm and a flame of truth on each fingertip.

The phone rings.

There is no hello. There never is when they call. She had known César was still in politics after the Invasion, but he never spoke of it till the end.

"If I die," he had said to her, "they'll still want to use the shop. Whatever they want, you let them have it, no questions."

Sometimes someone would bring messages, or leave packages, or just call on the telephone. Sometimes ones like the girl would come, wanting to join, and Señora Luque would have to pass the word.

She hangs up the phone.

The girl sits as still as the plaster saints around her. She is a pretty, serious girl, maybe thirty. It is just as well. Politics are dangerous. She looks up as Señora Luque comes to her.

"Dijeron 'no.' "

The girl's face tightens. "Por qué?"

"They don't explain. Solamente 'no.' " It was just as well.

The girl rises and goes to the door, pausing as if afraid to go out onto the hot street.

"Gracias," she says, and then is gone.

Señora Luque hurries back behind the register, crossing herself.

Rufo watches the girl come out from La Mano Poderosa. He is sweating already but happy to be out of the restaurant. She is pretty, in a stuck-up kind of way. Keeping track of her could be worse. And if it comes down to the other, yes, he can do that too. And then he'd be sure to sit with the men.

T W O

 "GAME TIME!"

Corky is on the loose again.

Luz frowns at the noise and continues to circle the day room, pills rattling in white paper cups on her meds cart. She shakes Franken gently, waking him only enough to wash his trank down.

"*Game* time, everybody! *Game* time!" Corky frisks into the day room clapping her hands and rolling her shoulders as if preparing to do a trapeze act.

"No sleepyheads," she calls. "Let's get in*volved*, people! *Game time!*"

Three old Jews play backgammon by the air conditioner. A pair of old Cubans play dominoes by the window. Garber sits in his rocking chair and plays with himself till Luz takes his hand and puts a Valium in it.

"Medication, Mr. Garber. Would you like juice, milk, or water?"

"Woodchuck," says Garber. Luz gives him tomato juice.

Epstein unboxes his puzzle. The pieces are supposed to come together to form the first page of the score to a Brahms concerto.

"You think *this* is hard," he says to Corky, "you should try Mahler."

"I'm not sure a one-person hobby is a good idea for you, Mr. Epstein. We're looking for interface here." Corky looks around the room. "Maybe you'd like to invite Mr. Weiss—"

"He touches one note," says Epstein, "I'm breaking his fingers."

Garber digs under his blanket, trying to remember where he left off.

A four-handed pinochle game starts at the center table. There is a Parkinson's who can't hold his cards steady and a woman who can only remember Russian and a Throat Cancer who has to mime out his bids. A hand on the chest for hearts, wiggling the ring finger for diamonds, a pounding motion for clubs. For spades he points to Roosevelt or Wilson or sometimes to Luz if she is handy and the Parkinson's laughs and drops his hand all over the floor.

Some of the old men just sit and watch Luz roll around with her meds. Her uniform is dazzling white against her deep brown arms and legs. She rolls her hips and smiles, white teeth and black eyes, smiles, and before they know it they've swallowed whatever it was they swore they'd never swallow again, they've offered themselves up to rectal thermometers and bloodsucking needles and catheter tubes, lulled by her sweet voice rolling like oil on oil, her words a soft massage as she takes a hand in hers and slips a Darvon onto a tongue.

"You move in circles," says Gold opening wide. Luz pops a mood-elevator in. Gold never takes liquid. "And those circles move."

"What's that mean?"

"It's from a poem," says Gold. "It's a compliment."

Luz smiles. "Thank you, then."

" *'I know a woman who is lovely in her bones,'* " he quotes as Luz rolls away.

"She got a nice ass, too," mutters Roosevelt.

Wilson digs an elbow into his ribs. "Behave yourself, man. Girl's not deaf."

Roosevelt slides cluttered lunch trays into slots on the big rolling rack. Wilson passes out cardboard sputum cups to the gobbers in the room. The kosher lunches are on black plastic trays and the non-kosher on blue.

"Will you look at that." Roosevelt stares at Luz's bottom as she rolls out of the day room. "Cuban women, goodgawd!"

"Isn't nothin under that dress they don't make in the USA."

"Not the same *thing,* Wilson. Got no feelin for adventure, do you? No spice a life."

"Least I got my wits about me. You got less chance of getting tight with that Loose than a camel does to pass through the eye of a needle."

"Man is meant to dream," says Roosevelt.

"Marmoset," says Garber, working harder at himself.

"That thing gone tear off, he don't let up."

"If you fellas aren't busy," calls Corky, "we'll be getting a little sing together in a few minutes. We could use a couple baritones."

"Got patients need me," says Roosevelt, getting into gear behind the big rack and aiming for the doorway to the hall. "I can hear em callin."

"Beaver," says Garber.

Wilson places the last sputum cup in Garber's free hand. "Put it there when you done, man," he says, and lights out after Roosevelt.

The hall is full of walkers and wheelers and a few poor stiffs left strapped in geri chairs. Luz rolls the noon meds to them, singing softly—

> *No sé si tengo razón*

She sings—

> *Cuando sueño podría ganarte*
> *Si tú quieres mi corazón*
> *Solamente debes besarme*

Bing!

The call lights over the doors begin to flash, ringing on as the patients hear her voice.

Bing! Bing!

"Noyse!" calls Getchel. "Noyse!"

"I'm drownding!" calls Shamsky. "It's op to the vinders!"

"I die now," moans Galindez. "Me muero."

Bing!

Roosevelt grabs the linen cart and Wilson joins him with the discard basket and they rattle down after Luz.

"Thing is," says Roosevelt, "with all those cheekbones she got and that slanty kind of eye, she look more Indian than she does African."

"Didn't have many Indians in Cuba, man. Least not for long."

"You learn that in college, Wilson?"

Wilson tosses a dirty drawsheet at him.

"I don't usually go for real dark ones," says Roosevelt. "Girl is two shades blacker than you, Wilson, and you they could melt down for shoe polish. But that Loose, goodgawd!"

"Shhh."

"Untie me," calls Babakin. Babakin sits with his wrists tied down to the metal arms of a geri chair. "Pliss, untie me."

"We let them hands loose, old buddy, you be throwin everthing in sight up gainst the wall. You already hit Nurse Leonard with you pee-jug."

"I give you twenty dollars for right hend, fifty dollars for left hend."

"Must use his left to crank it," says Wilson. "Just like you."

"If I was *ever* to have to make my own mookie," says Roosevelt, "I'd need *both* of ems to hold it. Like that jingle on TV—'Takes two hands—to handle a Whopper—' "

"Untie me, pliss," calls Babakin after them.

Luz is trying to irrigate Heller's bedsore when they catch up with her. Heller's is nearly an inch wide and cuts down to expose his coccyx. He is on his stomach, face red, thrashing his arms back at Luz like a turtle burying eggs.

"Would you each take an arm?" says Luz. "Mr. Heller don't want me to help him."

"He just don't want you messin with his boodie is all," says Roosevelt.

"Slaughterhouse!" cries Heller. "You're running here a slaughterhouse!"

DuPre sits up in bed, watching Luz pat the saline solution away with gauze. "Your friend is in today," he says.

Luz bends down and peers into the wound. "I got a friend?"

"The serious one. Our Lady of the Bedpans."

"Marta?" Luz shakes her head. The sore is getting worse. "She's not on today."

"She wasn't in uniform. Just in to see her old man, probably."

"I think you got your eye on her, Mr. DuPre."

Heller tries to swat her but Roosevelt and Wilson are clamped onto his arms.

"Torturers!" cries Heller. "Black bastards! I'm calling the D.A., he'll fix your ass. Back to the Congo!"

"What you talkin Congo, old man?" Roosevelt tightens his grip. "I'm outa Memphis. All my folks outa Memphis, right back from the git-go. And before that I don't even wanna *think* about it."

Luz spreads something like peanut butter on the wound with a wooden stick.

"What's that?" asks DuPre.

"It's supposed to promote healing. Dr. Masi wants us to try it."

"Dr. Masi is a quack. I'm calling the D.A.!"

"Used to be a Memphis in ancient Egypt," says Wilson. "Maybe your folks are from that Memphis, way back."

"Egypt is A-rabs, man, not black people."

Luz lays gauze over the hole on the man's spine. "Have you been sleeping on your side, Mr. Heller?"

"Sleeping? Who's sleeping with *that* one in the room?" He struggles to indicate DuPre. "In the night he's tiptoeing over with a pillow, with plans to smother me. A slaughterhouse I'm in."

Luz tapes the dressing down. She cleans up her gear and leaves the orderlies to prop Heller on his side.

"That Loose," says Roosevelt when she's gone. "Got a way with her hands."

"Means 'light' in Spanish," says Wilson.

"Huh?"

"The word 'luz.' "

"No shit."

"Memphis was an old capital of Egypt," says DuPre. "Just down the Nile from where Cairo is now."

"No shit. Man, it's a regular education hangin round with you two. I learn more shit that I don't want to hear about. On three—"

On the count of three they heave Heller over on his right hip, so his back is to DuPre.

"What I *want* to know from you, DuPre, is how you be tiptoein over here with that pillow"—Roosevelt claps Heller on the thigh—"when you got no *legs?*"

Marta sits holding her father's hand through the bedrail. The old man's other arm, the right one, is twisted stiff against his side. He stares up at the ceiling, his face pulled into a hard scowl.

Luz kisses Marta on the cheek and gives her hair a tug.

"Qué tal?"

"O—solamente visitando."

"Le entiende el viejo?"

"Of course he does." Marta folds the old man's good arm across his chest. "He understands everything I tell him. He just can't talk back."

The other bed in the room is empty, stripped to the mattress. Levy had gone out with a coronary two nights ago.

"You hear about that boy this morning?"

"Uh-huh." Marta looks tired. "On the radio."

"You know Blanca who works on the night shift? That's her cousin got shot. Right on the street. They're crazy."

"There must have been a reason." Marta lifts the covers up to check the drawsheet. The old man closes his eyes.

"My brother wants to go out with you," says Luz.

Marta looks in her father's night table. "How do you know?"

"He told me. He wants me to hint around. You know. See how you feel about it."

"Maybe sometime."

"You should get out more. Coming in here on your time off—"

"I've got a lot of things to take care of."

"Cómo?"

"Things."

"You probably got some guy on the side you don't want me to know about."

Marta pulls the covers off old Scipio. He lies in a puddle of loose shit.

"Serafín is really crazy about you, you know." Luz grins and gets up to go. Call bells ring in the hallway. "He says your beauty touches his soul. I saw it in a poem he wrote."

Marta turns her back to her father and smiles. "Está loco, tu hermano."

When Luz is gone Dewey comes in with three urinals sloshing in each hand.

"Oh. Hi."

"Can you help me with my father?"

He lays the urinals on the stand by the empty bed, embarrassed. They always make him do the shit jobs, Roosevelt and Wilson. Just because he's junior man on the floor. The shit jobs and the piss jobs. Tapping catheter bags, collecting the sputum cups from the day room, breaking up impactions, wringing out gauze for urine samples of the patients so gone they can't use a jug. The smegma detail. Just because he's the only white guy.

Dewey moves to the other side of the bed from Marta. He lets the bedrail down and peels the wet hospital gown off Scipio. They roll the old man on his side toward Marta. Dewey looks at her when he thinks she won't notice. Their hands bump once, both holding Scipio's bare hip. Dewey starts to sweat. He pulls the edges of the old linen from under the mattress and rolls it toward the far side, wadding it against Scipio's back. The vinyl mattress cover is still dry. Marta wipes her father clean with a damp towel.

"What did he used to do? Your father?"

"He can hear you," says Marta. "He understands English."

"Oh. Sorry."

Dumb fuck, can't keep my mouth shut. He tucks a fresh bottom sheet under, miters the ends, and smooths over the empty half of the bed.

"We lived outside of Camagüey. We had a cattle ranch."

"Oh."

She is a few inches taller than Dewey, but that doesn't make him as uneasy as the way she looks right at you. He pulls the plastic drawsheet back, wipes it dry, and tucks it under.

"Over here he was in politics."

Dewey wonders if they nailed the Cuban kid from a car or on foot. Take a lot of rocks to just walk up and drop the hammer. Cold. You'd have to be a cold sucker.

Dewey puts a fresh linen drawsheet on, raises the bedrail, switches sides with Marta. They roll Scipio gently to the new-made side, careful not to pin his bad arm underneath him.

Dewey walks up to the mark. The mark doesn't know him. Dewey asks for the time and when the mark lifts his arm to check he sticks it in the kid's ribs and squeezes off. You get both lung and heart that way.

Marta rubs lotion into her father's skin.

Dewey walks up to the mark. The mark knows him. They reach to shake hands. Dewey has it in his left hand and when they grasp hands he brings it up under the kid's eyeball and squeezes. The hand, the one he's shaking, freezes tight around his and he has to break the fingers to get free.

Marta powders the red spots and creases, talking softly in Spanish to the old man. Dewey pulls the old sheets through, careful not to spill anything, and tosses the heap by the door. He pulls the fresh sheets through, tucking them under, mitering the ends.

They might have done it by car. You had to be a better shot. Unless maybe you called him to the window to ask directions.

"Excuse me—"

"Qué?"

"Can you tell me how to get to the Dixie Highway?"

"Well, you see that light up ahead—"

Wham.

Cold. Like a poisonous snake. Walking through streets with somebody's number in your pocket, maybe going out to lunch with him, laughing, smiling, getting him ready. To see his face that split second as the gun comes up under the eyeball. That would be something.

"We had one of the biggest ranches in Camagüey," says Marta. "My father and my brothers."

Dewey tucks the top sheet in. "Like on *Bonanza*."

"Yeah." She checks her father's body over. He is dry and clean. "Only there was my two brothers and then there was me."

They roll Scipio on his back and pull the top sheet over him. Not a wrinkle. Dewey makes a tight bed.

Scipio lies staring at the ceiling, his face pulled into a hard scowl.

In a wooden pen. On a ranch outside of Camagüey, near the center of the island. In a wooden pen just beyond the smell of the feed stalls. The bull was Maceo because he was big and he was deep bronze and he hated to be penned in. El Mulato Maceo. The bull was no good. He would fuck them but nothing ever came of it. The bull doctor came and threw up his hands. They milked the bronze Maceo for his seed and tried it that way but nothing came. The bull was big but no good. For years Scipio kept him. Maceo ate tons of feed and tore fences down. He chased anyone who came near. Scipio would let him fuck from time to time but nothing came of it. His thing was like Scipio's thick arm holding a melon but nothing came of it. He had big, red-rimmed eyes. Scipio's friends made jokes. He almost killed one of the vaqueros one day. They managed to get him in the pen. Scipio carried the sledge they used to drive in fenceposts. When he tried to climb in Maceo thrashed and kicked and splintered wood. His son Blas was watching. He called for his .38. He stood on the fence trying to get a clear shot. His sons Blas and Ambrosio were watching. Maceo came forward to get a look at the gun. His red-rimmed eyes looked up into Scipio's. His head was as big as Scipio's broad chest. He snorted hot air from nostrils like wet black rubber. He leaned his enormous head against the fence, suddenly calm. He was no good. The first shot sent a chip of bone stinging back against Scipio's face. Ambrosio started to cry. He was no good. Maceo stumbled back a step, then his hindquarters slumped down. He stared dumbly at Scipio. He had bought the bull at an auction. The bull was big and deep bronze and hated to be penned in. He had a thing like a strong man's arm and could break the back of a young heifer. The second shot went through Maceo's eye and there was blood then and Blas came close to watch.

Scipio lies scowling, staring at a bronze bull.

"Done already?" Nurse Temple is writing in her charts at the station.

"Roosevelt and Wilson are finishing up the beds." Luz hands in her med sheet. "Katz threw up."

"How's de la Pena?"

"Shat the bed. Marta's with him and I sent Screwy Dewey in to help. Listen, I want to move DuPre in there."

"What about Levy?"

"Levy went out Monday night."

Nurse Temple flips through the weekly report. "Jesus. He had such good color."

"So I want to move DuPre in there."

"Is he complaining about Heller?"

"No. He likes Marta. And she's always in there."

"All she does is sit and whisper at the old man."

"So?" Luz searches the station desk for the room assignment chart. "He likes seeing her, DuPre. And it beats staring at Heller's ass all day."

T H R E E

➤ THE KILLING OUT FRONT is great for lunch business. Tío Felix has given the girl the day off and so is working the counter himself. Sometimes he still likes to work the counter.

"Chicharrón pollo!" he yells in to Hong. "Carne guisada! Seven-Up!"

They come and stand around the sidewalk looking for stains, arguing about who the boy was and why they had executed him and did he deserve it or not and then they come in to sit at the counter, still arguing, hungry.

"Serrucho frito!" Felix yells in to his old cook. "Yuca y moros. Dos pollo asado!"

Once he had posted a sign, *Prohibido Discutir de Política en este Restaurante,* but they ignored it. Hong is only a few feet away in the kitchen but Felix has to shout over all the arguing to be heard.

"Bistec salteado!"

"Tío," says Marta, helping him carry plates of fried ham to the end of the counter, "you know somebody. Tell me who."

"Nadie. I know restaurant, I know farmacia, I know newsstand, I know fishing boat. I don know politics."

"What do you talk all day with your friends out at the Big Five?"

"Deportes. Negocios. No política."

"You know someone, Tío. I know you do."

"Felix," calls Salazar, who runs the record store down the street, "sopa mondongo, para llevar. Para mi esposa."

"Sopa mondongo, para llevar!" Tío Felix is sweating already. When Felix works the counter he keeps three extra shirts hanging in the back.

"I don see why they kill him," he says. He nods toward the men arguing over their beans and rice as if they were the ones responsible. "What do they want? Is over. He's sending all the prisoner home."

"Después de quebrantarlos."

Felix points to a small man sitting alone in the corner. "Does he look broken to you?"

Villas sits eating fried fish, gazing out the window. The men who argue lower their voices a little bit when they stand near him. Marta wonders what he'd say if she came to him with her plan. She looks in his eyes for twenty years in prison.

"You were in the fighting after the Invasion, Tío. They used your boats. You know people."

"No conozco a nadie. The ones who are still in it go under. Nobody knows who they are. The only guy I hear talk that kind of política, I don know him."

When she was younger he could have shut her up with a milk-shake. She would come in, head barely over the countertop, laying down whatever little handful of nickels and pennies she had collected. "Batido de mamey, por favor," she would order, and then, politely, "Buenas tardes, Tío." She would be full of questions about why this and why that till the batido was ready. She never got any on her face and when the level in her glass was just right she'd fill it back up from the metal tumbler. She never used a straw, but closed her eyes and drank long and slow like a baby suckling, coming out of it to gasp for air between drinks. Felix would turn to look at her face when she closed her eyes, wondering at how everything was perfect on a small scale, loving how smooth her skin was, wishing for a wife and daughters of his own. He would make a big show of counting her change and ringing it into the register. She never wanted a batido for free, but when he pressed a silver dollar into her hand before she left she didn't complain. "Muchas gracias, Tío," she would say, with the half-curtsy the nuns had taught her.

"Who is he?" asks Marta. "The one who talks politics?"

"Why you want to know?"

"It's my business," says Marta. "Y el de mi padre."

"Felix," calls Padilla, who sells insurance. "Medianoche, chuleta, y dos cervezas. Denos Heineken por favor."

"Espere un momento, compa, espere." Felix has broken the point of his pencil and there are too many orders to keep straight in his head. Men are starting to come in the door, see the crowd, then go back out. He wishes he hadn't given the girl the day off.

"How can it be business for Scipio?" he asks.

"He talks to me. We decide things."

"No habla con nadie. No puede hablar."

"He talks to me." Marta stands blocking his way to the kitchen, tight-mouthed, daring him to challenge her. "We do it without words."

It is expensive for Felix to keep Scipio with the Jews but Marta insists the care is better there. A bed is a bed, thinks Felix, and immediately feels bad.

"Who is the one who talks that kind of politics?"

Marta has him blocked right under the fan. The sweat on his forehead goes cold.

"Nuñez," he says. "Señor Nuñez. He sells magazines. He's not a good man."

"Por qué dices esto?"

Tío Felix blushes. Marta remembers the first time he blushed when she kissed him, when she was just starting eighth grade and came to show him her new uniform. After that she tried to stand farther away.

"Because of the kind of magazine he sells. For the newsstand."

Marta nods. "Sometime," she says, "I may want to borrow one of your boats."

"You don fish."

They are quiet as Villas comes up to pay his bill. Marta tries to look into his eyes but he has put sunglasses on to face the street.

"You don fish," says Felix when the man is gone.

"You let other people use it. They didn't fish."

"That was diff'rent." Felix wishes he had never listened to them. But there was the bank loan and the liquor license and there was Scipio talking in his ear. "That was United States government."

"So? Son más importantes que tu familia?"

"Camarón enchilado," says old Hong, passing a hot plate through his portal. "No hay yuca."

"No. But I don want my family to get in trouble." Felix takes the plate to a man in the front booth, Marta trailing after him.

"You let Blas use it."

Felix looks around nervously. "Who told you that?"

"You did some big deal with him. Lots of money."

LOS GUSANOS 19

"No es verdad. Fué un favor."

"So do me a favor. Let me use a boat."

"For what you want it?"

"I can't tell you."

"I promise to your father—"

"No prometó nada a mi padre!" Marta startles herself with her shout. The men stop to look at her for a second, then go back to eating and arguing.

"When he gave you money to start a business," she says, lowering her voice, "did he ask you how you would use it?"

"Is too dangerous, what you get into, créeme. I been there, sobrina."

"Where? Where have you been? You never fired a shot."

He blushes again, a different kind of blush. "I was ready to," he says.

Hong lays two steaming plates of rice and beans on the portal ledge but Felix can't think of who they are for. The men argue whether there will be more executions. Hong calls out that they are out of Heineken.

"I was ready if I had to," says Tío Felix, touching Marta's arm, looking to her eyes for belief. "I was ready to die."

F O U R

➤ EL HALCÓN ALWAYS starts in the ass section. Most of the Spanish-language magazines are there, though he never reads the text. What can you say about ass?

There is a guy in a business suit hovering between the big-boobies rack and the black girls. There is a kid who can't be of age fingering the cellophane-wrapped come-shot albums. El Halcón likes the pictures where they lie on their stomachs with their panties down around their knees and arch their butts up at the camera. The ones in color. Blondes. Walt cruises in wearing his shades and white shoes and he has to go to work.

El Halcón picks Backdoor Bonanza, which means that Walt has to be in Barnyard Babies. It is dark inside but El Halcón knows where the coin slot is.

"I feel like I should be filling out a ballot." Walt's voice comes through the booth wall.

"Just put your quarter in the slot. The occupied light won't come on till there's change in the machine." It is a skinny white girl and a black guy with a rod you could hit fungoes with. "Qué insecta," says El Halcón.

"It's on," says Walt.

"Your flick?"

"Operation Flypaper."

Walt never likes to explain things, which is one of the reasons El Halcón doesn't trust him. He'll snap out a couple words from on high and expect you to believe that all the details, all the possible fuck-ups, are being taken care of. That was how it had been with him for the Invasion, that was how it had been with all the advisers.

"That kid they whacked this morning stirred things up," says Walt. "The pinks are crying for investigations so the Agency needs something to show them. We're on a three-month trial. If we turn something up they'll make us fully operational."

It always takes the first quarter's worth to get their pants off and start into the straight stuff. Girl on top. You get a better view of it going in that way.

"Trial?" El Halcón puts another quarter in as the screen goes black. "What's that mean, trial?"

"It means you get paid piecework. Five hundred a head. On delivery."

"Bullshit."

"You turn a few in the trial period and we'll get an expense account. Subcontracts, immunities, the whole deal. Like the old days."

"It's bullshit."

It is quiet from Walt's booth for a moment. "God," he says finally, "this is disgusting."

El Halcón laughs. "She with the dog or the horse?"

"There's a *horse?*"

"Five hundred a head is bullshit."

"Of course if you were to uncover something major—"

"You know what you guys are like? All you yanqui creeps? You're like the ones who come in here and watch the peepshow doors."

They're getting ready for the rear entry now. It's hard to believe something so big can fit.

"And when they see somebody come out playing with their wallet instead of their dick, looking like they run out of quarters, these guys they jump into that booth real quick and start the show cause they know they probly see the big payoff on just one coin. Piecework my ass."

"How much," says Walt, "do you think the girls in this thing got paid?"

"Maybe fifty apiece. Maybe some blow."

"But they did it, didn't they? Because it was all that was available. I'm just telling you what's available."

He's putting it in now. The girl pretends it hurts. Then she pretends it's driving her crazy. He has her bent over the back of an easy chair. The camera goes in for a close-up.

"Yeah," says El Halcón, "but they got to fuck the horse."

Both men laugh. "Le interesa o no? Debo saber el domingo."
Walt learned his Spanish in Madrid and still carries the accent.

"What about guns?"

"It depends. You turn enough people, I can put guns in their hands."

"Like the old days."

"Cómo no? Solamente necesitamos revolver una roca," says Walt.

"Y encontramos?"

"Los gusanos."

"There are things under rocks besides worms," says El Halcón. "You can get bit."

They always pull it out right at the end so things can drip and dribble, so you can tell it was for real.

"Are you in or not? My people have to know."

"What the fuck. I'm in." He can use the money, and if the immunity comes later that could be a blank check.

"I knew we'd work together again. La guerra no termina."

The loop is off a little and the black man and the white girl appear again in their clothes. The girl kneels down and begins to unzip the man's pants.

"Back in business," says El Halcón.

FIVE

PEOPLE KNEW THINGS that Walt didn't. They spoke languages he didn't understand, laughed at jokes he didn't get. They could comprehend mysteries of behavior, were party to intrigues, knew secrets of the body.

Doctors.

The doctors always kept you in the dark. It was a place Walt hated to be.

He wondered if they'd accept the kidney work as job-related. If he could stay operational another year he'd have his thirty in with the health coverage, but the deductible was better if it was for something job-related. He thought of all the late nights, the smoky cafés, all the rum and Coke and sweet killer coffee. The sugar they used, especially the fucking Cubans. Maybe he could tie the dental in too. Some men fought and bled for their country, jumped from airplanes and ducked bullets and committed murder with steely, clear conscience. Walt drank rum and Coke and nerve-jolting coffee and gossiped with third-world colonels. His kidneys were killing him.

A field agent was a sensor, the Agency's longest finger stuck in the wind of change and conspiracy. Walt was supposed to be the first to feel the breeze pick up, to hear the faintest whisper of revolt. He sat in smoky cafés, eating, drinking, joking, absorbing the mood of the moment, cataloging the jealousies and hatreds, spreading the lastest scandal around to see what might be stuck to it when it circled back.

The bladder problems started in Madrid during the War. It was a place Walt hated to be. Officially he was attached to the embassy as translator and typist but was under orders to the OSS. Men were dying in battle and Walt was parked on his butt collecting rumors.

Madrid was a patient in remission, a sick, broken city still smoldering from the Civil War, pleading neutrality but dealing with Allies and Axis alike. War posters celebrated the victory of God and the Generalissimo over the forces of darkness. The Generalissimo's artillery had pounded ancient buildings to dust in order to save the city, and ghosts walked the streets. It was a city overrun by men with guns. On the corners the officers of the Guardia Civil, vain as matadors in their lacquered hats, pierced you with their eyes. The falangistas shook the air through bullhorns, belligerent, feverish with dreams of race and destiny, while the Carlistas stood aloof in the certitude of bloodlines and glorious history.

Walt preferred the Legionnaires, tough and cocky, good old boys who'd fucked their way through a hundred Moroccan burdeles and ran to battle screaming "Viva la muerte!" They called him El Cowboy because he told them he was from Texas and because he looked a little like Randolph Scott. They could drink, the Legionnaires, flicking back glass pourrons or bulging goatskins to blast a hard stream of acid red wine against the back of their open throats, never losing a drop. Walt tried to keep up with them at first, then realized he could fake incompetence and let half of it splash down his chin or fly off into space. Still, he wobbled to bed each night after curfew and woke with the sun high and his bladder bursting. The wise guys at the embassy nicknamed him El Borracho and wondered who he was related to at State to be able to keep his job. The wine was awful enough, but what passed for cognac made his eyeballs rattle loose in his skull, made his tongue thick and sticky.

Each day at noon he would drag in to file his secret reports. What Iglesias had said about Cárdenas. What Cárdenas had done to Santurce. What Beltrán, who had been tight with the Condor Legion pilots during the Guerra Civil, remembered about the problems with the Stukas. Who Díaz thought was spying for the Italians. What they all thought the Generalissimo would do if his hand was forced. The men would drink and relive their adventures in the desert with los Moros and their adventures against the Reds and their adventures with women. The women more than anything. Walt looked at the Spanish women in the streets, covered in their black dresses as the wall posters decreed, tight and unsmiling, and he wondered who the Legionnaires could be talking about. Some of their stories were about putas, but the rest were about conquests of the widows and wives and girlfriends and daughters the Reds had left behind.

"They do it any way you want," the soldiers would laugh. "It's the one good thing the Reds accomplished."

Walt looked at the stern women on the streets and wondered at the secrets they would never surrender to him.

Men were dying in Italy, in France, in the Pacific. Walt applied for transfer but his applications were never acknowledged. Most of his co-workers at the embassy had no idea he was with intelligence, they saw only a kid with a weakness for the drink, some Stateside wheel's protected little boy. Walt attached long messages to his reports asking to be filled in on the Big Picture, to at least be informed exactly what he was supposed to be doing. Finally Dearborne, the station CO, brought him in.

"You go out drinking with these men every night?" he asked.

"I try to. My bladder's been giving me some trouble—"

"You talk with them? Drink with them?"

"That's my assignment, sir. To gain their confidence."

"Wouldn't you agree, then, that the less you know the less likely you are to compromise our security?"

Walt didn't agree but could tell he wouldn't get any further with Dearborne. Intelligence ran on a need-to-know basis, and Command had decided that Walt didn't need to know.

There were a few men he couldn't meet in the cafés or restaurants. They had fought for or supported the Republic against the Generalissimo and lived in dread of the moment his internal security would decide to act on their existence. Some were Reds, some seemed to Walt no more threatening than New Dealers caught on the losing side of a bad fight. He sold them hope. There was a chance, a long shot, that the Generalissimo would go back into business with Hitler and Mussolini, and if that happened Command wanted to know who was ready and able to form an underground. Walt hinted at weapons that might become available. He speculated about targets, personal and military. He spoke of a commitment to justice and liberty. Walt called his secret contacts los espectros, ghosts who walked the earth starving for any scrap of hope he might toss their way. They brought him stories of the Generalissimo's indiscretions with the Nazis and assured him there was an army of patriots waiting to rise. Walt began to be able to recognize them in public, eyes hurting with their secret knowledge, laughter careful and insincere. Walt wondered if that was how he looked to the Legionnaires, if they knew exactly what he was up to and were playing with him. Los espectros haunted his dreams.

It was a quiet war from Madrid. Walt tried to meet Spanish girls but only succeeded in a few drunken visits to the burdeles, flourishing again since the defeat of the Reds. Once when he was barely able to walk the Legionnaires threw him in with a woman they called La Gitana, a skinny, hawknosed puta whose eyebrows met in a wolfish point over her nose and who decided he was a German. She had something serious against the Germans, La Gitana, and chased him out of the room and down the stairs of the burdel with a pair of scissors aimed at his throat.

"Es mejor que La Gitana doesn't like you, Cowboy," they laughed. "If she fucked you she might have killed you."

Walt's bladder became swollen. The embassy doctor told him to lay off the booze for a bit till the infection disappeared. He tried to sit in the cafés with the men without drinking, but they wouldn't have it.

"We don't let monks sit at our table," they said. "No virgins, no Reds, no monks. Salud!"

Then they would throw their heads back and hoist a bulging goat-skin of wine and it was like they were squeezing Walt's own swollen, angry bladder, blood-red wine shooting out in a perfect arc.

One of the ghosts introduced him to Alsina. She was just past twenty, with thick black hair that she wore in a braid over one shoulder and eyes that seemed always on the verge of angry tears. She called him Señor Walt and came to him for help.

"Mi marido era miembro de la POUM," she said quietly, her eyes taking in the other tables at the café without moving. "Escapó a Francia en los últimos días de la guerra. Después de esto, no he sabido nada."

Walt couldn't stop looking at her lips. They were full in a way American girls' lips never were. He wondered what it would be like to kiss lips like that.

"So many husbands are missing in France," he told her. "To find a special one, eso es muy difícil."

"Solamente quiero saber si está vivo o muerto," said Alsina, tears welling in her eyes. "Dicen que usted puede averiguar la verdad, Señor Walt."

Walt smiled. Señor Walt, the finder of truth. He touched her arm. Her arm was strong, bronze-colored. "Si es posible," said Walt, "lo haré."

"Who wants to know?" said Dearborne when Walt put in the request.

"One of my contacts."

"A woman."

"Yes."

"Is this to get you laid?"

"It's her *husband*."

"So?"

"She's a contact. One contact leads to another. The guy was in POUM, a real diehard—it could lead to important people for us."

"Has she produced anything useful yet?"

"This isn't sensitive information I want. A guy's whereabouts, dead or alive—"

"You don't waltz in here and order information like a tin of beef at the PX, Walt. She puts out with something useful, we'll look into it."

Alsina often wore a blue uniform when they met. She had a job at the Prado guarding art treasures still on display. Alsina had studied to be a painter until the Generalissimo had returned from Africa to put Spain back on the path to God and honor. Then she had joined the milicianos on the barricades, learning to shoot in the first days of the battle for the university grounds.

Walt wondered what it would be like to peel the blue uniform off her body.

"The people who know about your husband," he told her, "want to know some things before they help you. I would do it as a favor, pero no soy jefe."

"Qué quieren saber?"

"Names. Solamente los nombres de unos enemigos del Generalísimo."

"No voy a ayudar a Franco."

"You won't be helping him. We're looking for people willing to fight for justice."

Alsina thought, stroking the thick braid that sat on her shoulder, and looked up at him with wet eyes.

"Tengo miedo, Señor Walt."

Maybe the husband would be dead. The Vichy government had

rounded up most of the Republicans and handed them over when the Germans moved in. Alsina would need somebody strong, somebody with connections to see her through, to protect her. When he took her hand she didn't resist.

"Trust me," said Walt. "Si no puedes confiar en tus amigos, no hay esperanza."

Alsina gave him six names.

Sometimes when he was sitting with the Legionnaires, pretending to listen to their puta stories, he would think about Alsina. In some of the scenes she was the more experienced, love-starved since her husband left, sitting in her blue uniform watching him undress then showing him what she wanted. In others she was still a girl, looking at him with her liquid eyes and calling him Señor Walt, shocked and excited by the way he touched her. He was the one who knew secrets, the one who could bring her the truth.

He saw her a few times in the next weeks. They walked through the Puerta del Sol together, talking about how she had met her husband, about the war against the Generalissimo, about how her life now was all deception, a shadow life of words she couldn't say, feelings she couldn't show. Her only victory over the fascists would be to survive. Walt hoped that people who saw them together would think that they were a couple.

"He didn't get too far into France," said Dearborne. Alsina's names had checked out. "A lot of the POUM members were interned right at the border and shuffled around till the Nazis came in. We have him at Port Bou, Carcassonne, Lyons. Then he was in a bunch of them shipped to a work camp in Austria. Mauthausen. The trail ends there."

"Alive?"

"No way for us to know. I wouldn't lay odds on it."

When he saw Alsina next he wondered if she could see into him, could see that he carried the information but wasn't letting her have it just yet.

"In matters of trust," he said to her, "one can never be too careful. To truly know another person's heart, this requires a type of closeness, un tipo de intimidad que todavía no tenemos."

Alsina nodded gravely and they walked. It seemed that they walked through all of Madrid as she told him more about her life, told him that she and the man had been comrades and lovers but never married in the bourgeois sense, that she ached for him, could

not breathe some days for worry about him. Walt listened and held
Dearborne's report in a lump in his throat. When they stopped
walking they were at the apartment building where Alsina lived.
She took him up to her room. While he sat on a broken chair she
took her uniform off and carefully folded it and hung it up. She sat
on her bed and waited till he hurried his clothes off and they lay
down and she let him into her. Her arms were slack around his
neck. When he was done he rolled away and sat up, looking at
him.

"Dígame ahora," she said, her voice calm and direct. "Está vivo
o muerto?"

When he told her what he knew there were tears welling in her
eyes but not falling, never falling.

"Gracias, Señor Walt. Please go away now."

He walked back to the embassy. *¡Arriba España!* cried the posters
on the walls. *¡España Resucita!* He hated the city. He wondered what
secrets the man in Mauthausen knew about her, what parts of her
were only for him. Walt walked back through the Puerta del Sol,
bending over now and again to ease the pain in his bladder, hating
every person he saw. Señor Walt, he thought, the great keeper of
knowledge. He decided to go somewhere alone and get drunk.

When the news of VE day came Walt was passed out at a table
in a café near what was left of the university. Galán the Andaluz
lifted Walt's head up from where it had fallen in a puddle of wine
and peeled his eyes back.

"Cowboy," he said. "Buenas noticias."

Walt tried to remember where he was.

"You won. Los Nazi están jodidos," said Galán. "Tenemos que
ayudarte a celebrar. Viva los yanquis!"

After the Legionnaires had helped him celebrate Walt made his
way back to the embassy, more dead than alive. There was a party
going on. Walt hugged the wall, swaying under the Goya originals
and trying to smile until he found Dearborne sitting in a corner.

"Great news, huh?" he said.

Dearborne looked at Walt as if he couldn't quite place the face.
Walt realized that he hadn't been to sleep for two days, hadn't
shaved or changed his wine-splattered shirt, that he and Dearborne
weren't really supposed to know each other in public.

"I need a list of your contacts," said Dearborne, looking past
him out into the party.

"All of them?"

"Just the underground prospects. Just the Republicans."

"What for?" The espectros had always treated him with respect. They had never urinated on his shoes when he was passed out or taken him to gypsy putas who tried to murder him. He had sold them hope and they had trusted him

"We won't be needing them now, will we?" Dearborne spoke as if to a child. "We'll hand the names to our friends here in the government. As a goodwill gesture."

Walt made his way to the head and pissed a hard, merciless stream. Collins, one of the drivers for the embassy, was in the next stall. Collins was the one who had started the rumor that Walt was some Congressman's wayward son.

"Party's over," he called.

"Yeah." Walt examined the urine in the bowl. He didn't like the color.

"We did it. We licked em."

"Yeah," said Walt. "We did."

"Just between you and me, Walt," said Collins, "just out of curiosity—who *do* you work for?"

Walt managed to get to the Prado before it closed. The suspicious guide, a Catalan woman with red hair, parked him across from a Velásquez painting while she went to search for Alsina. The painting was called *El Triunfo de Baco*. Bacchus was a beefy teenager, a farm kid naked but for a cloth draped around his hips and a laurel crown on his head, looking distractedly off to the left, stone sober. Another kid equally stripped down lounged behind him to his left, bored. To the right of them were a cluster of Spanish peasants, flushed with drink, eyes lit up with the stupid joy of too much wine. The one in the center, a farmer with his hat pushed back from a sun-burned forehead, looked directly out from the canvas like a party reveler suddenly noticing a camera, offering a cup of wine beneath his idiot grin. A friend reached over his shoulder, playfully trying to grab the cup, while the others to their right engaged in the slightly hazy looks between each other that background Apostles in religious paintings always seemed caught in, men necessary for balance but unblessed by light. Their faces were wicked with the crude humor of the Legionnaires. Alsina had always called the painting "Los Borrachos," dismissing the artistry in her solemn disapproval of the drunkenness it brought to life. Sometimes Walt thought he could smell the breath of the peasants, could feel it hot and too familiar on his face as the men swooped close to shout some boozy insult meant as a joke. Kneeling before Bacchus, being crowned with laurel, was another peasant, his face turned from the viewer, his shoulders slightly hunched, head bowed, arms crossed tightly up against his stomach. It was the exact position Walt knelt in next to his bed after a night of gathering information from the Legionnaires, trying to breathe deeply to keep from passing out or throwing up, his forehead resting against the cracked plaster wall, the floor swimming below him, clutching the bedframe like a drowning man.

Walt leaned back against the wall across from the Velásquez painting. There was something solemn and tense about the man being crowned—drunk or not, he knew he was joining something there could be no turning back from. Walt's stomach made one of its attempts to float up into his throat and he bent double and hugged it with his arms. The Catalan girl came back.

"Alsina se fué."

"Cuándo?"

"El jefe dice que desapareció hace tres semanas."

It had been three weeks since he told her, three weeks since he'd seen her.

"Y dónde fué?"

"Austria," said the Catalan girl.

S I X

"EVERYTHING IS A struggle for souls," says Padre Martín.

"*Van Camp's tuna*," calls one of the girls from the checkout line. Padre Martín pushes the intercom button. "Albacore or light?"

"*Grated, ten ounce.*"

Padre Martín checks his price lists. "A dollar four," he says and releases the button. Marta sits beside him in the booth, watching the White Pantry shoppers cruise through the aisles. Padre Martín is all in black. He still always wears black, without the collar.

"I don't know where to turn," says Marta. "Sometimes I feel like what I'm doing is crazy."

"You still think it's important though?"

"Yes."

He has a sad face, a face of much suffering, and a deep, solemn voice. Marta has loved his voice since she was a girl. In the booth, kneeling, she would hear the rasp of the screen opening and then thrill when it would be his voice on the other side.

"*Fleishmann's matzoh cracker?*"

"A dollar twelve."

A woman comes up to have a check verified. Padre Martín scribbles on the back of it and she goes away. He sits back.

"Marta, do you know the story of Saint Margaret?"

"The one with the boar in the arena?"

"No, no. This is Saint Margaret of Hungary. She was a daughter of the king. When she was ten years old she begged to enter the convent, but the abbess refused to take her. She prayed and she fasted and she struck herself with stones until finally her piety was notorious and she was accepted into the order."

"Thousand Flushes?"

"A dollar twenty. She was famous for her mortifications. She would stand still for days at a time until she dropped from exhaustion. At Easter she washed the feet of all the nuns and servants in the convent, hundreds of them, never leaving her knees. She would cleanse the sores of lepers with the veil she never took off. During Lent she ate only the swill that the beggars in Pest were given. When she was sixteen she was taken by Ecstasies."

"Vlasic kosher dills, jumbo?"

"Look on the bottom."

"Sorry."

Padre Martín writes a note to himself. "In Holy Week she would fall into a state where she relived the movements of Christ from his arrest in the garden of Gethsemane to his death on the cross. She would offer her hands to be bound, bow her head for the crown of thorns, writhe in agony from the flogging of the Roman soldiers. In between Ecstasies she would collapse into a coma, her skin cold to the touch. People came from all over Europe to see Margaret, peeking through holes in the wall of the special cell the abbess had ordered built for her. It was a time when many had lost the faith. Margaret's Ecstasies were a reminder, a symbol, the Passion of Christ brought to flesh again. The visitors would watch every move, debating what it meant. Some of them saw blood pour from her hands and feet on the final day. Some saw tears of blood pour down her cheeks."

"Nilla Wafers?"

"A dollar eight. After the crucifixion she slept for three days with her eyes wide open, never blinking, her heartbeat a whisper in her chest. When she woke she always said she had dreamed about sheep."

The checkout line at the far end is stalled, people giving up on it and scooting their carts over to other lines. Padre Martín pushes the intercom button.

"Larry, bagging on Number Seven."

"Sheep?" says Marta.

"She dreamed she was walking barefoot on an enormous white plain that stretched out to the horizon in every direction. Every once in a while the ground would shift beneath her, until she realized she was walking on the backs of millions of sheep, packed so tightly together there was no way for her to fall through. The sheep were moving slowly, all of them in the same direction, and Margaret felt an incredible joy in her heart. Her toes sank into the soft wool on the backs of the sheep and then a light came from up ahead, a light so brilliant it turned the miles of fleece gold, so brilliant she had to force herself to keep her eyes open. It was the face of God."

People are complaining even with Larry bagging the groceries. The young Puerto Rican girl at the register is fumbling with the keys, losing her place, having to open the machine and write things on the tapes.

"People today would say she was crazy," says Marta.

"People said she was crazy then, some of them. But the others were inspired by her example, even people who never got to see her. Lost ones were brought back to the fold."

An old woman is talking loudly, inches from the girl's face. The girl tries to pretend she isn't there and concentrates on her numbers.

"Cómo murió?"

"Of a disease she caught ministering to the beggars in Pest. It rained for a week after her burial."

"KalKan Bits'n'Gravy?"

"Three for ninety-eight, special." Padre Martín takes his glasses off and wipes them clean with his handkerchief. The frames leave a dent over his nose. "She won men's souls," he says. "Think of the grace in that."

They are silent for a moment. The cash registers chatter and ring, the sound system chips in with "Heartaches" played on the xylophone setting of a synchronizer.

"Do you ever miss being a priest?" asks Marta.

"Hay muchas formas de servir a Dios."

"But when Padre Esturo deserted you—"

"Franco was dying. The Communists were taking over. There were souls in need."

"We needed him here."

Padre Martín shrugs. "Padre Esturo no es cubano. Quería volver a España."

"Y la Iglesia?"

"There are politics in the Church and there are politics in the world. I was involved with the wrong politics."

"I want you to hear my Confession."

He gives her a sad smile. "That would be a sin, Marta."

Sweat is running down the face of the girl at the register. Customers are scowling at her. She tries to open a cardboard wrapper of pennies with trembling hands.

"A veces empiezo a perder la esperanza." Marta starts to cry. Padre Martín looks away, toward the meat department.

"There's no reason to," he says. "Keep your mind on your goal, hold on to your faith in God. Hope will come. That was the first thing I learned when they took my vocation away. The power is inside us."

Padre Martín shakes his head and writes on a report form. The girl at the register is on her knees, looking for spilled pennies.

"She's new but I have to report her anyway," he says. "They've done time studies. Standards have to be maintained."

"I need singles for a fifty."

"Coming." Padre Martín sighs. "It's my job," he says and steps down to help the girl on her knees.

SEVEN

THEIR TASTE IS even worse than the Italians'. Rivkin wanders discreetly around the apartment while Duckworth asks the father questions in English. He walks slowly, softly, hands in his pockets. You don't want to be hardheeling through the place when there's been a death. The end tables have to go. Enormous over-stuffed pillows float on a velour-covered couch that could suck you under like quicksand. There is glass and chrome everywhere. Naked women's torsos in gold and ebony glaze flank the couch and the floor lamp is silver chrome with five light-housing pods drooping down from a central pole. The shining, lacquered-wood coffee table holds a ceramic bowl of fruit and a pair of phallic leaping dolphins in translucent pink glass. Rivkin studies his face in the wall mirrors etched with gilt wading birds. It reminds Rivkin of his Aunt Esther's place on Long Island. The rug makes him dizzy.

"Organizations?" says Duckworth.

"Just the Committee," says the father. The mother and the little sister are in the kitchen with relatives, red-eyed and trembling. Rivkin always feels like an intruder, a trespasser of grief, but knows they are an expected part of the drama.

"Whatsat?" asks Duckworth. He knows what it is but asks anyway. He likes to watch their faces when they answer.

"They want to bring families together. Thas all. Down there, up here. So people won't be cut off. Thas all. No politics."

"He a member of the Antonio Maceo Brigade?"

"No."

"Socialist Workers Party?"

36

The father stiffens. "He was a good boy. No politics, jus families. He wants to help the families get back together."

Rivkin passes by a three-tiered birdcage with half a dozen yellow parakeets hopping inside. He shakes his head. Even the floor of the cage is immaculate. The Cubans' places are always like that. Shit for taste but spotless.

Duckworth's face is impassive. He speaks softly and listens without reaction. "Were there threats?"

The father nods.

"Whud they say?"

"I don know. They always ask for Gustavo." The father, sunken deep in the couch, shifts uncomfortably. "They call up everbody on the Committee."

"Was he afraid?"

The father nods.

Rivkin can hear them talking in Spanish in the kitchen over the drone of the air conditioner. Somebody is weeping. When Ochoa calls in Duckworth will have him do a follow-up.

"Why you think they singled out your boy?"

The father sits thinking. Rivkin looks at the photos standing in plastic gilt frames on the TV cabinet. Communion pictures, a wedding shot. The dead boy smiling in a Miami High basketball uniform.

"He was the youngest," says the father. "He had the most to live for, the most to lose by risking his life. If they kill him, the others know they kill *any*body."

Duckworth asks if they can see the boy's room and the father shows them where it is. When they are alone Duckworth lies back on the boy's bed and closes his eyes.

"I'm beat," he says. "Hep yourself."

Rivkin pokes through the boy's desk. The room makes him uneasy. There isn't anything he can recognize as Cuban about it, as if the doorway brought you into another world. It looks like the kind of room his son Stuart will have when he reaches college age. Posters of the Dolphins' wide receivers on one wall, a poster of a white shark and a big one of the actress who played Wonder Woman on the wall by the bed. The boy was maybe a little neater than Stuart, or his mother has already been in to tidy up. There are no death threats in his desk drawers.

"When my Daddy was on the job in the thirties," says Duckworth, eyes still closed, "they used to come up here and shoot each other sometimes. Had a little half-assed revolution going on and there was gun-runnin and rum-runnin to finance the gun-runnin and sometimes some of the real cowboys would come up and try to take a bank."

Duckworth's family has been in Dade forever and with the cops almost as long. "We're something Andy Jackson left behind," he would say, or, if he wanted to needle Rivkin, "There was a hundred years of Duckworths in this town before the first Jew swum ashore."

He opens his eyes. "But mostly it was straight crime. Gimme a good aggravated assault in a barroom any day. Gimme illegal gambling, narcotics overdoses, bad checks, extortion, gimme the damn Mafia. I hate this political shit."

Rivkin goes through the pockets of the pants hanging in the boy's closet. "It's all political, Chief."

"What do you know about it?" He closes his eyes again. "Every time Washington makes googoo eyes at that fat bearded bastard down there I got dead Cubans up and down Eighth Street. I been having dreams lately. I tell you that?"

"Ever think of seeing a shrink, Chief?" There is a half-smoked joint in the pocket of a jacket. Rivkin shakes it into a cellophane bag.

"Crackers don't have shrinks, Rivkin. They have bartenders."

Rivkin looks under the bed. He finds a short stack of *Hustler*s. He rolls one up and taps his boss on the leg with it. Duckworth opens his eyes to see the centerfold spilling out.

"Jesus you're sharp, kid," he says. "Get Vice on the phone."

Rivkin shrugs and puts the magazine down. "So he's probably not a fag."

"They didn't pop him because he was a fag. Put those in an envelope and bring them with us. No reason for the mother to find them when she's cleaning out."

"Sure."

"And look in the dresser for condoms. He sounds like a responsible kid."

The doorbell rings outside. Second wave of mourners, thinks Rivkin. He'll go eyeball them in a minute. He likes to know things. He checks out book and record collections when he visits people, looks in medicine cabinets, takes inventory in refrigerators. He eavesdrops on conversations at public phone booths. He reads murder victims' mail.

"In these dreams," says Duckworth, "it's bidness as usual, I go out on cases, go into houses, talk to people, the whole bit, only everbody talks in Spanish."

"It's pretty much that way now, Chief."

"I mean *everbody*. The cops, the suspects, the voices over the radio from the station, the old Jews wrinklin up in the sun on the South Beach, *everbody*. I got Ochoa with me and I look over to him to translate and the bastard smiles and repeats what they said in Spanish, only a little louder."

"You should take classes, Chief. There could be some good informants in those dreams, only you no comprende."

"I didn't learn Yiddish when your crowd elbowed in," says Duckworth.

"You weren't *born* when my crowd settled in. Anyhow, the Spanish started this place, it's only fair."

"Tell that one to the Seminoles."

The school notebooks are disappointing. Nothing personal, just classroom stuff. Poli Sci and Econ. "Nice handwriting."

Duckworth sits up and rubs his knees. "Rivkin, what are you doin?"

"What do you mean?"

"You lookin for *clues?*"

There is something nasty about the way he says *clues*.

"We're supposed to be figuring out who shot this kid, right?"

"I already know who shot this kid."

"Who?"

Duckworth swings his legs over the edge of the bed. "One of six guys pulled the trigger. Another of them drove the car. The other four helped them plan it."

"Six guys."

"Yeah. I got their phone numbers, I know where they live, I know who'd come forward to alibi for em if we wanted to piss people off and drag their names into this."

"So why are we in here?"

"We're in here, buddy," says Duckworth, "cause if we weren't those people out there would be yakkin bout how the cracker and the Jew came and asked three lousy questions and then split, that's how little they care about Cubans. This is how we pay our respects."

Duckworth stands and hitches his pants up, then smooths the bed out. "I had a bust going on three of these guys a couple years back, lookin good, and then our friends from Washington step in and make some noise about how they got a precedential investigation in progress, they got immunities promised, they got bigger fish to fry. I mean these guys *are* the fish, they don't come any bigger down here, but I got to back off. So I get a college boy dead on the sidewalk and the newspapers actin like we been sittin on our hands. Cubans. I hate this shit."

Rivkin puts the joint and the magazines and the condoms he's found into an evidence filer. He wonders if he should go through Stuart's room sometime.

"Damn good ballplayers, though," says Duckworth. "Kid in my old neighborhood, Jimmy Hidalgo, would've made the bigs if the color line was broke in '48. Went down and threw for the Sugar Kings. Sucker could *fire* that thing."

When they come back into the living room Post is there with the father.

"Looky, Rivkin. The Feds've landed."

"Fellas." Post is one of the local Bureau guys. He sits at the very edge of his chair, his back straight, as if being comfortable would be disrespectful. "Whatta you say?"

"Now that you're here," says Duckworth, "we can hang it up."

"Any ideas?"

Duckworth shrugs. "Omega called the radio stations and took credit. Why would they lie?"

The father is looking at Duckworth with a scared expression on his face, worried about what they might've found out about his son in the room.

"He was a good boy," says Duckworth, patting the man gently on the shoulder as he goes toward the door. "I'm real sorry for y'all. Rivkin?"

"Coming, Chief."

EIGHT

Lourdes watches the fiber of the beef separate under her spoon as she stirs the thick gravy. The smell soothes her, she feels safe within the pocket of warm, spicy air that it makes. Marta comes in from the street.

"Mami," she says. "Qué haces?"

"La comida."

"Pero si no son más que las cuatro."

She shrugs and Marta goes into her room. Why shouldn't she start cooking at four? What else is there to do? Lourdes dribbles oil from a square can onto her skillet. It is the same one she brought from Camagüey, the one old Esperanza gave her when the soldiers came. The one the soldiers at the airport tried to take from her when they were leaving for the North. There was a limit to how much what you took could be worth and to how much what you took could weigh and the big black skillet made Lourdes overweight. One of the soldiers, just a boy, had it by the handle and she had it by the rim, holding on grimly and scolding them all. And Him, He laughed about it, the first time He'd smiled since the notice that they were taking the ranch. "You don't even know how to cook," He said and it was true, always the girl had done the cooking, old Esperanza who they'd brought from the Oriente, whose wrinkled brown face had showed no emotion when the soldiers came to billet.

"You're free," they told her. "The Revolution has made you free." Then they asked if she would cook them dinner.

She didn't come out to wave goodbye, Esperanza, maybe because she was afraid to in front of the soldiers or maybe she really was glad to see them go like the soldiers said. What bothered Lourdes was that she'd never know, the girl would be dead now, she was at least sixty at the time and from the stories life was very hard there now. She was walking through the kitchen the last time, the day before they left for Havana, and Esperanza finished washing the skillet and turned and handed it to Lourdes. Lourdes was stunned at how heavy it was.

"Take this, Señora," she said, her face revealing neither kindness nor irony. "You'll have to learn how to use it."

Lourdes pours the hard, dry rice into the skillet, stirring the grains into the oil with her wooden spoon. She turns the heat on under the saucepan of black beans on the rear burner.

"Fuí al hospital a visitar a Papi," calls Marta from her room. "Luz te manda un abrazo."

She doesn't like Marta going around with Luz, or any of the other negras she works with. They are nice enough themselves, the ones she has met, but going around with negras is how a white girl will get a reputation. At least when Lourdes was a girl that was so. Times have changed, of course, though He always said, raising His voice that way He had when He would make a pronouncement, that since times were only changing for the worse there was no reason to keep up with them.

Lourdes hopes Marta will have some appetite tonight. It is sad to have so much left over always. Marta has always been a light eater but it didn't mean so much when He was home and even less when the boys were still there. It had been all she could do to keep their plates full. Blas stirred his beans and rice into a purpley mix and hunched over so the fork wouldn't have so far to go to his mouth and Ambrosio would eat his rice first, every grain, before he started on the beans, and at the head of the table He would mash His food together with the back of His fork and then shovel in hunks of it, never talking at meals but not minding if they did as long as it wasn't too loud, or later, when the boys were ready to go, if it was about politics and then there were the screaming fights and He and Blas standing face to face the way that made her heart close like a fist with fear. There are still grease spots on the wallpaper from one night when a plate was thrown and now He hardly eats at all, she has stopped sending special things to the hospital because Marta says they just go bad and they have special food there, bland things, probably Jewish, that are fed to Him by hand.

Marta always picked at her food, her fork skipping over her plate like a stick-legged shore bird hopping through the surf. When she said she was done the food had moved but none of it seemed to be gone. She would listen to her big brothers with her eyes wide and would laugh when they laughed whether she knew what they were talking about or not and Lourdes would think a prayer of thanks to San Cristóbal that they were all together and all alive and another to the Blessed Virgin to protect her sister and her nieces and her cousins left in Cuba. Her sister had asked her to stop writing at one point because the neighbors were all suspicious of people who got mail from Miami and she wanted this job at a school, so there was only prayer.

Lourdes stirs the beef. There is no fat, no gristle. He taught her the cuts of beef when He was bringing home pieces from the Jews. That was when Olga Mejías, Lord rest her soul, taught her how to cook in the place on 12th and He was working in the meat department for the Lomax brothers. They were fighting with their regular butchers, something about unions, and He came in for them and every day was covered with the blood of the livestock and every night went to night class, sitting in a metal folding chair next to busboys who had been doctors and taxi drivers who had been lawyers and criminals who had been police. When the Habaneros who knew English or thought they did would make fun of Him He would call them city scum and it wasn't long before the Lomax brothers had to use Jewish words to talk about Him while He was in the room. He had butchered cattle with His own father on the range in Camagüey and it was no problem to do it again with better tools. But to work for another man, to be paid wages in cash that were a fraction of what the yanquis were getting for the same work, that made His body tight when He lay awake in bed at night and she couldn't sleep either but that only made Him angry so she pretended she was dreaming. He wouldn't have her rolling cigars or stitching underwear no matter how they needed the money, no matter how He hated sharing an apartment with the Mejías family, so she stood in Olga's steamy kitchen day after day learning to cook. Olga was a Habanera but not stuck up about it. She didn't have English either and was afraid to go outside the apartment, not because it was dangerous but because seeing what was out there reminded her of what was lost and would never be theirs again. She stayed in the apartment surrounded by everything they had brought and she and her family got bigger and bigger, like they could carry their memory

of home in the fat of their bodies. Her boys were nicknamed Big
Gordo and Little Gordo and the daughter Irena looked like Olga's
twin sister by the time she was fourteen, all youth lost in fat. Lourdes
cooked and cooked but never ate. She would breathe it, test it, taste
it, but that was all she needed. Most nights she sat at the table
without a plate, watching the others, ready to bring more when it
was needed, like Esperanza, though Esperanza was expected to sit
just on the other side of the door that led to the kitchen in the old
house, listening.

Marta drifts through the kitchen again, casting an eye at the
stovetop.

"You make too much, Mami," she says. "Siempre haces demasiado."

"Qué pasaría si alguien viniera?"

"Cómo quién?"

She hates it when Marta questions her. She's worse than a priest.
At least with a priest you know there is forgiveness at the end of it.

"Tu hermano. Tu tío."

"Nobody's coming, Mami. Nobody ever comes."

Marta goes into the living room and turns on the TV. The news
isn't on yet, so she watches the end of a story. From the accents it
sounds like one of the Venezuelan ones.

Lourdes sets the table for two. She isn't hungry but Marta will
get mad if she doesn't at least pretend to eat. The plates come from
later. He had given her the money to buy them the week the yanqui
Government people had met with Him and His political friends to
plan the Invasion. The same week the bank said it would consider
His application for a business loan. Things were looking up, He
said, we may have some important visitors, so buy some decent
plates. That was the place on 27th and nobody ever came except
for the bad week of the Invasion when Elio Pujol brought his short-
wave radio over because they had more room and the house was
filled with men and cigars and cursing as the reports would crackle
over the box. All she remembered was making coffee, always making
coffee that the men would take from her and down in one gulp
without ever looking at her and she kept the plates in the cupboard
for fear someone would break them in a rage at the Communists or
the yanquis or the liars on the radio.

It was politics and it was money, two things she tried to know
nothing about, two things that scared her, two things that made

Him angry if she spoke of them at all. "They're considering the loan," He had said, "but if things go well we won't need it. We'll be going home." That phrase, "We'll be going home," chilled her the way the phrase "We have to leave" had years earlier in Camagüey. She wished then that she knew the black arts, the santería, the way Esperanza did, or at least people said she did. Her prayers seemed so small.

She cuts a plátano in diagonal slices and tosses the slices onto the little skillet, the one she bought up here. The boys, especially Blas, loved plátanos cooked sweet and golden and she still makes them though Marta isn't much interested. It seems right, some kind of celebration like how they still use bread and wine in the Mass. Marta was only nine when they came North so she is more of a yanqui than the rest of them and has strange tastes. She is always telling Lourdes she uses too much sugar in her cooking but why should she listen to what someone who doesn't like to eat says about cooking? And lately, since He is in the hospital, she's always telling Lourdes about other things, about money and politics, until Lourdes covers her ears with her hands and it is no wonder Marta is so late in marrying with that kind of thing on her mind all the time. A woman in her thirties never married is suspicious, you wonder if there isn't a good reason even though she is healthy and good-looking and comes from a good home. Blas, back when he was home, would call her Sor Marta de los Dolores to tease her, because she took everyone's problems onto her own back and was so serious if you let her be. Maybe it will be better when He comes home, when the Jews have helped Him recover from His stroke. Marta seemed happier when He was home, or at least less restless. It is so strange now that He will only talk to Marta, that she will come home with long stories about how He said He was feeling and what He thought and what He wanted and when Lourdes goes in He hardly seems to know her and the only word He manages to croak out over and over sounds like the name "Maceo," but they don't know anybody named Maceo or at least Lourdes doesn't. Marta tells her that she is a nurse and can read the signals He makes with His eyes and His hands but it still makes Lourdes feel bad. It used to be her who knew how He was feeling and what He thought and what He wanted, sometimes from watching His eyes and listening to His breath and seeing the way His body tensed or relaxed when He spoke and sometimes He would talk to her late at night when He couldn't sleep and He would say her name and she could stop pretending she was dreaming. He would look in her eyes then and tell her what was bothering Him, what He was hoping to do and she would love Him so then that it all made sense, coming up to this place where they pretended to be living their lives but were really only remembering who they were in their real lives back home. They were all dreaming, the kind of bad dream where you are always just outside your body watching yourself, unable to stop what is happening and go back to where you want to be. In the morning He wouldn't meet her eye and if she mentioned anything He had said He would be gruff with her, like maybe she really had been asleep and had dreamed the whole conversation, but that was understood between them, it was all right. And now He spoke only through Marta.

She hears the TV set click off and Marta comes into the room carrying Ambrosio's diary. She is reading the diary more and more, lately, almost every night.

"Todo está tan quieto," sighs Lourdes.

"You should get a job or something, Mami. Charity or something. It's not good, alone all day in here—"

Lourdes sighs and shrugs. "Cuando tu padre vuelva—"

"He's not coming back, Mami." Marta has that stern look that hurts her so much. "He doesn't get better. He stays the same or he dies. Tú sabes eso."

Luz's older brother, Serafín, brought the diary to them after he got out of the hospital. He had been friends with Ambrosio during the training for the Invasion and they had both kept diaries and exchanged them on the boat just before the landing, so if only one of them survived he could carry the other's words back home. Back North. Serafín came over to dinner at the place they were living in now, after the loan had been approved and He had the carnicería going. A very polite young man, Serafín, thin, not as dark as his sister, with his suffering held in his eyes. He said that he hadn't read the diary and apologized if there was any damage from being in the ocean. Ambrosio had spoken of them all many times in the camp. He had been a brave man and a good friend. Lourdes tried to picture this man he was talking about, seeing only a boy with curly hair and a bright smile who didn't like loud noises and was gentle with his little sister, who wrote poetry, whose skin was sensitive to the sun and who had cried and clung to her his whole first year because of a bad stomach. Lourdes could still sense the way his little hands had gripped onto her though she hadn't held a baby, anybody's baby, in years. The way she could still smell the first breath of the ranch in Camagüey, the rich brown smell of cattle everywhere the day He had taken her out to their home. The way she could still hear her daughter's cough the year she had pneumonia and tried so hard to be quiet, to be good, not to be sick and make even more trouble, but her poor little body was just filled up with the sickness and even fat, placid Olga would wince when a cough would echo in the tiny apartment.

Lourdes tries not to think about the baby and the way it held on to her. She puts food on the two plates. Marta sits reading the diary. When she was a girl and still came home from school for lunch Lourdes had let her read at the table because He wasn't there to object and her face was so pretty and serene. Marta's fork pauses over the steaming beef. Lourdes sits and eats a few bites so her daughter won't lecture her. They sit in the places they always did, next to each other in the chairs nearest to the kitchen. The other chairs are still there. The smell of the food, the heat of it coming up from the plate, makes her feel a little better, a little safer, but soon even that will be gone and a whole night will face her. She wants to slam her hand down hard on the table like a man, just for the comforting noise it would make. She feels full. Marta reads her dead brother's diary.

NINE

➤ YOU TRY TO MAKE the night liquid without getting sloppy. Luz feels the day's heat still coming off the parking-lot asphalt, wading through it up to her calves with Caridad clicking alongside. She can feel the percussion already beating in her blood, the rhythm pounding out on Calle Ocho, *pa*papapa-*pa*papapa, cars and lights and nervous energy driving the night, the night already percolating with the interplay of conga and timbal, timbal and bongo, an insistent and expectant energy that you can hook into or give yourself up to but that you can't ignore. The guy at the door winks hello and his eyes drop to check them out as the bandsound washes over them and they descend into the muggy pit of La Barricuda—

En las tinieblas de la noche—

shout the men on the bandstand—

Yo busqué un salvador
Oíste mis oraciones
Terminando mi dolor

Luz feels the moist heat of men's eyes touching them and smiles. Caridad is jabao, fair-skinned with African features and wears her little fake-leather skirt like taut skin ready to pop over her strong meaty thighs and butt. Her top is cut tight and low to show breasts and shoulders like molded butter and Luz loves to walk in next to her, knowing how fine they look side by side, the hardtails against the wall sucking in their breath and muttering ay de mí, la blanca y la negra! Her satiny white jumpsuit is cool and soft against her skin and she lets an effortless little smile light her face to mask the agony of her feet bound in high-heeled red torture traps. La Barricuda is boiling with people, hard, choppy waves of people, dancing, elbowing for space, up on their toes checking out the players, wet with promise and desire and Luz laughs a little because she loves it so, that first headlong dive into the light and the heat and the noise and poor Caridad is trying too hard, showing her gums like fucking Miss America strutting her stuff down the ramp. The conga and the timbales and the bongo and the maracas are rapping with each other, stirring the damp mess on the dance floor, the horns are screaming and the little whippetlike Venezuelans at the microphones are dancing and shaking and shouting, revving the motor that drives the night, that shoots your blood singing through your veins and Luz tries to stay loose and calm and see how the game is breaking cause if that electric charge is all you get out of the night there you'll be lying stone sober alone in your bed with the rhythm still percolating through your hands and feet and veins and nowhere for it to flow, so juiced that if music is playing and people having fun a hundred miles away you can hear it through your window. Luz puts her hand on Caridad's arm to steady her and checks the room for Hector, half hoping he'll be here so she can ignore him and half hoping he won't so the night can play out without a scene. He doesn't call and he doesn't call and then he does some night when he's got nothing or nobody else lined up and he expects you to roll over with your paws up in the air, like he's some kind of fantastic drug you're strung out on and you can't live without it, you're desperate or something and fuck *that* shit, you know?

"Qué tomas?" says the guy behind the bar, too busy to check them out and Caridad gets a whiskey sour and Luz opens with a rum punch, heavy on the punch. You got to start easy, just a little lubrication at first to keep things flowing, you got to relax and concentrate, not let the music sweep you away. Caridad is almost shaking with nerves beside her, flashing her teeth at the world, ready to go off with the first presentable guy with the nerve to hit on her.

"Se llama Caridad," the boys in high school used to say, "cuz she give it away for free."

Luz surveys the room, picking out Celia Rojas and waving, waving to Amado and Zoila, seeing who can move on the dance floor. One guy with a cute ass slides totally inside the beat around a tall redheaded girl sweating buckets and trying to dance in shoes that don't want to dance but he's either a pato or so stuck on himself he might as well be. Why are the ones who can dance always the ones who live in front of a fucking mirror? The band shifts into something slower and just as loud but to Luz there is only one song and if guys are singing it's about this girl and how fine she looks and maybe she's interested and he could have her or maybe he already has and now there's this other girl tempting him with her bold eyes or maybe the first one has left him and he feels so bad he isn't even interested in looking for the second one, a regular fucking soap opera. If a woman is singing the story is similar but even more pathetic and uh-oh, who's this guy in the corner staring at me?

He is young, not bad-looking, staring across the floor but not like the hardtails with their thumbs in their belts and their shirts open to their bellybuttons fucking you hard with their eyes whether you like it or not, bitch, but an interested stare, almost like he knows her but doesn't know her. Luz holds his eyes for a short moment, no big invitation but no putoff either, then looks away and when she glances back, pretending not to, he is gone.

Cada vez que me abrazas—

The singers are wiry little guys with cute little tennis-ball butts that they shake as if to answer the percussion players behind them, hard-muscled little guys with tiny waists and chihuahua popeyes and thin mustaches that seem penciled on—

Me empiezo a ahogar
Todavía tú me cazas—

The guy is coming toward her through the crowd now with another guy in tow for Caridad, which shows he's thinking—

Hasta el fondo del mar.

The thing about La Barricuda is that it's so saturated with noise and people that to even say hello or what are you drinking you have to take someone's arm and put your mouth close to their ear like you know each other a long time and you feel a little warm breath on your neck and there you are looking into eyes maybe six inches away from yours for an answer.

"Qué dijo?"

"Rufo."

"Qué?"

"*Rufo*. And this is Frankie Cruz. We call him Oye."

The friend is shorter than Rufo, and older, with a dark mustache and the cautious look of a guy who's been married or still is and isn't happy about it.

"Nice to meet you," he says, then nods to the swamp on the dance floor. "Some zoo, huh?"

Rufo is very gallego, white even with a tan, with light brown almost blond hair exactly the kind Luz doesn't trust cause they always make it a big deal going out with a black girl and think you're easy sex like Hector who thinks you're desperate for him cause he looks like the guy from the Who with the sky-blue eyes and fuck *that*, you know? But this Rufo is pretty smooth and manages to seem like he's talking softly even shouting over the music and doesn't seem too eager but without the here-it-is-bitch attitude that's going down these days and Oye and Caridad just sort of smile uncomfortably at each other because they're so far apart, almost four feet, and it's not slick to be screaming at each other at this point and no sort of a deal for the evening has been cut yet so it's really in Rufo's hands. He tries the old school bit.

"I thought maybe I recognized you. You go to Saint Mary's?"

Luz shakes her head. "Public school. Mi amiga Marta iba allí—"

"Marta—?"

"—de la Pena."

"La conocí. She was in my homeroom. Real serious girl, good-looking—"

"Yeah." If he went to school with Marta he's older than he looks. Which is no big deal if they're not married.

"What is she now, a nun?"

Luz laughs. "Nurse. Trabaja conmigo en un hospital de ancianos."

"And how about you?" He turns to Caridad, who is straining at the leash.

"Nurse's aide. But I'm studying."

"We run this warehouse—restaurant supply. Oye's my boss."

Oye laughs and says that is an exaggeration. He has a Puerto Rican accent.

"Pretty soon it's the other way around," he says. "Pretty soon Rufo is el jefe."

"Por qué?"

"Porque the Old Man is cubano y los cabrones cubanos stick together," he smiles. "Back home they own half of San Juan." He gives Rufo an affectionate shove. "Whatever that's worth."

Running a warehouse is kind of vague but he dresses nice so it can't be so bad. A girl in a red sheath starts crying hysterically on the dance floor, speeding her brains out behind something she bought in the ladies' room but still bobbing sweatily to the beat while the guy she's just met treads water with his feet, surprised by her outpour but hoping to ride it out and still take her home before she passes out. The hardtails against the wall have given up on Luz and Caridad for the moment, their eyes snake through the wet pressing bodies hoping to cut something loose from the herd. Rhinestones are flying off the timbal player's shirt and when he flicks his head back jewels of sweat fly into the lights. The horns are in a frenzy and the singers popping up and down like pistons in overdrive and one guy on the floor at the edge of the bandstand is just leaping in the air over and over, twisting and turning when he shoots up each time from the crowd like a stick tossed in heavy surf. Oye shouts something in Caridad's ear that she just keeps smiling blankly at and Rufo gives a small smile and settles his back against the counter next to Luz, acting like he's enjoying just being beside her and rubbing arms now and then. It's like there's something on his mind which if it's true is a big step up from Hector who is like one of those lower forms you study in biology where all their sense is spread out along their backbones instead of having brains. Serafín called him a Cuban surfer but Serafín never liked any of her boyfriends. Oye and Caridad step out to dance and Oye isn't much to watch but Caridad—when Caridad shakes it all moves in the right ways and there are guys *dying* at the other end of the room and you can tell Oye's mind is screeching around corners thinking Madre de Dios am I gonna get *this* and Rufo gives a little smile and turns and says she's a good dancer, your friend. Another rum punch, heavy on the rum, appears in her hand and her throat is dry from shouting over the music so down it goes and he asks does she like to dance but she says no, not yet. Caridad is dripping sweat down her neck and rolling in between her breasts when she comes back and Oye has his handkerchief out mopping his forehead and Caridad gives her a look then nods toward the ladies' room but it looks like five minutes of heavy seas to get there and it's clear everybody is interested so why bother, you know? Luz puts down her glass and makes an opening.

"I think I'm going deaf in this place," she says.

"Why don't we go to Tabú? The music's quieter and sometimes there's tables free."

Tabú has a heavy cover charge, these guys aren't going for the budget tour. Luz looks to Caridad who looks at Oye then back to Luz and her smile gets bigger if that is possible and they nod and follow in the path the guys make through the swirl of bodies out of the steamy maw of La Barricuda.

Luz doesn't know anything about cars but this thing of Oye's is big and smells new and rides like velvet and the top is down which is the only way to be going down Calle Ocho at night. The warm breeze brings Luz back a little and she feels this Rufo watching her next to her in the back seat while Oye tells Caridad all about his machine and what it can do up in the front. She can tell he's one of those guys who treats his car like Hector treats his cock, talking to it softly and stroking it and rubbing stuff on it and expecting the whole world to be impressed with it and fuck *that,* you know? It's nice and all but it's not like only guys could go out and buy one, a car, if she wanted she could save enough but she'd rather make the apartment nice. There are dozens of them out here on the Calle, strutting their machines up and down the way the hardtails in the clubs and on the corners strut their balls when you pass by, hefting them up unconsciously, or maybe just checking to be sure they're still there. And if she wanted that it wasn't so hard to get and it didn't have to be Hector's and whenever she told him so he would go crazy cause he knew how true it was and call her all those puta names that he said only guys should use. Oye is stroking the felt or velour or whatever it is on the back of the seat just behind Caridad's neck, stroking it the way he's dying to stroke her and it cracks Luz up and makes her feel the rum up and down her legs a little too and things are getting warm and liquid in a nice way.

There's a table free at Tabú and the guy singing is great and the band behind him makes her want to cry. Oye and Rufo are telling stories about each other the way guys do to pump each other up in front of their dates and it's clear they've gone out together before cause their timing is so tight.

"This guy, he works for me," says Oye, "you gotta see him to believe him—"

"This guy O'Hara—" says Rufo.

"O'Hara de las ojeras." They both laugh. "Every time you need him to do something, you can't find him, and when you do—"

Rufo makes a snoring noise.

"Exactamente. Siempre durmiendo, siempre borracho."

"He's like that guy you read about in school—"

"Rip Banuinco."

"Rip Van Winkle, yeah—"

"To find him you gotta sniff for the whiskey smell—"

"The other day we find him asleep in the bottom of a packing crate. Should have sealed him up and sent him to Chicago—"

"So why don't you fire this guy?" says Luz.

They look at each other. "I can't," says Oye.

"Why not?"

He shrugs. "La política."

"What's politics got to do with your warehouse?"

Oye gives one of those sighs that mean women can never understand the complexities of the world and looks to Rufo.

"Toda la vida es política," says Rufo. "At your hospital, there must be somebody who can't do the job but they still got it—"

Caridad laughs. "Hematoma Helen. The patients try to hide when it's her turn to take bloods."

"Y sigue allí?"

"Yeah, she's been there forever. The head nurse an her went to school together."

"Ves? La política. Like that boy today."

"I heard too much about that boy today," says Luz and Rufo shrugs and Oye asks Caridad to dance.

The music is slower here, dreamier, like a machine gliding along the coast at sunset, taking long easy curves, following the shore, the congas still thrumming steady underneath the horns, the horns sliding, cruising, timbales rim-rapping, metallic in the breaks, and the flat slap of the bongo punctuating the rhythm like roadsigns ticking by at regular intervals. The singer is floating above it, his voice sad and world-weary, eyes closed to feel the music better, holding the microphone lightly in both hands, telling it to them high and sweet—

Siempre que vuelvo a verte
Mi corazón está ligado en hielo
Mis sueños caen del cielo
Siempre que vuelvo a verte

"So is he married?" asks Luz, surprised to hear her own voice as she watches Caridad on the floor with Oye.

Rufo smiles. "He was."

"Divorced or separated?"

"Separated. But it's for good this time."

"Sure."

"He's not a bad guy."

"No dije eso. I'm just looking out for Caridad."

Rufo nods. "Good. That's the most important thing, looking out for your friends. Knowing who your friends are." He wasn't making fun of her.

Oye and Caridad come back to the table, Oye catching his breath and wiping his face dry with his handkerchief and more people keep coming in till it's hard to see the bandstand. Rufo looks around, sighing, and says, "I used to come to this place a lot," he says and then from the corner of her eye Luz sees Hector walking through the crowd smiling his dazzling smile with some little straight-haired blondie from Dade Jr. trailing behind him looking like Mr. and Miss Coppertone America USA. He gives a command to the blondie and she stops a few yards back from the table like a good puppy while he comes to stand right over Luz with his hands resting on her shoulders like the boxing managers do with their young boys on TV.

"Luz," he smiles. "Qué tal?"

Rufo gives him a glance so languid and disinterested it's like a slap in the face and turns back to watching the band.

"Hace semanas que no te veo," says Luz, trying to seem casual.

"It hasn't been that long," says Hector. "I've been busy."

Hand the guy a mirror and a blow dryer and he's good for half a day, she thinks. Busy my ass. "Yeah," she says. "Me too."

Oye is looking to Caridad for a clue but she is looking away pointedly, never a big fan of Hector. Once he called her a white nigger and she almost caused a major crash on the Dixie Highway trying to beat his brains in from the back seat. He was just kidding, he said, and Luz broke up with him for a month over it but he has this talent for apologizing so you feel you're the guilty one.

He gives Luz a last little possessive squeeze and eases away. "You're lookin good," he says, giving an amused glance in Rufo's direction. "I'll give you a call."

The little blondie follows him away and Rufo turns back as if no one had interrupted. "The thing about these places, though," he says, "is they're nice for a while, then every asshole in town hears they're nice so they come in and then it's not so nice anymore."

Luz orders another drink. Somehow Hector gets to walk away like he's marked his property and Rufo gets to sit here like he doesn't really give a shit but could eat Hector for breakfast if he wanted to and Luz ends up feeling like somebody's leg has been lifted on her. It always happens like that with guys when they sniff around each other and you're in the middle. You might as well be a parking space they both want but not enough to really fight over. Sometimes she thinks it would be nice to have one like Zoila Carrasco has, who would kill for you, who can't stand to share you with anybody instead of this big dick act of not really caring, but those are always the guys who want you on a leash and pretty soon you're tied with three feet of slack to the kitchen stove while they're out fighting duels of honor over some other little girl who's as dumb as you are and the hell with *that,* you know?

On the other hand now Hector knows she's not home in her bathtub crying her little heart out like she was a week ago so fuck him and she lets the music smooth away the picture of his stupid, beautiful blond head, lets the music into her like warm water flows into your body when you're cold, filling you up with its heat and the singer is still up there above the rhythm, his voice cutting through everything else happening in the room to talk only to her—

> *Eras el alma de la noche*
> *El fuego de mi esperanza*
> *Estar juntos nunca jamás*
> *Eras el alma de la noche*

Luz is drinking rum and Cokes now and she's had two or is it three and the singer isn't so handsome but with his voice he is beautiful and if only you could go up and put your hand on his chest to feel the voice purring out like the velvet rumble of a beautiful tiger, thick and liquid, and Rufo is even more handsome than she thought when she first saw him even if he doesn't sing and seems so far away over in that chair sitting next to her and Caridad's smile is looser now, more the way she smiles when there aren't guys around and the night is really down around them now, warm and thick and liquid. Rufo asks her to dance and he's not bad, not showy but smooth and strong and the way he holds her feels good, like his body is listening to hers not trying to bump something into it and she remembers old Gold talking poetry to her today at work and what a sucker for a soft word she is, what a pushover for somebody who likes to think she's tough. And those circles move in circles, she thinks as she dances, moving her hips and smiling, eyes half closed, more sensing Rufo than looking at him, moving and listening with her body so the band and the sad voice floating and the touch and smell of Rufo close to her and the warm buzz of the rum all flow together thick and liquid like the night that has no edges anywhere just circles moving in circles. . . .

Me dejaste triste y vacío

The singer's voice circles above the band like a beautiful hawk.

En los brazos fríos de la soledad
Sin esperanza ni deseo
Por el invierno eterno de mi vida

In the car again the guys are talking about going to the club whatever that is and Rufo is flowing into focus then out then in as they glide down Calle Ocho in and out of the warm yellow streetlights. The club is upstairs from some farmacia, just a single bulb burning over the stairs on the side and Caridad gives a worried look back down to Luz as they climb, remembering a night when a club some guys they didn't like so much took them to turned out to be the guys' apartment and it was two hours of wrestling and excuses before they could escape and Luz had to leave her best pair of shoes inside when they bolted out after a taxi. Caridad's face has softened as the night has melted her careful look, lipstick smearing a bit at the corner of her mouth, hair wisping out from its tight curls, eyes liquid with alcohol and Luz thinks ay chica, if I was a guy I would ache for you and smiles reassuringly as someone coming out opens the door at the top of the stairs and they hear the music. The people at the door know Rufo and they're led toward a table. It is dark

and close and dreamy and a round brown-skinned woman is crooning and sobbing into the microphone with five guys sleepwalking
their instruments in the dark behind her and the music is liquid and
smooth like soothing oil, the brown woman pouring her troubled
life into the song but gently, discreetly, her sorrow a quiet and fragile
thing—

> *Días de calor*
> *Noches de eternidad*
> *Horas de dolor*
> *Vida de oscuridad*
> *Esperando tu amor*

They pass a table of men ruled by a silver-haired character in
glasses who Luz has seen before on the street, who Serafín had told
her is with the Omega and she feels Rufo tighten beside her, looks
at his face and sees for the first time that he isn't any older or
smarter than she is and he smiles a little nervous smile and gives a
little wave to the old dragon at the table who returns an imperial
nod, really only a movement of the eyes and then the eyes turn and
look at her and the way they look at her makes things start to get
solid and she sees just how small and dark the room is with lots of
old guys in expensive clothes and mostly younger women in expensive clothes and by the time they sit at their table Luz realizes that
besides her and the woman singing everybody in the room is white
or thinks they are like Caridad and that Rufo has realized it too
and suddenly thinks it's a mistake to have brought her here. The
glass holding the drink she has ordered is hard and cold in her hand.
She wonders if it's only her imagination or if the brown woman
singing is looking right at her. Rufo's voice is tinny and sharp and
they're talking about the dead boy again.

"He was warned," says Rufo. "He was told the price and he
went ahead and then he had to pay."

"Cuban business," says Oye shaking his head. "I don't see the
point. You lost the war, man, Fidel got that island in his *pocket,* so
why be killin each other?"

"We know his cousin," says Caridad, almost proud. "She works
on the night shift."

Rufo looks at Luz as if to see what she thinks.

"My brother says they killed him cause he was the youngest," she says. "To set an example."

"He knows a lot about it, su hermano?"

Luz notices for the first time how sharp his features are. A face that will be hard when he's older. She shrugs. "Creo que sí. Estaba con la Brigada y todavía conoce a algunos de esos. He hears the gossip."

"With the Brigade, huh? He go to prison down there?"

"He didn't get caught during the Invasion." It makes her nervous talking about Serafín in here, something is wrong. "He got on a little boat with some guys and they got back alive somehow. Some of them."

Rufo nods, interested. The brown woman is singing right to Luz, tears in her eyes.

"He's a man in love, tu hermano," smiles Caridad. "He's crazy over Marta on our shift."

"The Marta I went to school with?"

"Sí. An he's a good-looking guy, too. Qué lástima! Total waste."

> *El dolor dura para siempre*
> *Pero la felicidad es solo un momento*
> *Puedo vivir con la pena*
> *Pero sin los recuerdos de amor*
> *Sin falta tendŕe que morir*

Luz orders another drink and the darkness of the room swallows whatever is hard and old around her, the music slides in with its soothing sadness, a sadness that holds her close and rocks her gently and Caridad is giving her little looks and flicking her eyes at Oye, uncertain, wanting Luz to give her blessing and Luz can feel a big warm yes of a smile spreading on her face not because Oye is such a catch but because Caridad looks like she did in the sixth grade, eyes set wide with hope on her flat, pretty jabao face, worrying her heart to death over a glance from some little boy. The brown woman finishes her song and Luz whispers to Rufo if they can go now and she can feel his body loosen with relief when they are on the stairs leaving, having walked along the far wall away from the dragon's table.

Caridad gets hysterical in the car, hysterical laughing the way she does when she's drunk and overtired and she insists they have to go out to the airport and watch the planes take off and Oye thinks it's the funniest thing he's ever heard.

"Estás loca."

"No, no," she squeals, "it's great! You got to try it—"

"Estás loca y borrachísima," says Oye with his arm around her. "Estás shitfaced, chica."

So they swing up LeJeune, the warm night breeze caressing Luz, Rufo's hand light and friendly on her thigh and she decides, she knows, that she wants it tonight if only she can keep it going right, keep it going warm and liquid and nice and her thing puckers a little thinking about it and she laughs out loud and Rufo gives her a nice smile thinking it's the airport she's laughing about and what he doesn't know can't hurt him, right?

There are a dozen cars parked with their lights off by the wire fence at the edge of the airfield, some young couples necking and some families with their kids sitting on cushions up on the car roofs and a few older people just sitting and watching.

"Cabró," says Oye. "What's the cover charge?"

"When I was little," says Caridad, "when we first got here, we didn't have a TV, we didn't have a radio, record player, we didn't have nothing. Only this old car my father fixed up and got a taxi license for. So this is where we'd come for a big night out. Siempre los sábados por la noche."

A huge jet rumbles over them, shaking the car, close enough when it's directly overhead to hit with a rock if you had a strong arm and Caridad squeals with joy and squeezes closer to Oye. It climbs and fades until they hear the car radios again, playing the same station by some unspoken agreement, a merengue echoing from the car speakers seeming to fill the deep night sky till another jet thunders above to remind them this isn't the people's nightclub of the stars but a bunch of runaways and exiles who aren't flying home, ever.

"When I was a kid," says Rufo, "they said you could come out here and hop the fence and crawl through the grass to this place just past the end of the runway. And they said if you lay down in the grass at the spot right where the big planes lift off, the suction would pick you right up in the air, four or five feet off the ground like you're flying without wings, and it would carry you forward a bit till the plane got too high and dropped you back down."

His arm is around Luz now and she presses close, feeling nice to be held, floating on rum again and in love with the warm night and the frogs chirping and the smell of the wet grass on the airfield and the kids up on their hoods and cartops watching airplane after airplane leave them behind.

"They said there was no feeling like it, flying on a cushion of air. I never did it, though, cause they also said there was one kid who crawled too close and when the plane lifted it picked him up twenty, thirty, fifty feet in the air and then he broke out of the airstream and fell and broke his spine."

Luz thinks of the dead boy on Flagler again and wonders if the boy who fell from the sky felt the same going down as today's dead boy did when he saw his killer point the gun in his face, for they all said he must have been looking right at it the way he was hit and she presses tighter against Rufo and lets the next screaming jet overhead tear the picture from her head because she is tired of hearing about the dead boy and thinking about the dead boy and seeing how people are more excited than sad, as jumpy as the bright eyes of a ten-year-old at a car crash. Nothing is said but then Caridad and Oye are clinching and making sex noises in the front seat and Luz is up against Rufo with their tongues flowing together and he is sort of on top of her but it's not hard weight but something warm and supple melting over her and she is so liquid from the rum and the night she feels like her body is rolling under him, rolling like Hector's fucking water bed the only time he talked her into using it to do it and she almost laughs thinking of her body as a sloshing water bed but doesn't cause they hate it when you laugh or even smile too much it throws them right off the track. She pushes around so she is on top sort of, wanting, wanting something, wanting to be held and touched and to wrap herself around someone hard and her thing does a little shudder as the jet plows overhead trembling right through both of them and she reaches to see how hard it is because that's what she wants even if some of them think if you do anything they don't tell you to do or make you do you're one of those puta words they think they own but if that's what he's like that's his problem and just fuck him, you know? Just fuck him.

T E N

Diario
12 de Agosto, 1960

➤ Soy Ambrosio de la Pena Cruz, 17 años de edad, soldado en la santa Brigada de la liberación, caballero de la nueva Cruzada.

(Marta moves her lips slightly as she reads, familiar with the text, as if praying—)

We think it's going to be Panamá, but we're not sure.
We think we are among the first to be sent, but it's hard to tell.
We think they'll tell us more when we get there, wherever it is, but who's to say?

(The handwriting in this part is shaky. She pictures him with the book balanced on his knee, the light dim, young men sitting tense all around him—)

I asked the yanqui who watched the needles on the machine, on the lie-catcher (they say they work for American businessmen who want their sugar back—we think they're from the CIA, but how can you be certain?) if it was going to be Panamá. Tío Felix said not to ask questions, that if you asked too many questions they wouldn't let you go and I said if it's a place where you can't ask questions I don't *want* to go, which is the difference between Tío and me, between people from Tío's generation and the guys sitting on this airplane with me.

62

We're going to do it right this time.

The yanqui with the lie-catcher hooked me up and asked me where I was born and who were the people in my family and had I sympathized with or fought for or collaborated with the General and had I sympathized with or fought for or collaborated with Fidel and was I now or had I ever been a Communist or a homosexual or both and why did I want to go back and fight against Fidel now? After an hour of this I figured I could ask him one little question back, like where are we going to train, but he only said they didn't know if they were going to take me or not and I thought try and *stop* me from going, this is our fight, not yours, but then I figure these people are sending a man to the moon, they have enough bombs to blow the island right out of the water, so I kept my mouth shut.

The yanqui with the lie-catcher is not the man in charge.

They say there are rich Cubans in charge who want their land back, and rich yanquis who want their sugar back, and that's who's paying me $150 a month to be a soldier.

They say it's really just the General and he's taking money out of the suitcases he left with and after we take the island he'll come down in a helicopter and it will be the same mess as before.

When we were marched in here the windows on the plane were painted black with black tape around the edges so we peeled off the tape and scraped away enough paint so we can look out at this empty field with no lights on it. Nobody told us not to. Yesterday they took my personal belongings and gave me an envelope with some fake papers and I had time to trade some cigarettes for this diary with a guy at the Frente house who isn't going yet. Nobody told me not to.

I've started smoking but I've decided to try to stop when we get to wherever we're going.

We've been sitting here for hours. I don't recognize any of the other guys. Blas isn't here, even though we went to the recruiting place together and asked to be in the same group. They sent him somewhere else, or on another plane, or maybe he'll be one of our instructors because of his experience. I don't know.

They let one of the guys get on with his guitar and some are singing with him up at the front. The yanqui who passes through now and then to say we should be leaving any minute has a funny accent that somebody says is Guatemalan and somebody else says is just lousy Spanish. I ran into Herbie Socarrás in Coral Gables after the lie-catcher test and he said he'd heard they were building a base in Guatemala but somebody else told me it would be Puerto Rico and another said we'll just go over the fence from Guantánamo but most of the guys here have heard Panamá. We don't know. One guy here says he heard we'll just be a diversion and the yanquis will send the marines like John Wayne and Teddy Roosevelt and make us into another state. But another guy says then they'd have to pay the guajiros their minimum wage and they don't want that. Another guy who says he was in the army but says he was against the General told us it's always like that in the army, the people at the top *know* and the people at the bottom *do*. Another guy who says he was in the mountains with Gutiérrez Menoyo says with the rebels it was the opposite—*no*body knew but *every*body *did*. They aren't too happy to find each other here. The guy from the army says something about the lie-catcher failing to weed out the Fidelistas and the guy from the rebels says something about it failing to get rid of the Batistianos. There are some others here who were in the army or in the police but only this one guy who says he was with Gutiérrez Menoyo. I don't know where they sent Blas. There are a couple guys you can tell are just playboys who think this is a game or something, up singing with the guy who has the guitar. There is only one negro, the guy sitting next to me, who says his name is Serafín. He says his father worked in the kitchen at the Hilton and sometimes brought home wonderful desserts, or at least pieces of what was left of them.

We're going to do it right this time.

Nobody is here for the money or because they were forced by the General or to make a career of the army. We want to be here. Patriot-citizens, says the yanqui when he smiles and claps us on the back. You are the sons of Martí, he says. That's what the Communists call themselves says the guy who was with the rebels, and another guy says sure, they're his bastards and we're his legitimate heirs, and everybody laughs.

They say we'll be fighting Russians and they'll have tanks and rockets and machine guns.

They say there are women and children guarding the beaches, that we'll have to kill them to take the island.

They say we'll step ashore and people will cheer and throw down their arms the way they did when Fidel reached Habana.

They say the bullet that kills you never hurts.

The worst thing, I think, is to die in ignorance. Not to know where you are, who you're fighting against, what you're fighting for, how you'll be remembered. Of course we think we won't die, not one of us on this plane, but we're not sure.

We think history will absolve us.

We think history is on this plane and to miss this ride is to regret forever. We want to make history, to remember and be remembered, and so I write in this diary, I ask questions. The yanquis at the recruiting place told us about a Code of Silence but we are here together now, and I ask questions and men tell me their stories. We have been here for hours and I've heard a lot of stories. Somebody makes a crack that anybody so curious must be a spy and the guy from the rebels, who calls himself El Chulo, says a spy among Cubans is anyone with ears. That in Europe monks take a vow of silence but in Cuba they only promise not to shout. Another guy says he hopes Fidel is as confused by all the rumors floating around as he is and another says it's supposed to be a secret invasion but the only people not in on the secret are sitting in this airplane and the guy from the army who says he didn't support the General says maybe they'll just keep us in this damn plane for a week while John Wayne goes in and takes over with the marines and then they'll have us show up for the newspaper photos. That we'll be the new provisioñal government of Cuba. In that case, says one of the play-boys, I want to be Minister of Pussy. And then we're all talking at once, carving up the government positions, saying what should be the same and what should change and El Chulo turns to me and says listen, he says, as the guys are shouting and laughing and arguing, listen, he says, it's the Cuban Code of Silence.

The engine just started. Nobody is talking or singing or throwing balls of tape from the windows now. We're going home to fight. I am Ambrosio de la Pena Cruz, seventeen years old, soldier in the Holy Brigade of Liberation, knight of the new Crusade. When you read this, whether I am dead or alive, there will be a free, Christian and democratic Cuba, won by our spirit, by our blood. We are the sons of Martí!

The negro, Serafín, is trembling next to me. I say it's wonderful, isn't it? Can you feel the emotion? He says that his family came north by boat, that he's never been on an airplane before and is afraid he's going to be sick. Patria o muerte!

(Marta moves her lips slightly as she reads, familiar with the text, as if praying—)

E L E V E N

⟶ THERE ARE ONLY a few cars parked by the units at the Cockpit Motel when she pulls in. The noon sun makes the blacktop gooey and wobbles the air above it. Enormous passenger planes lumber close overhead, coming in to land. She opens the glass door to the little check-in office and steps into a wall of air-conditioning. A man with a face pocked like the craters of the moon is slouched over the desk reading the Hialeah results. He glances at her legs, then back to his paper.

"Forty for the night," he says, "fifteen an hour."

"Is Mr. Nuñez in?"

"He's checking some of the units," he says without looking up. "Try number seven."

Nuñez has a face like a hawk. He is fumbling through a huge mass of keys on a steel ring and cursing when she finds him.

"Señor Nuñez?" she says. He looks to be about fifty. There is a skull tattooed on the back of his left hand.

"Sí?"

"Quisiera hablar con usted."

"De qué?"

"Could we talk in private?"

He finds the right key. The door sticks a little and he shoves it open with his foot. A wet, musty smell comes out at them. He gestures with his hand. "After you."

She steps in and he snaps the light on. There is red, fake-velour wallpaper. Empty beer cans, crushed and twisted, litter the floor. Some kind of liquid has been thrown against the screen of the TV set in the corner. The bedsheets, wadded in a ball, are crusted with something black and sticky. A table lamp lies on its side. There is a puddle on the floor by the bathroom and streamers of toilet paper crisscrossing through it. The ceiling over the bed is a mirror.

"They beat the shit out of this one," says Nuñez, calmly surveying the damage. "You never want to rent to kids." He turns to her. "Ahora, qué pasa?"

She doesn't look like a puta to him. Dark-eyed, serious, maybe somebody's wife checking up. *Just what I need today.*

"They told me," she says, "that you can get guns."

"Guns?"

"Sí."

"Who told you?"

"Lo oí."

"Dónde?"

"Here and there."

"You heard wrong."

"I heard," she says, "that if somebody wanted to do something for Cuba, something that was against Fidel, that you would help them get guns."

He shakes his head. "No soy pendejo. Who sent you?"

"Nobody sent me. I have some people. Queremos luchar contra el comunismo."

He smiles. "Patriotas."

She stares at him. He doesn't like the way she stares at him.

"So why come to me?" he says. "Por qué no va a Omega?"

"We're not like Omega. Look, can you help us or not? We can pay some, if that's the problem."

"You say you have people?"

"Yes."

"Who are they?"

She gives him a hard look. "No soy pendejo."

"Look, let's say I'm a patriot too, and anything that goes against that greasy son of a bitch is good in my book—so what? If I was to get guns for you—let's say for the moment that I could—if I was and you fuck up, you kill some kid like they did yesterday and you get caught cause you're not like Omega, cause you're amateurs, then I've got the cops down my throat when you talk—"

"We'd never talk—"

"How do I know that when I don't even know who you are?"
She sighs. "Me llamo Marta de la Pena."

"Y los otros?"

"The guns would be leaving the country right away. There's no
way you could be connected with them."

"Leaving the country?"

"That's right."

"Where are you going with them?"

She is silent. He picks up the bedsheet and tosses it over the
puddle by the bathroom, keeping his eyes on her.

"Cuba?"

She is silent. He steps on the sheet, soaking up the water. He
crosses to the TV set and flicks it on. An overlit movie buzzes on
behind the stain on the screen. The sound is hollow and tinny. The
boss is standing behind his desk with his fly unzipped behind his
secretary, who is bent over the desk. The secretary is moaning and
gritting her teeth, her glasses still on, skirt pushed up around her
hips as the boss talks on the phone to his wife, telling her he'll be
home from work soon. The picture cuts to the wife on the other end
of the phone, sprawled on the kitchen table in stockings and garters
with the plumber humping into her and the electrician mashing her
breasts with grease-covered hands. She tells her husband to hurry,
she hates to be alone in the house.

"They're both lying," he says blankly when he looks away from
the screen to her. She stands stiffly in the middle of the room, eyes
locked with his, as if to take in anything else could blind her. He
flicks the set off and sits back on the bed.

"If this was for real, if it wasn't just some half-ass bunch of crazy
people going to get themselves killed, I might be interested. You
ever do anything like this before?"

"Not exactly. No."

He smiles. "Not exactly, she says. Well I have. There's more to
it than guns and a boat. If I'm gonna help you then I got to be in
on the planning."

"Por qué?"

"Soy patriota," he says, face impassive.

"I can't do that. The people I have—"

"This isn't a supermarket, niña, you don't come in here and say
I want guns, I'll take one of these, one of these, one of those. . . . I

need to know what you're up to, how many people you have, how experienced, what equipment you'll need. Then I talk to my people and they check it out and they think it over, and then maybe you get guns and maybe you don't."

"Who are your people?"

"People who feel the same way you and I do about the situation down home. People who can back you up all the way if they like you."

"Like the Omega?"

"The Omega isn't shit to these people." He leans forward and pulls the back of his shirt up, then pulls a gun from a pouch strapped to the small of his back. He hands it to her. It is black and heavy, the handle a little bit sweaty from his skin. "You ever hold one of these before?"

"No," she says. She holds the gun in both hands.

He stands and moves close to her. "This is a .38. Let me show you—"

He takes it gently from her hands.

"This thing here is a safety. You move it like this and the gun is ready to fire."

He moves the safety off.

"The rounds go in here, como eso, and that means the gun is loaded."

He puts his free arm around her shoulders and presses the barrel of the gun just under her right eye. She looks straight ahead, trembling slightly. She can feel his breath hot on her neck. His breath smells like sweet coffee.

"If we do something together you have to be very careful not to fuck me over," he says, almost whispering. "This isn't a game. Si tu me jodes, I have your fuckin head."

"I'll have to ask the others," she says, and steps back when he lets her go. He lowers the gun. "If they're willing to let you in on it I'll get back to you."

She walks out of the room, stepping around the beer cans on the floor. Hot white light blazes in from the parking lot as the door sticks partway open.

A black girl in her teens wearing a rumpled yellow dress and five-inch yellow platform shoes clumps unsteadily out of one of the units just in front of Marta, squinting up at the fierce midday sun.

"Day shift a bitch, aint it?" she says as Marta hurries past her.

El Halcón lies back on the bed. Pretty, he thinks, but you'd have to thaw it out with a blowtorch first. He yawns, then lifts the .38 and aims between the eyes of the man watching from the ceiling.

TWELVE

IN LA HABANA when El Halcón was a younger man he fell in love with a girl at the House of Virgins.

For certain things he had done on the job he had been rewarded by the Colonel with the task of collecting from the houses in the Colonel's district. There was a natural order in the Colonel's district. The dueñas collected from the customers, taking a cut for themselves and a little for the girls, then El Halcón collected from the dueñas and took a cut for himself and then the Colonel collected from El Halcón and took a cut for himself and then the Generalísimo collected from the Colonel, collected from all the Colonels and there it ended, the big fish eating the smaller fish till you got down to the minnows who ate shit from the bottom of the pond. That is how the world is.

The yanqui gangsters, the smaller ones he dealt with, whacked El Halcón on the back and bought him drinks. The Cuban gangsters gave him expensive cigars and tips for the racetrack and sometimes information he could use on the job. The dueñas, who the yanquis liked to call den mothers, would always invite him in to chat and listen to the baseball games on the radio and drink and sample the new girls. He tried to spend a little time and fuck a few of the girls at each of the houses on his route each week, so no one dueña would be jealous.

The girls in the houses always smiled when they saw El Halcón step into the parlor.

La Habana was a party then, day and night, a party people from all over the world paid to attend. Part of his job was to make sure the party ran smoothly. He would stroll through the noise and the

lights and the music with the full-belly knowledge that he was working for the people who counted, he *was* the people who counted,
with a welcoming smile and no cover charge waiting wherever he
appeared. There was a natural order then. All you needed was
something to sell and a will to survive. The girls sold their bodies
and the dueñas sold their craft and El Halcón sold his nerve and
his skill as a hunter. His friends in the barracks called him El Halcón
because he could spot a suspect in a crowd blocks away, because
once he got his claws in he never let go. La Habana was a party
then and El Halcón made sure only the invited guests got past the
door.

In La Habana then wherever there was an appetite there was
something to feed it. In one club a huge negro did unnatural acts
naked on stage and then walked among the audience wearing only
a towel. Drunken yanqui businessmen would pay him a few dollars
and dare their drunken yanqui wives and mistresses to reach under
the towel to feel what the negro had there, billed as the eighth wonder
of the world. In another club a dancer named La Pitona would
swallow things with her bollo—cigars, men's glasses, bananas, long-
necked wine bottles. After the clubs there was Casa de Negras and
Casa de Chinas and Casa de Francesas, or, if you couldn't make
up your mind, Casa de Todos Paises, where girls from all over the
world or girls who said they were from all over the world could be
found. For the maricones there was the Riding Academy and the
Bullring and Casa de Muchachos. This disgusted El Halcón but it
was part of his work so he collected from the dueñas, some who
were men dressed as women, at the door. The casas for the maricones
paid the Colonel double so they were allowed to exist. There was
the Heartbreak Hotel, sometimes called Casa de Rock, where boys
from the University of Miami would come to fuck little blondie
Cuban girls who spoke good English and wore ponytails and blue
jeans just like the little blondie town girls they were afraid to fuck
back home. El Halcón liked the little blondies and the way they
would dance up to him and call him Daddy but he hated the music
they played there and hated the drunken yanqui college boys who
were too stupid to be afraid of him. La Habana was a party then
and if a man had money or knew the people who counted he could
have whatever he needed. Most people knew how to behave at the
party but a few were swept up by it, running up dangerous gambling
debts or drug habits or mooning over some girl they thought was

special in one of the casas, bringing presents and making promises till she'd let them do her up the ass.

"Oh no," the girls would always say at first. "I don't sell that. That I save for my novio." And men made fools of themselves instead of just going to Casa de Nalga, where it was the specialty.

El Halcón strolled through it, picking what he wanted from a hanging orchard of bollo, fucking half for lust and half for public relations. Then he met the girl at the Casa de Vírgenes.

She was raped by her brothers, the dueña would say to the new fish, and you are her first paying gentleman. The dueña had a story like that for all her virgins—molested by her father, taken by an old priest, ravaged by lesbian nuns in the convent. Only the new fish believed the stories, or cared to try to believe them. Some of the virgins were really not much more than little girls and some only looked that way. The old Chinese merchants, who especially liked the Casa de Vírgenes, called them fish-ball girls because their breasts were like the tiny fish balls they sold at their restaurants and market stands.

Mercedes was a guajira from near Bayamo, light-skinned with big brown eyes and freckles on her nose, her body skinny and boyish. The other virgins called her Mosca. When El Halcón fucked her for the first time she said she was thirteen.

He usually only fucked the virgins once, when they first arrived. Maybe twice if they were something special. After that it was hard to keep the thrill. The girls got bored, they got hard and looked tired and didn't pretend not to be anymore. The new fish, especially the yanquis, could still be fooled because the virgins were still little girls, they still looked like little girls, but if you came back a third or a fourth time the thrill wasn't there.

El Halcón was sitting in the parlor drinking a beer and joking with the dueña when he heard about her. Kittens were playing at his feet. The dueña was soft for little abandoned kittens and the casa was always crawling with them. By the time they grew into cats, though, she chased them away to live on the street.

"The trouble with this place," she said, "is that I always have to be bringing in new virgins, always have to be teaching new virgins how to act. After six or seven months as putas," she said, "they're no good for virgins anymore."

The beer was always nice and cold at the Casa de Vírgenes, frost on the bottles the way the yanquis liked it. The first words of English he learned as a boy, hanging around the cafés and hotels in Vedado shining shoes and looking for things to steal, were "Could I have some more ice, please?" The dueña bought two big blocks off the truck every morning and kept a little Puerto Rican busy in the kitchen shaving it into drinks for the visitors.

"What you need," said El Halcón, pressing the beer bottle to his forehead to cool it, "is to get rid of all these old hags and get a perpetual virgin. Like the starfish that can grow a new arm if you break one off? You need a virgin with a bollo that heals up as soon as it is torn."

The dueña laughed. All the dueñas in all the casas in the district thought El Halcón was funny. "I have one," she said, "sitting upstairs. Un milagro de la ciencia. Una virgen perpetua."

Mercedes was sitting by the window with a kitten on her lap, looking down on the street. When he stepped into the room she crossed to the bed and sat on the edge of it without looking at him. The sheets were always clean at the Casa de Vírgenes and the girls were supposed to make their beds up fresh after each visitor.

The first time he fucked her he didn't say anything. It seemed to hurt her and she cried a little and then he started thinking she was just a good actress and the dueña was downstairs laughing so he slapped her hard enough to leave a palm print on her face. Then he was sure her tears were real. She wasn't anything special really, a skinny kid, kind of clumsy at it. Her wrists were so thin in his hands as he pinned her down he felt how easy it would be to break her and that made him harder.

"Tell me about your brothers who raped you," he said when he was done.

She held her hand over her bollo like she was covering a wound. "That isn't true," she said quietly. "I only have sisters."

He hit her then because he had wanted to hear her struggle to lie. "Are your sisters putas too?" he said.

"They work in a big mill in Bayamo."

"Do you know who I am?" he asked.

She shook her head.

"You know what I want you to call me?"

"Papi?" she said.

He smiled.

"A lot of the men want me to call them Papi. And they call me the name of one of their daughters."

He put his hands on the back of her neck and pushed his face inches from hers the way he did when he was interrogating suspects on the job, familiar and menacing. "I am Señor Halcón to you," he said. "You call me Señor."

"I will."

"I might kill you," he said. He looked into her eyes, unblinking as a hawk, and felt her pulse jump at the base of her jaw. "If I do kill you nobody will care. Nobody will say a thing. They'll pick you up with the dirty sheets and throw you away."

She started to tremble and that made him hard again and he fucked her as hard as he could with his face just that close to hers, his eyes fixed on hers unblinking as a hawk, giving her sharp little slaps when she tried to look away.

It was early December and things were very frustrating on the job. Rebels had landed on the coast of Oriente and though most of them were slaughtered, some had escaped into the mountains. In La Habana there was an endless round of arrests and interrogations. El Halcón would handle the telephone book while one of the captains asked the questions. The Colonel had brought phone books from Miami because the local ones were too thin.

"Just talk to us," the captains would say in a soothing voice, and El Halcón would smash the suspect in the face with a telephone book.

"Just tell us what we already know," the captains would say. "We only need confirmation. Don't get my friend here angry. He's a very bad man."

El Halcón would hit them with the telephone book until they bled from the ears and the nose and the mouth, but in a few days if they were released there wouldn't be a mark to show the shit-eating newspapers. He would hit them fast—*whap-whap-whap!*—so fast they hardly had time to think, so hard they thought their heads would burst open. He would hit them till the telephone book was in tatters and then he'd go get a fresh one from the pile while the captains crooned that nobody would ever know if they talked, they'd been very brave and now it was time to be sensible. If the suspects had been found with a gun or with other incriminating evidence and if their arrest had been private enough, they were given special attention. This consisted of one suspect being tied down naked to a table next to another suspect tied down naked to a table. A corporal called Nudillos would be brought in with a big pair of pliers, the kind that are used for working with heavy wire. He'd get the first suspect's balls in the jaws of the pliers and make little kissing sounds as he smiled and squeezed a little.

"Amiga," he would say, "I'm going to make you a woman."

The captain in charge would ask questions then while El Halcón took the second suspect by the hair and made sure he kept his eyes open and watched the whole thing. If the first one wouldn't talk or didn't give the right answers Nudillos would press the jaws slowly together till the man's balls were destroyed. The second suspect almost always talked then. What was frustrating was that they knew as little as anybody about what had happened in the Oriente.

"Fidel is dead!" they would cry. "I heard it on the radio."

"He's in the mountains!" they would scream. "I heard it on the street."

Where exactly in the mountains he was or how he got there they didn't know. Some were defiant at first and some were scared and some were just mistakes, people arrested through bad information or guilt by association, but none of them knew anything valuable. At some point the second suspect would always lose control of his bowels and no matter how careful he was El Halcón always came out a mess and the other guys from the barracks would laugh. Some of the suspects would call for their mothers and some would call for God and some would yell the usual business about the 26th of July Movement, but it always ended with one or the other of them telling everything he knew, as worthless as it was.

Later they were shot trying to escape.

He hadn't been that interested in a second time with Mercedes, but when he came to collect the next week the only new virgin was a round and placid girl from Pinar del Río.

"This one was born a puta," he said to the dueña. "Look at her face." He squeezed the girl's round cheeks in his hand. Her head flopped loosely as he shook it. "She knows she belongs here."

But when his eye fell on Mercedes in the dark, far corner of the parlor, she froze, as still and tense as a panicked rabbit. El Halcón walked toward her very slowly, letting her dread sink in, then grabbed the front of her blouse in his fist and yanked her to her feet and pushed her toward the stairs. They had her in a silk skirt and blouse and some makeup that day. You could have them go change into pretty much anything you wanted. But she looked so small in the clothes, like a little girl dressing up when her mother was away, that he had her keep them on.

"You look like a puta now," he said when they were in the room.

She lowered her eyes as if he had hurt her feelings. As if the feelings of a puta, even a virgin puta, could be hurt.

"How do you like it so far?"

She shrugged. "I don't like the ones who make me be a boy."

"Cómo?"

"Some of the ones who come in, they like boys, but they don't want to be that way. They have me put on a hat and tuck my hair in and then dress like a boy."

Mercedes was skinny enough to see her ribs. Her buttocks were still small and hard, and her breasts were just bumps, not even fish-ball size yet.

"Sometimes they spank me, and then they all do to me the way men do to boys. It hurts."

El Halcón was hard from listening to this and made her lie on her belly and fucked her in the ass, trying not to think about the men and boys, which disgusted him. The only time he'd gotten in serious trouble with the Colonel was for beating up a pato who whispered something to him in a bar, a pato who turned out not to be a suspect but a rich yanqui pato with a rich yanqui father and you weren't supposed to beat them up without asking permission. To keep from thinking about them El Halcón took his time on her and told her to say things.

"Say 'Fuck me.' "

"Fuck me," she said.

"Say 'Fuck me up the ass.' "

"Fuck me up the ass," she said.

"Say it like you mean it. Say 'Please.' "

"Please fuck me up the ass. Please," she said.

She said everything he told her to but she never sounded like she meant it. She wasn't sarcastic or bored like the girls in the other casas or the virgins when they were too tired to act like virgins anymore. She really tried, but the words didn't come out of her mouth right. He hit her some when he was finished fucking her and she cried like she couldn't understand why he would want to hurt her.

"You see?" said the dueña when he came downstairs. "Still a virgin."

The Colonel was obsessed with finding a printing press. Old Faget had been brought in by now and was always telling stories from Machado days, how it was not guns or rebels or sergeants in the barracks that had brought Machado down, but the printed word. That the underground was worthless if its voice was cut off. So a few times each week El Halcón and some of the other guys from the barracks would charge into some apartment, into some garage or warehouse, and start tearing up floorboards and busting through walls. Anybody in the place they had been tipped to was a suspect and a few times they actually did find subversive literature but they never found a printing press. The Colonel would curse them and call them cowards each time, would accuse them of letting the subversives carry the printing press away right under their noses. Old Faget was on his back he said, and everybody at the Presidential Palace was going on about how they needed to find a printing press to prove to the yanquis they were fighting against Communists. How this would prove anything to the yanquis was beyond El Halcón, as was why they should care what the yanquis thought when it was the shit-eating yanqui newspapers who always kicked up the most fuss and made them set their suspects who were writers free. If you wanted to find a printing press you caught some writers and asked them questions and didn't go around worrying what the yanquis thought or didn't think but that was too simple for the shit-eating politicians to figure out. One day the Colonel got so mad he had them come and take away the press from a little guy who printed wedding invitations and flyers for the smaller nightclubs. Just so the Communists couldn't steal it, said the Colonel. The little guy who owned the business protested a bit but El Halcón and the sergeant the guys in the barracks called El Cura because he was so good at getting confessions took him into one of the interrogation rooms right next door to where Nudillos was working on a suspect and left him there. They came back an hour later with a complaint form and the guy was soaked in sweat and shaking, saying maybe it was better the police kept the press out of the wrong hands for a while. The interrogation rooms had very thin walls.

The rebels up in the mountains were nothing, said the Colonel, as General Tabernilla y Dolz had predicted. But the fucking Cubans have such fucking big imaginations, he said, that a handful of wild-men in the hills could be blown up into a real threat. So they kept kicking down doors and tearing up floorboards. El Halcón got a splinter in his finger that got infected from lousy treatment by the butcher at the barracks they called a doctor, a man who was only good for coming in and saying "He's dead," or "He's alive," when there was some question about the state of a suspect. The infection made it very painful to grip onto a telephone book so he had to switch to a sandbag, which seemed to hurt them as much but didn't make as frightening a sound when it hit.

Finally, they found one. No resistance, not a soul in sight as they broke into an apartment they had surrounded. The Colonel was there with photographers and had invited Faget to observe. El Halcón knew the apartment, having broken into it months earlier to catch a suspect who was later shot resisting arrest. He recognized the printing press too, having helped carry it out of the little wedding-invitation guy's shop. The subversive literature piled around was familiar from other raids as well. But as El Halcón saw Faget congratulate the Colonel and the flashbulbs go off, he realized this was politics and not police business, and kept his mouth shut.

The next time he went to see Mercedes they had her dressed in something white and lacy like the Catholic girls wore for their sacraments and her hair was done in braids. She looked younger and smaller and more lost than ever. The dueña smiled a wicked smile as he went right to Mercedes but he stared at her till she wiped it away. He took the girl upstairs and threw the doll that she kept on her pillow on the floor and chased a couple kittens from the room and then sat on the edge of the bed and had her kneel in front of him. He took his cock out, already hard, and pulled her head close by the braids but she just looked up at him like she didn't know what to do or was hoping he wouldn't make her. He told her to suck him. She wasn't especially good at it and he wrapped her braids around his fists to pull her head down. After she swallowed him he slapped her face, once, hard. She looked ashamed then, as if a puta, even a virgin puta, could feel shame.

"Are you afraid of me?" he asked.

"Yes." She stayed on her knees in front of him, still in the white lacy thing.

"Why?"

"People tell me things."

"What things?"

"They say you're with the tigres. That you take people and they don't come back."

"Is that all?"

"They say you torture people." She said it as if she wanted him to tell her it wasn't true, that really he was just an honest man who directed traffic downtown.

"It's true," he said.

He patted the bed next to him and beckoned her to sit. He put an arm around her shoulders and moved his face close to hers, so she could feel his breath hot on her cheek. She started to shake.

"Some day," he said, "maybe I'll kill you. I'm not sure about it yet."

Then he told her about the mechanic they had interrogated back when the Ortodoxos were getting out of control. He spoke to her with his arm still around her shoulders, spoke in a soft, almost expressionless voice, like a man telling a bedtime story from memory. They knew everything they needed about the mechanic and the Ortodoxos but the Colonel wanted to make an example. Most of the guys at the barracks were there and they attached the metal clips from the telephone machine to the man's testicles. Wires went from the clips to a battery setup and you cranked a lever to send the current through. The faster you cranked the more current. After a while the Colonel didn't bother to ask questions and it became a competition between the guys to see which of them could make the mechanic jerk on the table the most. When it was El Halcón's turn he put his shoulder into it and really got it going and after the Colonel called time the mechanic writhed and jerked on the table for a full minute. Then he didn't move at all. At first El Halcón was worried that the Colonel would be mad at him, because the idea had been to send the mechanic back to the Ortodoxos to warn them, but the Colonel just slapped him on the back and made a joke of it. Later the mechanic was shot while resisting arrest.

Mercedes was in tears by the time he finished the story. "God have mercy on you," she said.

After that he always asked them to put her hair in braids. He would wait in the parlor drinking beer with the dueña and listening to the baseball game on the radio while one of the other girls helped her.

He started to think about her sometimes on the job, when things were boring. He had been in on lots of interrogations and hadn't thought about them much, and talking to her was the first time he'd said anything out loud. It made things more real, somehow. The interrogations were always like a quick dream, one thing spilling over into another, lots of shouting and screaming, the guys daring each other with their eyes to take it one step further, to see what would happen, to see how far they could go. He started coming for Mercedes a couple times a week.

One night he got there at the wrong time and saw two yanqui businessmen going up with her.

"If you want her I can make them take someone else," said the dueña, smiling. El Halcón said no, that was okay, and sat and had a beer, chatting and listening to the ballgame, yawning a lot as if he was tired or just bored, then made his collection and left. He waited across the street until the yanquis came out, a long time later. He put his hands in his pockets and followed them. They were drunk and very loud. One was called Larry and the other was called Dave.

"You think it's true?" said Larry to Dave.

"Do I think what's true?"

"What they said. About her and her brothers."

"Nahhh."

"Well I think it is."

"Nahhh."

"I mean why else would some little kid like her be working in a knock shop?"

"Look, even if it is true, it's not like it would be if it was back home. These people are oversexed, they're notorious for it."

They walked on a bit. El Halcón had his hand on his gun. He tried to think how he would explain it to the Colonel if it was traced to him. He stared at the exact spot on the back of the men's heads where the bullet would go.

"Dave—"

"Huh?"

"What if her brother had the clap?"

He stopped following them then. You couldn't shoot a man for fucking a puta. That's what they were for.

He didn't see her for a while after that. Then in March the crazy students attacked the Presidential Palace. They got all the way up to the third floor but couldn't blow the door on the Generalísimo's office in time and he escaped. At one point the word went out that they had killed him and the Colonel ordered that none of the prisoners at the barracks be killed. Just in case there was a new government to deal with.

"Politicians change with the wind," the Colonel liked to say, "but the Army will always be here."

When the students were beaten back and it was clear the assassination had failed things became very busy. There was pressure on the SIM to find everybody involved and that meant lots of interrogations. El Halcón would drag himself to the Casa de Vírgenes after being up for two days at a time. It seemed to be the only place he could get to sleep.

"We had a girl today," he would say after he pushed himself inside of Mercedes. "A little student. You see this blood on my pants? I broke her nose with my fist," he would say and slap Mercedes in the face, still fucking her, his heart still beating fast from the interrogations. "We heated up a curling iron. You know? Like for your hair? We heated a curling iron and put it up her bollo." He would come and then he would fall asleep in her arms. Sometimes he would stay with her like that the whole night. The dueña didn't complain, though he was taking up the time of her best virgin.

Later in the month he was too tired to fuck and would just come and lie on the bed beside her and tell her about the day's interrogations till his eyes grew heavy and his voice began to drift.

"May God have mercy on you," she would say when he stopped talking.

Finally they caught almost all the students who had escaped from the Presidential Palace. Some of them really were shot while resisting arrest. It was quiet in La Habana for a while, but El Halcón still had a hard time getting to sleep. He was drinking a lot, which helped some. It wasn't that the job bothered him, no, he was too hard for that, all the guys at the barracks said he was the hardest, más duro que nadie, but there was a lot of pressure. Bad things were happening in Santiago, and the Colonel thought they were being directed from La Habana. There seemed to be more and more suspects. El Halcón would drink till he passed out and that would do for sleep.

He was drunk when he had the honey dream. Part of the time the girl's face was Mercedes's face and part of the time it was the face of some other puta or maybe one of the female suspects. It was hard to tell. But the body was definitely Mercedes's body and her bollo was oozing with honey. Thick, reddish honey that slid down her thighs to make a sticky puddle between her legs. It kept coming, like water out of a spring, more and more honey flowing out from her little lips. He was hard and wanted to fuck her in the dream, in spite of or maybe because of the honey, but the bees wouldn't let him. Hundreds of bees swarmed angrily around her bollo, zigging and zagging, and every time he got close they would gather and sting him on the cock and he'd have to move away. When it was Mercedes's face on the body she would look at him apologetically and then look down at her bollo as if it had a life of its own, as if it had nothing to do with her.

When he woke from the honey dream he was hard. He got dressed and went to the Casa de Vírgenes. It was the middle of the night but everyone was still up. The dueña smiled at him. The virgins all smiled at him. Mercedes was making her bed when he came into her room.

"Please don't hurt me," she said, the way she always did when he sat her down next to him. He answered, as he almost always did, by hitting her in the face. Then he told her about something he'd done on the job or told her things to say, like he always did. But this night, the night he had the honey dream, no matter how he hit her or what he told her he'd done or what he had her say to him, he couldn't get hard again.

"Puta," he said to her, "you're no good even for a puta anymore," and he took her by the hair and made her suck him but it didn't work.

"You have to want me," he said.

"I want you," she said.

"You can't just say it," he said. "You have to want me to fuck you."

"I'm trying," she said.

He put his fingers in her bollo and pulled them out. They were covered with a kind of grease the girls used to stay wet through all the visits. He made her wash it out and dry it off.

"Want me," he said.

"I'm trying," she said, but she was dry.

"Want me," he said.

"I don't know how," she said. "I've never had that happen."

He used his tongue on her then. He had done it once before to a woman, when he was younger. It was humiliating. It seemed like he had to do it forever and at first it was too hard and it hurt her.

"Maybe softer," she said and he hit her, but then he did it softer. Finally she was wet from his mouth but he could tell she still didn't want him and all the while he kept almost thinking of the things he'd done with the rich patos to take money from them when he was a little boy on the streets and he sat back away from her, still not hard. She looked at her bollo, upset, like she was looking at a piece of machinery that wouldn't work.

"I'm sorry," she said. "I don't know how." He didn't hit her again.

El Halcón didn't visit her for a while then, but he kept thinking about her and had the honey dream several times. In Cienfuegos there was a mutiny of navy officers and men who fell in with the rebels. They held the police and military barracks in the city and the fortifications at Cayo Loco for a few hours until the air force came in and they had to eat shit with hair in it. Some of the navy people who were captured were brought to La Habana and things were busy again. Then El Halcón was almost killed by a boy in Jesús María.

It was an apartment only a block away from a place where El Halcón had lived for a while when he was a boy. The stink and the noise of the neighborhood was just the same, the way the people stared full of hate at the police. The boy was supposed to know something or know someone who knew something and their chivato in Jesús María had tracked him to this apartment. El Halcón was about to kick the door in when the boy opened it suddenly and stuck a gun in his face so hard it left a bruise. The gun was something that should have been in a museum, a Spanish Star from before Machado's time, and there was no telling how or why the boy was carrying it. He pulled the trigger and nothing happened and then El Halcón blew his lower jaw off. The boy gushed blood from his throat, the stairs slick with it as the guys from the barracks dragged him down to the wagon by his feet. He didn't die till they got him back to the barracks and the guys all slapped El Halcón on the back and made jokes about almost getting his brains shot out and ruining a perfectly good suspect. When El Halcón lay down on Mercedes's bed he was still shaking.

"We shot a boy today," he started as she sat cautiously at the edge of the bed beside him.

"We shot a boy today," he said again, and then was silent.

He was quiet for a long time, and then, maybe because she thought she was supposed to or maybe because seeing him shaking on the bed scared her, she touched him softly on the face and the chest till he started to breathe slower, then took off his clothes and touched him more until he was hard and then climbed on him and fucked him, slowly and cautiously. She watched his eyes warily the whole time but he didn't hit her or ask her to say things. When he was done she lay on top of him. He marveled at how light she was, and then he fell asleep.

Gunfire woke him in the morning. She was sitting by the window, playing with a kitten in her lap and watching the street, excited and scared like a little kid.

"Maybe it's the Communists," she said.

"Maybe." He put his clothes on slowly.

"They say they're going to take over."

"Sure."

"What will happen if they do?"

"If the Communists take over," he said, "you will still be a puta. Men will still come and fuck you, but they won't have to pay. All kinds of people, guajiros from the country, scum from the streets, even the negros. That's Communism."

"And what will happen to you?"

He shrugged. "The pay won't be so good," he said, "but there will always be the Army."

The gunfire turned out to be nothing important, just some gangsters killing each other. But the following night Nudillos was shot in the head at close range coming out of the Casa de Nalga with his pants still unzipped. Bad things began to happen all over the island. The government would report on the battles between the Army and the rebels and always it seemed there were more rebels killed, hundreds of them, and then the government would say there were only a handful of lunatics left in the Sierra. But the next week there would be more fighting, more hundreds of rebels reported killed.

"Divide every number by three," said the Colonel with a wink, "and then subtract ten."

El Halcón's arms were weary from the interrogations at the

barracks. They had to hose the floors off every couple hours like at a slaughterhouse. Sometimes the interrogations were very quick. One afternoon they rode out to where a big canefield had been burned. None of the local guajiros had reported the fire till it was out of control. They picked up the first young guy they found near the field.

"Did you set the fire?" they asked.

"No."

"Can you prove that?"

"I was with Anselmo."

They went and found Anselmo.

"Did you set the fire?"

"No. You can ask Estrada and Ponce."

They went and found Estrada and Ponce, who had three other witnesses who could vouch for them. They found the three other witnesses and took all seven of the men and hanged them from the telephone lines on the road to Santa Clara. On the back of each man they taped a sign saying COMUNISTA and left a pair of young soldiers there for three days to shoot at anyone who came to cut the guajiros down.

El Halcón would go to Mercedes's room for the quiet. There was no way to rest at the barracks, what with suspects being interrogated and the guys drinking and singing and carrying on more than ever. El Halcón began to ask about Mercedes's life before she had become a virgin at the casa.

"We lived in the batey, my mother and father, two sisters and me. During the zafra and during the milling there was enough food. During the dead season there wasn't." She talked about her past in the same tone that he used to describe the interrogations. "My mother was sick and there wasn't money for medicine and she died. The next year, in the dead season, my father killed himself."

He wasn't sure what it was that he liked about the story or why he had her repeat it so many times. It seemed part of the natural order, part of the way things had always been before the bad things started happening all over the country. Before he had started having trouble sleeping or getting hard. Recently there had been a woman, a suspect, and one of the captains ordered that all the guys who were there take out their cocks and fuck her, one by one, hoping that that might work better than pain in getting her to talk. There was a lot of joking about who was going to go first and who was going to catch what from who and when it was El Halcón's turn he couldn't get himself hard but crowded close to her and faked it while the guys talked about the time he'd killed the suspect cranking the telephone and was he going to fuck her to death. The woman just looked him in the eyes but didn't say that he wasn't really in her. Later she was shot resisting arrest.

The Colonel told him to ask for a bigger cut from the casas.

"Tell them it's for protection against Communists," he said.

"The Communists won't bother us," said the dueña at the Casa de Vírgenes. "Without us the tourist industry would die. I was here for Machado and I was here for Batista and I was here for Grau and I was here for Prío and I'm here for Batista again. Politicians come and go with the wind," she said with a wink, "but there will always be virgins."

La Habana was a party that was getting out of control. The music seemed louder, the nightclubs brighter, the people more desperate, in a hurry to take what they could. One of the guys at the barracks passed out in the hallway and smothered in his own vomit. The smaller gangsters were shooting at each other a lot more. The girls in the casas still smiled when he came in but their smiles seemed mocking, like they knew something he didn't.

"The Communists will nail you to a tree," he warned Mercedes, "and then they'll cut your heart out. Fidel has said that all the putas who fuck Army men will be killed."

Mercedes had been in the Casa de Vírgenes for two years. No other girl had lasted more than six months. She still cried when El Halcón told her the things the Communists would do to her if they took over.

"They're fucking each other up there in the mountains, the barbudos," he said. "When they come down they'll be wild. They smell like goats and they only like to fuck up the ass. And after they've all had you, even the negros, they'll nail you to a tree. That's how Communism works."

In December one of the smaller gangsters, a yanqui named Tulio, said they had to talk business. Tulio was a man who brought girls from Miami to the island and girls from the island to Miami. They met at an outdoor café in Vedado.

"We have to talk about a parachute, pal," he said to El Halcón.

"Cómo?"

"The way I see it, you're a couple miles high, the pilot is about to take a powder, the engine's on fire and you're outa gas. You're lookin down from the hatch and you know you should jump, only for one thing. You got no fuckin parachute."

The yanqui was the kind that always smiled when he talked but was never really friendly.

"Can I have some more ice, please?" he said to the waiter.

"What do you want from me?" said El Halcón.

"The way I got it booked, the shit is gonna hit the fan here within the next couple months. You little guys, from captains on down, are gonna be left here holding the bag and the barbudos will be using you for target practice. What I got is a deal where we supply a ticket outa here, whenever you want it. A parachute."

"And what do I have to do?"

"There's this guy, businessman, up north who needs a favor. He's a legitimate character, this guy, good contacts with the government, the whole bit, and he needs somebody killed."

"Who is it? Where?"

"Who it is you'll find out when you come up. Where is Miami. So how bout it?"

El Halcón looked out across the traffic backed up on the Malecón to the Bay. Boats moved back and forth. The sun was shining.

"Never," he said. "They will never take La Habana."

Tulio smiled and stood up from the table. "You know where to find me, pal. Just don't wait too long to jump."

El Halcón tried to go to the Casa de Vírgenes early in the day when he could, as Mercedes was almost always with somebody if he came at night. There was a shortage of virgins.

"It's the rebels," said the dueña with a smile, "the barbudos in the countryside. They must have burned this year's crop of virgins."

Mercedes was more and more excited as the word of the rebels' advances spread. Not scared or happy, just excited.

"I wonder what would happen if they did come," she said. "Life would be totally different."

El Halcón snorted. "Same shit, different flies."

He didn't hit her nearly as much as he had in the beginning, but when he did she still cried. When he fucked her she still acted like it hurt.

"Maybe she's just too small," he said to the dueña, trying to explain it.

"As soon as it is torn, it heals again," said the dueña with her wicked smile. "Like the rebels—when you kill one group of them another grows in its place. Una virgen perpetua."

In the last days there was trouble at the barracks. Some of the guys had been leaving food around and all of a sudden there was an infestation of rats.

"Communists!" the guys would joke when they saw one and take out their pistols and blast away. El Halcón was the only one who ever hit one, being the best shot in the barracks. The ceiling was having problems too, as it had been neglected too long and big hunks of plaster were starting to fall down around them. Nobody seemed to be in charge of cleaning anything up. The Colonel seemed more interested in the collections going well than anything at the barracks and the captains were hoarse from screaming at suspects day and night.

"Somebody fix the fucking ceiling!" they would scream now and then, but because they didn't single anyone out nobody felt it was their job. One night one of the guys, a sullen negro from Bueycito who they called El Mudo because he hardly ever spoke shot himself in his bed. The other guys thought it was somebody shooting at a rat and didn't find him till morning, stuck with blood to the sheets. Then the plumbing went wrong, and when you turned on the tap you got something lukewarm and thick with rust. Liquor bottles rolled under the beds and the halls started to smell of urine and at night the men would tune in to Radio Rebelde and shout about the lies that were being told, about the towns they were claiming to hold.

Caimanera is taken, they said on Radio Rebelde. Trinidad, Cueto, Sagua de Tánamo, Baracoa, Mayarí—we are coming to La Habana, they said. Do not support the elections, they said. The people cannot be defeated.

The toilets in the barracks backed up and began to flood the floor around them.

"We'll drown in our own shit," joked the guys in the barracks, and made suspects clean the toilets before their interrogations.

On New Year's Eve La Habana was a party on a sinking ship. El Halcón walked the streets to the Casa de Vírgenes, people dancing and shouting among the traffic, bottles smashing to the pavement, the little homeless boys running this way and that among the crowds, looking for something to steal the way he had when he'd been one of them. In the Casa de Vírgenes there was a costume party in full swing. The dueña, dressed as a she-cat with a row of hanging teats, greeted him at the door.

"La virgen is upstairs," she said, smiling, her whiskers almost touching her pointed ears, "esperándote."

Pushing through the crowd of screaming people he ran into El Cura from the barracks, dressed as a country priest and dragging a new virgin, a little girl dressed as a rag doll, behind him.

"I'm going to hear her Confession," said El Cura, slapping him on the back, then, leaning close to his ear, he shouted over the noise. "They're leaving tonight," he said. "Batista, Tabernilla, some of the other big ones, they're flying out tonight." El Cura had a crazed smile on his face, telling it as if it were a joke. "We're on our own now," he said, and made a sign of the cross with his hands like the Catholics did.

On the first landing of the stairway there was a kitten playing, pawing at an earring that had dropped to the floor. El Halcón picked it up and stroked it for a moment, thinking that when it grew up to be a cat there would be Communists walking the streets of La Habana, then he wrung its neck and threw it down the steps toward the party. He looked at his watch. He had to leave for Tulio's boat in an hour.

Mercedes was dressed in the white, lacy thing like the Catholic girls wore for their sacraments. Her hair was in braids and she sat by the window looking down at the people celebrating in the street. The kittens in the room scattered and ran out the door as El Halcón stepped in.

"The Communists are coming," he said.

"I know," said Mercedes, sitting on the edge of the bed. "Maybe everything will be different."

She looked young and lost and full of hope, as if a puta, especially a virgin puta, could have hope.

He pushed her back on the bed and fucked her with his pants only halfway off, staring at her face, his eyes unblinking as a hawk's. She was looking at him strangely, and he realized there were tears on his cheeks. When he was just about to come he took the pillow from beneath her head and put it over her face and pushed down onto her with his whole body. She thrashed and jerked but he was able to stay in her until she didn't move anymore. He straightened her dress and straightened the sheets under her and crossed her hands over her chest. He put the doll that she kept, which had fallen on the floor, on the bed next to her and put the pillow back beneath her head.

"She's still a virgin," said El Halcón to the dueña as he passed her on the way out downstairs. "Una virgen perpetua."

THIRTEEN

~~~~ NURSE TEMPLE WAGGLES the hit list at Dewey. It is Enema Day and somehow Dewey's number has come up again.

"Do Gold first," she says, handing him the list. "He's got family in this afternoon and I want him cleaned up in time."

The philosophy in Basic used to be that it built character, the shit and piss details, policing the grounds, KP, latrine duty. The way Dewey sees it he's got character coming out his ears. What he needs is action.

"What's wrong with Wilson?" he says. "It should be his turn."

"We're moving Rothschild today. I need Wilson to be with Roosevelt on that."

She turns and squeaks back toward the station in her new white orthopedics. Dewey snaps into the Weaver stance, supporting his right hand with his left, and aims his finger at the base of Nurse Temple's skull—

The back of the woman's head was gone. Blood was starting to dry on the floor of the corridor when Dewey reached her. Sgt. Brick trotted by, crouched low, his MP5 held ready.

"No time for that, kid," he snarled, pressing himself against the wall. The terrorists had their hostages spreadeagled face down in the day room. The nurse had been the third victim, after they'd gunned the two cringing orderlies, Roosevelt and Wilson. They were threatening to throw a new body out every ten minutes until their demands were met.

"Waco and the Indian are coming in through the sun porch," said the Sgt. "We go in the front door. If they're clustered, we might have a shot at saving the hostages. If they've set up a crossfire—well . . ." Brick shook his head grimly.

"I figure we zap whatever moves," said Dewey, hefting his Mauser, "and let God sort em out."

"Yo! Screwy Dewey!"

Roosevelt and Wilson are pushing a bed with the guy Wilson calls the House of Rothschild in it down the hallway. The guy is three-fifty, three-sixty pounds of dead lox and Wilson calls him that cause Wilson has been to college and is always saying stuff that's like jokes only not really funny. Roosevelt eyes the IV stand and enema bag Dewey is lugging.

"Man, they got Dewey on his favrit gig again. Sucker be the Paul Bunyan of the Hershey Highway."

"You be careful, Dewey," says Wilson. "Most had us a Jewish astronaut, last time you worked that thing."

The House of Rothschild rolls his huge head toward Dewey, a massive jowl plopping against the bedrail. He struggles to pull each breath in, phlegm rattling thickly in his chest. The House of Rothschild can sweat through a new sheet in a half hour and has to be rigged like a horse and slung from a hydraulic lift to change his bed.

"Help me," he croaks to Dewey, his constant words, his only words for years. "Help me."

"Help me."

The old man had caught one through the lung, blood bubbling scarlet from under his shirt.

"Help me."

Dewey crawled over on his belly and put his hand over the man's mouth, then managed to roll him till he was behind the concrete stairs. The Equality Police were patrolling on foot now, some of them with tracker dogs.

"Shhhh," he whispered into the old man's ear. "They're still out there."

The old man rolled a terrified, liquid eye toward Dewey, pleading not to be abandoned. Dewey pulled his Beretta from his back holster. To be caught with it meant an automatic death sentence under the Gun Law. They could have it when they pried it from his cold, dead fingers, he thought. He sensed that they were closer.

"Blood tracks, man." The voice came from the left, ten, maybe fifteen yards on the other side of the stairs. "We musta hit that fat dude."

Dewey lifted his head just enough to see. Two of them. One big, dark brown and bullet-headed, the other thin and wiry, lighter skinned. No dogs. Dewey slid the Beretta into his belt and slipped his bolo knife from the ankle sheath. A gunshot would bring the others down on them, but with a knife there was still a chance. The big one spoke.

"Blood movin this way. Les put that ugly sucker out his mizry."

If there had been dogs, no way. Dewey was good with the bolo, but not that good. The old man began to choke on his own blood.

"Yoo hoo!" called the smaller one. "We come for your ass, Porky."

Another few steps and they'd see him. Dewey dug his feet in, ready to spring. He remembered the phrase Brick had used before he went underground.

"The last great act of defiance."

Cold comfort, but it had a ring to it.

Brick was gone now, maybe dead. Dewey's fist tightened like steel on the grip of the bolo knife. The big one had his AK slung cockily over his shoulder. It looked like the other hadn't cleaned his in months.

"Yoo hoo! Fat boy! Where are you?"

He'd go for the smaller one first, trying to get jugular and vocal cords with the same swipe. If that didn't work, there was always the Beretta and what would inevitably follow.

Remember the Alamo, he thought, then jumped. . . .

"They won't take you till you're eighteen," says Dewey. "Which is a serious waste of manpower. Does it hurt?"

"I don't recommend the experience," says Gold, lying on his belly.

"You tell me if it hurts. By sixteen you've got the stamina, most of your growth, the ability to follow orders—"

"He's in a hurry to follow orders."

"There's a Haitian guy on the night shift—try to hold it in now— he says he knows where you can get a fake birth certificate. I get that, prove I'm eighteen, I go Marine Corps, then I go Rangers." Dewey slips the nozzle out and positions the bedpan. "Rangers is where it's at."

"He's in a hurry to die."

Dewey helps the old man sit up on the bedpan.

"What, you kept this in a refrigerator? Sitting on ice is not conducive to bowel function. You're old enough to join the paratroopers, you should know that."

"It was by the air conditioner." Dewey sits in the wheelchair at the foot of the bed. "There's plenty of people in history fought in wars before they were sixteen. Plenty of people."

"Of course there were."

"I'm serious."

"I'm not arguing. There's David, still in short pants when he went against the Philistines and brought Goliath down. There's Saint Joan, there's—"

"Saint Joan who?"

Gold rolls his eyes. "Saint Joan who, Saint Joan of Palm Beach. What are they teaching now in the schools?"

Dewey shrugs. "Nothin."

"And we wonder there's a generation of cutthroats running the streets."

"I went to public school," says Dewey. "We didn't learn saints."

"Saint Joan of Arc," says Gold. "The Maid of Orléans. The burning conscience of her people."

Marta steps into the room. Dewey straightens in the wheelchair and Gold covers his privates with his blanket.

"Dewey," she says, "DuPre just got added to the list for a Squibbs. Come in when you're done here, okay?"

"Sure."

Marta leaves.

"Like ice, that one," says Gold softly.

"Serious," says Dewey, the blush fading from his face. She had to come in when he was just sitting around.

Gold shifts uncomfortably on the pan. "She hears voices."

"What?"

"She hears voices, Saint Joan, and off she goes. A little peasant girl, younger than you, out in the yard doing peasant things, churning butter, whatever, she hears voices and she's off to save France. Catholic people. The Jews, let's face it, since the Old Testament days the Jews have gotten a lot more suspicious. They hear a voice they'll argue the Talmud a little, check references. Catholic people, there's one whisper it's off to the races."

"Is this like ancient times?"

"This is like knights in armor we're talking, the English and the French, an old story of bad blood. I'm certain you didn't get it in school."

"I've seen movies."

"So picture Errol Flynn—"

"Who's—?"

"A cultural illiterate as well. Picture your favorite star of the day—"

"Harrison Ford."

"This is an actor? It sounds like a car dealership—Oh, my God, I think it's coming—" Gold closes his eyes to concentrate, tensing his body. He relaxes, opens his eyes. "False alarm."

"Don't push."

"At first they laughed in her face, a sixteen-year-old girl with no military training, claiming she was sent to save France. Then, certain predictions she made came true, their backs are against the wall, who's going to turn down a shot at divine intervention? They put her in a suit of white armor, give her some troops to lead, and sure enough she boots the English out of Orléans. Who knows what she was as a fighter, but for inspiration you couldn't ask for better."

There is a sudden rush of something liquid into the pan. Gold closes his eyes again.

"So what happened?"

"Why is it," says Gold, "that most of my pleasures these days are only the relief of pain?"

"What happened to Joan?"

"Joan? She was betrayed by her own people, declared a witch and burned at the stake by the English. A little girl, seventeen years old."

"Seventeen," says Dewey.

"Then years later," says Gold, "they decide to make her a saint. Catholic people, go figure."

"You're a girl," he said. In the dark, with her leather jacket and black pants, the hat and scarf that she wore, it had been impossible to tell.

"And why not?" She was very young, barely in her teens, and her voice held only a faint trace of a French accent.

Dewey hurried to gather and bury his parachute. "They told me the maquis would be sending their top officer in this section."

"I am the top officer."

A cloud shifted to let the moonlight through, giving him a better look. Her face was beautiful but touched by sorrow.

"The Boche, they are out tonight," she said, a sneer of hatred curling her lip. "You must come with me."

"It's GI Joe," says DuPre when he sees Dewey come in. "Just the man I want to see."

Marta sits by her father, speaking softly in Spanish. Old Skip is cranked up high in his bed but barely focusing on her. DuPre sits watching them, hands lightly grasping the trapeze bar overhead.

"On your belly," says Dewey.

"You mind closing the curtain?"

"It's just a Squibbs," says Dewey. "Just a squeeze bottle."

"You mind?" DuPre nods over toward Marta.

"She's a nurse—"

DuPre tries to reach out for the curtain and Dewey sighs and draws it around them. Marta keeps whispering in Spanish.

DuPre swings himself over on his belly. "Would you want to lie down with a plastic bottle up your ass with her in the room?"

"I'm not a patient," says Dewey, and pulls on a rubber glove.

"I hope you never are, son."

Dewey searches through DuPre's nightstand for a jar of vaseline. "If I am it won't be in this hole."

DuPre is thin and stringy as a plucked chicken, but still strong in his upper body. There isn't much lower body left.

"So who are we fighting this week?" he asks.

"The Ayatollah."

"We haven't nuked him yet?"

DuPre is another one with the jokes that aren't really funny. "That damn gutless Mr. Peanut," says Dewey, "lettin em shit all over us. Take a deep breath."

DuPre takes a deep breath and Dewey squeezes the solution in. "Do me a favor, son," he says through gritted teeth, "and stick that bedpan over here in the sun for a minute."

Dewey pulls the elastic covers off DuPre's stumps and shakes some talcum powder onto them. He puts the covers back on.

"It was the macaroni and cheese," says DuPre. "Every time they serve it I get stopped up."

"Try and hold it in another minute." Dewey looks at the scars on DuPre's back. "I read your chart the other night."

"Not exactly a page-turner."

"It said war-related injuries. About your legs."

"That's right." DuPre is concentrating, his hands balled into fists.

"You were in World War One?"

DuPre laughs hard enough to fart out a little water. "I'm not that old, son. I was in Spain."

Dewey frowns. "The Spanish-American War?"

"Where do you go to school?"

"I dropped out."

"Doesn't matter, they probably don't teach it anyways. Spain was in '36, at least for me it was. I fought for the Republic against the Fascists."

"That's like the Nazis?"

DuPre rolls over on his back and Dewey slides the bedpan next to him. "Sure. Mostly at that point it was Moors and the Foreign Legion and some of Mussolini's people." He pulls himself up in the air on the trapeze bar and Dewey slides the pan under. He settles down onto it. "The thing is," he says, "I *like* macaroni and cheese."

"The *French* Foreign Legion?"

"Spanish, but it's the same difference to me. Mercenaries."

Dewey sits on the edge of the bed. "And who were you fighting for?"

"The Spanish people. The Republic."

"They paid you?"

DuPre laughs again. "They paid us in food, in shelter, in kindness."

Dewey is confused.

"It was a cause," says DuPre, gently. "For freedom."

"Like going to Nam."

DuPre shakes his head. "No. I don't think so. Not like that at all."

DuPre sighs and looks out the window down onto the street. Old women wearing sunglasses are walking short-haired dogs.

"What did you use?" says Dewey. "M-1's, Brownings, Enfields?"

"You do know some history." DuPre smiles. "We used whatever we could get our hands on and could find enough rounds for. Personally I carried something made in Russia, I wouldn't remember the name, it was bolt-action and came packed in grease."

"In *Russia?*"

"They were the only ones who sent arms."

"This is before or after the Communists?"

"This is *during* the Communists. This *is* the Communists. How old are you, son?"

"Sixteen."

"That's old enough you should know these things. You should be taught history. It's a disgrace."

"And you stepped on a mine?"

DuPre sighs. "I'm a Jew from Toronto, in a hurry to live, to experience, and here is a noble cause. I scrape for the ticket to France, sneak across the border when sneaking wasn't hard, lie about my age and they put me in the Internationals. I'm with British, Irish, Americans, Cubans, other Canadians—a real hodge-podge. We train for a few weeks with broomsticks on our shoulders, then we're thrown in at Jarama. The grease is still shining on the rifle they gave me, I still haven't shot a round. I charged out of a trench with the rest of my unit, went three steps and took machine gun rounds in both thighs. That was my war."

Dewey doesn't know what to say. DuPre continues to look out the window, brooding. Marta is quiet on the other side of the curtain.

"Fifty-caliber babies," says Dewey, finally. "Those'll do a number on you."

"I'd do it again," says DuPre. "Even knowing how it came out."

"We beat the Nazis."

"Not in Spain. Not in a lot of places."

Dewey is confused again.

"But you, GI Joe, you wouldn't understand that. You just want to be a soldier, a mercenary—"

"A pro*fess*ional—"

"Somebody who shoots where somebody else points. In my war the soldiers discussed politics, they debated topics. In my war if the men weren't satisfied with the officers, the officers were replaced."

"No wonder you lost."

DuPre smiles again. "You might be right, there." He looks down to where his legs used to be. "I still dream about walking sometimes, and when I do, sometimes just before I wake up, I swear I can feel them."

Dewey wiggles his toes. Old Scipio is snoring from his bed on the other side of the curtain. "You said you lied about your age."

"I was sixteen years old," says DuPre, his eyes growing distant. "In a hurry to live."

The Cuban woman held the boy under the arms, trying to drag him off the street. Rounds from the Shi'ite AKs burst on the pavement all around her.

"Stay put, kid," said Sgt. Brick, but Dewey was already up and running.

Draw fire, he thought as he dashed past the Cuban woman, then return it. He dove, rolled, and came up on one knee with his RPK spitting death. By the time he'd burned 40 rounds the Cuban woman was in the clear. Sgt. Brick leaned out and gave them a pop with the grenade launcher, and when it lit up Dewey sprinted back to cover, bullets whining past his ears.

"You John Wayne it one time too many," grumbled Brick, "and those tent-heads'll make hamburger out of you."

Dewey grinned and crawled over to check out the boy. The Cuban woman had slit down the front of both pants legs and it was a mess.

"You a nurse?"

She nodded, her dark eyes locking with his. "That was a very brave thing you did."

Dewey shrugged. The boy was pale and scared, looking down at what used to be his thighs. Dewey clapped him lightly on the shoulder.

"Lighten up, son," he said. "In a year you'll be out running relays."

The Cuban woman caught his eye again. It was a lie but he didn't want the boy to panic. Her hand touched Dewey's as he helped her tie the tourniquet, and an electric charge of desire went through his body.

"Here they come," called Sgt. Brick. "Let's kick ass."

The door closes on Dewey and Marta in the elevator.

Dewey looks at the wall, trying to think of something to say. He can never think of anything to say to her that isn't about the patients. It's supposed to build character, abstinence from relations, being the lone wolf. Dewey figures he has character up the wazoo, what he needs is action. Marta turns and looks at him in that solemn, unblinking way of hers. He feels himself start to flush.

"Why do you want to be a soldier?" she asks.

He shrugs. "Fight for freedom, I guess. Fight Communism."

She nods.

"I figure it's something I'd be good at. I'm in training right now." He hopes she doesn't laugh. So many of the others laugh, they think it isn't serious, think it isn't real until they're in a killing situation. Then it's too late.

She just nods, thinking. "You were talking about guns."

"Uh-huh. You name a conflict, from the Civil War up to now, and I can probably tell you what weaponry was involved."

Dewey's stomach feels funny and he can't tell if it's the elevator going down or being next to Marta. She is so beautiful, solemn and beautiful. Dewey has seen her smile once or twice when she's with

Luz or sometimes with her father. When he does himself a lot of the times he tries to imagine her face, her body.

She looks away from him. "I'm interested in learning about guns," she says, voice tentative.

Dewey grins. "What do you want to know?"

The door opens.

FOURTEEN

➤ WHEN DUCKWORTH CATCHES the first whiff of it he stops. The smell sits in the hot noon air thick as glue. Rivkin stops beside him, expectant.

"This is as far as I go," says Duckworth.

"What's the matter, Chief?"

"I seen a dead Colombian before. You want to stick your nose in it go ahead." Duckworth opens the passenger door of one of the patrol cars and sits inside. Patrolmen are thick and officious around the Lincoln, one of them angling a sun-gun into the open trunk so the photographers can get their fill. His legs hurt. "Send Ochoa back and make sure the prints are on the wire."

Rivkin hurries off toward the Lincoln. There are civilians in the parking lot, coming back from their lunch breaks. They rubberneck to see over the flock of patrol cars, minds buzzing, then they step into the smell and their faces change. Duckworth looks up at the curious mugs pressed to the windows of the office building. *I saw the worst thing today.* He slides farther into the car till he can put his legs up on the seat, shutting the door against the smell. More patrolmen wheel in and take their turn hovering over the mess in the trunk of the Lincoln. *Day off tomorrow.* Duckworth closes his eyes and tries to imagine sleeping late. *Marion in the kitchen, bacon smell, sports section on the couch—*

Danny from the *Herald* knocks on the window.

Danny from the *Herald* pushes his nose against the glass and Duckworth waves him away. Danny covers his heart with his hands and pleads with his eyes. Duckworth puts his legs down and lets the reporter in.

"Think you'd be used to this scene by now," Danny says, sliding in behind the wheel.

"Used to it doesn't mean you need to climb in the trunk with it. You're on my shit list, Danny."

"What for?"

" 'Authorities are baffled.' *Baffled?* What is that? Even you know who killed that kid."

"If you know who did it why don't you bust somebody?" Danny pulls out a pad and pen.

"Put that away."

"What?"

"I'm not talking to you."

"Look, Harlan, I tried to run a story about your hands being tied by the Feds, but—"

"But they killed it upstairs. You want a medal?"

"You give me names and places, hard facts—"

"Danny, I'm not talking to you. You go ahead and make up your stories, but I'm through giving you ideas for em."

Ochoa opens the door and the odor rolls in. Danny sighs, steps out onto the pavement. "This is what happens to you guys when you smell retirement," he says. "You get cranky."

"Go interview the corpse, Danny."

Ochoa slides in next to Duckworth and closes the door.

"Are you *baff*led, Ochoa?"

"I don't think so."

"Good. Fuckin reporters, they give me a pain. You tell em the truth, they say, 'Sure, but what's the *story?*' Bunch of fiction writers."

Ochoa waits for a moment, then unfolds a sheet of paper. "We got a male, mid-twenties, probably Hispanic, took a .38 in the left temple. No ID on clothes, patch of skin missing on the back of the right hand, another on the left bicep, probably distinguishing tattoos."

A bright kid, Ochoa, bit of a Boy Scout but very thorough. When the Cubans take over the town he'll be sitting pretty to move up. "Prints?"

"No fingers," says Ochoa. "Cut off clean at the knuckles."

"Cute." Duckworth rubs his eyes. "You said on the phone I'd want to come down. So far this is not interesting."

"The Lincoln belongs to Justo Camejo."

A bright kid, Ochoa. Follows the politics without taking it personal. Or at least he doesn't show it. "Camejo got an office here?"

"Twelfth floor." Ochoa looks back to his sheet. "They reported the car stolen three days ago. Then this morning it was back. They called for the Bomb Squad, thought it might be wired."

"What's the old man say now?"

"His secretary says he never deals with the car, it's just the driver. All we got on the driver is a moving violation last year and that he did time in Cuba in '61."

Duckworth shakes his head. "Most of the best and most of the worst guys in the Community did time in '61. That was the Invasion, '61."

Ochoa smiles and shrugs. "Before my time, Chief. Want us to pull Camejo in?"

"Naw," says Duckworth. "I'll take Rivkin up. He's never met any of the old boys."

"Forget about the Colombian."

A Muzak version of *Jamaica Farewell*, all synthesizer strings, is playing in the elevator.

"You wonder who he is," says Rivkin. "If he's got a family, money problems maybe, he sees a quick way out. Or maybe he's just a wise guy, some greedy little fuck in over his head."

"Forget about the Colombian," says Duckworth.

"Who said he was a Colombian?"

"Anybody gets hisself stuffed in the trunk of a Lincoln with their fingers clipped off is automatically a Colombian," says Duckworth. "Ask Danny from the *Herald*."

"He was on me about that Cuban boy last week. I gave him no comment in three languages."

"Good. I want to cut the fucker off for a while, teach him some manners. 'Authorities are baffled' my ass."

"Yeah." Rivkin hums along with the Muzak for a moment. "Harry Belafonte sang this."

"Mmmn."

Rivkin makes a face. "That smell—"

"They let him ripen in there a couple days before they brought the car back. It makes more of a statement."

"I hope it was just some schmuck with a hungry nose," says Rivkin. "You hate to think of the little guys, never had two nickels to rub together, get sucked in looking for one big score. They walk into somebody else's game, don't know the players—"

Duckworth scowls. "Another fiction writer. You should work with Danny and Edna at the *Herald*." Too much education, Rivkin, and not enough sense. Too much imagination. "Maybe the Colombian is a Cuban, maybe he's a Guat, maybe he's some guinea with a suntan down from Jersey, it's not important. What *is* important is he's been sent as a calling card to our friend up here. What *is* important is who sent it and what the old dragon does about it. Cause of death, time of death, victim identification, forget it—that's for forensic and the soap-opera writers at the *Herald*. It's not important."

Rivkin sulks. "It is to the guy in the trunk."

"The guy in the trunk," says Duckworth, "is out of the conversation."

Monochromatic paintings of geometric shapes hang on walls painted cobalt blue. The air-conditioning is a cool whisper. The receptionist is blond and frosty, eating plain yogurt with a plastic spoon.

"Mr. Camejo dealt with the police earlier," she says. "His driver can answer any questions you might have."

Duckworth takes a seat without being offered one. "He could talk to us here," he says, settling in, "or we could go shoot the breeze with the wife and servants down in the Gables till he gets home."

The receptionist very deliberately sticks her spoon upright in the yogurt. "I'll just be a moment." She goes into the inner office.

Duckworth rubs his knees. Rivkin pokes around, checking out the decor. "Nice," he says, approving of the art on the walls. "This is nice."

"We finish, you can ask Camejo for a job," says Duckworth. "You could be his rent collector. Get a key to every apartment, get to poke around people's business, check out their trash—"

"Nobody likes a landlord."

"Lots of people like Mr. Camejo," says Duckworth. "And if they don't they try to keep quiet about it."

The receptionist comes out. "Mr. Camejo will see you now."

"That's good of him." Duckworth takes a long time to get to

the door, the receptionist freezing her face in a haughty deadpan. Rivkin breathes in her perfume as he goes past.

The carpet is thicker in Camejo's office. Scattered around the room are photos of him shaking hands, blasted by flashbulb light. Camejo and Johnson, Camejo and Humphrey, Camejo and Claude Kirk, Camejo and Nixon, Camejo and the Mayor, Camejo and Ford, Camejo and Carter, Camejo and lots of other beefy white men who look important. The old man sits behind a desk empty but for a telephone. You can look through the floor-to-ceiling window behind him and see Biscayne Boulevard and the causeway to the Beach.

"Gentlemen?" he says, rising to greet them.

He's one of the Cesar Romero ones, silver hair, yachting tan, manicured nails, lots of white teeth. He speaks softly, with only a slight accent. Duckworth nods and sits in the one available chair. "This won't be long. I'm Duckworth, this is Rivkin."

The old man sits down. "How can I help you?"

"Why did somebody leave a dead coke dealer in your car?"

Camejo gives a slight smile. "Only a coincidence, I'm sure."

Duckworth nods toward the window. "All that ocean out there to lose someone in and they coincidentally pinch your car from a guarded lot then return it to the same place three days later."

Camejo doesn't register a thing. A tough old cookie. "Perhaps they have me mix up with someone else."

"Or maybe they don't."

Rivkin is scrutinizing the little models of housing projects on the display table as if there might be little suspects running around in them.

"Maybe," says Duckworth, "there's a tenant from one of your buildings, he's unhappy with the utilities bill, he decides to send you a message."

"There are many disturb people in the city these days," says Camejo. "This is why we must all cooperate with the police."

Duckworth gets up slowly and moves to the window, looking down at the traffic on Biscayne. "Or maybe," he says, "there's a fella, older fella, involved in a certain kind of politics, and he thinks these politics are so important that it's all right he should do his fund-raising through criminal activities. Let's say drug-related activities, that's very popular now, and let's say he steps on somebody's toes during the course of these activities—"

Camejo leans back in his chair. "If you have a question I can answer, Lieutenant, please ask it."

Duckworth turns to look at the photos on the wall. "Where's Kennedy?"

"Pardon?"

"You got every other big cheese came into town in the last twenty years, why not him?"

Camejo speaks very softly. "I was not an admirer of President Kennedy."

The receptionist steps in. "Lieutenant Duckworth? A call for you. Line seven."

Camejo offers his phone. Duckworth nods and looks to Rivkin. "That'll be Harrison. You take it." He locks eyes with Camejo as Rivkin picks up the phone.

"Hello? . . . Yeah, we're here. . . . No. . . . I'm not sure. . . . I'll tell him that." Rivkin hangs up.

"What the hell are we doing up here and cease and desist immediately," says Duckworth.

"Yeah. Something like that."

The old man cocks an eyebrow. "Is something wrong?" Very solicitous. Cute.

Duckworth starts for the door. "Somebody doesn't like you, Mr. Camejo. Besides me, I mean. Maybe you know who it is. We'll be paying attention to whatever you do next." He smiles at the receptionist. "Have a nice day."

The elevator Muzak is playing *Guantanamera* on the way down.

"What did that accomplish?" asks Rivkin.

"Maybe he doesn't ice whoever stuffed his dealer, maybe he waits till my day off to do it or does it out of the county, keep me off his back. Maybe it didn't accomplish anything. That prick is one of the people did the boy on Flagler, you can bet on it. I just wanted to spoil his lunch."

"Harrison was steamed."

"Harrison can stick it. He knows as well as I do that Camejo is knee deep in shit. I'm too old to play nice with these characters."

They ride in silence a moment. Then Rivkin starts to sing along.

". . . *guajira, Guantanamera—Yo soy un hombre sincero—*"

Duckworth scowls. "Don't do that."

Rivkin shrugs. "I learned the words at Interfaith Camp, for the singalong. It's a poem by José Martí."

"That fuck," says Duckworth. "That fuck is behind half the trouble in the hemisphere. Every time one of these half-assed Cubans, left, right or center, breaks a law they say José Fucking Martí told em to do it."

"He's dead, Chief."

"I *know* he's dead, Rivkin. They got his head planted on a pedestal across the street here. If he wasn't dead I'd bust his Cuban ass and stick it on the first boat back to Bananaland."

Rivkin looks at his shoes. A fountain of information, Rivkin, none of which you want to hear. The Muzak bounces cheerfully over the melody.

"You want to know what the words mean?"

Duckworth just gives him a look. The elevator door closes behind them, cutting off the song. The Lincoln and the patrolmen are gone from the parking lot.

"Two possibilities," says Duckworth. "There's a fella, Juan Escobedo, lives in Bogotá, does his banking up here. He lost a lot of outlets when Camejo's people came into the trade. Camejo's people keep it out of their noses, they got more discipline than the usual cowboys. That's what a cause will do for you." Duckworth tosses the keys to Rivkin. "You drive. The other possibility is a character deals out of Tampa, Blas de la Pena. State's got a want on him so I'd be surprised if he was trying to get back in the game down here, but you never know. He's got some kind of political beef with Camejo, goes way back. Whether it's them or somebody else, anybody tries to move on Camejo and it's gonna be ugly."

"What do we do?"

"Try to keep score." Duckworth sits and starts to untie his shoes. "So what the hell is Interfaith Camp?"

FIFTEEN

THE AIR HANGS solemn with echo as she walks up the aisle. Marta kneels at the altar by the tilted bank of candles in their colored glass—red, blue, deep royal purple. It is her favorite part of the church. The church hasn't changed since she was a girl. The whiff of vinegar on her fingers from the holy water, the saints watching from the walls, the echo, the smell like old women in black pinching their ivory beads with grief, kneeling, heads bowed, moaning in a whisper. Thick air held inside for ages, light that is never bright, small voices lost in vaulted stone. Marta feels at home here.

The lit candles flicker in colored glass. The sound they make in the near-empty church is thick and liquid, like moving your tongue when you wake from a dream. Their glow—red, blue, deep royal purple—is the never-sleeping heart of the church. When she was small her mother's hands lifted her by the hips and she leaned over the padded rail, reaching with a long wooden taper, holding flame to a wick and watching as it caught life and glowed color. The purple was her favorite. It was the holiest, the most powerful. On the nights of the Vigil, when her brothers were lost on the dark Island, her mother would bring her here. Marta in white Communion lace, her mother in black, weary from tending the men by the radio—they would join the mothers and sisters who tried to pray arrows of fierce love into the dark Island night, tried to bring God's powerful shield down to protect their lost boys. Each night Marta would light purple for Ambrosio and red for Blas. Ambrosio was the younger, the one who took the most care with her and played with her and would always listen. Blas was more like their father, a man with moods and a loud voice.

"Ahhhhhh!" the women in black would sigh as her mother brought her forward. "Mira a la niña!"

Marta in Communion lace, walking straight and solemn and feeling like an angel. The women in black would cry and nod and press their fists to their hearts, moved by the glowing, innocent girl lighting candles of hope for her brothers.

"Rece, niña, pray for them all."

All through the Vigil she lit the candles, purple for Ambrosio and red for Blas, then she'd kneel and bow her head into her folded hands and pray, the women behind her hissing with the power of it, moaning in their whispers.

She tried to separate the words and think about what they meant the way Padre Martín had taught her, but in the excitement of the Vigil, of the men clustered by the radio at home and no bedtime and the groups of people arguing on every corner and the whole bank of candles lit now—red, blue, deep royal purple blazing hope in the heart of the church—with all that she settled into the usual chant, closing her eyes tight and squeezing her hands together hard, the laced knuckles aching, straining to let God know she was sincere.

And when her mother took her back out the women in black who knelt on the aisle reached out and touched her the way they touched the holy water or the relic of Santa Margarita or the hem of the bishop's gown the time he visited for Confirmation. Marta's face glowed, not with shyness like usual but with knowing that she stood for something in their eyes, stood for something more than she was, like the wine or the Host was more than it was.

"Qué angelita!" the women said each Sunday as she came forward, folded hands pointing like the prow of a boat, eyes to the floor, gliding in a state of grace to Communion. "Qué bonita hija de Cristo!"

Their eyes and their whispers lifted her nearly off her feet as she went forward, floating serenely to the altar.

"Trained her like a damn dog," said Blas. That was back at home and Blas was what Padre Martín would call a tormented soul, even before the yanquis kept him from fighting, his candle low and wet in its red glass, struggling to take flame, sputtering and popping. Blas didn't go to Mass anymore, like their father didn't. Home belonged to the men with their moods and loud voices. At home Marta blushed if something brought their eyes on her, she sat near her mother with her hands folded in her lap and helped with the food and tried not to spill. Liquid ran from her at home, no meal was without the tension of her father's sharp eyes, the glass growing huge and treacherous in her moist fingers, her heart sinking as it slipped free or suddenly appeared in front of her sweeping hand. Her father's eyes, like nails, first on her, then on her mother, asking What's wrong with it? Why can't it do the simplest things? Ambrosio would be the one to help her mop up and tell her not to worry, while Blas would laugh and say she'd been taken by the spirits again.

Blas teased her about the spirits because of the time she'd had the fever so bad that they gave her cortisone and she went into a state. The saints had talked to her then, not the plaster ones on the walls of the church but the ones that came up close by your pillow, whose breath was hot in your ear and on your neck. She cried because she was so tired and they wouldn't let her rest. Her body tingled with the saints, it shuddered and sweated with the hot words they hissed into her ear.

They said she had to do something for them.

She had to.

It was so important nothing else mattered.

People were waiting for her.

Marta soaked through blanket and sheets, poured fever sweat through her damp hair and down her neck till they threw her pillow away, till her mother filled the tub with icy cold water and Ambrosio carried her in wrapped in a sheet and laid her gently down into it. Her cheeks glowed red as they sponged her body all over and her father appeared at the door, his hard eyes on her in the water.

What's wrong with it? asked the eyes. Is it crazy? Is it going to die? This girl, this late mistake of his life with her female moods and secret thoughts, crying, "Make them stop! Make them stop!" as if possessed.

Marta dreamed in a fever.

She was on the hill. The hill covered with sharp rocks and yellow dust, the hill Christ dragged his cross up to die. She was Verónica, offering her veil, but Christ was her brother Ambrosio, a bloody tear streaming from each red eye, the crowd jeering, and when he took his face from the veil the imprint was not Christ's face or her brother's left in blood but the outline of the dark Island, a Cuba blood-red like the one she'd cut from construction paper for the cover of her report for the nuns at school. Ambrosio looked deep in her eyes and nodded, as if there was something she understood now, something she had to do when he was gone, then the torturer's whip sang out and Ambrosio shouldered the heavy, splintering cross and turned up the hill.

Marta dreamed in a fever and she was very small at a table where men were talking, deep voices and dark moods. It was the table for the Last Supper but she was on the floor and could barely see over the edge of the table to the men. They were bearded men but not John and Luke and Paul but Fidel and Che and Raúl and all the other barbudos the friends of her father cursed and made jokes about, and at the center of the table sat her father. He was not Jesus there but God the Father, the one with eyes like nails who knew all and saw all but he didn't see that the bearded ones were planning to kill him. And the saints, the real saints, were hot in her ear complaining that their places at the table had been stolen, telling her she had to warn her father. But the thunder of the men's voices drove her back, her father's eyes could not see her and she could find no way to touch him.

Marta dreamed in a fever that she was the angel with the sword and could fly. A painted statue of the angel stood in a nook as you entered church, a girl with long blond hair and eyes so blue and clear she could see into men's souls. The angel held a sword as high as her shoulder and carried a defiant, proud look on her face. Marta was the angel flying, swinging her sword before her, driving the Dark Hordes back from the land, terrified but soaring, her family below pointing up to her with the other people she was saving, thousands of them, pointing up at her with Mami and Ambrosio and Blas and her father, his eyes soft now, streaming with tears of pride.

Padre Martín said the words over her, the Extreme Unction, but she didn't die. The fever broke, and after that Blas would tease her about talking with the spirits.

Marta lights her candles. Purple in mourning for Ambrosio, red for the troubled soul of Blas, blue for her father, for her mission. Women in black are scattered in the rear pews, moaning in whispers, working their beads. Marta opens herself to the power of the church. People will try to stop her, people will says she's crazy. But her father is counting on her now. Her people are waiting.

The word came back in bits and pieces on the radio, in hints and rumors, words carried on a dying wind. The slaughter on the beach, the confusion, the airplanes that never came. It was weeks before there were lists of who was captured and who was killed. They learned about Ambrosio first, and then the mystery that none of the lists, not from the government, not from Fidel, recognized that Blas existed. The day that Ambrosio's body was sent back, Blas walked in the door.

"Me llamaron fidelista sin Fidel," he said, bitterness twisting his mouth. "A danger to La Brigada. They put me and the best of the fighters in a stinking porqueriza in the middle of the jungle. Prisioneros de los singados yanquis. Y a La Isla they send carniceros Batistianos. Butchers and children," he said, thinking of Ambrosio.

Her father, a butcher still for the Lomax brothers, would not look at Blas, would not speak to him. If the yanquis did not trust him, did not trust any man who had fought in the monte for the Revolution, they must have good reasons. Blas sat in their kitchen with bitterness twisting his face, a ghost in his own house, as the women in the bedroom prepared the body of his brother.

Marta walked in front of the men who carried the coffin to the gravesite, solemn in her white lace, holding a huge wreath of flowers before her like a shield. Dozens of people lined the path to the grave.

"Volveremos!" cried the men, eyes fierce. "Libertad o muerte."

"Mira a la niña," sighed the women. "Mira a la hermana. Parece una angelita. Look at her face. All she needs is wings to fly."

Marta didn't cry at the burying or at the Mass later for Ambrosio and the others. Some praised her strength and some were a little frightened by her. It was that day that she knew her eyes could see into men's souls. She saw the shame tugging at Tío Felix, his eyes darting from face to face, dreading judgment. She saw the bitterness twisting inside of Blas, the bile in him burning against the yanquis, against the old men crying volveremos who had not gone in the first place, who always stood on the side and let others do the dying. And she saw into her father for the first time, past the eyes like nails and into his heart, beating now as much with pride as with sorrow as he buried his son, his son the poet, the sensitive one, the one who cried when he slaughtered cattle. A hero now, a patriot and a martyr. Marta saw her father look through Blas like he was air, the way he had always looked through her, a ghost at his table. He saw only Ambrosio now, saw him for the first time, strong and heroic and a man.

"Qué ojos!" the women whispered as she went down the aisle, leading what was left of her family. "Eyes to burn you with."

Padre Martín spoke from the pulpit that day. He was not much older than the boys they had just buried, and there was anger in him that scared the women and made the men standing at the rear step forward to listen.

"These men," he said, "our sons, our brothers—they are part of God's Army now. Shoulder to shoulder with Michael the Archangel, swords of righteousness raised in their hands! They have not *left* us," he said. "They are not gone but are part of La Isla forever, their names burned in blood on the pages of our history, their bodies bonded with the soil of our beloved Cuba!"

The men in the back began to nod and repeat his phrases, and old Padre Esturo, tall and noble like a dream of a bullfighter, smiled with pride behind him.

"Next year in La Habana," said Padre Martín, "I will say another Mass for these men, our crusaders. They are waiting for us there right now—waiting in the churches of La Habana, in the silent churches, the ravaged churches of Santa Clara, of Ciego de Ávila y Holguín, of Pinar del Río y Matanzas y Camagüey y Santiago de Cuba, waiting for us to join them in God's holy battle. Vendremos, compañeros, hermanos, hijos—we are coming!"

And it seemed to Marta when he said the last, when the men in the rear stood to shout and the women cried to Jesus and her father's face flushed with pride and determination, it seemed that Padre Martín was looking straight at her, straight into her soul, his words burning there and lifting her, lifting her up above the congregation till she floated over their voices, that much closer to God, and she whispered her own secret promise.

Padre Martín moves away from the women in black, hoping they won't recognize his face. He sees Marta by the candles and waits, kneeling. He feels strange in the church again. He goes to Mass, when he goes, at a church across town, a new church with no memories. He feels like a secret visitor, an invader. When he was still serving he would sometimes watch the santeros, usually poor, usually black, come in and plant themselves at the foot of one or another of the statues on the side wall. They'd whisper their pagan words, think their pagan thoughts and the saint would be renamed, made wild and African. Once or twice the janitor found offerings when he cleaned in the morning—liquor and flowers, a twist of tobacco. Padre Esturo thought it was a desecration and wanted them caught and punished. Padre Esturo had not wanted to let the blacks in at all. There was the Haitian church for that.

Padre Martín did not worry much about the santeros. It was at least a faith, a faith in something beyond the television set and the automobile, a belief in something more powerful than man, if not higher in its purpose. God knows they are in His house, Padre Martín reasoned, and maybe He will touch their souls.

Padre Martín kneels, waiting. He feels like a secret visitor, a santero of despair. He looks at the statue of Saint Peter and re-members only pulling it from its crate, the screech of the nails wrenched from dry wood, the smell of the packing hay, the statue cold and waxy to his touch. He sees the votive candles lit but can only think of them two dozen to a box, the boxes piled high in the tiny bathroom of the rectory. He remembers the catalog number for reorder. He recalls conversations with the man who repairs stained glass, billing arguments with the power company, the day the microphone was installed in the pulpit, all the annoying de-tails of running a large operation. But the power it held for him, the magic of faith, is not there. It might or might not wait up at the head of the aisle, by the altar, but he doesn't like to go up that far.

Once he stood beside Artime on the pulpit, when Artime was freshly ransomed from Castro's dungeons, and with Artime listening he spoke to the moral center of La Comunidad, spoke with such fire and strength that some weeks half the men crowding to hear his sermons were not even Catholics.

"Don't forget God," Padre Esturo would whisper sometimes just before he spoke, "and don't forget Jesus. Fighting the Communists is good, pero aquí tenemos una oportunidad. We can win souls here. Try to mention the Pope."

It hurt Padre Esturo that so few Cubans were Catholic, hurt him to see them taken by the Baptists and Methodists, even some of the old families, the gallego families. Tall and sad-eyed like the great Manolete, Padre Esturo seemed always to be near the end of a losing battle.

"Our glory is in failing," he would say. "In trying though we know we will fail. Success," he would say, "is not for this life, but in the next."

But Padre Esturo had gone home to wait for the Generalísimo to die, to see his dream grow old and fail, and Artime had died young, and the crowds in to hear Padre Martín fight the devil of Communism had grown smaller and smaller and the Bishop had asked him to think more about God and less about politics.

"When our island is under the thumb of Satan," said Padre Martín, "when souls go through life there and can never be touched by Christ, how can we separate God from politics?"

Padre Esturo would have told him again the story of how he shouldered a rifle in the fortress of Toledo, how he knew for sure he'd sent at least three of God's enemies to Hell during the great siege there, how a priest was not only the voice of God on this earth but the razor edge of His righteous sword. The Bishop told Padre Martín to seek guidance in contemplation and prayer.

Padre Martín was photographed with some men at a demonstration, holding a banner and shouting slogans. He was on the radio for several months, spreading the word, raising the alarm, until the Bishop or somebody above him heard the show and he was told to stop. When the Cuban plane exploded and Omega was suspected, he answered some questions for a TV news reporter. He said something about chickens coming home to roost. He said something about the Hand of God. There were calls to the Bishop and he was forbidden to make public statements.

Padre Esturo would have told him again about the Guerra Civil in Spain, how he had walked the line of the Communists and Anarchists and simple criminals about to be executed, offering the Last Rites, offering a prayer, a benediction, but Satan was in them and they spat on him. How he had turned to the Commandante and the soldiers of God's Army, waiting with their rifles, and said, "That is enough. Send them to Hell." But Padre Esturo was gone and there was only the Bishop.

"I try to do God's work," Padre Martín said to the Bishop, "and you give me church politics."

"Do you speak directly to God?" asked the Bishop.

Padre Martín knew this was a challenge, a test. "What is a vocation," he said, "but a feeling from God? I have a feeling that what I do is right, is God's work. Church politics," he said to the Bishop, "do not concern me."

The Bishop was a very calm man, a yanqui with a yanqui way of doing hard things without showing emotion. He nodded at what Padre Martín had to say. "I think you may be right." He laid his hand on Padre Martín's shoulder and looked him straight in the eye. The Bishop had cold blue eyes, eyes that made Padre Martín regret the pride he had shown, the anger. "Church politics do not concern you, not nearly enough. Maybe what God wants you to do must be done outside of the church. You're a young man. If this feeling you have is truly from God, it won't go away if you're not a priest anymore."

Padre Martín felt he was falling, falling like Lucifer through the universe, a fall with no end. He wanted to take it back, to restate his position, but the Bishop walked away then, the audience over.

It wasn't the very end, not quite. The diocese offered him a post in the desert in Texas, minding a shrine that Polish immigrants had built after the War. It was a simple life—a congregation of old women, a painting of a black Virgin that had been slashed by the sabers of Mongol invaders, a cactus garden behind the cinder-block box of a chapel. A good place to reflect, to remove oneself from worldly matters. It was that or out. He could have made a public show, could have asked the few who kept the faith of la causa alive to lobby with the Bishop, but politics, church politics, disgusted him. His last Sunday they brought in a guest speaker, a missionary from Africa, and he did not even have the emotional farewell he had planned. He served the Mass, muttering the Latin by rote, and when he took the Host he could barely swallow.

Padre Martín kneels waiting for the girl to join him. God knows that he is in His house, he hopes, and maybe He will touch his soul.

The girl always goes to the candles first. Padre Martín started watching her at her First Communion. It was grace, Padre Esturo said, not just the pretend holiness of little girls, but true grace.

"Quizá va a ser monja," said Padre Martín, watching the way she moved, the cool solemnity as she crossed herself, the strength in her eyes.

"A nun would be a waste," said Padre Esturo. "Nuns we will always have. One like that—" He shrugged. "One like that is very rare."

Padre Martín fell in love with her. Not in the carnal way, the way that had happened with a few women since seminary and that he could always pray and work to get out of his mind. Marta was still a little girl. He thought about her and sometimes dreamed about her, he tried to hold her eyes as he gave his sermons, tried to be near her when her class would come for instruction. He was jealous, too, of her brothers, and of the nuns who taught her and spent time with her at school. He wanted to be the one to teach her, to be with her. Sometimes, catching her eyes or being caught by them during Mass, he thought that her gaze, her strong searching look, meant that she understood his unspoken feelings, that she loved him back. Other times he thought she was seeing through him, clear through to the weakness in his heart.

Marta turns and sees him. She genuflects in front of the middle of the altar and starts back. Padre Martín doesn't like to go that far up anymore.

"I have news to tell you," she says, kneeling beside him in the last pew. "About my mission."

Padre Martín sighs. "Not here. Anywhere but here."

"I think he's a bad man," says Marta, "un alcahuete. But I think he'll do what we need."

Padre Martín shrugs. "One can do God's work without knowing it. The Virgin rode to Bethlehem on an ass."

He is embarrassed to have her see his room. The smallness of it, his clothes hanging in the open from an extension cord strung from the bathroom to the galley kitchen, the hotplate crusted with grease splatter by the sink, the little cans of food from the market piled everywhere. The cell of a secular monk, everything mean and small, nothing holy. He sits on his unmade bed under the poster of Martí, Martí with a glow like a halo around his head, his eyes fixed on a glorious future, and wishes they'd met in the park instead.

"He says he can get us guns," says Marta. "He says he'll have to come with us."

"Do you trust him?"

"I believe he hates the barbudos."

Padre Martín nods. Marta is sitting on his one chair, the clattering fan on the table riffling her hair. If she has an opinion about his room her eyes don't show it.

"I can get one of my Tío Felix's boats."

"And when do you want to go?"

"The anniversary. To be there on the day my brother was killed."

"They have a holiday on the anniversary. Una tertulia para todos. Es muy peligroso."

"I know. But whatever we do will speak much louder then. If you can only be a small flame," she says, "you have to burn brightly."

Padre Martín smiles. It is a saying he has used from the pulpit many times. Now she is the teacher and he is the one who learns.

Her eyes dig into him. "I want you to come with us."

He feels himself blushing. "Yo?"

"If you come we will be blessed."

"I'm not a priest anymore."

"Yes, you are. En los ojos de Dios, siempre lo serás."

She says it with such finality that for a moment he feels it must be true. He thinks of Padre Esturo, pistol in one hand, crucifix in the other, fighting for Catholic Spain.

"I don't know anything about guns," he says. "I'm not a soldier."

"None of us are."

Padre Martín looks around the room. There is a simple cross hung on the door. There is a pile of cans from the White Pantry under the sink—canned peas, canned fruit, canned tuna. Over the sink is his list of what he eats each day of the week. He knows it by heart now but has never bothered to take the list down. Canned ravioli on Monday. Ham and potatoes Tuesday. Wednesday is hot dogs and beans. He still doesn't eat meat on Fridays. The ancient Jewish woman with the sores on her legs in the next apartment gives him baked things sometimes, heavy, gluey apple things with names he can't pronounce. She calls him her bachelor friend. There are mice that he never sees but hears at night when they gnaw on the chair legs.

If the feeling from God is true, it won't go away because you're not a priest anymore.

He feels himself falling, falling not like a bad angel through the universe but like a man, a man who knows where hard ground is and how it can hurt. It is an exciting feeling.

"I have to confess," says Padre Martín, "that I get sick in boats."

SIXTEEN

SERAFÍN DOESN'T LIKE the waves. The Beach is okay, crowded with people, noisy. But the waves won't be ignored, drawing his eye out past the waders and splashers to the empty sea beyond, out to the flat unbroken horizon. Serafín has long ebony fingers, their joints knobby as walnuts, and he presses them into the sand making patterns and tries to keep the waves from drawing his thoughts out to sea. Radios are blasting salsa and rock, groups of teenage boys cruise up and down the beach checking out groups of teenage girls who toss their hair and throw their shoulders back, eyes safe behind their sunglasses. Mothers stand calf deep in the water ready to grab their toddlers from the tumbling surf. Kids race by, spraying sand. A tall Haitian man, a few shades darker than Serafín, stands fully dressed at the edge of the wet sand, looking out across the water.

Serafín can feel the few inches separating his bare arm from Marta's. She sits on the blanket beside him, drawing something in the sand with her foot. If he leaned just a little his arm would be against hers. Maybe in a minute or two he'll try. Marta has on a black one-piece bathing suit and wears a small golden cross on a chain around her neck. His sister, Luz, sits on the blanket in front of them in a mustard-yellow bikini, rubbing lotion onto the back of this new guy Rufo. Rufo is maybe a little too good-looking but an improvement over the last one Luz had. Serafín turns his face away and looks down the line of pink and white Beach hotels. It's embarrassing when Luz tells stories about him.

"He was king of the Coca-Cola boys," says Luz. "If you wanted to sell sodas on Playa Santa María you had to deal with Serafín first."

"Es un exageración," says Serafín.

"There was a whole pack of boys," she says. "They'd go swimming in the morning first thing, and then when the people started coming and it got hot they'd run around selling Cokes."

"We didn't swim at Santa María," says Serafín. "Santa María was segregated then, a causa de los yanquis. We had to swim down by the river and then hitch a ride up to Santa María to work." Luz is trying to pump him up in Marta's eyes, which is okay, but she should get the facts straight. He can't tell if Marta is listening or not.

"And he always sold the most, Cokes that Papi stole from the hotel."

"He didn't steal the Cokes," says Serafín. "He borrowed the bottles. The empties. Then I'd go down to Chucho Martínez, who had the fountain, and he'd fill them up with his own stuff, which cost less. Papi didn't steal. He borrowed some bottles. And maybe some ice."

"You don't *borrow* ice, hermano," says Luz. "Ice melts. He stole some ice from the Hotel Nacional kitchen for you to put the soda in. And at the end of the day you went around and fought with the other boys to pick up the empty bottles."

The yanquis didn't like it if you hung close waiting for them to finish so you could take the bottle back. Serafín kept track in his head of every bottle he left off and when he'd see that family getting up to go he'd send one of the Muñoz brothers over to fetch. The Muñoz brothers were little and skinny with big brown eyes and sold more than half his Cokes for him because the yanquis thought they were cute. He would give them each one Coke to drink at noon and when the sun went down he'd take them to the alley behind the Nacional kitchen and Papi would feed them scraps from the hotel lunch. They were street kids, their parents guajiros who'd wandered into La Habana after they were evicted from the land they were born on. The father was in jail for stealing and the mother sometimes got work cleaning fish. Serafín put the word out that the Muñoz brothers were under his protection and if they got beat up he would find the kids who did it and put it right.

"Serafín was the king of them all," says Luz. "You had to fight to keep your territory, to keep the other boys out. Some days he brought in as much money as Papi."

You had to pay Chucho Martínez for the soda. You had to pay the cop they called Botas Negras, who was in charge of the Beach, to let you sell there. You had to pay Gato Oliviera, who ran the neighborhood, so that his gang wouldn't rob you of your profits on the way home.

"The boys would have fights," says Luz. "Sometimes with knives. That's how Serafín got his scar." She points.

"It was a bottle opener," says Serafín. There is a long horizontal scar, raised and angry pink against the brown skin of his stomach. "Me corté con el filo."

It had been a new boy, a big half-Chinese boy with one eye that didn't focus right. A sullen-looking boy who showed up one day and started selling by the south wall. Pepito, who usually worked that area, came complaining.

"Serafín," he said, "you got to get this jodido chino off my sand."

"Por qué?" asked Serafín. He hated the fights, hated being the boss, but that was the way it had worked out. "No me molesta," he said.

"Porque eres el jefe," said Pepito. "And the boss has got to keep order. I pay you five centavos a day—"

"Métate tus cinco centavos. Maybe the chino will pay me six."

Pepito knew Serafín couldn't do this without fighting every kid on the beach. "Get him off my sand," said Pepito. "Es tu carga."

Serafín left his icebox and Cokes with the Muñoz brothers and walked down to the south wall. The other vendedores kept selling but watched him, knowing what was cooking. Pepito walked a few yards behind, trying to look indignant. When they found the new boy he was sitting on his box drinking a soda. He hadn't sold much. There was nothing cute about the new boy, nothing the yanqui ladies would want to take a picture of. He looked up at Serafín, emotionless, his bad eye wandering off to the side so that Serafín wondered if someone were coming up behind him.

"No puede vender aquí," said Serafín. "Esta arena le pertenece." He jerked his thumb over to Pepito, who stood breathing heavily a few feet back. When Pepito got excited you heard a faint wheeze in his breath, could see his skinny ribs stick out as he fought for air. Pepito slept under the pier, and when a cold mist rolled in you could hear his cough boom out like a foghorn.

"Quién lo dice?" asked the new boy.

Serafín sighed and tapped his chest. "Yo."

"Ya le pagué al jodido patrullero," said the new boy. "Botas Negras told me I could sell here."

Botas Negras had done this before, taken a boy's money without checking with Serafín. He was a thief, Botas. But none of the boys he'd sent had been as big or as mean-looking as this one.

"You pay Botas just to be let on the beach," said Serafín. The new boy had a steel bottle opener tied around his neck with a piece of string. The new boy was so beefy he almost had tits, and the bottle opener dangled between them, the sharp end pointing down. Serafín's opener was tied to his icebox, back with the Muñoz brothers. "Once you're on the beach, if you want to sell, me tienes que preguntar a mí," said Serafín. "And I say no."

The new boy stood up. He was at least as tall as Serafín and a lot thicker. He pulled the opener over his head and began to twirl it on its string. "Make me leave. *Make* me."

The other vendedores were there now, ringed around, faces solemn, most still holding their iceboxes. We're going to make a killing today, thought Serafín, knowing that the Muñoz brothers, who were obedient and would keep selling no matter what, would have no competition during the fight.

Serafín walked straight at the new boy. Usually if you walked straight at them, pretending to be unafraid, they'd run. Then he'd split the abandoned Cokes among the other vendedores and there would be peace again. The new boy stood still and took a hard grip on the bottle opener. The sharp end, rusty red, peeked out of his fat fist.

"Ven, negrito," he said. "Come and get it."

Serafín and the new boy began to circle each other, the new boy feinting with the bottle opener, Serafín with his left lead. He had seen Benny Paret fight once when Paret was not much older than he was. He had once sold a Coke to Kid Gavilan and the Kid had demonstrated his famous bolo punch. Serafín was very fast and had a long reach, but for some reason he was too close when the new boy swept a hard backhand with the bottle opener and he was cut. Maybe it was the bad eye, throwing him off as to where the new boy was looking, but he was cut sharp across his belly and the other boys, watching silently up to then and screening them from the turistas on the beach, all gasped.

"He's cut," they hissed. "El chino ha cortado a Serafín!" And Serafín, feeling only the sudden electric shock of it, danced sideways and crumpled to his knees in the sand. He had been down before. The time that he fought Big Colón to stay on the beach, to become el jefe de los vendedores, they had rolled in the sand trying to put each other's eyes out with their thumbs, punching and choking till Serafín bit such a piece of Big Colón's nose off that it sprayed blood and he panicked and quit. That time a bunch of the yanqui men had gathered around shouting and making bets and when he was the winner one of them gave him five yanqui dollars.

The new boy walked toward him. Serafín didn't look at his stomach but could feel hot blood running down his thighs. He dug his fingers into the sand, taking two big handfuls, and when he was close enough he threw them into the boy's eyes, the good one and the bad one, and as the boy's arms went up to protect his eyes Serafín kicked him hard in the huevos with his heel. He grabbed the boy's wrist and jerked it down and around, pinning it behind him, then jerked up till the boy cried out and dropped the bottle opener and then he felt the boy's elbow pop inside his muscle, the way he felt the chicken bones pop when he helped Papi in the Nacional kitchen. The boy fell down then, fell to his knees with his forehead to the ground and Serafín kicked him in the head as hard and as many times as he could, his bare foot hurting more than the slice on his belly, kicked until the new boy fell on his side and his bad eye popped out. It was glass, and Serafín wiped the sand off it, examining it like a new shooter won in a game of marbles, then threw it far off into the waves. He left the new boy heaving and moaning on the ground and walked down to the water. The other vendedores were already splitting up the new boy's Cokes, Pepito taking the most cause it happened on his sand, coughing with excitement as he counted. They would leave a respectful number for Serafín to take if he didn't die from the cut.

Serafín walked in up to his knees and looked for the first time. His belly and shorts and thighs were a mess of sand and blood. It was hurting now, hurting like he'd been cut in two by a hot wire. His knees trembled and he lowered himself into the waves, hoping the salt water would cool the burning, would clean the cut the way it cleaned the cuts on the fishermen's hands in his grandfather's village. Serafín sat in the water, watching the threads of blood wash around him in the waves. The waves stroked him, carried him, soothing.

Whack! The side of his face burned as he was slapped hard over the ear and lifted up under the arms by somebody much bigger than he was, clear out of the water. It was Botas Negras, dragging him off the beach by his arms, rocks and seashells scraping his back, past the new boy heaving in the sand, past Pepito counting his new-won Cokes, past the big yanqui with the red face, talking loud through his nose the way they did—"Git that nigger outa the damn water whatta they pay you for?"—and finally past the Muñoz brothers, skinny and big-eyed, posing for a two-centavos photo a blond yanqui lady was taking. She had her face in the viewfinder and didn't notice the black boy, bleeding across his stomach, being dragged past her feet by a uniformed officer in wet motorcycle boots. The Muñoz brothers smiled at the blond lady and waved to Serafín as he went by.

"That's how you got the scar?" says Marta, looking at it with a professional eye. "I always thought it was from the Invasion."

Rufo stirs under Luz's hands for the first time, turning on his belly and raising his sunglasses to look at Serafín. "You were with La Brigada?"

Serafín nods. Marta looks at his face.

"I'm impressed," says Rufo.

"Don't be."

The Beach pounds with music from radios carried on the shoulders of young boys. Black boys, brown boys, white boys, skinny Vietnamese boys with crew cuts and surfer shorts, carrying radios nearly half as long as they are, blasting music. Old Jewish men pick their way slowly through the edge of the surf, pants legs rolled up, noses coated with white sun block. Old Cuban men argue and laugh up on the platform beneath the palm trees, clacking their domino tiles on stone tables. Women in bikinis, glistening with oil, jog up and down the waterline, feet kicking up spray as they weave through little boys and girls tottering unsteadily in the waves. The sun is bright and warm and this beach is okay, this beach is fine with

Serafín but there is still that tall Haitian standing fully dressed at the edge of the wet sand, staring out into the ocean.

"Debes de estar orgulloso," says Marta. "Everybody who served in La Brigada should be proud."

Serafín shrugs. It isn't something he likes to talk about.

"You were in the dungeons?" asks Rufo. "How long did they keep you?"

Serafín looks away. Luz answers. "I told you, he got back on his own. Serafín and some other guys. They sailed a boat all the way back."

The thing Marta has been making in the sand with her foot is a little island. It looks like a map of Cuba. "You should be proud, Serafín," she says.

There wasn't a sail. It was only a rubber raft, made for four, maybe five people. It was for hauling equipment in, not for survival.

Serafín and the others in the Second came off the *Houston* in the dead of night at Playa Larga. The little fiberglass boats were too light and shallow for the size of the waves and the one Serafín rode in was swamped halfway to shore. He was crouching in the middle of the boat, knees bent against the slamming of the hull against the black water, tracer bullets streaming overhead as the *Houston* returned the machine-gun fire they were taking from the beach. There was already water over his ankles and then the boat smacked down into a deep trough and he felt it give, water over every side, choking the motor, sucking the boat under. He held his rifle in both hands over his head the way they taught in training and went straight down, gasping a breath and waiting to feel bottom. It took too long and he frog-kicked hard for the surface, his heavy boots dragging on him, holding on to the rifle as long as he could till he finally let go and felt it bump him on its way back down. When he broke surface there were a few scattered shouts in the dark and the tracers glimpsed overhead as the waves crushed down on him, filling his boots, his uniform. Serafín let himself go under and swam as far as he could between breaths under the waves, swam toward the lights that weren't supposed to be on the beach.

He crawled out of the water tangled in seaweed and saw men, his men, moving out across the beach. There was some firing but scattered, more like rioting than the war he had imagined. It was real though, he could feel that it was real, that somewhere across the dark beach there could be someone pointing a gun that would kill him.

"Fucking boats," said Conejito, his squad leader when he found him. "I knew those fucking boats were no fucking good. There's only two left working. The sun's coming and we're still bringing in the Second."

"I lost my rifle," said Serafín.

Conejito shrugged. "Stick around, compadre," he said. "Somebody's bound to get shot."

Oliva was ashore then and gathered a bunch of them to move into the scattered bohíos just in from the beach and take up a position facing the road that led out to Girón where the rest of La Brigada was landing. Serafín went along, stripping off his shirt and undershirt and wringing them out, shivering in the night air, feeling naked and cowardly with his empty hands among the armed men. There were grenade explosions off to the right, and there were mosquitos, silent, hard-biting mosquitos you only noticed after they'd punched into you. Serafín sat behind three riflemen he didn't know very well and waited for the sun to come and warm him. The men said there was a radio tower that wasn't supposed to be there sitting under the lights that weren't supposed to be there right by the beach, that the yanquis had fucked them with bad information and the stupid plastic boats.

"All we have to do is hold for a day," said one of the men, "y después vienen los Marines."

"A la mierda sus Marines," said another. "We don't need them. Just a little air support."

"I hope Fidel is pissed," said another. "I hope we woke him from a good, deep sleep."

There was firing then, Serafín lying flat out on the ground, seeing only the muzzle flashes of the milicianos who crept out of the woods at them, never close enough to see more than a glimpse of body but seemingly all around them. The men fired back with rifles and machine guns and Serafín felt things crawling on him. They were land crabs, dozens of them, red and black, scuttering around on the ground while the men tried to kill each other. Serafín felt them climbing over his legs and back but didn't move to get them off for fear somebody was watching him from the dark woods, trying to make out his shape. The milicianos came and went all night. Serafín wished they would go away for an hour or more so he could take his boots off and dry his socks. The three men with rifles stopped talking and Serafín could only tell they were there when they were firing or slapping mosquitos.

The sun came up hot and with it came the planes. Serafín didn't know the names of planes, but he could tell they were Castro's, coming in low over the mangroves, five, maybe a half dozen.

"Here come the planes they're not supposed to have," said one of the men.

The planes passed over them toward the beach and there were explosions.

"I hope everybody got off," said one of the men. "I hope everybody got off that fucking ship."

It was past noon and they hadn't slept and they hadn't eaten when the first tank arrived. By then two of their own tanks had come up from Girón and the men had dug little trenches in their spots facing the road. Oliva had been up and down, telling them what to expect. Serafín had borrowed a shovel and dug himself a pit but without a gun it felt wrong to sit down in it so he sat on the edge killing mosquitos and waiting.

The order had gone down the line to hold fire, and they sat in their shallow trenches at the edge of the trees, looking across the swamp to the road. The Castro tank came straight down the road, followed by trucks with men in them and more tanks and then they just stopped. Soldiers got out of the trucks. Men started setting up mortars.

Don't they know we're here? thought Serafín. Then the ground erupted underneath the tanks and trucks and men and things were lifted into the air and everyone around him was firing. Serafín lay at the front of his pit watching the others being slaughtered, men running and falling, stumbling across the swamps to be cut down by machine guns, trucks torn apart by shells and then, overhead, two planes of La Brigada diving in and dropping their bombs, firing their rockets. Serafín had thought about bullets and dying in training camp but he wasn't ready for the way the men came apart. They were men like him and when the bullets or the shrapnel hit they tore apart. They were men like him and they tore, hunks of cloth and meat and blood and gristle ripping off into the air, spilling out onto the ground. Men were hit in the face and their heads exploded, nose and teeth driven back through their skulls. When the firing lifted Serafín could feel the ground still shaking, but it was his body trembling uncontrollably. One of the men with a rifle was spitting blood as he had bitten part of his tongue off without knowing it during the fighting and there was nothing moving out on the road.

There were heaps of soldier left lying on the ground. Smoke. Nothing moved. Then the shadow of something crossed over Serafín and he looked up to see vultures, dozens of vultures floating overhead, wheeling lazily around the open ground, cautious at first, then flapping in to roost on what was left of a body, one by one, till the road was glistening black with them.

"There wasn't a sail," says Serafín to Luz. "It was just a rubber raft."

"I met a guy," says Rufo, sitting up, "who swam it. Only a couple years ago. Him and his wife, they coached sports and they wanted to leave, but when they asked for exit visas they just lost their jobs. So they started training, taking longer and longer swims, and they learned how to navigate by the stars and built this little raft from inner tubes or something and one night they split. The raft breaks up right away, they were pushing it in front of them, so they're just out there swimming and they keep going. Ninety miles they swim. The guy said they were both about to go under, it was night and a bit cloudy and they think they're lost, only all of a sudden they see lights in the sky over Key West. Explosions. It's the Fourth of fucking July, right? Fireworks—qué suerte, huh? That saves them. That and all the training."

"They only trained us to take the beach," says Serafín. "Not to run away."

Marta frowns. A pair of yanqui maricones, slender and deeply tanned, spread their blanket a few feet away. They wear their T-shirts on their heads, knotted into turbans, and talk loudly about what foods make you bloat.

"Ustedes nunca huyeron," says Marta. "It was a retreat."

Serafín looks her in the eye. "In a retreat you keep your face to the enemy and your rifle in your hand."

"Who wants to swim?" says Luz, standing up. She won't listen to talk about the Invasion.

"We would have died on the beach for no reason, or else been caught like the others," says Serafín. "I don't feel bad that I ran away. But that's what I did."

"Come on," says Luz. "Me estoy quemando aquí."

Marta gives Serafín a long, sad look, then stands to go with Luz. Serafín and Rufo watch the women walk down to the surf.

"Qué pareja," says Rufo, smiling. "La agonía y el éxtasis."

By the time they had moved up to the Rotunda somebody had handed Serafín a rifle. He felt much better. Not that it would protect him or keep him from getting killed, but holding it meant that he was supposed to be there, meant he didn't worry about the others wondering what his story was.

The Fourth had joined them with their heavy weapons, and more tanks, but there was still no food or water and the rumor was that the whole Fifth Battalion had drowned when the *Houston* was hit in the morning, or were eaten by sharks, or had run into the swamps, or were somewhere hiding, sitting out the battle. Nobody had seen any of them. The rumors from Girón were not good, and nobody knew what had become of the paratroopers up ahead. Serafín tried to think water out of his body and into his tongue. It had just gotten dark when the shelling started.

At first there were explosions and a pause and then more explosions, the ground seeming to leap out from underneath Serafín, the way his abuelo would hold him firm in his two arms then jerk them down quickly so he would feel like he was falling, only to land back into the old man's arms. His abuelo had arms knotted with muscle, arms that smelled of brine and fish scales. The ground leapt out from under Serafín and then there was nothing but explosions with no space between them, with the concussions sucking the air out of the sky and Serafín lying curled up with his hands over his ears, bouncing on the hard ground with each shell that came close, his rifle hopping around next to him. The land crabs stayed in their holes. In any tiny break of sound between explosions there was the *ping, ping, ping* of flying slivers of metal, the cracking of palm branches and the cries of men who were hit. Serafín wished he could grow roots and grip into the soil, wished he could burrow deep into it like a mole, dig under the waves of concussion and whipping shrapnel. A tree was sliced by singing metal just overhead and a large branch as thick as his arm hung down bleeding sap as papery shreds of palm bark fluttered in the air. Nobody ran. They dug in and waited for it to ease up but it didn't ease up, the earth shook and ripped apart hour after hour. Serafín's jaw ached from trying to clench his teeth together, his ribs were sore from the pounding. It was almost midnight when the shelling finally stopped and then the tanks rolled into the Rotunda.

The Brigade tanks moved up to meet them and they blasted their cannons at each other nearly point-blank till there were two tanks grinding up against each other tread to tread, turrets banging and wrestling for position to get a shell off like great dinosaurs in a death struggle till the barrel of the Castro tank split and then there were soldiers coming, lots of them, rifle flashes coming through the trees at them and Serafín was firing his gun. He didn't see men, didn't see faces, but they were out there all around him and he fired at the flashes and tried to keep low, taking his time, firing and firing till he had no more ammunition. Then he lay facing the enemy, his gun pointed toward them as if this could do any good and he waited for what would happen next and tried to stay awake. The Brigade's mortar started firing the fósforo vivo and the electric white flames burst out in the trees ahead along with screams, human screams but it was as if the white flames themselves were screaming. Once Serafín saw a flame in the shape of a man running, screaming, and there was a concentration of firing and the shape fell and burned on the ground, suddenly silent. Once he saw the outline of a tank moving up through a wall of the white flame. He pounded his forehead against the ground to stay awake, stay alert. The firing thinned out but didn't stop and the night went on. Serafín bit down on his dry, swollen tongue to keep himself awake. He strained to see past the burning tanks into the trees where the enemy was but couldn't make anything out. It got colder. Serafín saw his abuelo, sitting near one of the burning tanks, mending a fishing net, holding it up to the flame now and then to examine his work. He thought he should crawl forward to tell him it wasn't safe there, that he could be hit by the bullets, but his abuelo seemed to melt into the flames. Serafín saw shapes start to appear out of the darkness, trees and bodies and armored vehicles but it was only the dawn approaching.

They were told they were falling back to Girón to get more ammunition. Serafín climbed into the back of a truck, the men around him so tired they could barely gossip about what they thought was happening.

"They blew up the *Río Escondido* yesterday too," one said. "Did you hear that big explosion yesterday morning from Girón? It went right under."

"The jets are coming," said another.

"What jets? Whose jets?"

"No sé. Solamente he oído que vienen."

"No tenemos jets, hombre."

"But the *yanquis* have jets and they're on our side."

"If they're on our side," said the man who knew about the *Río Escondido*, "where the fuck are they?"

It was light out when the trucks reached Girón. Serafín joined the others walking toward the beach, stretching his cramped legs out, asking around for more ammo and then there was more shelling and then the part of the earth Serafín was on lifted up into the air as all the wind was sucked out of his body and his eardrums were driven into his head and he was slammed to the ground, the weight of the world crushing on top of him and there was white fire in his head but no screaming, just the whooshing of the wind as he fell through space, fell through white dry space with no bottom.

"She's a serious one, your Marta," says Rufo.

"She's not my Marta," says Serafín. "Es solamente una amiga de mi hermana."

"Qué lástima."

Serafín shrugs. This Rufo is a nosy one.

"You think we could have won it if the yanquis had kept their promises?"

"If they brought in the planes and the tanks and the Marines and killed half the people in the country. Or maybe just burned everything down, de Pinar del Río a Santiago de Cuba. No fueron rusos contra nosotros en la playa, hombre. Fueron cubanos."

"Cubans with Russian machine guns."

"And our guns were from the yanquis. As far as those milicianos cared, we *were* yanquis."

"Some of them helped us."

"More of them didn't."

Rufo scowls and looks out to the women bobbing up and down in the surf. "So you ran."

"I got in a raft on the beach. Everybody else was gone."

"And you sailed all the way back here," says Rufo. "Not bad."

There wasn't a sail.

Serafín came out of the falling whiteness on the floor of a little shack on Playa Girón. His nose had been bleeding and was crusted and sore and he had a headache but he could stand and wait for the world to steady itself under him. There were two dead men lying in the corner of the shack, their arms folded over their chests, handkerchiefs covering their faces. Serafín staggered out onto the sand and saw men running every whichway, saw trucks and tanks and machine guns mounted on armored cars abandoned on the beach, stranded without ammo or gasoline, and the sky crossed with swooping airplanes strafing them. He tried to stop someone to find out what was happening. The men were mostly paratroopers, who were supposed to be far inland now, and they were tired and angry and scared.

"They got on boats and left us!" said one of the men.

"They ran off into the swamps," said another.

"They're all dead," said another. "Massacred. The tanks are heading for the beach and we'll be next."

There were some men swimming out to a sailboat that had been anchored in the bay and a few others had little rubber rafts the frogmen had brought equipment in on and were trying to push them out into the battering surf. Serafín sat on the sand and held his head, feeling that there was blood crusted in his ears, and watched the men run. The last of the rubber rafts was hundreds of yards from shore when it occurred to him to swim for it.

There wasn't a sail. It was only a little rubber raft, made for three, maybe four men and some signal equipment. There were already seven or eight men on and around it, with others swimming out ahead of Serafín. The men on board paddled away from the beach with wooden slats pulled from the floor of the raft, calling out to the swimmers but not slowing to bring them in. Now and then one of the planes would buzz low over them, strafing, bullets chopping up the water in parallel lines. The waves slapped Serafín back as he struggled to reach the raft. He twisted under the surf and managed to yank at his boots till they slipped off. He had always been a good swimmer. "My little fish," his abuelo called him when they visited the fishing village Papi had grown up in.

"Mi barracudita."

The old man would stand out in the surf, brown and wrinkled as a nut, and spread his arms wide. "Ven aquí, barracudita."

Serafín would dive under the waves, eyes clenched tight, frog-kicking till his arms found the old man's knobby knees, then burst through the surface like a dolphin into a wet embrace.

"Qué es esto?" his abuelo would cry, hugging him. "Qué monstruo del abismo?"

"Adelante, adelante!" called the men in the boat. "Los aviones vuelven!"

But the planes didn't come back after them, fading back over the swampland up the bay. The man swimming just ahead of Serafín coughed once and went under the waves. He didn't come back up. Serafín gasped in a breath between waves and dove under. Without his boots he felt free, frog-kicking hard beneath the pounding surface, coming up halfway to the boat. The men kept paddling with the planks.

Soy barracuda, he thought as he went under again. I cut through water like a bullet cuts air.

He swam hard, pulling his stomach in hard and driving with his legs. Finally his fingers found a leg and he pulled up into air. Two of the men hanging on shifted so he could grab onto the side of the raft.

There were eight men aboard, one hit so badly it was clear he was going to die. All of them managed to get most of their bodies out of the water. The raft rode low in the high swells, the men bailing it out with their cupped hands. They gave up paddling as the current took them and the beach grew smaller in their sight. They drifted past the oil that marked where the *Río Escondido* went down, drifted away from the bay, the island.

"I don't see any fucking marines," said one man. "They told us the marines were coming in right behind us."

"It's a good thing they didn't come," said another man they called Chiste, who had been shot in the ankle. "This boat is too crowded already."

Serafín could still see the beach, a khaki-green ribbon of seaweed bobbing at its edge. Or maybe they were the bodies of the ones left behind. In the village of his abuelo the beach was always littered with palm fronds after a big storm. He would run through them, chasing the ghost crabs from hole to hole, excited by the damage a serious blow could cause. Sometimes fish were beached and he'd scare off a cluster of seabirds feeding off the carcasses. Vultures wheeled high over Playa Girón, floating, wings never moving. It was too late for the marines.

The sun fell in the sky and the current took them away from the island, till it was only a dark green line crowding the horizon. Now there were no other boats in sight. The men decided they were probably drifting toward Mexico.

"Is anybody an officer?" asked one of the men. "Somebody should be in charge."

"The hell with that," said another. "We're all fucked together on this raft, we should just agree on rules and cooperate."

"Shit, a Communist," said Chiste. "Throw him overboard."

The men laughed at this till they discovered the one who was badly hit was dead.

"Anybody know who he is?"

Nobody knew.

"Well, we have to make room."

"The sharks will eat him."

"The sharks will eat all of us if this raft sinks from too much weight. Adiós, compañero."

"El soldado desconocido."

"Al fondo, amigo."

The man floated alongside them on his belly for a moment, then was flipped on his back in a swell. He looked peaceful despite the high waves rocking him up and down, and then he seemed to fade down into the water.

The men were quiet for a while then, watching the island disappear into the dusk. They couldn't hear gunfire anymore. Serafín looked at his body. A few bad cuts, nothing more. Three of the other men besides Chiste were wounded. They sat with their eyes closed, minds retreating into the pain and the buffeting of the waves. The waves lifted the raft high, holding it still for one small moment at the top, then smacking it down into a hard trough.

"Maybe the people who landed on the other side are winning," said one of the men. "Maybe we were just a diversion and the ones who landed up north will take the island. If they take the island and we're out here we'll all be cowards."

Chiste laughed. "Pendejo," he said. "Even if there were others, and they did land, and they did win, what makes you think we'll get off this boat alive?"

Luz and Marta come out of the ocean. Marta sits by Serafín, beaded with water, breathless from swimming. Serafín wonders if he could help her dry off, then just hands her a towel. She was only a little girl when he met her first, when he came back and Ambrosio didn't. He got out of the hospital and went to see the family and brought them Ambrosio's diary. He had crammed it into his shirt pocket when Ambrosio gave it to him and they joked that maybe it would stop a bullet from his heart like in the war movies. The diary was stained by sweat and seawater but still readable. Marta sat next to him, as close as she was now, solemnly watching him as he answered Señor de la Pena's questions about Ambrosio in training camp. He saw her every year on the Anniversary after that and then she and Luz got to be friends at the hospital. Serafín wasn't sure when he started thinking about her as a woman. Maybe the time he saw her and they talked in the parking lot at the Versailles or maybe when he saw her with Luz all dressed up the first time or maybe, somehow, on that first day in their sad little sitting room when she kissed his cheek and thanked him for being her brother's friend. She felt like something he'd lost and wanted back. He had been with women on and off, twice with marriage ideas, but always it ended.

"I'm drowning with you," they would say. "Your moods. You're so quiet I can't breathe."

"You let life take you wherever it wants," they would say. "I want to *do* things. I have dreams."

"You're eating me up with sorrow," they would say. "Our children would be born sad."

Marta rubs her legs dry with the towel. The maricones are basting themselves with oil. A blond boy with a peeling nose squats in the sand in front of them, fooling with the controls of his wailing tape player, nodding his head to the bass line. Gulls fight over a piece of hard roll overhead. Serafín can smell the salt of Marta's skin. It's good to still long for something, he thinks.

"Your brother thinks the Invasion was a mistake," says Rufo.

"No hablen de política," says Luz. "It's so boring all the time."

"Do you really think that?" Marta is looking at him with her direct gaze.

"No dije eso," says Serafín. "I said we never had a chance of winning."

"But it was important," says Marta. "As a symbol."

Luz shakes her head. "You live in the past you might as well be dead. I like it fine here. Down there, even without Fidel, what could I be?"

"La Reina del mar," says Rufo, stroking her leg and smiling. "La Perla de la Perla."

"You got to forget the past as soon as it happens. Or else it drags you down."

Rufo moves his hand up under her buttocks. "How could you forget me?"

"I don't know who you are *now*," she says. "I won't have to forget you."

Marta is hurt. "You don't want to go back? You don't miss it?"

"The last time I saw Cuba," says Serafín, "it tried to swallow me."

On the seventh day Serafín woke with his head hanging over the side and found himself staring at a man's foot being eaten by small fish. The foot belonged to Chiste, and it had swollen and turned colors, stinking sweet with gangrene, till the men in the raft had asked him to hang it over the side. Chiste lay on his back under the patchwork canopy they'd made of shirts and pants, staring dully out at the horizon. The sun was still low in the sky, slanting under the canopy to sear their blistering skin. Chiste didn't notice that his foot was being eaten. It was a deep, angry purple, the toes cracked and oozing and little fish darted around the toes, worrying tiny pieces of flesh away from them. Serafín silently reached to find the net he'd made from an undershirt on a hoop of wire. He let it drag in the water a moment, leaning far over the side, then brought it toward Chiste's foot and scooped. He caught three little ones, each a few inches long. They weren't big enough to cut so he looked around to see who was conscious. There was Chiste and the man who wept at night and the one they called El Pescadero because he hated to eat fish.

"If fish is all we have to eat on this little ocean voyage," he said on the second day, "I think I'd rather starve."

It was the seventh day and he was awake so Serafín gave him a fish to share with the man who wept at night, one bite apiece. He gave a whole one to Chiste because he had provided the bait and kept one for himself.

"If you eat a shark that has eaten a man," said El Pescadero after tearing his fish in two with his teeth, "does that make you a cannibal?"

"A cannibal once removed," said Chiste. "Maybe you get a century in Purgatory instead of eternity in Hell."

A pair of sharks had followed them for most of the fifth day. Their dorsal fins would cut through the waves, then disappear. The men named them Che and Raúl. At dusk a third shark appeared to join the others. The men wanted to name him Fidel but Chiste said no, he should be named Kennedy. That was who had put them on this boat. That was who lied to them.

"See?" said Chiste, pointing to the shark. "He even swims crooked."

Serafín didn't tell the men who were awake what the fish he'd caught had been eating. He put his fish sideways in his mouth and bit down into its middle, sucking on the livery insides. He chewed for a long time, unable to swallow the hard part of the head because his throat was so dry.

It was a day too much like the other days. The sea was calm and relentless and there was too much of it, as there was too much of the sun and too much empty sky above. There was nothing for the men to look at but each other, which was to face death. The one they called Guajiro, the curly-haired one who stuttered, had a kind of green pus coming out his eyes and made a small, bad noise with each breath. The sea and sky were monstrous around them in their vastness, their lack of detail. Time seemed to refuse to pass, only to bake into their skin, to rock them gently to nowhere.

"I'm bored," announced Chiste. Most of the men were conscious now. "Somebody drink seawater and go crazy."

"I don't have the strength to go crazy," said El Pescadero.

"Somebody sing a song."

Yesterday the one they called Canario, who in the first days had sung them every song he knew in a sweet high tenor, had the green pus run from his eyes and died.

"Nadie tiene fuerza para cantar."

"Somebody tell a story. That doesn't take any strength."

"Serafín, read from your book."

"Qué libro? Alguien tiene un libro?"

"He has a Bible—"

"No es la Biblia," said Serafín. "Es un diario."

"A diary? So read it! Tell us your secret thoughts—"

"No es *mío*. Pertenece a mi amigo Ambrosio."

"Ambrosio? El Poeta?"

In camp everybody had a nombre de guerra, given sometimes in fun, sometimes with cruelty. Serafín was called El Angel Negro and Ambrosio was El Poeta.

"Léalo, hombre. We don't care who wrote it."

"Un diario es privado—"

"*Nothing* is private on this raft, compa," said Chiste. "We don't even get to die in private. Read it. We're the best audience El Poeta will ever have."

Serafín pulled the little diary out from under his shirt. The black leather cover was stained white with seawater and with his sweat from the first days. Nobody had sweated after the fourth day. Nobody had urinated anything but blood after the fifth. Serafín flipped through the book looking for something that wasn't too personal and that wouldn't start a political argument.

" 'Los Gusanos,' " he said.

"Qué dice?"

"Los Gusanos. Es el título del poema."

"En voz alta, compa," said Chiste. "Poetry should be read loudly y con confianza."

" 'En nuestra esperanza los gusanos no encuentran comida,' " read Serafín. It was hard to make out some of the words, stained and run together.

The worms find no food in our hope.
Our passions crackle over them,
A distant and useless lightning
Bearing no taste, no weight,
No twitch of sustenance.

The worms take no warmth from our glory.
Our greatness cannot move them.
Even our names,
First blush of understanding,
Will not pass their mouths.

The hero corrupts beside the coward.
The hangman slips wetly through the thief.
The battlefield dead are joined,
All brothers before those
Who live in what they eat.

Our conquests flutter, thin as words,
Tossed on a failing breath of time.
There is no meal in our legend
For those who wait below
Passing through us without longing.

The waves rocked the men in a long silence. Serafín pictured Ambrosio sitting apart from the others in camp, watching, not judging but watching clearly and with sympathy. Serafín felt what would be tears if there was liquid left in him to weep.

"Nos atravesamos sin anhelo." El Pescadero repeated the last line.

"This is the best poet in the world, your friend," declared Chiste. "El mejor del mundo."

"I would eat a worm if I had one right now," said Rubio, one of the paratroopers. "A nice, big, juicy worm."

"I got a worm here you could eat."

"I said a big one. Yours wouldn't feed a minnow."

"If a shark ate one of us," said El Pescadero, "and then followed the raft and we caught it and ate it, would that make us cannibals?"

"Not this again!"

"I wish we had a fucking shark we could feed you to!"

While the men again debated the mystery of the Body and Blood and whether it could be pulled down from metaphor into something useful on a raft in the middle of the ocean, Serafín went under. He took hold of the piece of rope they'd hung and lowered himself down, deeper, till the water was cold and darker blue. He tried to stay under as long as he could. The blue cold came in and lifted some of the dryness out of him and he thought about letting go and trying to sink but he floated back up and pulled himself into the raft with the others.

"I'm warning you," Chiste was saying when he came back up, "if any of you eat me after I die I'm putting a curse on you."

"You're full of poison, compa, who would want to eat you?"

"Cuál es la maldición?"

"The curse is that when you die you will come back to sit on this fucking raft forever," said Chiste, meaning it. "And there won't be poetry."

When the sun was at its highest Serafín tried to catch fish. They had made a line with bootlaces and tied El Guajiro's dog tags onto it for a lure.

"Serafín," said Rubio, "you should make it hop up and down."

"No, no, Serafín, you pull it up *slow*, then let it drift back down."

"Catch a big one this time, Serafín. No more fucking minnows."

"Cállense!" said Chiste. "Let the man work. Creen porque es negro es su esclavo? If we land on some desert island we'll have five Robinson Crusoes and only one Friday—you'll run the man to death."

Serafín let the line hang loose in his hand, listening with his fingers for any action. His abuelo would use his medal of San Cristóbal as a flasher when there weren't any of the little silvery fish the barracuda usually took.

"Es muy poderoso," the old man would say, shining it up on his pants. "El Santo me ayuda."

Serafín's abuelo was not a religious man, he didn't go to the church and pray for the future like Papi did, but he believed in power, in spirits. Papi would sit on the sand with only his shoes and socks off while the old man taught Serafín how to fish. Serafín would swing the line over his head and fling it out over the surf, then draw it back in fast, trailing it over one hand to listen with his fingers for any action. If there was a hit he'd run full tilt back through the surf and up onto the beach, running up past Papi till the barracuda slid out of the water on its belly, silvery blue like a new pistol in the open sunlight. Serafín would dig the hook out and bury the fish in the wet sand with the others so the pigs wouldn't eat them. Papi would watch him but never say a thing, thin and dignified in his Sunday clothes and long-brimmed hat. Papi never went in the water and the rule was on Sunday you didn't ask him for anything. All week at the Nacional it was gringos snapping their fingers for him—Boy! they would call, Muchacho! they would call, Hey Pedro, over here! Nobody who worked with Papi in the kitchen or at the bar at the Nacional was named Pedro, but it was what they all answered to.

Papi wore a spotless white jacket at the Nacional and had learned an elegant way of serving. He was the oldest of the busboys and steady, never late, never drunk, so the headwaiter made him the king of butter and ice. When the gringos sat down to eat in the café he was there at their elbows, a quick spirit who never splashed and never blocked the eyesight of a guest engaged in conversation. And there were a few of the gringos, the ones Papi called los grandes Señores, who didn't call him Pedro but called him by his real name and slipped him a tip, though tipping the busboys was not necessary. Once he had iced the drink of the famous Hemingway and once he had found a hundred-dollar bill on the floor that he turned in to the headwaiter and the person who had lost it came down and personally shook his hand.

It was one of the grandes señores who got Papi a job at the Eden Roc when he came to Miami. Papi became thinner and more elegant but reduced somehow. He shrank the way lots of the ones who never learned English did, a kind of fearful shrugging in from the world. Serafín felt he could feel every one of Papi's bones when the old man hugged him on his way to training camp.

"Puedes ser el gran libertador," Papi said, proud and frightened. "Puedes ser nuestro próximo Antonio Maceo."

The fish were not hungry for dog tags that day, and Serafín gave up and pulled them in. El Guajiro was dead and they rolled him overboard, struggling to pull his shirt off to add it to the patchwork canopy they had rigged overhead. There were a few good seats in the shade of the canopy and they took turns sitting in them except for Chiste, who just sat with his leg, ugly purple up over the knee now, dangling into the water and a shirt he kept dipping in plastered over his face. The green pus was coming out of El Pescadero's eyes now but nobody told him.

Near dusk Rubio drank seawater and went crazy.

"I hate to think we have to wait till the old bastard dies," says Rufo. "Who knows how much damage he'll have done to people's heads by then."

"I don't see why you want to go back." Luz is carefully brushing sand off her legs, intent as a cat cleaning itself. "What's so wonderful down there?"

"I've never been there," says Rufo.

"Really?"

"My parents were up in Tampa when all the stuff happened and they never went back. I was born here."

"You mean I'm going out with a real American? Qué suerte!"

"I'm a Cuban. What do you think, Serafín, do we have to wait for the old bastard to die or could we take it back? If we really had the government behind us—"

"I drive the limo from the airport," says Serafín. "I hear these guys talk all the time—estos hombres importantes, estos grandes señores—they have their own world. Cuba doesn't matter to them. If they could build a hotel on it tomorrow, maybe. They don't think about us."

"If they hadn't lied the first time—"

"Si no hubieran mentido la primera vez seríamos puertorriqueños," says Serafín. This Rufo is after something, pushing it. Marta is watching him, serious, upset. "Either we wouldn't have gone or they would have taken it with their own people and we'd both be shining their shoes on the Malecón right now."

Rufo shakes his head. "Tu hermano es pesimista."

"Mi hermano," says Luz, "es el hombre más sabio que conozco. He knows what he's talking about. You got some dream about paradise somebody has handed you."

"Es mi patria."

"Great. You can have it."

Marta stays fixed on Serafín. "It would have been something if we had won," she says. "If the time had been right. You could have been the next Antonio Maceo."

Serafín has to smile a little. "Quería ser pescador," he says. "A fisherman with a boat and a good net. That's all I ever wanted to be."

It was a day too much like the other days. Too much sea, too much sky, too much sun. There was only Serafín and Chiste left now, and Chiste was out of jokes. He had hung on as the others died, despite the angry color that moved up his body, rotting him from the inside, as if his sense of humor had kept him alive. His smell was a huge wafting cloud of sweet decaying meat that enveloped the raft, that became the air they breathed. He was barely conscious, moaning softly, and Serafín had stopped being sickened by the smell and had begun to think about eating him.

"When this is over, I'll live at the bottom of a lake," said Serafín, talking whatever came into his head to push away the thoughts of eating Chiste. "A cold lake, the kind you see in movies that freeze over in the winter, the kind with water so clear you have to move it with your hand to make sure it's really there. Do you know that you can live in the bottom of that kind of lake? No te jodo, Chiste, es la verdad. You don't have to breathe in that kind of lake, just drink in the cold water to live."

His abuelo lived at the bottom of that lake now. It was very cool. Sometimes they would swim up toward the surface together till they saw the green Cola bottles bobbing on the surface, marking the border to the hot world. Giant turtles, white ones, swam around them, curious, and diving birds flew by, stroking gracefully, looking for fish to eat. Sometimes he felt sad because he missed people who lived up in the hot world—Papi, maybe his sister Luz. You couldn't live in both, you had to make a choice.

"When this is over," said Serafín to Chiste, who he thought maybe was dead, as he had stopped moaning, "they'll let me have my job back selling soda on the beach. You have to fight sometimes, but you can make good money."

Serafín saw himself sitting on the icebox in the hot sand, drinking cold soda, bottle after bottle. There was a slice across his belly where it bubbled out and ran down his thighs, but that didn't matter because there was always another bottle of soda and he never got full. Children, skinny little black and white children, yelled to him from where they played together in the surf. He sat in the hot sand drinking Coca-Cola and played with the ice that wouldn't melt.

Chiste had stopped moaning and there was a seagull standing next to him. He had to be dead. If he was alive his eyes would focus and he'd snatch the bird and kill it in a stroke and then make a joke about Serafín getting the feathers and claws and him eating the rest. But the seagull stood on the edge of the raft right beside him, the line of its beak turning up in a smile, staring at Serafín with button eyes. There hadn't been birds in the sky for days and Serafín didn't know how this one could just appear. Then he realized it was Chiste's soul and once it was gone his body would just be flesh and Serafín could eat it or not. The gull heard his mind, croaked and spread its wings and flapped up into the monstrous clear sky.

Chiste's body was all smell now, a smell that burned deep in Serafín's nose and throat. It was work to move over by the body and nearly beyond his strength to push it over the side. Serafín lay on his back searching the sky for Chiste's soul escaping. He wouldn't be tempted anymore. The smell of Chiste hung around the raft though his body was gone and the black rubber burned his blistered skin where he touched it crawling over the side.

Serafín swam down till the water was blue and cold and swallowed. But the salt water burned his throat, burned the insides of his belly and suddenly something was fighting him and it was his own body, wrestling with his soul to pull him back up, beating its way up through the deep blue water to the surface, dragging him back onto the raft. Serafín lay face down on the floor of the raft, sides heaving like some poor beached fish torn from the bottom, and felt all the strength ooze from his body. If he wanted to drown himself now he could, but he'd have to get over the side first and that was a journey he'd never manage. Serafín lay on his face on the floor of the raft and let the sun take him, gave himself to the waves and imagined his body baking into a fossil of cured black leather.

A tanker picked him up drifting off the coast of Louisiana. They gave him to Coast Guard people who didn't believe he had lived at the bottom of a lake or been to an island that tried to eat him. Then at the hospital there were men with Federal badges who hid him from cameras.

"We want to spare you the front pages," they said. "We're trying to let the whole sad mess blow over a bit," they said. "Besides, amigo," they said, "you look like you been to Hell and back."

Serafín walks down and stands next to the Haitian man staring out into the ocean. Waves have soaked his shoes. Serafín looks out across the water for a while beside him, silent, then speaks softly.

"Have you lost something?"

The man notices him for the first time, nods.

"Ma femme," he says. "My wife was in a boat that turned over. Out there."

Serafín looks out past the jumble of people playing in the shallows, out to where the big waves are formed. He doesn't like the waves and he knows there is nothing to see but he keeps looking, standing silent by the Haitian man, helping him honor the dead.

SEVENTEEN

➤ 0630 HRS. REVEILLE

Commando up, morning drills—strength, endurance, agility.

Dewey rolling from bed to rub warm tap water over his eyes. Fifty push-ups, one hundred abdominal crunches, curls with the ten-pounder. Catfooting past the Old Woman, waxy as death on her fold-out bed, down through the lobby to Ocean Drive. Tiny lizards flick away from his running feet on the dew-wet sidewalk.

"Mira," say the old Cuban men with their guayaberas hanging over their pants, pointing, "el corredor."

"Already it's eighty degrees," say the old Jewish men, belts yanked up under their sagging pecs, shaking their heads as Dewey runs by them. "This is *healthy?*"

Cutting over to the beach on the way back, digging hard through the sand, pigeons and gulls scattering in front of him. Back through the lobby, slaloming around the geriatrics, spinning, head-faking to the stairs and up, two at a time. Final burst. In past the Old Woman, gray face over gray oatmeal, and into the water.

0730 HRS. SHOWER

0745 HRS. MORNING RATIONS

Energy Stix. Power Shake. Protein and carbohydrates, calcium, riboflavin, zinc. Pumping his calves under the table, ready to rock.

0800 HRS. ROLL CALL

Commando present and accounted for.

Dewey time-punching his card with Roosevelt and Wilson stacked up behind him, sniping.

"Screwy!" calls Roosevelt. "My *boy!* We gonna kick some geriatric butt today or what?"

"What's the word, Dewey?" says Wilson. "Been keepin the South Beach safe for democracy?"

"Dewey gots to stay on his *toes,* man. Bad guys be comin, A-rabs or some shit, you *know* they be comin up that beach in submarines, take all them wrickledy old babes hostage. Dewey got some major responsibility."

"Don't think we don't appreciate it, Dewey. You're our hero."

Dewey ever moving, advancing, accepting his losses but taking ground—

0820 HRS. ORDERS OF THE DAY

Nurse Temple is CO. Marta is on but not Luz, who is good to look at but says things that sting. Roosevelt and Wilson make faces at each other while Nurse Temple runs down the shit list, the blood list, the PT and OT lists.

"We have a new admission," she says. "Room 312, logged in last night at one forty-five, a Mr. Edgar Gelmis. 'Upon admission the patient was confused and disoriented—' "

The patients are always confused and disoriented upon admission. If they weren't, thinks Dewey, they wouldn't be there. Will. What none of the patients have enough of, what his grandmother lacks, sitting in her nightdress watching soap operas through a thick fog of static. The will to overcome. Will as compact and sharp as a diamond point, will that can slice through the defenses of others with laser heat, a stone kernel of will that can't be broken.

" 'Patient is diagnosed as diabetic, extreme care recommended to avoid abrasions—' "

Dewey stands at parade rest, eyes forward, gut sucked, listening to the top outline the day's program and mentally trying to center his chi.

0900 HRS.   CALL TO ARMS

Patients up and dressed. Breakfast.

Hitting them fast and hard before their defenses are up—bedrails down, sheets torn away, teeth rinsed and pushed in, a blitzkrieg of activity. Ambulatory cases pulled upright, johnnycoats changed, robes and slippers on, into the geri chairs. Roosevelt has a technique of opening the milk cartons with one hand, a special pressure point Dewey has never mastered.

"Wake *up*, people!" booms Roosevelt, clanking down the hall with the feed cart. "Today is the first day of the rest of you misable lifes!"

Dewey feels a sweat breaking under his shirt as he zips through his patients. He makes it all efficiency, no wasted motion, yank, tuck, pull, lift, carry, set, open. The patients are used to him not talking in the morning and the ones still with the program try to cooperate. The others he handles firmly but without anger. Anger is counterproductive. A cold fury is needed in combat, clear thinking, a force of will. Roosevelt barrels through the rooms, banging trays, spilling juice, shooting his mouth off. Wilson is almost motherly in his contacts, easing and pleading his people into their geri chairs, talking even to the cases where nobody is home. But Wilson has no bulk, no upper body power, Wilson is not a serious person. He doesn't even think in a straight line and Dewey knows to steer clear of him.

Sliding the wheelers into their machines, cranking the bedbounds up and sitting, closing his nose to the heavy breakfast food, oatmeal and egg and sausage. Color drains into ashen faces, cheeks take shape, eyes focus. The troops are assembled. Dewey sets the last one up and then passes in review, cruising down the hallway past Wilson and Roosevelt still working their rooms, turning eyes left to see his own people, strapped in or upright on their own, facing their first test of the day.

1000 HRS.   MEDEVAC

The injured pile up by the elevator. Legs riddled or missing, arms palsied, clenched rigid with stroke, the blind the lame and the spastic. Dewey moving the worst casualties out first, no more than four to a ride. Propping the shaky ones against the wall, staring straight at the door till it slides apart to reveal Corky and Donna oozing progress and good intentions, hands reaching to catch the wounded.

1030 HRS.   QUARTERS INSPECTION

A GI bed is key to a disciplined soldier.

Stripping down the old linen, tossed into the hamper. Undersheet spread and tucked, wipe and tuck plastic drawsheet, set and tuck linen drawsheet, spread and miter linen top sheet, spread and tuck top blanket. Dewey motoring the beds to his work level, hands flying, the tightest units in the facility. Bedrails up and wiped shiny, breakfast debris policed, personal articles stowed, twenty push-ups in every room, four beds per room, eight rooms plus Intensive Care. Dewey working in a controlled rush, sweating a round spot through the back of his white shirt, sweat dripping from his face to the tight-pulled linen on the beds. Doors and cabinets shut, everything square. The top always brings prospects into Dewey's rooms to see what care their parents will be getting.

1130 HRS.   HONOR GUARD

Roosevelt finds Mrs. Pincus dead in the mop-up operations after breakfast. Ancient Mrs. Pincus, eyes and ears shot, mind unsprung, muttering in Czech and German and Yiddish to a world no wider than the reach of her arms. Dewey gets the detail. Washing the body, slack and gray under his hands, putting the teeth in, new gown for transport, arranging the arms across the chest before rigor hits—the facility sends its people out looking sharp. Wheeling her through the halls during visiting hours, head propped and lids pulled down so she seems to be napping, no public display of death on Day Shift. Dewey in the freight elevator studying her face, her face like his grandmother's in the morning when he catfoots past her for his run. Baum from the mortuary is waiting with the van in the back lot, the Jews always gone and planted in a flash. Transferring the remains. Baum presses two dollars into Dewey's hand and calls him Sonny.

1200 HRS.   CLOSE-QUARTERS COMBAT

Dewey waiting for the opening, timing his move with the man's breathing. The movement is forceful but not violent, insistent but not brutal. Siaga has wild animal eyes, powerful hands. Dewey and Roosevelt are the only ones strong enough to take him on, and somehow Roosevelt is always busy elsewhere when the time comes. Dewey pins Siaga's wrists with his left hand and works the spoon with his right, his upper body tense, ready to duck away. The facility doesn't allow you to tie them down during visiting hours, so Siaga's hands, which have a life independent of his ruined mind or his desperate appetite, struggle to claw free. Dewey focuses on the old man's mouth, the rhythm of his breathing. He feints with the spoon, touching the lower lip, then pushes it in. Siaga takes it down, eyes widening as he swallows. Dewey tries another but this one blasts back past his ear, peas and carrots spreading like buckshot as it flies.

"Yo, Dewey," calls Roosevelt, passing by with Thorp in a chair, "watch where you be pointin that sucker. People gots to *walk* here."

Siaga glares up at Dewey with his wide animal eyes, bony arms tensed, straining to be free, mouth gaping with his hunger.

1330 HRS.   AFTERNOON RATIONS

Dewey popping suspension push-ups between chairs in the cafeteria while Wilson and Roosevelt count out loud, fifty the hard way. The nurses sit at one table, nurses' aides and laundrywomen at another, orderlies at the one by the vending machines. Swiss steak, french fries, green beans. Fuel for the fighting man. Marta is at the nurses' table. Roosevelt plays basketball with his fries, tearing off little pieces and set-shooting them over Dewey and Wilson's heads into the trash barrel. Dewey cleans his plates, wipes his tray and puts it back at the bottom of the pile. He pockets the plastic tub of butterscotch pudding for the Old Woman.

1400 HRS.   MEDIC ASSIST

Holding arms steady, bodies still as Marta takes blood samples. Dewey arm-locking the patient as Marta strokes the vein, a long and sensuous stroking that gives Dewey chills to watch. She is quiet and efficient, Dewey smelling her soap, her hair, the starch of her uniform as they stand close. Blood running up into the vials, labeled and sorted on the cart. Marta works without speaking to Dewey till just after the last blood then checks the door to see if anyone fully conscious is nearby. She whispers. Time and location of rendezvous, necessary precautions, she touches his arm and is gone.

1500 HRS.   WASTE DISPOSAL

Dewey hustling between the male patients and the bathroom, urinal bottles sloshing, two in each hand, pausing to measure output on the watch-fors. Bedpan detail. Holding the bottle for the ones with no aim, running the tap for the suggestible ones, tapping the bags of the catheterized. DuPre takes a full five minutes to pee, prostate shot to hell, weaving some long tangled web of Red propaganda he expects Dewey to believe while he dribbles from his little inch. Old Scipio in the next bed doesn't release but once every three days, holding everything in for messy, day-long explosions of piss and loose stool, shitting with a kind of acid malice just after new linens are put under him. A way Dewey will never be. Legless, mindless, dickless. Killed in action, maybe, wounded, sure, but you keep that last round in the chamber. Death before Dishonor.

1600 HRS.   TACTICS

Dewey punching his time card, jogging in his whites over to the Beach. Dodging the relics in the lobby, up the stairs two at a time. The Old Woman is watching *Gilligan's Island* reruns and eating animal crackers with tea. She separates them by species, making little piles on her TV table, then eats the carnivores first, then the ungulates, finally the primates. She asks Dewey how his day was and he says fine and retreats to the rear of the pullmanette.

"I need to see you after work," she whispered. "It's important."

Dewey sits with the new mercenary manual he ordered through *Soldier of Fortune,* packed with the how-to stuff that will make the difference between coming back in one piece and not coming back at all. Dewey reads and works his Power-Grip Hand-Flexer, switching it from right to left and back. When he thinks of how she looked at him, of how close she stood when she asked, his stomach makes a fist. Dewey reads a chapter on ninja mind control and practices moving his chi around his body. *Hogan's Heroes* begins on the TV.

1800 HRS. SPECIAL OPS

Dewey in his camouflage field jacket riding a city bus full of geriatrics across the causeway to the city. It takes forever to get them all in and seated. Dewey has the brass knuckles, sold as a novelty only, in his jacket pocket and his Legionnaires' Assault Boot Knife, nine inches of cold serious steel, Velcroed under his pants leg around his ankle. Dewey is combat ready. He waits for the geriatrics to creak off at the downtown stop. Dewey practices his urban infiltration walk down Flagler, looking ahead for potential escape routes or sniper nests, checking the reflection in the parked car windows to see if anybody is tailing him. It is still hot. Cuban men sit drinking coffee outside little bebidas counters, talking, always talking. Dewey sweats inside his field jacket, the assault knife chafing his ankle bone. He cuts down Marta's street. He is early, walking around the block three times, passing on the opposite side of the street. All clear. He is pumped, pumped to the max as he climbs the outside stairs to the second-floor landing, finds the door.

1915 HRS. CONTACT

"My mother will be back soon," she says. "We have to do it quick."

The apartment is smaller than he imagined. There are religious pictures on the walls.

She calls from the bedroom. "In here."

Dewey moves his chi to his diaphragm to calm himself as he enters. There, lying on the bed. He's seen thousands of pictures in magazines but never in real life, never to touch and to hold.

"Go ahead. It's yours if you want it," she says softly, looking into him with her piercing eyes. "If you're willing to do everything I say."

He lifts it up in his arms. Lighter than he expected.

"It's Belgian," says Dewey. "Fairly new model, based on the Kalashnikov."

He sights down the barrel.

"Gas-operated, takes a thirty-round magazine, NATO round, can be set for automatic, semiautomatic, or three-round bursts for snapshooting. It can fire rifle grenades."

Dewey takes aim at a picture hanging on the wall, a picture of a girl in white armor. He lines the sight up with the red cross on her breastplate.

"It's over eight pounds, which is kind of a load these days, and it's got a heavy trigger—you really got to squeeze this baby."

He lowers the rifle.

"For firepower and accuracy, though, it's a good deal. This isn't a sport model—where'd you get it?"

Marta hasn't taken her eyes off his face. "From somebody I don't trust," she says. "Can you get bullets for it?"

"Not so easy, but possible." Dewey drops to a knee and snaps the rifle up to aim at the girl in white again. She is holding a sword half as big as she is. She is as pretty and fierce-looking as She-Ra but not as developed.

"I want you keep it," says Marta. "I want you to hide it somewhere."

"Any tools with it?"

Marta pulls a small canvas satchel from her bed. "You're with me?"

"Semper fi," says Dewey.

2030 HRS. TRANSPORT

Dewey sitting on the bus back across the causeway with a cardboard box on his lap, the semiautomatic broken down inside. Black kids in the rear, making noise, might be trouble. Blood sticky in Dewey's sock from where the knife is rubbing. Replaying the moment. At the door, she takes his hand in both of hers, looks into his eyes.

"This isn't a game," she says. "This is real."

The thrill goes through him again. A well-trained commando and his rifle, the deadliest weapon in the world. The rifle has a smell to it, almost a taste, a weight to it that he can feel in the box. The black kids are yelling, throwing something across the aisle to each other. One of them has a joint out in his hand. Dewey wonders if they know where to score some ammo.

2100 HRS. BARRACKS

The Old Woman sleeping in front of the buzzing TV when Dewey tiptoes in. He stashes the box, turns the set off. He stands close by her. A pillow maybe, or a plastic bag. Death by asphyxia-

tion, half the CODs at the facility said that. Dewey kisses his grandmother's cheek, flicks her lamp off.

Dressing the raw ankle with supplies from his med kit. Ten tiger
push-ups from a handstand against the wall, fifty slow crunches,
isolations with the free weights to top off.

2130 HRS. SHOWER

2145 HRS. LIGHTS OUT

2200 HRS. DISCHARGE

Her lips, her arms. A long, smooth stroking. Her thighs, the way
her skirt rides up when she bends to draw blood. Her eyes. Her lips,
whispering his name. Saying his name. Her breasts, strong and big
and up-pointing like She-Ra's. Her lips. Dewey catching it in Kleenex, sitting up, pumped, ashamed.

2210 HRS. SHOWER

Extra cold penalty.

2220 HRS. NIGHT CALLS

Fifty-push-up penalty. Hanging from the doorsill till his fingers
scream, thinking ninja thoughts of stealth and self-control.

2245 HRS. LIGHTS OUT

2300 HRS. NIGHT MANEUVERS

Dewey sweating under the thin sheet, eyes open, operating the
rifle in his mind, stripping it down, cleaning it, sensing the enemy
and opening it up full throttle, a thirty-round pull.

The most dangerous weapon in the world.

EIGHTEEN

SOMETIMES HE WONDERS why he bothers with the dogs. Horses, horses were something else, horses were big and sleek and noble, thundering past you like a crushing wave till they rolled over the finish line. That was the Sport of Kings. This, these dogs, was the Sport of Bus Conductors.

Walt sits in the upper tier under the hard white neons, pondering his moves for the Third. There was no consistency with the dogs, no pattern. They needed a steady hand to guide them, needed to carry somebody with some brains on their back. It was "collided" one week, "never a factor" the next, "won in a waltz" the next, "collided" again, "left at the gate." No pattern, no excellence of blood showing clearer and clearer with each performance, just wild stupid speed unleashed and pointed in the right general direction.

"I like this Linda's Twist," says one of the conductors behind him.

"How much do you like her?" says his friend.

"She's my key for the Trifecta."

"You seen her run before?"

"Nah. I just got a feeling."

It's a mixed crowd at the dogs—black, white, hispanic—but to Walt they all look like Jackie Gleason in *The Honeymooners*. Heavyset guys with big plans and polyester souls. A field of white hair and bronzed bare skulls shines up at Walt from the seats below, a regiment of porky old duffers in their Sammy Snead panamas wafting funnels of cigar smoke into the night sky. Walt wears the white yachting cap his Cuban boys gave him as a joke when he was running the boats. The Admiral, they called him. El Almirante de la Marina Secreta.

There is a nice kind of man-made buzz at the dogs, the constant rumble of the air conditioners like big friendly bombers coming to bail you out of a tight spot, the happy yakking of the bus conductors, surf sounds from the Beach a block away and the white electric hum from the light towers above. Walt feels good, feels hopeful. The plan to tear this place down will never go through, he thinks. This is culture here, people's culture, people's lives. You can't tear down people's lives.

"What's your take on it, Mort?"

"Midland Minnie and Burnt Toastem for the Quinela."

"Tough to hit that one-two."

"I won with a Midland something-or-other a couple weeks ago."

"It's a *name*, Mort."

"So? It comes in, it pays a bundle."

"Half of these dogs are so happy to get out of the box they forget to run."

Walt walks under to the ticket windows. There are little video tote boards and TV screens hanging everywhere from the rafters. A lot of the plungers never leave the bunker, spending the night under the eerie fluorescence, shuttling between the snack bar and the ticket windows and the replay screens. The Second is playing over again, digital time clicking off in a box superimposed at the bottom of the screen, a half-dozen men kibitzing underneath. There is a carpet of ticket stubs under Walt's feet that will thicken as the night progresses, mostly violet with a sprinkling of green. Walt approaches the comforting mechanical clacking of the ticket machines, sellers in white shirts and blue ties solemn in their duties. Walt finds his line and falls in.

"Aquí los perros están mimados," says the man in front of him, rolling sweat in spite of the air conditioners. "Los alimentan demasiado."

"Nunca he oído esto," says his friend.

"La verdad. Hay que hacerlos pasar hambre para hacerlos más rápidos."

Colombians. Walt recognizes the accent. More and more of them in town these days. Some drogueros, some honest working stiffs who've heard it's no longer a disadvantage to speak only Spanish, some political refugees and then the tourists like these two, banking their profits from home up here in Miami, going to the same restaurants and clubs as the ladrones from everywhere else Down There who are sucking their people dry. Like Fat Stuff here and his friend decorated like a Christmas tree with gold chains and jewelry. Wonderful people. Wonderful people if you need a brother in arms or a friend or someone to help you get shitfaced. To plan a mission with or stay on a schedule or to keep a secret they were hopeless. Walt smiles at the two in front of him. No control, no sense of the big picture, just emotions, raw hormones. In the boat years he had felt like the camp counselor in charge of an orphanage, a troop of violent and lovable children. They needed his steady hand to guide them and he was buoyed up by their energy, their heart. When that steady hand was lifted—well, that was the mess we have today.

"La otra cosa que nunca deja permitir," says the dog expert, "es la penetración. Pueden verla, olerla, lamerla, pero nunca penetrarla. Es la ruina de un perro."

Walt places his bet and goes to the Men's. The beer seems to run right through him these days. The wall above the trough urinal is stained from guys too drunk to aim, from guys who keep reading their racing forms while they piss.

El Halcón interrupts Walt in midstream.

"I have a vision," he says, appearing at Walt's elbow. "Fossil Fuel."

"A slug," says Walt, having to concentrate now to get it all out. "Not happy unless he's got his nose up some other dog's asshole."

"A vision is a serious thing," says El Halcón. "Hay que atenderla."

Walt zips himself in and they walk upstairs together.

"Did you see the name or was it a picture?"

"I had a dream. A dream about no gasolina."

"The shortage."

"Sí. Y luego, I come here, look in the program, third race, and there is the name. Fossil Fuel."

The Third is about to start below them. Young men trot across the green infield to their spots along the rail. Handlers, boys in red shirts and white pants, wearing white yachting caps, lead the dogs onto the white sand track. The dogs are nervous skeletons, all ribs and buggy eyes, wrapped in their shiny colors, their rear legs spread apart a little as they walk.

"Andan como si tuvieran hemorroides."

"That's good," says Walt. "You want a wide base for power. I always back the ones with the tails that curl up. Look at that Ponca Flash, in the yellow there."

"Lots of them got that kind of tail."

Walt shrugs. "These dogs are so damn flighty, you have to have something to go on."

"Qué juegas?"

"I'm boxing a six-dollar triangle. With that you can play your hunches but everything isn't riding on one dog. You want to have something to fall back on."

"You don't bet brave," says El Halcón, "you don't win big."

Walt shakes his head. "That's the problem with you people. No sense of proportion."

High-pitched squeals and barks come from the starting box as the last of the dogs is pushed in. The neon lights overhead blink off. El Halcón scowls and looks away, not ready for another "you people" conversation with Walt.

"I know how they feel in that box," he says. "Crowded together in the dark where some pendejo stuck you, your heart banging away."

"I'd feel better if somebody with a whip was riding them."

"Cómo no? You always want something to fall back on, Walt. You go with putas and wear three rubbers on your dick."

Walt shoots him a look. "You have anything to report?"

"I had another vision," says El Halcón. "Vi a una mujer. Una guerrera."

Walt checks the bus conductors around them, talking loudly as the post approaches, excited.

"And your woman warrior," he says, "what does she want?"

"More equipment."

"How many people does she have?"

"Three, maybe four."

"Who?"

"Aún no me ha dicho. No confía a mí."

"When?"

"En el Aniversario de la Invasión."

"Sentimental." Walt smiles. "You people are so sentimental."

El Halcón leans closer to Walt. "She wants three more pieces like the first one. And fireworks."

"What kind of fireworks?"

"She wants to make a very big noise."

"Here comes *Rusty!*" cries the track announcer over the PA system as the mechanical rabbit hisses around the red rail. Walt holds up a hand and begins to breathe in a steady, measured rhythm as the bell sounds, gate flying open, dogs a blur of color spraying white sand behind them, men shouting their names out. It is over in seconds, the dogs yelping in a hysterical knot at the rail, handlers running to separate them, the deep rumble of disappointed bettors peppered with a few cackling winners. Numbers spit out on the tote board.

"These dogs are such a quick fuck," says El Halcón. "Me gustan más los caballos."

"They don't know how to win," says Walt, watching as the dogs are dragged off. "It's all hormones with them. No sense of the big picture."

"How did you do?"

Walt is still breathing deeply. "I had Ponca Flash, Nocturne and Movin Moe, any order. Ponca Flash didn't finish."

"Qué te dije? Fossil Fuel, el segundo."

"Ponca Flash," says Walt, "got left on the beach."

El Halcón grins at the private joke. "What about the equipment?"

"This woman sounds like a flake."

"She is a vision. Muy sincera, muy religiosa, muy obsesionada. Estoy seguro que ella hará algo."

"It doesn't matter if she *does* something. It has to be something we can use. I'll give you one more piece, no fireworks."

"She promised a meeting. Para planear la operación. If I bring fireworks it attracts more flies."

"Not yet." Walt lowers his hand and begins to breathe normally. El Halcón looks into his eyes.

"Estás enfermo?"

"It's the racing," says Walt. "My doctor says I should control my heart rate if something exciting is happening. The breathing helps."

"So when you're feeling good, getting excited, you do something to make it go away?"

"A distraction."

El Halcón shakes his head. "You people," he says. "You people."

NINETEEN

CHEESE WAS HARD to come by in the Dominican in 1950. Something he ate, something he drank. It caught hold and wouldn't let go. After the War Walt caught on doing public relations for the Sugar Company, working out of Puerta Plata on the north coast. Use his Spanish, decent pay, live like royalty in a house on the beach. The Sugar Company issued him a sidearm and a machete and he sometimes went out with both strapped to his hips. The cutters called him El Flaco because he looked like the character in the Mexican movies and because he had lost so much weight with the dysentery. Nobody he knew of had the dysentery or seemed familiar with its effects. Walt's insides had liquified into a seething bog of wastes, he had the chills each night and was sick with a queasy sweat each day. His stool was a thin, acid soup. The Sugar Company doctor in Havana said he picked it up from the water. The embassy doctor in Ciudad Trujillo said he had probably eaten a poison grouper. The German ex-patriot doctor in Puerta Plata, who ran the seafood restaurant, went into a long Conradian dirge about the maladies of the Western soul in tropical climates and told him to eat a lot of cheese.

But cheese was hard to come by.

Walt started an amber collection and carried American toilet paper with him wherever he traveled. He organized lectures the cutters had to go to, printed pamphlets they couldn't read, even produced a short movie that was shown at all the bateyes called *La Companía: Padrón y Amigo*. His secret job was to play the Uneasy American with the Dominicans, the halfhearted flack with a sympathetic ear for a complaint, an open mind for a nationalist argument. The Sugar Company was fueled by the muscle and blood of the macheteros, any organized discontent among them had to be torn out at the root. In this their great ally was El Caudillo. Any threat to the best interests of the Sugar Company was also a threat to the state of the nation, to the rule of the strongman. El Caudillo had the island firmly under his thumb in 1950, his serious rivals dead or in exile, but was convinced the northern canefields were thick with conspiracy. Since it was known that any coup attempted without the backing of the Sugar Company would fail, there was pressure to put his fears to rest. Walt spent his time hinting that support for El Caudillo among the yanquis might not be as firm as it seemed, that men with idealism and democratic principles were always of interest. He dangled the bait of collusion and waited.

It was a long wait. The Dominican cutters were not a loose group of people. Each drink they took would plunge them deeper into a moody silence, an oppressive quiet that thickened the air till Walt oozed sweat. He'd make a comment, ask a question, and it would hang for a moment in the dark rum silence, then slowly sink unanswered. He'd retreat to the men's facilities for one of his asssearing discharges, ever grateful for his soft American paper, then return to a table unchanged in the smallest detail, as if the cutters had been locked in amber while he was gone.

Walt sat in his little house on the beach and despaired of ever breaking through with the Dominicans. He worked on his collection, polishing the pieces, turning them over under a magnifying glass searching for bits of insect or plant caught in them. Every few nights the power would go down and Walt would be in the dark. A terror would creep into him then, feeling alone in somebody else's world, so much of his life a fiction, so weightless. He could disappear without a ripple. The terror would squeeze him till he could get the candles lit and see his amber around him, reassuring, glistening like honey.

The cutters are a witless bunch, he thought. Forget the cutters.

Walt tried the field bosses, but they were the sharp end of the Company's stick, hungry men with a feeling for power or just for organized meanness. They growled down Walt's misgivings about the Sugar Company's activities.

"These people," they would say of the cutters, of their brothers and sisters and cousins and neighbors who worked in the fields, "these people need discipline. They *like* it, the way a dog likes a strong master.

"Y si no les gusta"—they would laugh—"siempre hay más haitianos."

There were, in fact, always more Haitians if you needed them. They were the curse the Dominican cutters toiled under, living proof of someone hungrier, more desperate, willing to work harder for less pay.

"The Haitians don't feel pain," the field bosses would say. "They sweat, but they don't really feel the heat."

Walt didn't bother to talk with the Haitians. Their ambitions stayed on the other side of the island and never cost El Caudillo any sleep. Walt dangled discontent in front of the field bosses but none bit. They began to avoid him. He tried the journalists, but the journalists were all copywriters for El Caudillo. He tried the local schoolteachers, but they all seemed to be relatives of the local politicians who all seemed to be relatives or business associates of El Caudillo himself.

The Sugar Company people in Ciudad Trujillo were not happy with Walt's skimpy reports. What the hell was going on up there?

Mostly what was going on was the deterioration of Walt's lower intestine. He saw that he was a doomed man, a professional Judas on an island where nobody wanted to play Christ. He became more and more impatient with the Dominicans, his diatribes against the paternalism of the Sugar Company and the atrocities of the yanqui-puppet Caudillo and his murderous henchmen louder and more inflammatory.

"What is *wrong* with you people?" he would shout, smacking the flat of his hand against the tabletop. "Don't you *care?* Don't you have any pride?"

A dark ripple would energize the room for a moment, eyes regarding him flatly, then it would be absorbed into heavy, liquid silence.

Walt was called down to Ciudad Trujillo.

"We've been getting reports from your turf," said Hasbrough, the PR chief. "Somebody stirring things up."

This was news to Walt. "Who told you that?"

"We've gotten complaints from several different sources."

"Give me a name. I'll check it out."

"It's *you*." Hasbrough clearly did not think it was funny. "You're up there to help us put out brushfires, Walt, not start a goddamn banana rebellion."

"I have to seem sympathetic if they're going to trust me."

"Sympathetic is one thing," said Hasbrough. "Putting ideas in their little pendejo heads is something else. First and foremost you're a representative of the Sugar Company. There is a certain dignity that comes with that." He ran a cold eye over Walt. "Cut down on the rum punches, fella, put on a little weight. You look like shit."

Walt bought some cheese, goat cheese, in Cuidad Trujillo, but when he got back to Puerto Plata it smelled too bad to eat.

Things picked up in the tiempo muerto. Most of the cutters had no work, their children were hungry. There was more time to drink. Father Graham arrived in the tiempo muerto.

He was a young Jesuit from Montreal, off on his first mission. Walt didn't like his eyes. They were light blue, with a sharpness to them that made you uneasy, that said I've got your number, pal. He brought two steamer chests full of baseball equipment with him.

"To bring people to God," he said, "first you have to bring them to each other."

The cutters were different people on the ball field. Walt would sit and watch them from the rickety bleachers at the abandoned mill where Father Graham had set up his leagues. The men and boys would grin and hotdog during warmups, calling to their friends on the sidelines, calling to their wives and girlfriends and children who clustered by the stands. Father Graham would be working the crowd, a healthy do-gooder sweat dampening his black short-sleeve shirt, holding babies, joking with the men, helping to set up the bases and draw foul lines for the umpires. He had appointed some of the older cutters as umpires, black men from the British islands who had been great cricketers in their youth and had a passion for rules.

Walt had never seen a baseball move around an infield with the snap the Dominicans put on it, one-handing bad hops off the scabby dirt and whipping their throws with acrobatic cool.

"Quite an operation you've got here," said Walt when the priest sat by him, eager to give his Spanish a rest. "You're quite an organizer."

"For the amount of work the Sugar Company gets out of these

people," said Father Graham, eyes crinkling in an untrusting smile, "you'd think they could do a little organizing of their own. You'd think they could afford a few balls and bats for the dead season."

Walt could never play his part with Father Graham, the priest always beating him to a complaint.

"We pay them a wage," said Walt. "What they do with it is their choice."

"The wage you pay won't keep a family alive," said the priest. "I don't think choice has anything to do with it."

In the early mornings when there was nothing to do Walt would walk the beach near his house and sometimes he'd run into Father Graham. They would talk about baseball, about the places on the Spanish side of the island Walt had been to and Graham hadn't, about the people and the food and Walt's intestinal difficulties.

"I had the same thing when I got here," said the priest. "Then one of the old women made this brew, some bark, some crushed leaves, coconut milk, some other things, and I was as good as new."

"The power of faith," said Walt.

"You should try it."

"This island has it in for me."

"This island," said the priest, "is my test. If I succeed here, I'll know my vocation is real."

"You mean you aren't sure?"

Graham smiled. "Nobody came out of a cloud and ordered me to do this. I don't know if I'll be any good at it. You can do a lot of damage in God's name. What about yours?"

"My what?"

"Your vocation here?"

Graham was giving him that look again and Walt could feel himself flushing. "I'm just a working stiff," he said.

Graham didn't change expression. "If you ever need someone to talk to," he said, "you know where I am."

They met often, talking about Graham's life and how he had come to be a priest. When the conversation turned around to Walt, Graham let him lie, listening with his little half-smile. Walt began to look forward to the ballgames, to seeing the priest on the beach.

Father Graham never scolded his people for missing Mass on Sunday. "His house is always open," he would say. "Come when you need Him." If a man was drinking too much or beating his wife or hurting his children, Father Graham would go first to the old cutters, wiry men who sat unmoving as lizards in the sun against the wall in front of the church in the zócalo.

"Talk to him for me, will you?" said Father Graham. "Men can't do these things and keep respect. Tell him to think about our children and what they see, what they think a man should be."

The old ones would talk to the man then, leaving the priest out of it. Sometimes a man changed for the better and sometimes people were only reminded of a way things might be. The younger cutters began to hang around the church, standing in the back at Mass or smoking on the steps until Father Graham came out.

"Is it true," they asked, testing him, "that God says all our reward will be in the next life? That our task on earth is to suffer?"

"Our task on earth is to help each other through life," said Father Graham.

The men smiled. "There are some things we would like to help each other with," they said, "that we are afraid to do on our own."

Father Graham sat by Walt the next time he came to a ballgame. Los Tigres were playing Los Elegantes in the young men's league. There was a kid on Los Elegantes who Walt was sure could make the majors if they were really serious about letting the colored play, a skinny, dark brown shortstop who could spray line drives all over the lot. Walt had been toying with the idea of talking the Sugar Company into sponsoring an All-Star team from their bateyes all over the island. If there wasn't going to be a revolution to crush maybe he could do some real public relations work.

"With the amount of money the Sugar Company makes on these people," said Father Graham, "you'd think they could build them some decent housing."

"The housing was decent when it was built," said Walt. "How the cutters keep it up—well. The Company doesn't like to interfere on the home front. We can only provide the raw materials."

The priest laid a hand on his shoulder. "We have a petition for you to present to the Company."

"We?"

"I helped to translate. The men would like to improve their quarters. They'd do all the work. All they want from the Company is to provide the raw materials."

"Is this a demand?"

Father Graham smiled. "A petition. It's something like a prayer."

Walt watched the Elegante shortstop snatch a one-hopper and nail the runner by a step. "I'll pass it along. Don't get your hopes up."

"Our prayers are not always answered," said Graham, "but we can never stop offering them."

When the Sugar Company ignored the petition Father Graham supervised the cannibalizing of the abandoned mill for lumber to make repairs on the housing. The men were happy to have something constructive to do during the tiempo muerto, were happy to have free wood and roofing tin to work with. They tore the old mill buildings apart with a communal joy, wives and girlfriends and children coming to watch and lend a hand. Walt drove by to watch the end of it. Father Graham greeted him with crowbar in hand, beaming a big do-gooder smile.

"They go down fast with a lot of hands, don't they?"

Walt leaned out of his window to take in the scene. Women were talking and laughing as they stacked sections of roofing. Little boys and girls worried nails from the boards that had been pulled down. The men sang and insulted each other jokingly as they worked.

"You know this is still Company property?" said Walt.

"Of course we do. Otherwise this would be stealing."

"No comprendo, Padre. Clue me in."

"The Sugar Company owns all this. The Sugar Company owns the housing these people live in. They're not using these buildings anymore, so—"

"So you're tearing them down and stealing the lumber."

"We're transferring a few of the Company's assets," said the priest. "Very simple. Improving the water situation will be much more difficult."

Father Graham helped the cutters petition the Sugar Company for a new well. He helped them petition for a permanent doctor in a clinic instead of the traveling alcoholic who would never come during the tiempo muerto. The petitions were ignored. His league grew to include teams from bateyes all over the north and wherever there was a team there was a group of men with a petition or a proposal or a list of complaints to send the Sugar Company.

Walt was summoned to Ciudad Trujillo.

"What's the scoop on this character?" asked Hasbrough. "Commie?"

"He's a priest."

"That's no guarantee these days."

"He's a do-gooder. Civic improvement, running water, education stuff. Nothing political."

"The Caudillo thinks he's building a power base."

"For what? To take over the island for the Vatican?"

"He's going to end up costing us money."

"Have you seen the places these people have to live in?" Walt could hear himself, recognized the tone he always used when he played the Uneasy American, but couldn't stop. "There are people starving out there, people sitting in filth, kids dying from the shits and it would cost us *pea*nuts to give them a little relief. You want to keep these people from turning on us, give them some breathing room."

Hasbrough sat behind his desk, staring at Walt. "We want him out," he said quietly. "The quickest way to do that, we'll need the word from certain parties in the Church. For that we need a field report marking the guy lousy."

Hasbrough jerked a thumb at a desk in the corner. There was a typewriter with a fresh piece of paper rolled up in it.

"You write the report. 'Suspicious activities,' 'Communist influence,' 'fellow traveler,' the usual. You know the buttons to push."

"He's not a Red."

"If we can't figure out a way to get shed of the guy," said Hasbrough, "I'm sure the Caudillo will."

Walt had one of his attacks while at the typewriter and had to run to the bathroom. When he came back, Hasbrough was reading the letter.

"Who's Machiavelli?"

"An Italian. He—"

"Subversive?"

"Yeah," sighed Walt. "A subversive."

"Then we should have him on file."

Graham said goodbye on a night when the power was down, a night when a dangerous wind rattled the boards of Walt's house on the beach. Walt was crawling in the dark, patting the floor for the candle he had dropped, when a flashlight beam caught him between the eyes.

"Don't worry," said the priest. "It's only me." He was dripping from the storm. He played the beam over the floor till Walt found the candle and lit it. They sat across from each other at the table,

Graham holding Walt's pieces of amber up to the flame and bringing his unsettling blue eye close to look into them as the tropical storm roared outside.

"It looks like some kind of bug got caught—"

"It's an ant. It gets caught in the tree sap, the sap petrifies—bingo. You're in the Hall of Fame."

"It's very old?"

"Centuries and centuries. Before Christ. Before people."

The priest nodded, turning the amber over in his fingers. "I'm going to be leaving."

"Oh?"

"Orders from the bishop. They've decided my services will be more valuable back in Canada."

Walt couldn't manage to act surprised. "Just as well," he said. "The tiempo muerto is almost over—your people will have their hands full with work pretty soon."

Father Graham looked at Walt over the candle flame. "Somehow the bishop got the idea that I was becoming a problem."

Walt shook his head in sympathy. "It's this island. Why'd you come here in the first place?"

Father Graham smiled. A jolt of wind pounded Walt's little house, nearly blowing the candle out.

"To save your soul," he said.

TWENTY

◀ IN THE KITCHEN there are two men, a woman and a boy. The kitchen smells like coffee, though only the ex-priest is drinking any, his cup balanced behind him on the edge of the sink. The overhead light bounces hard on the balding spot on his forehead. His hands lie together in his lap, fingertips touching as if in prayer. He can't quite believe he's really here, doing this thing, saying these words. He watches the face of the man who sits against the wall in the shadow of the refrigerator.

The man who sits by the refrigerator, the killer, is smoking, flicking the ashes into an empty beer bottle on the floor. He has bad skin and a hawklike nose. His legs are crossed, left ankle on right knee, and he takes in the room with a cold, superior gaze.

The boy is wearing a sleeveless black T-shirt and pacing between the stove and the pantry, wired for action, squeezing a tennis ball first in one hand, then in the other. He keeps looking at the clock on the wall, though time is not a factor here. There is a bronze-plated crucifix hanging beneath the clock, a sinewy Christ with the legs bent double at the knees and twisted to the side. There is a poster of the Cuban flag with a José Martí poem written in Spanish beneath it taped over the refrigerator door. The boy can't read the Spanish or the face of the man who sits in the shadow against the wall. The boy paces and keeps glancing over the woman's shoulder to the pistol on the kitchen table.

The woman is still in her nurse's uniform, sitting at the head of the little table. The pistol is an antique, a Spanish Star her father used during the fighting against Machado in '33. She doesn't know what kind of bullets it takes or how to load it but has laid it on the table as a symbol of the purpose of their meeting. She feels the boy pacing behind her, restless, feels the uncertainty of the ex-priest. Her mother is at church making a Novena, praying for her family. The woman touches the barrel of the pistol and faces the cold eyes of the man in the shadow of the refrigerator.

"Necesitamos más," says El Halcón.

"Mi tío vendrá con nosotros." She knows that Tío Felix lives in doubt, knows that the only way to get him in is to pull him along at the last moment with no time for doubts. "Iremos en su speed-boat."

"He says we need more people," says Padre Martín to the boy.

Dewey shifts the tennis ball and shakes his head. "The more people you have the greater the security risk. You only need a few good men."

"I see only one man here," says El Halcón in English, deliberately. He glances at the ex-priest. "Maybe one and a half."

Dewey stops pacing and gives El Halcón what is meant to be a withering look. Marta lifts her father's pistol, hefting it in both hands as if checking its weight. "What we need is more rifles," she says. "Y explosivos."

"Por qué explosivos?" says El Halcón.

"To blow up the power station at the Playa Girón. That will be our mission."

"Y por qué eso?"

"Because we'll do it the night before el aniversario de la Invasión. Cada año los fidelistas celebran su victoria. If we take out the power it will show everyone."

"Show them what?"

"Que el espíritu de la libertad vive todavía. That the war is not over."

"Y por qué la electricidad?"

Marta's face hardens. "To turn the lights off. Qué si no?"

Padre Martín can't believe he's sitting here, considering this. If he says this won't work, this is a mistake, will it all stop? He knows other men, men of action, who have done these things. He wonders if they have had the same feelings, the sense of unreality as the details are discussed, the sense of doom.

"It was her brother's mission," he says softly. Marta stares at the old pistol. "Her brother was with a team who were supposed to destroy the power in the area. To cut off communications."

Dewey sits against the stove. "Your brother was in the Pigs thing?"

"He was killed there."

When Marta was little Ambrosio would take her to the drawer where the pistol was kept. Ambrosio would open the drawer and they would look at it and he would tell her how their father had shot people with it in the troubles during Machado. Marta felt its power, felt its holiness just looking at it.

"Cómo se llamaba?" asks El Halcón. "I might have known him."

"You were there too?"

El Halcón sighs and looks at Dewey. "If you were a man then you were a part of it."

"Ambrosio de la Pena Cruz," says Marta.

El Halcón shakes his head as if the name means nothing to him.

"I have a map." Marta pulls a folded restaurant placemat from the silverware drawer in the table. She opens it and Dewey comes close to look. He puts his hand, as casually as he can manage, on her shoulder. A smile flickers on El Halcón's face. He lights another cigarette. There are food stains on the placemat and a map drawn in ink with lots of things crossed out and relocated.

"There is a Marielito in housekeeping at the hospital. He worked at the Playa Girón. Every year he would help clean up after the celebration. He drew this for me."

El Halcón pays no attention to the map. "Necesitamos más," he says. "No puedo obtener explosivos sin que tengamos más en la fuerza. My people will only give them if they think we will be a success."

Marta pretends to ignore him. She places her father's pistol carefully to one side and smooths the placemat out on the table. The boy stuffs the tennis ball in his pocket and puts his other hand on her other shoulder, holding his breath. The ex-priest, to be polite, pushes his chair closer to the table.

"The power station is not far from the beach," she says. "There are three different places we can set our charges."

"Necesitamos más," says the killer, sitting in the shadow of the refrigerator.

TWENTY-ONE

➤ WILSON. Wilson needs a chance to talk to Luz without some white man's shitty ass between them. Every morning when he pops his ticket he checks for her name on the punch-card rack. Days when she's off are like swimming in glue for him, another tour in Wrinkle City. Wilson looks across the bed at her, wiping hard, and wishes it was sandpaper. The old man whines.

"Gentle," says Luz, without looking at him. "You have to be more gentle."

I be gentle with you, sweet girl, you give me the chance. You get the best out of me, I swear, all kinds of things in me nobody knows, saving them up for somebody. For you. Sweet pretty woman with a killer smile, Florence fucking Nightingale. For *you*.

Luz flirts with the old man, old Jew, old white sack of shit. How can she be so happy? Doesn't she know? Or is Papa right and they think that much different?

Wilson follows her out of the room, arms stuffed with shitty linen. She is half a head taller than he is, more with the nurse's cap. A stallion. She shoots a burst of Spanish at one of the Cuban girls in housekeeping as they pass and the girl laughs. Wilson knows buenos días, buenas noches and cállate. Shut up. Luz says it whenever they go in to deal with Stern, the lunatic in restraints with diarrhea of the brain. Man shits words out his mouth a mile a minute, not one of them mean diddlysquat, veins in his neck popping blue he shouts so hard and she gets him to stuff a rag in it with a word and a smile.

"Inamawannagowahowstoyuheardemgetgowakbysipdostikstik-stik—" yells Stern as they enter.

"Cállate, viejo," says Luz, moving to the head of his bed, stroking his shoulder and cooing all her little pigeon words in Spanish. Wilson sits in the corner, waiting. Sanjurjo, as deaf as he is blind and six years older than dirt sits on the edge of his bed with a huge expectant grin on his face. Fucker is too stupid to die. Luz is almost singing, sitting to put her mouth closer to Stern's ear. The old man's fists start to soften into hands. Wilson grinds his teeth, his stomach in a knot at ten in the morning, and longs for somebody to croon his anger away.

"We go back here all the way to the Spanish," Grandaddy would always say, as if that were some big fucking deal. "Our people run off the plantation in Cahlina and never look back. Come back here and jungle up with the Indian."

Grandaddy was real loose with his *we. We* could mean him and Granmama or *we* could mean people in the near family or *we* could mean all black people since Creation.

"It was King George people up north of us then and they was always knockin heads with the Spanish, which was to the south of us. Spanish left us be, knowin them King George people got to cut through *us* to get to *them*. Also they had them a degree of respect count of they had fought the Moor for so many centuries. The Moor was us, see, the colored man."

Grandaddy said colored till he died, refusing to move with the times. "In my day," he would say, pausing to pull off a chaw of Little Yara, dixie cup half full of black-red spit in his hand, "in my day *black* was the last word you heard before the *fightin* broke out.

"Now the *In*dian at that time was a runaway too, keepin clear from the same white man as was after us. The Indian took us for a brother. You got Indian *blood* in you, son. You be proud of that."

The only Indians Wilson had met at that age had cracker accents and sold baskets in the Parrot Jungle parking lot. Nothing he saw in the mirror conjured up Grandaddy's stories of Wildcat or Oceola. Indian my black ass. If their blood was running in the family it skipped around Wilson. When he was at the U later he hit the library looking for the connection, but that was before the whole Afro thing was being taught and he couldn't find a single book. That was before the bad shit started. Before the first riot.

*　　*　　*

Stern seems blissed out now, like the wild alligators they turn on their backs in the swamp shows. Wilson moves to the bed and starts to work on the knots holding the hand restraints, yanked solid with the old man's thrashing. Luz swishes past him and he tries to breathe her in, but all he gets is a white smell. Starch.

Luz. Luz wonders sometimes if it's healing or just stalling for time.

"He's an old man," Dr. Masi is always saying after an exam. "We can't expect too much."

But some of them are not so old and still no one expects them to get better, just to fall apart at a more dignified rate. So far she's seen only one patient walk out on his own steam and that was just Rednose Fisher sneaking off for a bottle and turning up next in Jacksonville.

Luz wraps her hands around Stern's wrists, raw and oozing from the restraints. She washes them gently, puts on the salve and the gauze. Stern's chest has stopped heaving but he stares pop-eyed at the ceiling, the muscles in his jaw clenching till she puts her hands under them and rubs with her thumbs till they relax. They tiptoe out, Luz giving sweet Mr. Sanjurjo a pat that fails to stir him from his grinning fog. The evening shift will complain about the restraints being left off Stern but he's the one who needs to heal, not them.

Gold and Epstein are easy. Good spirits, still with the program, always complaining about each other but always checking at the desk about the other's health.

"He doesn't eat right," says Gold, nodding toward his companion. "He gets involved with his music and he forgets lunch."

Luz irrigates Gold's infected ear. Epstein sits on the next bed, radio headset on, lost in opera. Wilson, moody as always, hangs by the air conditioner.

"I got this ear when they took me to that swamp-hole Memorial to have the spleen yanked out," says Gold. "Or was it the gallbladder?" He puts his hand to his heart the way he does to recite. " '*Today we have the naming of the parts.*' "

"That's a strange poem."

"It's about weapons, not bodily organs, but to me it applies. I got more hollow places than a chocolate rabbit. How's it coming in there?"

Luz pulls the syringe back and takes a look. She holds his ear, gently slipping her middle finger inside. There is a heat, a bad heat.

"La verdad?"

"Sock it to me."

"I think it gets worse before it gets better."

"I can't sleep on that side at night now. Usually I have my best dreams on that side."

"Qué lástima."

"Sometimes I dream about you."

"You say that to every nurse on the floor, Mr. Gold. It's on your chart—'Watch out for Mr. Gold and his dreams.'" Luz packs up the irrigation kit. Wilson hooks the towel into the linen cart. Gold puts his hand over his heart.

" *'She walks in beauty like the night—'* "

"You must be dreaming about Blanca on the eleven to seven. I only work days." Luz squeezes Epstein's arm, waving to him through his music. Losing weight too fast, Epstein. Have to watch him. His skin doesn't feel right. Have to make up something medical sounding so they'll pay attention at the desk. Cyanotic. They love that one. Patient found listless and cyanotic, monitor intake.

Old Señora Godoy, the one they called La Bruja and ran from when she came out on her patch of lawn, used to scare Luz shitless with the touch business. She'd grab onto Luz's hands, thumbs digging into her palms till she nearly cried, and close her acorn-shell eyelids.

"Tienes el toque, niña," La Bruja would croak as Luz tried to pull away. "El toque dulce."

She tried to ignore all that spooky stuff, all the old-country mumble-jumble the guajiros and pescadores had brought up with them. That stuff didn't apply in America. Then her brother was lost in the fighting and she developed a raging thirst.

"I need water," she told her father, who seemed to shrink with each day of no news from the island. She drank glass after glass from the tap till her little belly swelled taut, then she sat on the toilet crying and peeing it out and then she drank more, direct from the faucet in the bathroom. There wasn't enough water in the world for her thirst. Her father called Dr. Cifuentes, who was a taxi dispatcher then because of his license, and he came to look at her in case it was cholera or worse. She was fine, healthy except for the stomach pains from the water.

"He needs me to drink," she told the doctor. "Serafín needs me to drink for him."

Dr. Cifuentes took her seriously the way not so many adults did and thought for a long moment. "Drink, then," he said. "We have to do whatever we can for them."

And then when they heard he'd been found on the raft and Luz got to see him and hug him she could feel the thirst on his blistered skin. Mortal thirst, a thirst that ran up her arms and hammered in her skull. She could feel the sun and the ocean too big and too empty, could feel the terror and beyond that a sadness that went to the bone, that oozed from Serafín and threatened to fill her up like cold, dead water and she had to fight to keep it from pulling her under. She felt all of it through his skin before a word was spoken, and when they let her stay in with him while he slept she held Serafín's hand in both of hers and there was a heat there, a loving heat she could feel coming out through her and into him and she wanted Señora Godoy to be right. If she could heal. If she could heal.

Luz looks into Epstein's eyes, lost in opera, looks until they come back to the world and see her. She touches his cheek with her hand. He fumbles by the nightstand, claps his upper plate in and then smiles back at her.

Wilson. Wilson wants to know how she thinks. Maybe if you think in Spanish you think different. Maybe if you're Spanish and a woman then black isn't so much to have in common. Wilson watches her flirting with the antiques and wants to know.

"Knowledge is *power*," Grandaddy would say whenever he'd go into one of his stories about Mr. Flagler. All these stories had to do with some time where old Flagler was caught between a rock and a hard place in his business and Grandaddy would wander in with a tray of steaming biscuits and Flagler would turn and say, "So what do you think, Thomas?" and Grandaddy would put him straight. Grandaddy worked meals on Flagler's private railroad car. In the only picture he saved, hand-tinted to color, he wore a white linen jacket, red sash and a big Uncle Ben smile.

"Mr. Flagler *made* this state," Grandaddy would say. "Built it up from swampland. And I was *there*."

Papa would have to cut in then if he was around. "Funny he didn't leave you no orange groves," he'd say, "you givin the man most his good ideas and all."

Papa was Grandaddy's bad boy, the one who liked to cut school and fish and run around after women too old for him. The one Grandaddy loved the most and fought the hardest with. By the time Papa came up there wasn't any private cars, wasn't hardly any railroad service left at all, so Papa cut bait and put it on white people's hooks. When the marlin were jumping his family ate pork chops and beefsteak. Other times they stewed the bait and called it Papa's chowder.

Grandaddy wouldn't hear a word against Flagler. "The man open up a world to me. A world of knowledge. That count better than any orange grove."

"Look, Daddy, Flagler wasn't gonna listen to no colored man's opinion less it was to make a story of him later at the Planters' Club. White don't wanna hear what we got to say."

"I served *quality*, boy. None of your fat northern trash down here to drink and chase they boats around."

"And you was the same nigger to your quality that I was to my white folks! Serve it with a smile then make your black ass scarce."

Grandaddy would get all stony and quiet then and when Wilson was little there were times when he thought he could see it coming through. The Indian blood. He thought of it as something thicker, rusty red and hot with anger. Grandaddy didn't use any nigger talk and wouldn't hold for it in his earshot. Papa only did it when he was hurt bad or drinking too much.

"Aint no niggers in this family," Grandaddy would start, quiet and simple. "We been free people since we run off from Cahlina. White man pulled them first chains off and we was *gone*."

They would be silent for a long time then, Papa staring blackly off the porch into the sawgrass, Grandaddy moving his chaw from one side to the other till he'd shake his head and sigh.

"You don't know, boy. You don't *know*."

Wilson trails Luz in to check on Garber and Galindez. Galindez is moaning his sad shit and Garber is yanking his crank.

"Good morning Mr. Garber," says Luz. "How you doing?"

"Sprocket-hole," says Garber as if it means just fine.

Luz moves Garber's business hand away and inspects his joint. "Wilson, would you put some vaseline on Mr. Garber here? He's rubbing himself raw."

Any other nurse he'd tell them to shove it, grease up the man's dick their own damn self if they wanted but leave him off that case. Wilson digs out a rubber glove and wriggles it on. He fingers out a gob of vaseline the size of a baseball. Luz smiles.

"Don't be afraid, it hasn't bit anybody in years."

And nobody's bit *it* for years neither, which is a large part of Garber's problem. Wilson begins to slather the stuff on.

"Boogie," says Garber, looking Wilson in the eye and cheerfully trying to say that feels good. All Wilson hears is boogie. Garber starts to get hard and Wilson gives it a sharp flick with his gloved forefinger.

"Boogieboogieboogie," says Garber.

Luz. Luz puts her hand on Galindez's forehead and pushes his damp hair back.

"I die now," says Galindez. "Ahora me muero."

"Dónde te duele, viejo?"

Galindez indicates an area from his breastbone to his groin. "Los gusanos," he says.

"Qué?"

"Los gusanos están comiéndome."

There is no mention on Galindez's chart of worms, no mention of any infection or bacteria or anything else eating him but he is convinced that he is dying, dying at that very moment. Luz pulls his johnnycoat up and runs a hand over his chest and belly.

"Los sientes?" he asks. "Están comiéndome."

She doesn't feel worms but something *is* eating him, there is a hollowness, a dry, light feeling in his chest cavity like he has been emptied out and packed with loose sawdust. If Dr. Masi were to open him up there would only be dust and stale air.

"Qué tipo de gusano? No los siento."

"Nos entran cuando somos jovenes," says Galindez. "Me entraron en mi niñez, hace muchos años."

Luz tries to imagine him as a boy. Did he know he had the worms then, feel himself emptying out as they grew and grew? She tries not to think about it too much, tries to stay lost in the fullness of her life, but sometimes she can't help but feel it. A whole life reduced to dream and memory, still breathing but connected to living by the narrowest thread, a phrase, a sensation, a knot of pain. Was there a moment when Galindez let the rest of it go and gave himself up to his worms? Or did he feel himself losing it, bit by bit, his own force shrinking as they grew fatter? Everybody had to die, she knew that, there was no final healing and nobody was safe. Not even her. But it was bad to have to face it with every breath, to feel its weight on you every waking moment.

"Grandes," says Galindez. "Los gusanos de la vida. Me han comido."

She touches his head then and looks into his eyes and can tell that he is right. He is dying now, not as quickly as he would like maybe, but dying just the same, eaten by his great worms of life. She fluffs his pillow, yanks out the wrinkles in his bottom sheet, rubs his back with TLC lotion.

"Sí que te estás muriendo, viejo," she coos to him as she works into his muscles. "Como todos. But I have to make you more comfortable."

Her hands can do nothing to keep it away. But maybe she can draw some of the terror out for a moment, and a moment's less terror in somebody's life seems worth the effort. Galindez lets a full breath out, a breath he seems to have been holding in for days, and his moan turns to a weary purr. His thick muscles melt under Luz's fingers.

"Estás mejor?" she asks.

Galindez purrs and closes his eyes.

Wilson. Wilson can't see it. The ones who are still with the program, the walking wounded, okay. But spending time and effort on a gone sucker like Galindez, forget it. They get old and they die, let em go. Should be part of the job description—suckers want to die, *do not get in their way.* And here's Luz doing a major tune-up on this stiff. Waste of those pretty hands. Think what those hands could be doing. Wilson finishes with Garber and Garber goes back to work polishing his bayonet. Make that thing *shine.* Wilson peels the glove off and sits on the edge of Garber's bed. No danger, man been cranking on it for years and it hasn't gone off yet. What Grandaddy used to call a dead issue.

It was Grandaddy's saved-up money that sent him when Wilson was ready to go to the U.

"We never had one into college before," Grandaddy said, all proud like it wasn't Wilson who got accepted but the whole family back to slave days. "We movin up."

They were good about it at the time, Grandaddy trying not to lord it too much about his money and Papa trying not to resent it that he didn't have much to throw in. He'd been out of work for so long but he still took Wilson aside and pressed a wad on him, folding money he called it, maybe a hundred in fives and singles and some of it smelled like fish. The first couple weeks at the U before he made friends sometimes Wilson would pull the money out and look at it. Smell it.

"This is all I got right now," Papa said. "You do good there. Learn up. Find you some way not to come back to this life."

When the fishing had ended for Papa he tried catching on at the hotels or driving taxi but by then it was all Spanish. The middle bosses were all Cubans and they did the hiring and firing on that level and if they wanted black they had their own or the Ricans and Dominicans. Papa spent his days drinking rum with his old dock-rat buddies and bitching about how the Spanish had come between the black man and the white man.

"Shit was gonna *happen,* see, good or bad. Some kind of respect or justice or maybe just a *war,* see? Only then the Spanish come and the white man don't need us no more, don't need to *deal* with us no more. Build them a fast highway right by us, so long, baby, been nice knowing you. So we left with nothing. I mean *nothing,* we been left the shit you throws to the gulls. Best thing would be, that

Fidel Castro eat him a bad oyster, falls out dead, and all these Spanish go home and boss they own niggers around."

The war happened at the end of Wilson's first semester.

He was out with friends from the U watching a ballgame at a bar in North Miami and people kept coming in saying shit's gonna happen tonight. Shaking their heads, ordering hard liquor to calm them down, a little scared and a little excited. In the bar it was all purple light and air-conditioning, though, and Vida Blue was working a two-hitter and Miami was a long, long ways away so it wasn't till they stepped out into the hot rush of the night that they felt it in the air. Shit *was* happening. Lots of it. Glass breaking. Sirens. Fire. Little scary pops, like kids with plastic bags, scattered around the night. Wilson and his friends started walking fast through it, catching the mood, and then a half-dozen brothers ran by yelling come on, come on picking up things to throw and he and his friends were pretty Afroed then with the do and the attitude and the energy of it all, they were running, looking for rocks, bricks, sticks, anything to throw at what they didn't know yet but running toward the glass and sirens and fire and gut-grabbing little pops of gunfire till they were *it*, front lines, tear gas rolling, pigs in helmets, news at eleven. Wilson gave it his outfielder's peg, run-hop-longstep throw it sizzling straight overhand into the line of blue and his eyes exploded with flashbulbs, the Media returning fire on him from every angle, freezing his moment for Can We Save Our Sick Cities? in the special edition and then the brothers faded around him and the blue wave hit Wilson all alone, chopping him down and rolling him under till somebody had him by the feet and he was swept, strangest sensation, swept like his body was rags head bouncing back under the wave of blue and hurled sprawling and soaked in his own liquid into a hard metal wagon. There was nigger talk and more from the helmets, slamming down the hallway at the station, fingertips pounded in ink, thrown into the tank with a full house of brothers swapping war stories and nursing their wounds. One of the helmets kept stomping past on the other side of the iron looking in through all the black faces to Wilson's and pointing his club and screaming it was you, it was you you little motherfucker boogie you're not gonna live through the night and the other brothers hooting till the helmet slammed his stick on the iron again and again, gone with fury and Wilson started to shake inside, wondering if they'd pull him out and give him to the helmet, feeling his face swollen out inches from where it should be and numb, not like his skin at all and then there was Papa's voice. Papa's angry voice that Wilson used to hide out from, and it was just in the next room threatening to waste any white motherfucker touched his boy and the helmets telling him to shut up and get out and then he was there, arms pinned behind his back, tossed into the tank himself with the other brothers giving a round of applause. Wilson was embarrassed a split second and then felt like he might cry. Papa found him sitting on the floor against the wall, touching the top of his head where it scraped on the pavement, trying to stop the bleeding with his fingers.

"You all right?"

"I'm fine, Papa." It was hard talking with his lip swollen out so far.

"They got you for something?"

"Being black."

Papa smiled. "Got me a regular little wild man here. I mean they got you for a crime?"

"I threw an orange."

"Orange?"

"They were all over the street. Somebody bust open the White Pantry and there was food all over. I couldn't find no stones."

Papa nodded. "Never can when you need to. Hurt your head?"

"Naw."

"Might be that big ole hair you got be good for something. Your mama and me heard the sirens, called that dorm, but it was busy."

"You been out there looking for me?"

Papa shrugged. "I seen your friend Rodney, he said they run you in."

The other brothers in the tank started to chant. Papa looked around at them, shaking his head.

"Never seen one like this," he said. And then, "You ought to visit home more. Your mama miss hearing from you."

"I been busy."

"Thowin oranges."

"Yeah."

They got shy after that, and it was hard to talk with the chanting and the yelling from everybody. They took Wilson out separate after a cop with his eye bandaged ducked in and put the finger to him. Nothing Papa could say could stop them but Wilson wasn't embarrassed at all when he tried, wanting the other brothers to know that was his old man. When they brought him down the hallway for booking the helmet who'd been so crazy before marched right past him, staring through him without a speck of recognition.

The detective looked like he'd just gotten out of bed.

"Son," he said, "you seen the mess out there?"

"Seen some of it."

"Well somebody's gonna have to *pay* for that. What's your name?"

Luz. Luz checks out the new one, Rosen, pale and shaky, in the bed Levy used to have. She feels bad about Levy, though she did what she could. He had complained about his stomach, but they all did that and nobody paid much attention. She felt over his liver and there was something, not a heat but an activity, something that didn't belong. She mentioned it in report and Nurse Temple shrugged it off but it was there on the next shift and the next, a tingling almost that bothered her fingers, Levy looking gravely into her eyes as she said, "I don't know, you could be right. Pero no soy médico."

She bugged Temple about it enough so she brought it to Dr. Masi on one of his visits. Dr. Masi was a good man but he had his blind spots.

"He's an old man. To really check we'd need an intrusive procedure, cutting, the whole bit. I can't go opening patients up because a nurse has a superstition. Monitor his output, put him on a bland diet."

Luz felt it hardening after that, the activity growing denser, becoming a thing. Levy was not a happy man. He spent a lot of his day scowling out the window. Luz read his chart for background.

"Mr. Levy, somebody told me you have a daughter in New Jersey."

"We don't talk."

"I have relatives up there. You have grandchildren?"

"We don't talk."

"Why not?"

He gave her a look but she could feel that the daughter was something hard and hurtful in him, something he needed to talk about.

"Who she married."

"Who she married?"

"She married *him*. For me she's dead."

"I'm sure she doesn't feel that way."

"Marrying him was a knife in my back. She pushed it in. She knew it and she pushed it in."

"Her children should meet their grandfather."

Levy scowled out the window.

It wasn't easy keeping his health out of the phone call. The daughter was wary, afraid of being hurt, proud.

"He couldn't come to the phone himself?"

"You know how he is. He's just talking about you so much, I thought—"

"Is he dying?"

"I'm not a doctor. The doctor says he's fine."

"Then he could get up and come over to the phone—"

"I'm not calling from the hospital. I'm at home."

"You're calling me long distance from home?"

"He talks about you all the time. He really wants to see you."

"Is he very sick?"

"He's an old man. You can never tell."

Luz could tell though. His liver was hard, swollen and hard. Even Dr. Masi could feel it but it was too late. He didn't say anything to Levy, the usual we'll have to keep an eye on this. But Levy knew.

"A cancer," he said. "I knew it. You knew it."

"I thought maybe I felt something."

"Just as well."

The daughter came in like she might change her mind at the door and fly back to Jersey.

"When he talks about me," she asked when she tracked Luz down in the cafeteria, "what does he say?"

"About you when you were little. You know. My daughter this, my daughter that. The way parents are."

"Is his mind okay? I mean he doesn't think I'm a little girl still or anything, does he? He'll recognize me?"

The daughter dressed nice and looked like she was doing fine. She had jewelry, blond frosting in her hair.

"You'll be a wonderful surprise for him."

Luz tried to stay away for a couple days, getting the other girls to cover his room so he wouldn't suspect that she had called. When she finally did go in she didn't mention the daughter. Levy watched her as she felt the liver. There was heat now, spreading. Levy was turning a bad yellow.

"She has two," he said, out of the blue. "Megan and Jeremy. A Megan in my family."

"Is a pretty name."

"She's eleven. The boy is eight. They leave gaps."

"Gaps?"

"The kids nowadays. Have a baby, recover for a few years, maybe have another. In my day it was *bam, bam, bam.* No gaps."

"You only had one."

"Her mother wasn't well." Levy looked away, out the window.

"You never told me about your wife."

"She's none of your business," said Levy, grumpy, and then went on to describe a young, beautiful woman, how he met her, what they'd do on a Sunday with their little baby girl, how her illness changed her body, the way he never really got started with his life again. Temple came in to get her finally, wearing her boss hat.

"I thought you went home, Luz." Ice in the air. "You have other patients waiting, don't you?" Then, her voice all creamy, "How are we today, Mr. Levy?"

"I don't know about you," he said, "but I'm about to croak."

He was on tubes when the daughter came back with the children.

"My husband doesn't know we're here," said the daughter. "He thinks I took them to Disney World."

Luz ran ahead and pulled his nose tube out and detached the glucose IV. She pulled the top blanket down over the output bag and cranked him up a little higher.

"Visitors, Mr. Levy."

His eyes were yellow, yellow and lidded like the giant turtle at the Seaquarium. They rolled slowly from the window to her.

"Your grandchildren."

"I'll scare them," he whispered. "An old man dying."

"They passed up Mickey Mouse for you. You got no choice."

"What do I say?"

Luz tried to think of herself as the little girl, the Megan who looked nervous and awkward out in the hallway. What could she want, what could she use?

"Tell them about your wife, Mr. Levy. They should know that."

The daughter took them back to Jersey the next morning and then Levy went out just the other day, went out in a cloud of morphine. Luz checks over Rosen and tries not to put her hands on the bed. If she felt anything left of Levy there, in the dead plastic and linen, that would be too much to carry, too spooky. It's enough that she can feel Rosen's nerves shooting thousands of frenzied messages every whichway under his skin, can feel the paranoia prickling out from Heller as he holds on to his bedrails, positive that she's going to come over and hurt him next, can feel little Wilson's slow anger and boredom as he mopes by the door. She feels too much, Luz, it gets noisy sometimes. And what she can't feel, can't get even a hint of through her touch or his is what that damn Rufo is up to, so sweet and distant, making love like he's lost to her but not lost, not lost at all. She can touch him all she wants and never know what's under his skin. Some touch. Qué toque más dulce, Señora Godoy, que puede sentir la muerte pero no puede sentir el amor. When it comes to her own life, her own feelings, her fingers are blind.

"You lay a hand on me," says Heller, tightening his grip, "I yell for the bulls."

Wilson moves over by his side. "Easy, man. She's just trying to help. Trying to get you better."

"She's a witch, that one. She put a curse on me."

"No soy bruja," she says, turning to Heller, suddenly weary. "I'm a nurse. We have to turn you over now."

"Over my dead body."

"That can be arranged," says Wilson and begins to pry the old man's fingers off the rail.

Wilson. Wilson doesn't really like to touch them but it's the job and he needs the money. He had doctor dreams, once, Wilson, back when he started at the U. Doctor, lawyer, Indian chief. Some bigshit job that paid serious coin and kept you out from under white people. No trains, no fish, no big Uncle Ben smile. Fuck-you money, that's what he was going to make. Wilson pries Heller's fingers off the rail, deaf to his shouting, and flips him, swift and gently as he can cause Luz is there, flips him with a quick twist and tuck that leaves his ugly bed-sore ass pointing up at the ceiling.

"Thank you," says Luz.

Decubitus. Wilson reads the medical journals when he's on graveyard and the antiques are all sleeping. The nurses do their nails and talk about their kids and how little sleep they got during the day but Wilson gets his head into pulmonary edema and ideopathic meningitis. He understands the shit, too, which surprises him a bit sometimes, after a couple of years of this asswipe job he's started to feel like he maybe belongs here, that this is what he was aimed at all along, this or some other dead-end slave. Luz and Wilson look into the gaping decubitus over Heller's coccyx, an angry Grand Canyon of bedsores, and then trade a glance.

"Shouldn't let him on his back for a couple weeks," says Wilson. "Thing is getting bigger."

"I tell them you said so in report."

He doesn't know if she's mocking him or not. She seems serious, laying out her artillery to clean out the sore.

"I can't breathe on my stomach," says Heller, voice muffled in his pillow. "How the fuck am I supposed to breathe on my goddamn stomach?"

"Gills, man," says Wilson, sitting across Heller's legs to keep him from kicking when Luz treats the sore. "Grow you some gills like a mud-hopper. Then we could stick you underwater, tone down that mouth of yours."

"A witch and a torturer," says Heller. "A pair of demons from the dark continent."

"This might hurt a little bit, Mr. Heller," says Luz as she prepares to put the salve on. "I'm real sorry if it does."

Wilson was one of the few they hung charges on, his face plastered all over the nation in the flashbulb glare, his mouth open in a grimace, his eyes two buttons of reflected flame, his arm extended in a spearthrower's follow-through. The picture helped a half-dozen different cops remember him as the one who had the knife, who had the gun, who set the fire. The picture put a face on their nightmare.

The lawyers from both sides played their game and Wilson ended up with only three months on the county and six months suspended. He managed to get his ass bounced out of the U, though, and it was right around then that Grandaddy fell out with his stroke.

"We never been that kind," Grandaddy said the first time he saw the picture in the paper.

"You mean we run off but we never fight back," said Papa.

"I mean we never been this kind of trash to join up in a mob. Never." It wasn't easy for Wilson to be around the old man in those days, bumped out of school, tuition lost, face still healing from the riot. Grandaddy didn't like his friends, his attitude, his clothes, his hair.

"You ever see a colored man, an African man, with his hair growed out all woolly like that? Black Power my butt. Just another excuse for the young boys to lip off at they elders is all."

"It's a war, Grandaddy," Wilson tried to explain. "Us against the white man."

"Don't tell me no war. Don't tell me no white man. I *knows* the white man. Served with him fifty years, seen the state come up from swampland."

"We ain't serving no more."

"You ain't *warrin* neither, boy. We had some *wars* with the white man. This piddly-shit you done aint nothing like that. We took on the King George people, kept their ass outa this country. Then come the Americans, want to take us back for slaves, they got to bring a whole damn army down here. Indian man, Wild Cat. Colored man, John Horse. They was the generals. They had the *knowledge*. White man needed a whole army to pack them off to Oklahoma Territory. Only some of us lit out, went down to the swampland with Billy Bowlegs. White man never brung him in. Boy throw a damn citrus fruit at some cracker, be talkin bout *war*."

After the stroke the old man just lay in stony silence, a frown stamped on his face. He changed color, turning dull copper like a used penny, his cheekbones coming out as the rest of his face sank away and when Wilson came by all he could see was the Indian blood, thin and bitter now, tired from too many battles lost. The last time Wilson saw him he waited outside for Papa to finish.

"Wilson gone back to school, Daddy," he heard Papa say, lying. "He promise to straighten out and they let him back. Boy got a mind on him. Gonna make us all proud. We movin up, Daddy."

Papa's eyes were red coming out through the doorway. He nodded for Wilson to go in. Grandaddy's fingers were bone, clamping onto Wilson's hand in a way that sent a chill through him. The old man's eyes had gone nearly clear and Wilson looked down into them and thought he saw no living focus, just his Grandaddy's soul and the souls of all that *we* he always talked about, the Africans run off from the Carolinas and the Indians joining blood with them, all of them in there pulling the old man down, pulling him back into something old and charged with spirit and suffering but calm in the face of it. Wilson felt for a moment that he might fall in, the eyes went so deep, and it gave him the willies. When he could work his hand free he kissed his grandfather goodbye and got out.

Luz and Wilson walk for the end of the hall, the last station on their rounds. Luz is thinking about Rufo, how it's happening to her the way it always does, getting drunk with the idea of him, letting the hard part of her, the part that is suspicious and wary slide and giving in to the hot, comforting idea of him being there against her, his size and his smell and his man's body while Wilson is chewing at his fate, supposed to be so damn smart and emptying piss bottles for a living, whole libraries full of useless knowledge, history and medicine and politics in his head, and he can't think up an opening line to break ice with some Cuban nurse. She has a long stride and he hurries to keep up with her, not to follow a step behind like he works under her but like they're in this together, health professionals on the job like fucking Temple is always barking about. They come into old Skip's room and he's relieved to see that her friend Marta is not in, the white Spanish make him uneasy enough without her extra weirdness on top of it. DuPre is on his side reading and old Skip is red like he's about to explode. Luz is wishing Marta was there so she could ask has Serafín made any move and sensing as he moves past that maybe, could it be, is little Wilson carrying something for *her?* She'd be the last one to know and Wilson the last to confess it, always a half step behind her, cruising in her blind spot. En cuestiones de amor she is one big blind spot and really doesn't have the energy to deal with Wilson if there is something going on in his head. Enough. Enough men, enough problems.

DuPre looks up from his book and smiles.

"Hola, Luz. Qué tal?"

Smartass, thinks Wilson. Showoff motherfucker.

"Nada de particular. Y tú, te gusta la nueva sala?"

DuPre nods toward Scipio. "She draws the curtain when she talks to him. But sometimes she'll visit with me. How's Heller?"

"Mean as ever."

"He's scared. His body is committing treason."

"Tienes razón."

DuPre watches Wilson move to the window that opens on the parking lot.

"You look so much like a kid who was in my outfit."

Great. More fucking war stories.

"So?"

"So nothing. You look just like him."

Luz examines the chafing on DuPre. "It's getting much better."

"Todos sus enfermos están mejorando."

She smiles. "If it's true why shouldn't I say it? All my patients *are* getting better. Does anybody die on my shift?"

DuPre laughs and turns to Wilson again. "I don't remember his name. Age is a terrible thing."

"Why should you remember his name?"

"We were comrades. Brothers."

"Sure."

"That's what we called each other. Brother. Compañero. Hermano."

"You talked Spanish?"

"We were in Spain. It seemed like the thing to do."

"Spain. Right."

"You don't even know when that was, do you?"

"Between the First World War and the Second. Paul Robeson was there."

DuPre makes an impressed face to Luz. "A historian. He knows who Robeson was."

Luz has her hands on Scipio's shoulders, looking into his eyes. "How has he been, Mr. DuPre?"

"This is hard to say. Mr. de la Pena is not tuned to the same broadcast the rest of us are. He doesn't speak."

"Marta says he does."

"Marta is an angel of mercy. She hears thing us mortals are not privy to. He seems to have been voiding fairly regularly, for what that's worth."

Luz feels like she's holding a volcano in her hands, pent up, nearly senseless, ready to blow. Hot juices are flowing in Scipio, biles and resentments, violent gases. A rumbling under the skin. His hard, yellow lion's eyes scare her a little.

"I don't know what to do for him. Maybe Marta does."

"Wish somebody knew what to do for me," Wilson lets slip, bored, looking the other way. Stupid fuck, what I say that for?

He does. He does like me, maybe a little bit, maybe more. Qué lástima. Luz smiles, looks at him as kindly as she can.

"I'm a nurse," she says, "not a miracle worker."

Scipio opens his mouth and a moan of rage blisters out.

Scipio opens his mouth and a moan of rage blisters out.

Brujería. The girl was strange. Sick. Female problems. Woman things, mysteries. The older boy was strong but bad. A wild young bull. The girl was sick. The younger boy cried. When the second bullet went through the eye he exploded in tears, the bull quivering in the dirt and the boy puking sobs till Pedro took him away. The girl was strange. Hard to look at. Thin and breakable, a thing he didn't understand. What he could hold tight and shake in his strong hands he could know. The girl was strange, dark water. Bad blood. The bull had bad blood. El Toro. He was a bull. He was a bull with a lion's eyes. El Toro, his nombre de guerra. When the Machado people knew about him, when he was quemado, he died and became León. Ojos de León. The man from the country. We need a man from the country, they said. One who can kill. Ojos de León. Un desconocido en La Habana. A face nobody knows. For a killing. Execution. And his father. His father. It had an octagonal barrel. His father had used it against the Spanish in La Guerra and then against the yanquis. Execution. He would not know the man. Enemy. Killer. The man would not know him. Blind justice. Blind. It was noisy, una pistola vieja, an antique from La Guerra. Con cuidado, his father said when he was a boy. It makes a big hole. The man had a white skimmer on his head, a white jacket, white pants. The finger, the mulatto, was standing by the door of the café. Men in summer clothes sat outside drinking coffee. A touch to the nose. The finger. A pause behind the man in the skimmer and a touch to the nose. Enemy. Machado man. Desconocido. A touch to the nose and a man was killed. Execution. Ojos de León does one in La Habana. Someone from here does one in Camagüey. Blind justice. A handsome man, white teeth, in a white skimmer. It was noisy. Birds exploded, screeching, from the trees when he tested it. He was supposed to drop it. Walk away. A pause behind the man in the skimmer, coffee cup raised to his lips, skimmer tilting back. Ojos de León. Corazón de Toro. It had an octagonal barrel. It was noisy. Men in summer suits exploded from their chairs. What the pistol took flew across the plaza. He was supposed to drop it, walk away. He held the Spanish Star to his chest and ran, slipping, bad blood and teeth on the stones, men in summer suits screeching. He didn't know the man. Un desconocido. He ran, body of a bull, eyes of a lion. Ambrosio puked tears and the vaquero had to take him. A man from the country. El Toro. Blas in the monte with the barbudos and Ambrosio puking verses and the girl sick with a holy fever. Brujería. What he could hold tight and shake in his two strong hands he could kill. Execution. The girl was dark water, slipping through his thick fingers. Women's business. A curse. A curse. Blas in the monte, Ambrosio puking romance, the girl sick. The bull was strong but no good. No good. Let him fuck sometimes but nothing came. Nothing good. Execution. Brujería, a curse in the teeth of a handsome man drinking coffee. The Spanish Star burning in his hand, burning next to his heart, back to Camagüey. A man from the country. Men in summer suits everywhere. New Machados springing from the old. La política was a child puking tears. What he could hold tight and shake in his strong hands he could know. Family. Land. Enemies. It was noisy. The noise shocked him, the noise pounded apart the quiet of day. He was supposed to drop it. Walk. The Spanish Star burned against his chest and he ran, ran over a curse in a handsome man's teeth clattering on the stones of the plaza. Bad blood. Teeth.

The girl was strange.

Scipio opens his mouth and huffs for breath, face red, nostrils flaring like an angry bull.

TWENTY-TWO

"TAKE HOLD OF THE WHEEL," says Tío Felix, stepping back to let Marta slide in front of him. "Apúntalo a este channel marker acá," he says, pointing. "I be back before we get there."

Marta looks around at the people in the other boats moving past in both directions, trying to seem like she's done this a thousand times, practicing. It isn't as hard as driving a car. The rest of the world seems to be on vacation, seems not to care that men are rotting in prisons, that souls are burning in torment. The sun kicks off white hulls and blue vinyl sail covers, gulls swoop and splash, radios thump out disco hits. Three men in a small boat with a big motor wave as they pass and Marta waves back. The rods they carry are not as big as the ones rigged on the sides of Tío Felix's boat, there is no power winch, no deck space. She wonders what they do if they hook onto something really big. She can't imagine cutting loose once you were started into a fight. Her uncle returns, hitching up his pants, face glowing with sun and beer.

"I don't use the head so much," he winks. "Out on the water, when there is no womens on board—" He shrugs. "What harm is my little drop going to do? The ocean doesn't care."

She'd caught him in a good mood at the lonchería, a lazy Sunday afternoon when he could leave Gustavo on the register and take his boat out. She had never liked the boat when she was a little girl, the wind and the spray and the noise too overpowering, had never thought of it or needed it till now. Tío Felix props his depth-finder up on the instrument panel and squints close to the screen.

"Aquí está el fondo. Pero aquí"—he points—"aquí is just some fishes. Don't get fool."

"How deep is it here?"

"Quince pies."

"And where does it say that?"

He taps the screen. "Aquí. But I don't use this where I know the water."

"Y cómo sabes la profundidad sin esto?"

"You know the tide from a chart, from your memoria. If you know where you are and know the tide—"

"If you don't know where you are? Or if it's night?"

He indicates the instruments on the panel. "Todo esto. Pero antes, cuando era un joven marinero en los años de Machado, we didn't have none of this. In those days we use the sun, the star, los mapas—"

"Teach me how."

"Por qué?"

"You know why, Tío."

Tío Felix frowns and looks out over the bow. They are coming out of the channel into deep water.

"If this boat is going," he says finally, "I am going with it."

"If you got hurt, Tío—gracias a Dios no—pero la cosa podría ser peligroso. If you got hurt somebody else would need to know."

The first real wave smacks the hull and Tío Felix pushes the stick ahead to bring the bow down a bit.

"Como siempre me dices, Tío—anything can happen at sea."

A pair of little sporting boats are moving up ahead, rigged for marlin, a handful of pale tourists grinning back over their wake. A strong breeze is working up from the west, a Gulf breeze with a pleasant whiff of rot to it. Medium swells thump the boat almost broadside.

"Tío? Qué dices?"

Tío Felix takes the wheel from his niece.

He had never dreamed of going to sea.

"The ranch is too small for two sons," his father said. "And when brothers fight it is a sin against nature."

Felix was the little one, the fat one, the timid one.

Mi Pequeño, his mother called him.

El Gordito, his brother called him.

Mi Segundo, their father called him.

If Scipio climbed a tree that was forbidden, it was Felix who was discovered still stuck in its branches. When Scipio decided to be a pitcher, Felix was shanghaied to be his catcher, though he served more as a target than as a fellow player. When Scipio discovered girls, Felix was left tending the cattle alone, inventing excuses till his brother could sneak back on the job. And when Machado closed the University and Scipio came home to share in running the ranch, their father decided that Felix should go to sea.

"The soldiers in the army are all thieves," he said. "I won't have a son in the army."

"They're thieves in the navy too," said Scipio. "Floating thieves."

"You shut up," said their father. "The navy will make a man of him."

"The navy will make a thief of him."

"He'll go to sea. The ocean doesn't care about politics."

Their father had read books about young men who went to sea and had often said he wished he'd had the chance. If he hadn't had to beat the Spaniard off the island instead.

"The sea is a hard master," he told Felix. "We've spoiled you in this family, but in the navy they don't care who you are. They don't care and the ocean doesn't care."

"And the putas on Calle San Isidro don't care either," teased Scipio, "so watch yourself."

"He won't be in La Habana—"

"Padre, La Habana is where all the marineros are. We had to step over them sleeping on the street when I was at University—"

"Shut up, you."

"Sí, Padre. But it's true."

Felix had never dreamed of going to sea but was glad to be leaving home. Scipio would stay and mind the cattle and he would go to a place where nobody knew or cared who he was, where nobody knew his nicknames, nobody saw him as the small shadow of his older brother and if he bought a woman the entire city of Camagüey would not know it by the next morning.

The day he left, their father called them in to his study. He had two gifts, one for each son. To Scipio he gave his Spanish Star, the one he had used to beat the Spaniard from the island in '98. It was heavy, with an octagonal barrel, and he had always kept it in a case on the wall over his desk.

"This gun was used to make us a free people," he said.

"If we were a free people," said Scipio, "we wouldn't be kissing the ass of the yanquis." Scipio had been infected with politics at the University and spent his days in exile haranguing the cattle about the insidious bondage to the Colossus of the North and his nights plotting revolt with his friends in town. "If we were a free people we wouldn't be eating Machado's shit."

Their mother was not in the room, so their father didn't take offense at Scipio's language. It was the language their father used for the politicians in Camagüey, for the norteamericanos he dealt with in business.

"We needed the yanquis," he allowed. "Now we are stuck with them."

"Why did we need them? The Spanish would have left anyway."

"And the negros would have taken over and what would we have then? The negros and the guajiros. If the Maceo brothers had not been killed and the yanquis had not come—it would have been anarchy."

"The Maceo brothers are heroes."

"Yes, they are heroes. If they had lived they would have become tyrants."

"And so now Machado shits on our people—"

"You boys," their father said, meaning Scipio and his friends who had been turned out when the University was closed, "you boys call yourselves revolutionaries. You don't know. This, today, this is nothing. It's a game. When I was young, there were *men*—"

"Padre—"

"José Maceo. Calixto García. Antonio Maceo. Máximo Gómez. Giants."

"Padre, they've been sold out."

Their father shook his head the way he did when the unsurmountable barrier of age and wisdom separated them. "I'll give you this gun, niño, and maybe someday you'll learn what it means."

"Sí, Padre. Gracias."

Scipio took the gun and hefted it and then held it tight against his chest. When they were little boys he would climb on their father's chair while Felix had to stand watch, nearly peeing from nerves, and he would take the pistol out from its case.

"Someday he's going to give this to me," he would say.

"No he's not."

"He is. He killed the Spaniard with this pistol and if they try to come back I'll shoot them with it."

"He won't give it to you."

"You'll see Felix. You'll see."

Their father gave Felix a Bible to take with him to the navy.

Felix picked it up and looked inside but there was no inscription. It was a thick Bible with a leather cover, nothing special. Felix looked at the Bible, then at the pistol that Scipio cradled in his arms.

"It's a Bible," he said finally.

"In case you go to La Habana," said their father. "In the city you might need it. On the sea—the sea is not wicked. The sea is hard and dangerous and doesn't care who you are, like God. But not wicked."

"But the pistol—"

"They'll have guns in the navy," said Scipio, looking smug, sighting down the barrel of the Spanish Star.

"I've never read the Bible," said their father, "but your mother tells me it's a great comfort. Sailors read it when they're becalmed at sea."

"Sí, Padre."

"I have friends who have friends in the navy. They'll look out for you."

"Sí, Padre."

"There are no politics in the navy," said their father, eyeing Scipio to shut up before he could say anything. "Just the sea and hard work. It will make you a man."

"Sí, Padre," said Felix. "Gracias."

Because he could see that his segundo was disappointed with the gift, their father took him into Camagüey the next day and had a navy dress uniform tailored for him. When Felix stood by the train to say goodbye their father looked him up and down, proudly, the way he examined his prize bulls.

"You look like a seaman," he said.

The officer who received Felix into the Cuban Navy stared him up and down like a buyer at a cattle auction, then snorted.

"You look like a cook," he said.

Felix was sent to work on the patrol boats that were trying to stop the flow of weapons being smuggled down from the north. The base was at Bahía de Sueños, a cluster of rickety wooden barracks with hammered-tin roofs next to a town full of starving people. It wasn't a town so much as a nightmare with a road through it. It was a place where the little children and the dogs and the chickens all looked alike, scrawny and tough, sharing their lice and fighting over what few scraps of food made it to the heap behind the sailors' mess. A few of the adults made charcoal or tried to fish, but most sat all day in front of their bohíos slowly getting drunk on fermented guarapo or on the acid home brew they made from whatever fruit they could find that the rats and the pigs didn't get to first. The marineros called them las pulgas after the fleas that hopped in the little children's hair, and El Capitán gave orders to shoot any of them who came near the boats. There was a rumor that the year before a marinero had wandered too close to the bohíos and was bitten either by a dog or a small child and had died in the navy hospital in Guantánamo. At night sometimes the marineros would go out with flashlights and pistols and shoot at fruit rats in the trees for fun.

The day that Felix arrived he and the three others who were new were ordered out on a patrol boat with all their gear. El Capitán came out with them that day and they anchored on the lee side of a key that the marineros said was ruled by wild goats. El Capitán was short and thick and powerful-looking, his head shaved bald and tanned from the sun, with a smile that made Felix want to pee in his pants. Felix and the other new ones stood at attention in front of the marineros while the mate dumped the contents of their sea bags onto the deck. The mate was tall and had a thin, thin mustache at the edge of his upper lip, looking like Gilbert Roland in the yanqui motion pictures. He nudged the contents of the bags around with his foot, kicking anything valuable or of interest over closer to El Capitán. El Capitán would grunt at the things he was interested in and if he nodded the mate would put them into a mail sack. When the mate picked up Felix's Bible El Capitán took it from him.

"De quién es esto?"

"Es mío," Felix managed to say.

El Capitán walked up and put his face so close to Felix's he thought their noses would touch. "*I* am God here," he said, and threw the Bible overboard. He looked Felix up and down, poked him in his soft middle. "Usted es el cocinero?"

"Si Capitán. A sus órdenes."

"Sabe cocinar?"

Felix had never done more than boil water in his life. He had seen the women who worked for his mother cook but had no memory of how they went about it except that it involved pots and flame. "No Capitán."

"You'll have to learn then. I don't want this one on a boat," said El Capitán to the mate, "unless we need shark bait."

The mate picked up the dress uniform Felix had gotten in Camagüey. "Who brought the sailor suit?"

The marineros laughed. Felix had to swallow several times before he could answer. El Capitán's face had not moved from his.

"Otra vez el cocinero," said El Capitán. He snapped his fingers and the mate handed him the uniform. He held it in front of his body, squinting to size it. As short and round as Felix was, El Capitán was shorter and rounder. He threw it back at Felix in disgust.

"I've only known you for two minutes," he said, "and already I'm sick of you."

The mate threw the rest of the belongings El Capitán didn't want overboard then and Felix and the other new ones scrubbed the deck all afternoon while the marineros took naps and the mate and El Capitán fished for grouper.

Felix became the cook, working in a tiny hotbox of a kitchen attached to the mess, rising hours before anyone else to try his cooking out on himself before he faced the wrath of the marineros. The cook who'd been there before, a chino with years in the navy, had been skillful and popular with the men till everyone got sick one day, vomiting and shitting at the same time, an hour after dinner. The chino blamed it on bad pork he'd been sent but El Capitán, who never trusted chinos, said the man had poisoned them on purpose and sent him off to Guantánamo for discipline.

Felix had an assistant, an Indian boy the marineros called Gerónimo after a character in the yanqui motion pictures. Gerónimo was small and skinny and mostly silent, and the marineros spent long, bored evenings speculating about him as he dished their food.

"No puede ser cubano," was the opinion of Diego from Matanzas. "El Español killed off all the indios here in the first days. He must be a Mexican."

"Es demasiado pequeño para ser mexicano," said Alcides from Cienfuegos. "He looks more like los indios de Guatemala. They're to the Mexicans what the negros are to us."

Gerónimo would flip Felix's slop onto their plates dispassionately, as if he didn't understand a word of what they were saying.

"El Español would hunt them like wild pigs," said Diego. "He'd catch them and put them on a spit and turn them over a fire till they burned to death. He couldn't get the indio to work, so he hunted them for sport. When he killed them all he had to bring in the negros para el azúcar."

"Los negros para el azúcar y los chinos para el ferrocarril," said Alcides.

"I think some of that indio on a spit got into this stew," said Enrique from Trinidad. "Felix, what did you put in this shit?"

Felix would shrug and give the answer he gave every time the men complained and El Capitán was not near. "No soy cocinero," he would say. "Soy ranchero."

He hoped they would hear this and nickname him El Ranchero or El Vaquero, but mostly they just called him Felix you poisoning-son-of-a-whore or Felix you miserable-excuse-for-a-cook or Felix you less-than-a-chino piece of worthless shit.

Felix tried his best to learn how to cook and yearned to go on the patrol boats if only to get out of the stinking oven of a kitchen. As hot and overworked as he was, he didn't call the indio boy Hatuey or Cacique or any of the other names the marineros had for him, not even Gerónimo, which he answered to though it wasn't his name. He didn't make the boy do extra work or blame him when the cooking failed and soon they were friends, or at least co-workers who didn't hate each other.

The boy told Felix how a patrol boat had stopped his family at the mouth of a river near Baracoa when they were turtling and asked how old he was and when he didn't know exactly they took him aboard and told his parents he was in the navy now and could get out in a few years if he followed orders and didn't try to run away. He had never been away from his family, not even for a night, but the marineros took him away to where nobody he knew could find him. He knew how to make soups and stews and showed Felix what to do with the turtles and iguanas that he'd bring in from the walks he snuck off on early in the mornings. The only thing he liked about the navy, he said, was the rice they got to cook for the marineros, something he'd heard about but had never eaten before.

The marineros were unhappy about other things besides the food and having to live in Bahía de Sueños. At least once a week they'd go out hunting for gunrunners, Felix packing enough food for each of the two boats for three or four days, but they never caught anyone. In fact, whenever they got close, El Capitán would order them to start shooting before they could even see the smugglers or call for them to surrender over his bullhorn and the smugglers would get away. A few times they had the enemy bottled up in the mangroves, certain that there was no way out, and then El Capitán and the mate would take the skiff in to negotiate surrender terms. El Capitán and the mate always came out unhurt but nobody ever surrendered and the marineros would be told it was just a group of honest fishermen, hiding because there were some capitánes in the navy who would stop them and steal their catch. El Capitán and the mate spent more and more time away from the base and whenever they came back they would have cases of beer for their personal enjoyment shipped in a truck, along with blocks of ice. Felix's most important job was to keep this ice from melting. In his nightmares it wasted away into puddles in moments, and El Capitán would come for him knee deep in the meltwater, brown bottles of warm beer bobbing in his wake. Felix would bolt upright, covered in sweat.

"Qué pasó?" Gerónimo's soft voice would come from the bunk above him.

"The ice is melting," he would say, a cold finger of dread creeping into his heart. He would put his shoes on and flap through the clouds of nightbugs down to the little icehouse he and Gerónimo had built to keep the beer in. The ice was always melting, the way ice did in the tropics when there was no refrigeration, and once he discovered marks left from the marineros or las pulgas from town trying to pry in and steal El Capitán's beer. As the ice melted away so did Felix, and despite handling food all day he continued to lose weight from worry. Even when the ice was fresh and there was plenty of it El Capitán always pressed his beer bottle to his temple and then cursed and said it wasn't cold enough, the son-of-a-whore cook couldn't even bring a beer from the icehouse without ruining it. The sight of El Capitán or the mate strolling past with a cold beer was always good for mutinous speculation among the marineros.

"If we're going to be pirates," said Ramón from Santiago de Cuba, "we should at least have a share in the treasure."

"I wonder how much El Capitán takes from the contrabandistas."

"Enough to buy a lot of beer."

"If we're not going to catch them, why doesn't he let us just stay in bed?"

"If we didn't almost catch them sometimes they wouldn't bother to pay him."

"I hope that one of them brings in the gun they use to shoot Machado," said Diego.

"I hope one of them brings in the gun they use to shoot El Capitán."

"At least when it was rum we'd catch them sometimes. Cuando tenían la Ley Seca en los Estados Unidos. We'd catch them and El Capitán would take half of their rum and let us drink some of it."

"It's all the fucking yanquis' fault. This job was fun when they had that law. It was nice with us drinking and them going dry."

"The pirates would share everything," said Ramón. "Gold, rum, women. They decided before each raid who would get what share, and if a man was injured there was a fixed rate of compensation. So much for a hand cut off, so much for an arm, so much if you lost an eye."

"How much if you lost your pinga?"

The marineros laughed and touched their pingas under the table.

"Then you'd be un pirata rico for the rest of your days."

"Somebody lost their pinga in this soup. Felix, you poisoning hijo de puta, what is this shit? Did you stick that Indio's pinga in this soup?"

"He stuck the Indio's pinga somewhere, but it wasn't in the soup."

"Qué honor," said Diego. "To serve in Machado's navy for Capitán Cerveza. Qué honor, qué oportunidad para servir a mi patria. To make sure the contrabandistas arrive safely but with empty pockets."

"At least we'll never die at sea," said Luís from Las Tunas.

"Instead we'll catch a disease from the pulgas—"

"Or choke on this food from this less-than-a-chino piece of shit. I wish El Capitán had kept the Bible and thrown *him* overboard."

"Los piratas," said Ramón from Santiago de Cuba, "ate like kings."

Because their father had friends who had friends in the navy, Felix was granted a leave of one week in the middle of the summer.

El Capitán brought him in for a face-to-face before he was allowed to go.

"Piensas que eres muy inteligente, ay, chico?"

"No, Capitán."

"You think you're so smart your capitán doesn't know what you're up to. What you're planning."

"No tengo planes, Capitán."

"You think you can escape me, that you can get a transfer away from me. No hay esperanza, chico. What's mine is mine."

"Sí, Capitán."

El Capitán let Felix go finally, after promising he would bring back a case of beer or two to prove his good intentions. Gerónimo was left in charge of the mess.

On the train to Camagüey, Felix changed into the dress uniform their father had bought him, though now it was much too large for him in the chest and seat. Scipio was waiting for him at the station.

"Qué ladrón tan guapo," said Scipio, hardly smiling. "What a handsome, well-dressed thief I have for a brother."

Scipio took him to a café where old men argued about the past and sat him in the darkest corner.

"The uniform has to go," he said.

"Y por qué?"

"Have you been underwater all this time? Don't you know what's happening?"

"Contrabandistas are trying to bring guns to the bandits and terrorists," said Felix, quoting El Capitán. "I am serving in the front lines of the nation."

"Los soldados y los marineros de Machado," hissed Scipio, "the loyal dogs of oppression, are helping their master bleed our country dry. That uniform could get you shot in this city."

"Por quién?"

"Certain people."

"Do you know these certain people?"

Scipio looked tired and older. He looked around the room at the old men taking their coffee, reading their papers, arguing yesterday's politics.

"Men are killed every day," he said, something almost like sadness in his voice. "Sitting at a place like this, living their lives, thinking their thoughts. Then somebody comes up behind them and *bang!*" Scipio slapped his hand down on the table, then sat back. "The uniform has to go."

Felix was frightened the way he was always frightened when his brother went somewhere ahead of him, somewhere forbidden and dangerous.

"Have you done things for these certain people? Are you still with the students? The ABC?"

Scipio gave him an exasperated look. "Machado's porristas are everywhere. Men of action prefer not to talk." He got up to leave. "Our father is waiting to see you."

"I think they've made a man of you," said their father when he saw Felix, though there was a tone of doubt in his voice. "You've lost your baby fat."

"Sí, Padre."

"Is the work hard?"

"Sí, Padre."

"And is it dangerous?"

"A veces, Padre," said Felix, thinking of the times when the marineros would throw their tins at him and Gerónimo, of the time when Leopoldo from San Cristóbal tried to hang him from a tree outside the mess on a night the marineros had gotten drunk on aguardiente.

Their father nodded solemnly. "And do you still have the Bible I gave you?"

Felix tried to sigh and seem scarred by action, the way Scipio had in the café. "It was lost at sea," he said.

Their father frowned and nodded and clapped him on the shoulders. "I understand. And was I right about the sea?"

"Sí, Padre. Es un maestro duro. May I take my uniform off now?"

In his week at home Felix spent as much time as possible watching the women who cooked for his mother, asking a few shy questions and gaining weight rapidly as they made him dish after dish. When it was time to go back to Bahía de Sueños his dress uniform fit perfectly again. He ran off the train at Nuevitas to buy a case of beer.

Gerónimo was in the kitchen when Felix returned, sweating, his face bruised and swollen on one side. He was cutting a chicken up and tossing it into a stew.

"Qué pasó, hombre?"

Gerónimo wouldn't answer, wouldn't look at Felix. He tore the old hen apart with his hands, cracking the bones, twisting the flesh away and flipping hunks of it into the big iron pot that could cook for two dozen.

"Did you fight with somebody?"

Gerónimo continued to ignore him. Felix crossed to the barracks. Only Teodoro, the big machine-gunner from Santa Clara, was in, lying on his bed with a wet towel over his forehead.

"Qué pasó con Gerónimo?"

Teodoro moved the towel aside and lifted one red-rimmed eyelid. "It's you. If you were smart you wouldn't have come back."

"Qué pasó?"

"El Capitán has declared war. Somebody stole his beer. He blamed it on the Indio."

"Who took it?"

"Who do you think? Everybody. But he decided the Indio stole it and sold it in town and he took him in front of everybody and taught him a lesson."

"And nobody said anything?"

"You mean confess? Estás loco? He had his pistol out and was threatening to shoot us all. He's been out of his mind since the attack."

"Qué ataque?"

"The other day. Coño, you're lucky you haven't been around. We had one of their boats trapped, corked up in a little inlet, the usual thing. El Capitán and the mate start rowing in to discuss terms—you know, that mierda—but this time they get halfway to shore and whoever is behind the trees lets loose with a burst."

"Tiraron al Capitán?"

"Just a warning. At that range they could have shot them to pieces. Hombre, nunca he visto al maestre remando tan rápido! He just about lifted that boat out of the water, he was rowing so fast. Then the contrabandistas blew out of the inlet and nearly swamped them—qué lástima que no lo hicieron."

"I thought El Capitán had a deal with them."

"So did he. By the time El Capitán got back on board they were gone and he was screaming why didn't we open up on them, even though his last order was to hold our fire and wait. He says tomorrow we go out for blood. He's got them all down at the boats getting them ready."

"Y por qué no está con ellos?"

"Hombre, I passed out and banged my head on the deck. Too much beer last night."

Teodoro winked at him and put the towel back over his face.

In the kitchen Gerónimo was still working on the stew. A dozen yellow-brown frogs were laid out on the cutting block, their pale bellies pointed up at the ceiling. Gerónimo took each one and pressed a sticky, clear fluid out of a sac beneath each cheek, dripping it into the stew. He gave Felix a hard look as he shook one of the little bellies over the pot.

"Para el sabor," he explained.

"And what does it taste like?" Felix asked.

"Sweet," said Gerónimo. "Como la venganza."

Felix let Gerónimo finish the guisado while he set about making some loaves of bread and frying a mess of plátanos. The men came back surly and sunburned, weary after a full day of El Capitán's personal supervision. They were hungry and paid no attention to Felix or Gerónimo as they ladled the food out. Gerónimo didn't eat at all and Felix decided he only felt like a little bread. The mate and the captain didn't show up at mess and when Felix went to their quarters to see if he could bring them something they weren't in.

"El guisado era muy dulce," said Teodoro, patting his belly as he left the mess. "Just what I needed to feel better."

It hit them about four in the morning. Felix woke to the sound of retching, the barracks air thick with sulfur. The marineros collided in the dark, staggering out to the slit trenches or just crawling as far as the front steps. Somebody started weeping, and Felix could make out Orlando the mechanic from Placetas cursing rhythmically on the floor, doubled over with cramps.

It was not long after that the lights snapped on and Felix and Gerónimo were yanked out of bed to face El Capitán and the mate. Most of the marineros were still outside, though a few stood pale and wobbly around the bunk. Felix heard Teodoro moaning from his bed in the background, claiming that he was going to die.

"Qué haces con las comidas?" hissed the mate.

"Nada de particular," answered Felix. "Lo hice como siempre."

"And him," said El Capitán, stepping up to stare Gerónimo in the eyes. "What did he do?"

"He cut the vegetables. He cut the meat. He cleaned up. Como siempre."

"You'll pay for this, you know," said El Capitán to Felix, without taking his eyes off Gerónimo.

"Maybe it was some bad pork, Capitán. I should pay more attention when it comes in."

"I'll see you at the boats in an hour," said El Capitán, then pushed Gerónimo to the floor and stomped out. The mate gave Felix a withering look, then went about checking which of the marineros would be well enough for duty.

Felix was thrilled to finally be out on the water. There were only enough marineros standing to crew one of the patrol boats, and they were yellowish and unsteady, sitting in the stern desperately gripping onto ropes and cleats and occasionally heaving into the wake. The sun rose golden directly behind them as the boat chugged along the coast, a string of green keys off to their right. Wood ibis and white herons flapped up from the shore as the boat interrupted their feeding. A flock of blue-green parrots wheeled overhead, then settled in the treetops to the left. The mate was at the wheel, El Capitán watching over his shoulder, grim. Felix and Gerónimo had been ordered to sit out on the bow, unarmed, their legs dangling down into the spray. Felix had hitched a line over his hand like he did riding temperamental horses on his father's ranch, concentrating on matching the rhythm of the bow with his body and ignoring the spray slapping his face. Gerónimo held on tight with both hands, the bruise on his cheek livid with exertion. Behind them Teodoro was slumped at the forward machine gun, still predicting that his intestines were going to explode.

There wasn't a chase. Shortly after noon El Capitán nodded and the mate turned the boat left into a muddy, winding channel that cut into a thick mangrove forest. On the port side Felix could see turtles sunning themselves on the twisted roots, now and then a lizard darting across the branches. Felix realized that he and Gerónimo were up front in order to draw fire, and immediately the branches were full of snipers, each bend in the channel held an ambush. He calculated how he could flatten and roll back toward the little bridge, hoping that El Capitán would be too involved in fighting to shoot him with his pistol as he crawled past to shelter. The marineros were taking their positions now, faces pinched with concentration, sensing that this time El Capitán was in it for real.

A half mile in the water turned a deeper, redder color and the mate cut the engine.

"Get in," El Capitán called to Felix and Gerónimo.

Felix looked back to see if he had heard correctly. El Capitán had his pistol out.

"Get in the water," he said.

Felix crossed himself and slid off into the tepid, murky water beside Gerónimo. Gerónimo paddled over to the bank, stripped his shirt off and began to cover his face and neck with muck. The mate came forward and looked down at them.

"You two swim ahead. No noise, and when you can touch bottom stand up until we catch up with you."

Felix felt himself pee in the water, the certainty that they were going to be executed and left floating in the channel draining from his body. He began the swim forward against the weak current. Gerónimo snaked into the water and was soon a couple body lengths ahead of him.

Felix swam desperately, trying to keep his face up, the water thick and reddish-brown like the guisado Gerónimo had concocted, full of slithery tidbits and sudden cold spots. When he tired he made his way toward the bank till his feet found purchase on the slimy tangle below. He would bounce on his toes till the patrol boat slid into view behind, the marineros taking turns on long poles to keep it away from the bank and push it forward. El Capitán would see him then and wave his pistol and Felix would struggle back into the middle, trying to swim out of their sight again.

Gerónimo swam easily, steadily, head caked with mud, eyes and nose floating just over the waterline like a caimán stalking a marsh bird. A tiny breeze continued to ripple the surface and Felix saw a snake wriggling straight at him, a snake with a big wedge of a head and a smooth, sambalike rhythm that erased the ripple from the water in its wake. Before he could decide to scream, splash to the bank or backpaddle, the snake dove straight under, disappearing into the red stew. Felix realized his mouth was wide open with terror as he took in a brackish mouthful, then went under, hugging his knees and elbows into his chest and bracing for whatever the snake was going to do. He hit bottom, feeling his ankle slip in between some ropy tree roots, then pushed off for the surface. But the bottom wouldn't let him go and he had to squat back down to it, scrabbling with his fingers at the awful muck till he felt free, and then bursting up gasping to stare into the eyes of Gerónimo, who had come back to make sure he was okay. The boy looked into his eyes, then turned effortlessly and headed back up the channel.

The attack came when the breeze had died to nothing. Felix and Gerónimo had come to a spot where the channel narrowed rapidly and the bottom came up to where they stood waist deep. Gerónimo scooped up more muck, slathering it on his chest and back, as they waited for the boat to come around the last bend. Felix tried to swat the mosquitos that had begun to gather as quietly as possible, aware that El Capitán must know that someone was back in the channel if he had bothered going hunting with a sick crew. The mosquitos were small and nearly silent and agitated, zipping randomly in and out at first, then there were more lighting boldly from all directions till Felix had to sit down into the putrid water and try to splash them away from his face and then as the patrol boat eased around into view the air was filled with them, he was breathing them, they were in his eyes and his mouth and biting his skull through his wet hair and he began to bob under to try to lose them but each time he came up there were more till all he could think of was getting back to the boat and wrapping himself in something, crawling inside something where they couldn't get at him and he was thrashing across to the bow, hung up now on a shelf of mangrove roots, but climbing up was worse, they were all over his back his neck the small behind his knee biting him through his wet clothes flying down his nose and throat as he gasped, panicked again, clawing his way up onto the foredeck and there were the marineros and the mate and El Capitán all swatting and twitching in a Saint Vitus dance of revulsion, bodies black with mosquitos, blood-starved swarming mosquitos, the men too overcome to curse or cry out, Ramón pouring a can of gasoline over his own head to keep the mosquitos off then screaming as it got in his eyes, Teodoro rolling himself up in a piece of canvas and swatting underneath it while Alcides peeled his sweat-soaked shirt off and hopped in a small circle flagellating his body with it, small clouds of mosquitos shifting with each wet flap. Felix tucked himself in a ball and rolled over and over on the deck, running his palms over every bit of exposed skin as if washing himself with freezing water, all too frenzied in their slapping and rolling and shuddering to notice until the machine gun burst into life.

It was Gerónimo, caked with mud, solid as a statue behind the gun Teodoro had deserted, blasting into the trees to the right, branches snapping, bark flying and then return fire from the trees, splinters exploding off the side of the bridge, the marineros throwing themselves flat onto the deck as the mosquitos continued to drain them through it all, Gerónimo locked onto the gun roaring out into the mangroves and Felix seeing men running back through the trees, turning to fire as the engine jolted to life, El Capitán gunning it into reverse, churning bottom till the boat yanked free and began to plow back out of the channel. The return fire stopped but Gerónimo continued spraying the machine gun, yanking it first one way, then the other till the mate realized he was trying to turn the gun around on them and ordered everybody to keep down while El Capitán steered them expertly back through the twists and overhangs. The machine gun was bolted so that Gerónimo couldn't quite get it around to play on the bridge and finally it jammed and he just sat and wept, tears channeling through the mud on his cheeks.

El Capitán turned the boat around at the mouth of the channel and ran it out a little way before he had the anchors thrown out. A late-afternoon breeze had picked up and the mosquitos decided to stay ashore. All the men but Gerónimo were red and puffy with bites, El Capitán's face like an angry boil as he poured half a bottle of rum on his skin then drank the rest, cursing the marineros, the contrabandistas, the shit-eating políticos in La Habana, the army, the navy, the pendejo God who invented mosquitos but especially Felix and el indio loco, who had stolen his beer, poisoned his crew, tried to sink his boat and lead him into slaughter. When he was finished with the rum he took out his pistol again and had Alcides and the mate lower the skiff. He ordered Felix and Gerónimo into it.

"Back into the channel," he said. "I know this coño hit somebody. Come back with bodies or don't come back."

The channel was easy with the skiff. The breeze kept up and the mosquitos seemed to be done feeding by the time they got in deep. Felix rowed and Gerónimo sat in the bow staring glumly ahead into the trees. Little crabs were scooting around the mangrove roots now, the sun slanting low through the branches. Felix rowed hard and fast, barely able to see through his swollen eyelids, the work helping take his mind from the sickening crawl of his skin as the insect bites began to percolate. He wanted to roll in sandpaper, to scald his body in boiling water. Gerónimo touched his shoulder and they drifted silently toward the final bend, listening. Listening. Parrots rustled and squawked to each other as they settled in for the evening. An owl was waking up, its cry sad, penetrating. Frogs set up a throbbing wall of sound for the birds to call above, and the mangrove branches creaked in the breeze. When Gerónimo was satisfied that the contrabandistas hadn't come back he nodded and Felix rowed them around the bend.

"No vuelves, hombre?" asked Felix.

Gerónimo shook his head. He was still half covered in dried mud, skinny, forlorn-looking.

"Voy a buscar a mi familia," he said, waved, and slipped into the mangroves as if he knew where he was going.

"El mayor problema," says Felix as he runs his boat along the coast, cutting the waves on a right angle, "is that men cannot breathe water. If this were not true, la cosa sería fácil."

"People can swim," says Marta. She is noting landmarks on the coast, trying to imagine what will be visible and well lit at night.

"People can swim as fish can walk. You catch barracuda, he can live on deck all day you don't hit him to death. But he can't sur*vive*. The ocean"—he indicates the water around them—"the ocean doesn't care. The ocean es un gran guisado, a big stew, and everything that floats in it es solamente para sabor. It lives, it dies, cuál es la diferencia?"

"Where we're going is not so far."

"The ocean can kill you in three feet of water. The sun can be shining and the water is blue and the whales and the delfines y todos los otros peces can be happy, going on with their business, you know? But in the middle of all that if some little thing is wrong there you are in the ocean with them, and if you can't breathe water, chica, estás perdida."

"So you'll be our captain. And on the water you'll give the orders."

"Capitán." Tío Felix gives his niece a sad smile. "The ocean eats capitánes for breakfast."

During Batista, the second time, Felix caught big fish for yanquis and smuggled in guns for the 26 de Julio through the Jardines de

la Reina islands. The yanquis called him Capitán or Cap or sometimes just Pedro if they were very drunk or very rich or both. The
precaristas who were his contacts to the 26 de Julio called him Viejo,
though he was only just forty. He had a big Bertram Hull with twin
Merc 150's and all the rigging the yanquis liked for fishing and
drinking. The section of the hold where he kept the ice for drinks
and the catch was built up and hollow underneath. He would hide
the guns and other supplies that were left at the drop-offs in the
Jardines de la Reina and ferry them to a spot just down the coast
from Manzanillo. Things were going to change on the island and
he wasn't going to be caught on the wrong side twice.

It was probably Nidia at the El Ritz who recruited Felix, though
he liked to think he'd made the decision on his own. Nidia ran the
bar at night, strong and big-shouldered with dyed-blond hair and
the nalgas of a rhumba queen. Any man who worked on boats along
that section of coast came into the El Ritz sooner or later, ordering
drinks, then standing up on the rail for a better view as Nidia swung
her wide hips away from them. The ones who voiced their compli-
ments were pinned into silence by Nidia's icepick stare.

"She could cut your throat," the regulars said, "then ask the
man at the next stool what he was drinking."

The story was that Nidia's man had been killed by the tigres,
doused with gasoline and burned to death after organizing a cutters'
strike during the zafra. The story was that Nidia didn't cry at the
funeral, that she disappeared a day later and before she turned up
again two of the four men who'd done the killing were found hacked
to death with a machete and the other two had fled to the Dominican
to work for the Caudillo. The regulars who drank at the El Ritz
considered Nidia's strong arms, her flat, impassive face, and shuddered to think of what would happen to a man who betrayed such
a woman. They watched her rhumba-queen hips, watched the sweat
run down between her mammoth breasts, watched the round, beautiful nalgas working under her tight skirt and thrilled to the fantasy
of fucking her.

Felix liked to watch Nidia work the bar. There was nothing
random in her movement, refueling the steady drinkers, ignoring
the stiffs and sponges till there was money on the pine, watering the
nasty drunks so they never got nastier, keeping a dozen tabs in her
head as she worked to the rhythm of the jukebox mambo, sliding

big and graceful through the smoke and the heat and the noise. Felix liked her because she looked you square in the eye like a man but had a voice like honey, because she could break a coconut in two clean halves with one chop and defuse an argument with a sweep of her bar rag. He liked her because she had a tattoo on the inside of her arm and a bracelet of three bleached seashells on her wrist and because sometimes he could make her smile, a wide, dimpled flashing smile that showed a pair of gold teeth, that made him think of how she must have been before her man was killed. A smile that made him jealous.

On nights when the thought of sleeping alone again was too depressing Felix would stay in the El Ritz, sitting at the corner of the bar drinking black rum till morning, smiling at the joking stories the pescadores and dockworkers and patrulleros told about him, the worst charter fisherman on the coast, nodding in agreement with anyone who had a passionate political point to make or a sad tale of betrayal or a boozy confession of hopelessness. Often at dawn he would be the only one left, and Nidia would talk with him as she cleared the tables and he helped her stack the chairs.

"They say you were in the navy," she said one morning.

"Es verdad. I was a cook."

"But you went on patrols."

"A few times."

She took this in, rolling something over in her mind. "Do you ever go out on your boat alone?"

"A veces. But only when the weather is good. I'm still a better cook than a marinero."

"Do they ever stop you? Las patrullas?"

"No. They recognize me by now. They bring the new fish on deck and point to me and say, 'There goes Felix de la Pena, the worst charter captain on the coast. Steer clear or he's likely to run you over.' "

Nidia smiled then and Felix felt the same glow he got from the first big gulp of rum he took every night.

"If you were really so bad," she said, "you wouldn't have such a beautiful boat."

"I have this boat because if I didn't my brother would have to take me in as a partner in the cattle business. I'm even worse at cows than I am as a marinero."

"I've seen some of the fish you bring in. The big ones you hang on the scale for the yanquis to stand next to and have their photograph taken."

Felix felt himself flush. It was true, he wasn't bad at the fishing, just lazy and not interested in the business part.

"Fish are stupid creatures," he said. "Even more stupid than patrulleros. The yanquis talk about how crafty the fish are to flatter themselves, but if fish were smart there wouldn't be so many on the walls in here."

There were dozens of trophy fish mounted on the walls at the El Ritz, marlin and yellowfin and tarpon and swordfish and wahoo and a huge green sea turtle suspended over the bar by wires, swinging gently in the breeze of the ceiling fans, seeming to float above the patrons with a disapproving frown lacquered on its face.

On the mornings Felix stayed Nidia would signal that she was leaving by turning off the fans and opening the front door to the hot, white morning light. Then Felix would lose his nerve, again, swallowing whatever invitation he'd rehearsed in his mind all night and saying a simple good morning, sleep well, to Nidia as he stepped by her, not quite touching, then watch her climb the outside stairs to her tiny apartment over the bar. He would wait till she was out of sight, then roll toward the dock, ground heaving under his legs like a gentle sea, till he reached the *Vaquero*. He always slept on the boat mornings after the long nights, the gull cries and mooring sounds and pescaderos' voices comforting at the edge of his rum-thick dreams, the life in the little harbor easing the sting of his loneliness.

Sometimes Nidia was in his dreams, rolling under him warm and firm, Felix lost in the pillows of her breasts and thighs and buttocks, her strong arms holding him tight. She was a floating island in the dream, a warm, safe place to be. He'd wake in the afternoon with the sun shining on deck and drink a cold beer to clear his mouth, then pee into the oily harbor and feel enormously grateful that he wasn't living on a ranch.

"When you were in the navy," Nidia asked him another time, another early morning, "was there fighting?"

"Un poco."

"And you were in it?"

"It was during Machado. We were supposed to chase after contrabandistas."

"You fought for Machado." Nidia held her eyes down, fishing with her words, wiping the bar counter.

"I was in the navy. I cooked for the marineros." Felix shrugged. "En aquellos tiempos no me interesaba la política."

"Y ahora?"

"Con Batista?" Felix sighed. Complaining about politics because they were bad was like complaining about the sea because it was wet. "The first time he was a disappointment. This time he's a disease."

"Un asesino. Un monstruo." Nidia threw the rag into the bucket at her feet. "Something has to be done."

"Como siempre."

"The guerrillas are doing something."

Scipio was always going on about the guerrillas.

"Punks," he would say. "Schoolboys. This," he would say, jerking his chin up in the air to signify the distant Sierra Maestra, "this is nothing. We were serious. We had *men*. Giants."

Felix would never point out how many of the giants were sucking up to Batista now, how many were gangsters or had sold themselves to the yanquis. He would never point out that Scipio's son Blas had been on a list when the University was closed and was now in the monte with the guerrillas. It was no use pointing things out to Scipio, loud and bullish in his opinions, pacing the room and poking the air with a thick cigar to drive home his point.

"The ones who aren't killed will turn into bandits," he would say. "You can't make a revolution with guajiros, with precaristas. Those days are over."

Felix shook his head and looked to Nidia apologetically. "I'm too old now to be running with guerrillas in the monte."

Nidia poured la última, the last little stiff one she gave to Felix in the mornings, and put the bottle away.

"There are other ways to fight against him," she said. "We have to rise up together. Si no luchamos juntos, vamos a ser barridos hacia el basurero de la historia."

Felix tossed la última down, mild and sweet on top of all the others he had drunk that night.

"Tienes razón," he said. "But right now I'm too tired to do anything but sleep."

He wondered who Nidia had been listening to. El basurero de la historia. It was not the way Nidia spoke. When he was back on the *Vaquero* staring out over the harbor he tried to imagine what it might look like. The dustbin of history.

It was a comfortable place to be, he thought, a place with no ambition or fighting or famous men, a place where the sea was always gentle. The beer was not as cold as the yanquis liked it, but it was cold enough, and the food was simple but well cooked. People slept when they felt like it and felt like it often. There were no mosquitos. On reflection it seemed a good place for a man like him. The sea didn't care about history, and the sleek dolphins that leapt in the wake of his boat and the seabirds that floated lazily overhead and the white sun that burned away the boozy chill of morning, none of them cared about history and had been leaping and floating and burning long before history had been invented. If only he could have a woman like Nidia to live there with him he wouldn't care either. But he knew it was more likely she would pull him struggling into her world than that he would persuade her to slide into his.

Nidia kept at him. She was right, of course, something had to be done and people had to rise up together. He began to believe the 26th of July was serious, more serious than all the other groups and rumors of groups that had come before. Would a woman like Nidia be involved if it wasn't serious?

It would be like a sudden storm, he thought, the kind that left fish surprised and gasping on the beach, the kind that lifted small boats into treetops. To miss such a thing would be shameful, and he thought of Scipio's dumb surprise to learn that his little brother, the segundo, the gordito good for nothing except failing at the sport-fishing business little brother was one of the secret ones who sparked the fire of revolution. Let Scipio be swept into the dustbin of history, Felix thought, let envy chew his stomach as he stood knee deep in cow shit.

There would be boxes left buried in certain places, Nidia told him. He would be informed of the locations and he would dig them up and take them in his boat to places on the coast of the Oriente and hide them there. There would be signs to follow.

"How can I fight the tide of history?" said Felix one morning. "I'll do it."

"We'll win this time," said Nidia. She seemed to be glowing from within and Felix ached to touch her.

"We've won before."

"You'll see," she said. "You'll be a part of it."

The game started.

"Sabes dónde está Boca de Tiburón?" Nidia would say to Felix under the din of the El Ritz on a busy night, setting down his drink and smiling her dimpled smile.

"I know how to find it," he would say.

"They tell me the fishing is very good near there."

"I'll have to try it."

There were plenty of times when they were alone when she could have told him the pickup spots, but she was in love with the drama of the game or thought it was part of seducing Felix to join.

Felix didn't need to seduce Pedrito to come along. Pedrito slept in a crate that a refrigerator had been shipped in, a crate with a rusted scrap of tin for a roof that sat at the edge of the dump behind the cannery. Pedrito was fifteen but looked nine, undersized and filthy in tire-rubber sandals a T-shirt and shorts made from a sugar sack. Felix took Pedrito out to cut bait and scoop chum and untangle lines when he had a charter and sometimes let him come along when he went out on his own, the boy sleeping in the sun on the deck as they drifted for bass, a life vest for a pillow. Felix never heard him speak. Felix would begin to ready the *Vaquero* for a trip and Pedrito would suddenly appear and sit on a piling, watching silently till Felix motioned him to come along. He didn't smile or seem thankful but did everything Felix needed before he even thought of it and when Felix paid him at the end of a charter he accepted the money without looking in his hand to count it. It was like having a very useful cat on board.

There were little inlets on the coast or in the keys where a small boat could hide, Boca de Tiburón or Fuente d'Oro or Las Gaviotas, places unlisted on the maps that the pescaderos and contrabandistas knew, places Felix had been in the navy and in his years of running the worst charter business in Cuba. He would anchor in the late afternoon and dabble for baitfish, netting mullet and menhaden to toss into the live well under the cockpit, watching the shore and the open sea all the while for anything unusual. The fighting chair would be gone to make room for the little flat-bottomed skiff he used for bonefishing, and at dusk he'd leave Pedrito on board and lower it in, scanning the treetops as he rowed into the inlet.

The sign was always the same. Never more than a quarter mile in, hanging over the left bank. Two hoops tied from vines, the lower one strung with a trio of bleached seashells. A patrol boat searching the inlet would be watching the bottom for depth, watching the sides for ambush. At least that was what Felix comforted himself with on the way in.

The crates were in a shallow hole, covered with undergrowth and a thin layer of dirt. Felix poked around the base of the tree till he heard wood and then dug. The first few times he levered inside to see—mostly older weapons, Garands and San Cristóbals, a tommy gun, some ammunition. But as the game went on he just loaded whatever there was into the skiff and covered the hole. It would be getting dark then, Felix pausing at the mouth of the inlet, listening. He carried a roll of caiman hides in the stern, ready to dump the crates if a patrol boat rushed him and claim he'd been in to trade for hides with some skinners. When it was fully dark he'd row out to the *Vaquero*.

Pedrito helped him winch the crates and the skiff on board, then they'd wrestle the crates below to hide them. The ice he buried the big fish in was shifted on top of the crates and a canvas tarp laid over it all. Pedrito's solemn cat face showed no sign of emotion or interest in the crates.

Felix loved running at night. He'd swing the *Vaquero* out away from the coast, navigating by the stars if it was clear, making a test of it. He ran with his cabin lights on, the worst charter captain on the coast lost at sea again if anyone was to challenge. He never saw a patrol boat. Sometimes Pedrito would throw a line over and shine the flashlight down it, waiting a bit, then hauling it in hand over hand faster than the pan-sized squid could think to unwrap themselves. Felix would set a course then and leave Pedrito at the wheel while he made arroz con calamares the way the women who had cooked for his mother taught him, sautéing the squid in their ink and mixing it with the rice. He'd stand on deck with Pedrito as they ate, watching the stars, breathing the night air, smelling the coast without seeing it, feeling the sea roll beneath them. On the land things were changing, men were killing each other for money and revenge and ideas and nobody knew how it would end. But the sea didn't care who they were or what they were carrying and at night the land was just a whiff of green in the air. At times it was hard for Felix to believe that he had become part of the inevitable struggle that Nidia talked about, instead of just a man floating on the surface of things, drifting with the current.

At first light the *Vaquero* would be off the coast by the delivery spot, Felix swinging in close enough to anchor, the skiff loaded and lowered. It was the part where Felix felt danger, always a chance that he'd been betrayed, a patrol hidden in the inlet. But there never was, and he'd find the sign hanging in the trees, always wondering who was small enough to climb that high. He'd pull onto the bank and start with the spade, smiling every time, thinking of the pirate books their father had given them to read, especially the *Treasure Island* he told them was set on the Isla de Pinos. Felix would dig a shallow hole and set the crates in, still wet and cold from the ice, then cover them with a thin layer of soil and arrange undergrowth on top till it looked natural.

The guerrillas were still mostly a rumor, the government claiming to wipe them out every other day, and sometimes Felix wondered if anyone really came to pick the guns up or if they might lie there secret and rotting forever, unclaimed treasure.

On the way back if the weather was good, Felix would troll for wahoo and bonito and take naps, Pedrito at the wheel. In his dreams Felix sailed under white canvas in blue water, sun shining gold, dolphins racing alongside his bow. Pedrito and Nidia were in the dreams and sometimes Nidia was the land, seductive and dangerous, a sweet smell in the air. Pedrito would be the sea then, indifferent, killing men like he was chopping baitfish. And sometimes there were coffins floating on the water. In the good dreams the coffins spilled open to reveal rifles, shiny and new, with gleaming steel bayonets attached. In the bad dreams there was only one coffin, a sinking one, and Felix knew that if he looked inside he would find himself.

When he woke Felix would bring the boat into harbor and Pedrito would help to put things right, then carry the catch over to the cooler at the Miramar. It would be late afternoon by then and soon the El Ritz would be open.

Mambo limped in most nights around eight. Felix knew him from the charter fishing out of La Habana after Machado and before the Big War, before Mambo went into the navy. Now he ran the patrol boats on Felix's section of coast and worried about the weather.

"When Cubans start getting serious," he would say, "it is a very bad sign. You know how it is when the squalls come down from the Gulf, the color the sky gets?"

"I never go out in that kind of weather." Felix would watch Mambo's cigar smoke rise and spread past the giant turtle hanging overhead.

"Of course not. You're the laziest charter captain on the coast. You only go out to take naps on the water."

"I have the best dreams there. I dream about Nidia."

They'd both watch Nidia for a moment, gliding big and lovely behind the counter.

"En los sueños, sí, Felix. Pero en la vida—hombre, in real life she'd cut you for shark bait."

Felix would smile. "Ahora. El cielo."

"El cielo." Mambo continued. "The sky gets that color, like blood from a bad wound, and if you're out too far or in too close you know you're going to get pounded. That's what I see in our future. People are going around with serious faces, people are whispering. When Cubans whisper it's a very bad sign."

It was Mambo's job to stop the contrabandistas, to make sure that nobody was bringing guns by sea to the guerrillas who were a rumor in the Sierra. Mambo had been a contrabandista himself at one time, in the days when they had the Ley Seca in the States and everybody was shipping rum. Now he sold much of the gas the government gave him for the patrol boats to Echevarría who owned the marina. His patrols never had enough fuel for a real chase if they happened to see somebody smuggling. He had been in the navy long enough to know how the wind blew.

"If the radio is correct," he would say, "the guerrillas have been wiped out several times. It would be wrong to waste the time and gasoline to go searching for a threat that doesn't exist. And if they lie, que es muy posible"—and here Mambo would give his sad smile, turning to look at the other regulars crowding the El Ritz, talking, laughing, arguing, filling the air with noise and smoke—"there is the chance that the guerrillas will win. If this happens it would not be healthy for me to do too good a job chasing them, verdad? Those are very serious boys in the mountains, with long memories and no sense of humor."

"Things might be better if there were a change."

"En Cuba? Felix, things are always better after a change. After the squalls pass, the fishing is best, the sea is most beautiful. But then things will always slide back again."

"Es posible."

"Es seguro. What happened after the Spaniard? And after Machado? If Batista leaves the same will happen. Cubans are too good-hearted to be serious about change."

"Pero las guerrillas—"

"Los guerrilleros son jóvenes y hay pocos. The real problem is that they infect the people up there, los precaristas, los negros, and after they're gone it's hell to quiet things down. Maybe the guerrillas will be wiped out. En ese caso"—and here he would always look Felix in the eye and smile gently—"in that case it would not be healthy for me to do too *bad* a job chasing them. It's like the tides, Felix. You be careful not to be caught in the wrong place at the wrong time."

Felix was not sure if Mambo suspected his night trips or not. They'd spend long hours drinking side by side at the El Ritz, talking about the weather and the fish and the conditions around this or that key the way they would if they were two charter captains killing time. But at times Felix thought he heard a soft note of warning in his friend's voice.

Soon the radio was reporting so many guerrilla units wiped out each day that there was no doubt the army was failing to control them. Rumors flowed of police barracks raided for weapons, of army patrols throwing their rifles down to run away. Nidia smiled more and sometimes sang along with the songs on the jukebox, doing a little rhumba step as she stood mixing drinks behind the bar.

"Big winds coming," she'd say as she left Felix his black rum. "Big winds blowing all over."

In that time Felix spent his days out on the water thinking about how he was going to tell her he loved her, that he wanted to be with her, to hold her, touch her, watch her move through the day. If the winds came or if they didn't he wanted her, and he didn't know how to let her know it. He was afraid. Not because he knew the story about her and the tigres and believed it was true but because he respected her the way a man respects another man and thought that since he had joined in the inevitable struggle she felt the same about him. If he told her, if he brought love and all those other feelings into it, who knew how she would react? It would be a hard thing, losing the respect of a woman like Nidia.

"A woman like that loves only once," Mambo would say as they watched her moving through clouds of cigar smoke. "If she loses him, everyone else is just company."

When he was young Mambo had been a shark for women, earning his nickname in the clubs of La Habana, dancing office girls and widows and tourist ladies into woozy surrender.

"The only difference between dancing and fucking," he said in those days, "is that you don't fuck in front of a live band."

Finally he had danced too often with the favorite of a certain jefe de policía and his boat was burned in the harbor and both his legs were broken in several falls down a flight of stairs at the station house where they took him to identify suspects. After he was released from the hospital he bought himself a position in the navy.

"Una mujer como esta," Mambo would say, rubbing his knees under the table, always sore now in the humid season, "is a ship doomed to sink. If you're near her when she goes down she'll pull you under."

Since he had stopped dancing Mambo's feelings about women were almost always gloomy, and Felix tried to ignore his warnings. But at times he would get the same uneasy sense from Nidia, a whiff of desperation in her smile, and it made it harder to tell her what was in his heart.

"Conoces Los Tortugueros?" Nidia asked one night at the El Ritz in the month when the navy had tried a coup in Santiago and failed. The bar was full of talk of what it meant and who had chosen which side and who was going to come out of it alive. Mambo was not there because all the navy had been called to quarters.

"I can find it," said Felix.

"I hear the fishing is very good there. But you'd have to go right away."

Nidia had never indicated any hurry before. Felix drank a few extra stiff ones that night and barely smiled at the jokes the pescadores called out about him and watched the giant turtle swinging overhead, wondering how many winds had swept the island in its life before somebody killed it and stuffed it and painted it with lacquer. It could have been alive before Martí, alive in slavery time, and Felix knew it cared as little who ruled the island as whichever ignorant pescadero who netted it had cared, as little as Felix himself, drifting lazily on rum, cared at this moment. Then Nidia sat by him, which she never did, her round, strong body pressed warm against his side, and whispered in his ear.

"If I were a man," she whispered, her warm breath like rum through his veins, "I would do what you are doing."

When she put her arm around him and kissed him on the cheek the pescaderos who saw called out jokes and churned with jealousy. Felix drank one more stiff one and left to get the *Vaquero* ready.

When he got to the boat Pedrito was sitting on a piling, hugging himself with his skinny arms against the chill of the night. They had never put the boat ready in the dark before, but there he was. He held the flashlight while Felix checked the motor and plotted the course, staring down over Felix's shoulder with no hint of understanding in his eyes. They were out of the harbor at sunrise.

It was not the kind of weather Felix went out in. The sky was like a bad mood and the swells were high and sharp-edged, smacking hard into the bow till they'd lurched out past the harbor, then washing over the sides as he ran along the coast. Pedrito was soaked within minutes. When Felix handed him an extra sweater he misunderstood and buried it under a pile of canvas to keep it dry. The sea pounded them through the day, the sky never changing. Felix's jaw began to ache from bracing himself against the impact of the swells. He knew it wasn't the sea that was to blame but the boat, for being in its way, for trying to move against it. But he began to hate the swells anyway, to dread the monotony of their blows, to imagine a malicious will behind the brutal conspiracy of water and wind. The barometer warned of rain all day but the clouds never opened and the air grew thick with water, till Felix, dripping at the wheel from every crashing swell, felt he was more under the sea than on top of it. Pedrito squatted in the stern, a line fastened around his waist and secured to the U-bolt that ordinarily held the fighting chair, methodically working the hand pump as if he could keep up with the spill.

The swells dropped as Felix came in on the lee side of the key. It was still rough, and he ran the *Vaquero* past the inlet and out far enough so if it dragged anchor with Pedrito aboard it wouldn't run aground too quickly. The skiff was a nightmare, smashing against the hull when they lowered it, the little motor whining as the prop was lifted into the air at the peak of each swell, taking water fast and hard over the stern.

It was too late to turn back. It had been too late from the moment they left harbor, and Felix tried to concentrate on the thought that he would tell Nidia everything if he got back alive. If he was going to risk his life for this shit he was going to need more than her respect.

They would have a bar and restaurant on a hill overlooking the coast. Nidia would run the bar and Felix would grill mariscos and cook arroz con calamares and carne asada. Men would come to watch Nidia move behind the bar but be very respectful and she would smile all the time. The regulars would make jokes about Felix how did you land a woman like this and he would smile and cook and take their money. The restaurant would be called La Perla and the sign would be a large, rough oyster, jaws open to reveal a gleaming neon pearl inside. At closing time they'd send the waiters home and put something soft on the jukebox and dance a little before going to bed together. They'd make love and then listen to the waves rolling in, gentle waves, sleepy, rocking waves.

Los Tortugueros was wide at the mouth and Felix managed to motor the skiff in without breaking apart and then it was peaceful. The trees wrapped around him and the water lay flat and murky red below. He searched up in the wind-bent branches for the sign but there was none and he chugged deeper and deeper, the inlet narrowing till he heard a human voice and nearly jumped out of his skin.

It was a man standing on the bank only a few feet from him, bearded, dressed in green fatigues. He had a rifle slung over his shoulder. He grabbed the stern before Felix could react and hopped in.

"Vámonos," he said.

"I was looking for the sign. I couldn't find it."

The man in the fatigues shrugged, then jerked his head toward the sea.

"Vámonos."

Felix supposed that if the man wanted him to know details he would say something. The man slouched in the stern, a lump of fatigue green, his rifle across his knees. When they came to the mouth of the inlet Felix heard the motor of the *Vaquero*, then saw that it had been dragged past them and in and that Pedrito had the engine up to half throttle, bow pointed out into the swells, anchors still down, holding it almost stationary in the water. It was something Felix had never taught him to do.

"I hate boats," grunted the man in the fatigues.

The sea calmed for the trip back but it rained cold all night, Felix running on instruments and memory. The man in the fatigues sat in the hold, shivering, climbing out only to throw up over the side a few times. Pedrito crawled onto the pile of life preservers and slept.

The sun burned through as it came up in the morning and dolphins played around their wake a few miles from the drop-off. The color of everything was brighter, the sea light blue, the island a dark bottle green. The man in the fatigues looked yellow and weary in the back of the skiff going in. Felix had made him a sandwich with eggs and fried ham which the man regarded with a queasy eye and tucked into a pocket in his fatigues.

"Buena suerte," said Felix as he pushed off from the bank in a hidden crook of the inlet.

The man in the fatigues nodded slightly, then turned and walked into the trees as if he knew where he was going.

When Felix got back to the El Ritz he found Mambo alone behind the counter, pouring himself a drink. He had his pistol snapped to his belt. He looked like he'd had a worse night than Felix.

"The weather was very bad yesterday," Mambo said, finding another glass to pour a stiff one for his friend.

Felix sat across the counter from him. "El peor que he visto este año," he agreed. "A real pisspot."

"You were out on your boat." Mambo sounded suspicious.

"I thought it would get better. It never did." Felix looked around the deserted room. "Where is everybody?"

"They were told the bar would be closed tonight."

"Por quién?"

"By the ones who took Nidia."

Felix felt the floor shift, unsteady beneath him. He'd been awake and on the sea since early the day before and now he had to grip the edge of the bar for support.

"They came in when the place was full and said it would be closed till further instructions and then they carried Nidia away." Mambo pushed the rum he'd poured over to Felix. "It took four of them."

"Y por qué?"

"You know the stories about her."

"They can't take you away for stories."

"Hombre, pueden hacer lo que desean. They can take you for something you say, for something your neighbor says about you, for something they think might be true. They can take you for going fishing in bad weather."

The first gulp of rum burned all the way down. "You think she'll be back?"

Mambo sighed and leaned his elbows on the counter.

"There is nothing you can do," he said. "If they do let her go she won't be the same."

"Who was it?"

"You can't do anything."

"Which four?"

"Bad ones. Zayas and his big friend with the wavy hair and the one they call Cabroncito and one I didn't know down from Manzanillo. Heces."

Felix tried to think of Nidia scared and that made him think of what it would be that would scare her and then he tried not to think of it at all. Mambo squeezed his shoulder.

"I hear the fishing al norte is very good. En Florida hace buen clima."

Felix wondered how much Mambo knew, wondered if he'd known before they came for Nidia.

"I don't want to go to Florida," he said. "Soy cubano."

"If the weather changes for good," said Mambo, "if our friends from the mountains should win, I might want to charter a trip."

She wasn't dead yet. It wasn't final. It could turn out okay.

"If that happens you can take my boat," said Felix. "There's an extra key taped under the seats on the port side. I'll wait as long as I can before I report it stolen."

Mambo nodded and poured them each another drink. He limped around the counter and fed the jukebox a coin. The orquesta of Osvaldo Farrés filled the empty room and Mambo stood with his drink in his hand, eyes closed, swaying with the music for a moment. He gave Felix his sad smile.

"Some things that you lose you can't get back," he said. "I didn't know that when I was young."

After that night Felix spent his days sitting on the deck of the *Vaquero*, tied up in the harbor, drinking beer. There were no more charters anywhere because of the fighting. Pedrito came and sat by him a few times, watching the gulls, but finally he realized Felix wasn't going out anymore and disappeared from town.

Nidia came up in a net about ten miles down the coast. She was naked, swollen, her breasts cut off. Felix was there when the pescaderos brought her in, laying her wrapped in ragged canvas under the scale they used to weigh the big fish for the yanquis. Felix recognized the tattoo on the inside of her arm, blue seahorse against a red heart, and didn't stay to see the rest.

The El Ritz opened again soon after but the rumor was that the man running it was a cousin of Zayas from the policía. The regulars stayed away till Christmas night when a bunch of them broke in after closing and cleaned it out. Felix took the giant sea turtle from over the bar, carting it home in a wheelbarrow at three in the morning, drunk out of his mind on looted rum, the pistol Nidia kept below the counter stuck in his belt. He hoped some comemierda in a uniform would stop him so he could shoot holes in them, but nobody did. He used the turtle as a footrest in his cabin on the *Vaquero*.

Early on New Year's morning Felix went to the harbor and found that his boat was gone. He hadn't been able to sleep the night before because the skin on his chest was burning from the tattoo he'd gotten, blue seahorse on a red heart. As he walked back into town he heard that it had happened, that they were coming. Some people hid and some lined the streets waiting to cheer and some went about their business as usual. Felix joined a group of young men and women who said they were going to storm the police headquarters. They were chanting and running and as he fell into step running with them his heart quickened and he thought of the bundle of ragged canvas winched from the fishing boat and swung over the dock, streaming water, and Nidia's arm, bluish white, working free to hang loose in the air.

"Paredón!" shouted the ones running with him. "Paredón! Muerte a los perros!"

Then Felix was chanting too, shouting curses and phrases of revenge with the others and he felt he was part of a hurricane about to break loose, part of something fast and powerful and irreversible.

When they reached the headquarters only Cabroncito, the one everybody said was retarded, was left standing on the steps with his pants half buttoned, still drunk from last night's party and wondering where his comrades had gone. He squealed as the crowd boiled up the steps and threw him down and dragged him into the street, squealed like a scalded pig. His pants fell down and tangled around his ankles and the men took turns trying to kick him in the testicles while the women slashed at his face and arms with their nails, screaming and spitting. One of the younger men tried to urinate on him but the others kept dragging him down the street and he couldn't keep up and pee at the same time. Felix knew Cabroncito had been one of the ones who killed Nidia and if he'd met him alone on the street he might have done something but now he could only watch and catch a glimpse of the terror in the man's eyes as the people swarmed over him. He wondered if Nidia had been that scared or if she had her hatred to keep her fighting to the end. He'd killed big fish, fish bigger than men, and seen their eyes go from something living to something dead, but the terror was usually played out of them by the time they were on board. When Felix left, Cabroncito was rolled in a ball coughing up blood, a ring of screaming people around him, gathering the last bit of collective fury to stomp him into the pavement.

The guerrillas rode into town in the afternoon, piled onto a stolen jeep, a flatbed truck and a DeSoto taxi. People lined the streets to cheer and bang things together. The jeep came in the lead, and Pedrito was sitting on the hood of it, wearing a fatigue cap and the sweater Felix had given him. He wasn't smiling or waving or holding a rifle over his head like the other guerrillas. Felix gave him a small nod as he passed and he nodded back and then the men in fatigues began to fire their rifles into the air.

Felix walked to the dock and sat with his legs dangling over into the slip where the *Vaquero* used to be. The cheering and the gunfire faded and he watched the waves, rainbow slicks of motor oil glistening as they rolled in, and as the sun fell the enormous chilling hole of Nidia's death crept into him. Nidia was gone from his life, was gone from the earth and there would never be anyone like her again. He had never gotten to know her and never would. Felix put his hand over the raw blister of the tattoo on his chest and started to howl, long piercing cries broken only with sobs, the sound wailing out across the deserted harbor to mingle with the squalling gulls above, then be swallowed by the sea, constant and uncaring.

Tío Felix pushes the throttle, pointing them south into open sea. Marta has never been this close before, not since they left, and a quick thrill tickles along her shoulder and up her neck. They could just keep going and they'd be there. Tío Felix points.

"La Isla está allí," he says. "A unas tres horas."

"At night?"

"If the weather is good is just as fast. You only go slow when she's near."

Marta stares ahead across the water as if trying to see it. She remembers a shade of green, the smell of cows, the creases in the skin of old Esperanza, who cooked for her mother. She watches her uncle at the wheel for a moment, his wide face tanned and leathery, shirt unbuttoned and sprouting with tufts of white hair, his tattoo, blue seahorse on a red heart, that she used to trace with her finger when she was a little girl. He doesn't look like a warrior.

"Piensas que vale la pena?" she asks him. "El ataque?"

Tío Felix thinks for a long time, the wheel loose in his fingers.

"Other attacks have made a difference," he says. "Other attacks have changed our life forever."

"Y esto? Piensas que es importante?"

He frowns. "Sometimes when I hook on the big fish, and I fight him and I fight him and maybe I pull him in and maybe he swims away y por qué? The sea doesn't care and the other fishes doesn't care. Pero es importante para *mí*."

Tío Felix checks the position of the sun, looks at his watch. He pulls back on the throttle a bit and looks ahead where the island will be if he keeps running south. The idea of setting foot on it again makes his throat go dry.

"And the fish," he says to Marta. "He cares too."

Felix had named the first place La Perla Perdida. It was high up on Calle Ocho, away from the center of town, six little tables, a counter and a sweatbox of a kitchen. By the time Felix arrived Mambo had already sold the boat and was set up in business getting refugees their driver's licenses.

"You don't honk your horn or curse during the test," Mambo would say in his first session. "You call the yanqui 'Sir' and one time tell him what a wonderful country is los Estados Unidos. After you pass you drive how you want and say what you want. Eso es la democracia."

Mambo was doing well except for his knees which hurt him folded up in his little training car every day. He paid Felix what he could for the *Vaquero*. Scipio was already up with the family by then and was working for the Lomax brothers and there was a doctor they knew from Camagüey sitting as night clerk in a hotel for men

by the bus station and a jeweler from La Habana who had helped
to finance the rebels cutting grass for rich yanquis in Coral Gables
and the best chess player in Santiago who had never worked in his
life on his knees squeezing shoes onto the feet of schoolchildren in
downtown Miami. It was a crazy time, faces and names from the
past popping into Felix's life, stripped of wealth and position, lost,
stunned, angry. Families still in Cuba sent their children up to live
in camps run by Irish priests, former enemies found themselves
side by side in the waiting rooms of social agencies and employ-
ment bureaus, grown men walked the streets trying to hide copies
of *My Weekly Reader* inside their shirts. People needed something
to hold on to, needed a center, and when Scipio was able to dig
up an impossible two thousand Felix bought the mortgage on the
lonchería.

La Perla Perdida became the center of Felix's section of Calle
Ocho. Mambo drove him to Tampa to pick up a jukebox filled with
the songs of the grandes orquestas of the forties and fifties. A famous
portrait artist who was painting signs in Hialeah made a mural on
the west wall that included Columbus, Maceo, Martí, Adolfo Luque,
and Desi Arnaz. Felix did all the cooking himself, starting with a
short menu of medianoches, lechón asado, moros y cristianos and
strong, sweet coffee, then expanding as he learned the suppliers and
got faster on the burners. He hired Chang, the first in a long series
of Chinese-Cuban exiles who cooked for him awhile and then left
to start their own restaurants.

Over the counter hung a large green sea turtle Mambo had pulled
from the *Vaquero* before he sold it.

The food and the music and the mural on the wall supplied the
atmosphere and the men who used La Perla as their community
center supplied the talk. It was loud and excited and musical, Cuban
talk, and it reminded Felix of the grandes orquestas, of Pérez Prado
and Tito Puente and Machito in his heyday. This man or that man
would stand for a long solo, playing on his favorite theme with
variations, holding the floor, then as he went out at high pitch the
supporters or dissenters would jump in with counterpoint, arguing
in staccato call and response till they fell back into the general
rumbling body of the conversation, laughter beating percussion
around the edges. Sometimes it was hot and driving and angry,
sometimes light and lyrical, happy memories, and sometimes, early

in the morning or in the meandering aftermath of the lunch rush, there would be the slow sad tango of a broken man.

The sweetest were the memories, love songs for the lost island, la perla perdida. How things used to be, how they might never be again. The most bitter were the military marches, driven by the thumping of tables and the shouting of a single word.

Betrayal.

Betrayal.

Betrayal.

And though they were all sinking in the same boat the factions of before had not died. The Batistianos argued strategy, drawing lines of battle on the green map of Cuba in the center of the paper placemats Felix had designed. The ones who had supported Fidel and some who had fought in his army spoke of plots and counterplots, argued that Raúl was the Communist and Fidel only the dupe, found hope in news from home. There was much talk of what one or two well-placed bullets could do. There were MRP men and DRE men, men who followed the 30th of November and a few tough old birds who had cracked skulls for Rolando Masferrer. And almost from the beginning there were rumors of a return.

"Batista is putting together an army," said some. "The Dominicans are joining him and they'll take over in a month."

"Batista couldn't keep an army together when he was in Cuba," answered the skeptics. "And why would the Dominicans fight for us?"

"Eloy Gutiérrez Menoyo is in the monte with a thousand men," said some. "He'll do the same thing Fidel did and do it better."

"Eloy Gutiérrez Menoyo is a maricón izquierdista," countered the old Batistianos. "If he has a thousand men then Fidel has emptied the lunatic asylums."

"The yanquis are fed up now that Fidel is queer for Khrushchev," said some. "They're going in with the air force and the marines and they'll make us a state."

"Fuck being a state," said a joker by the coffee machine. "Have them make Jackie our queen."

"La Reina del Caribe—"

"And Frank Sinatra the king—"

"That's what we need in Cuba. La monarquía."

"Everything else has failed."

"Y la democracia? Cómo aquí?"

"Cómo aquí? Who wants la democracia if you have to wear a poker in your ass?"

"Qué bello inglés."

"Gracias. Lo aprendo from the yanquis en mi taxi. La escuela de la calle es la mejor."

"Qué quiere decir el poker en el culo? Es un juego de naipes?"

"Not *cards* poker, pendejo. Hurgón."

"Bueno. Y what this means?"

The ones who spoke English would laugh at the ones who didn't.

"The marines better attack in a hurry or this one is lost."

In time, though, the rumors began to take weight. Some of the younger men stopped coming in and some of the older ones had ideas about where they had gone.

"Something is up," said Mambo, sitting with his back to the counter, rubbing his knees. "They're starting to whisper again. Mira como los derechistas won't sit near los izquierdistas anymore. Something bad is going to happen, I can feel it in my legs."

"Tus piernas always hurt, hombre," said Felix, refilling the sugar bowls after the lunch frenzy.

"Eso más bien parece un hormiguero. Like when you think you have a fish on the line but maybe he's only playing with the bait."

"Whatever it is, we are too old for it, Mambo."

"Sí, estamos viejos. La historia has passed us."

Men began to come into La Perla to be surrounded and congratulated by their friends. A force was being recruited by the yanquis, a brigade of Cubans who would be armed and trained and backed with the might of Tío Sam and these men could brag that their sons had been accepted. Cigars passed hands, toasts were offered. If I were younger, the men would say. If they'd only take me. One day Mambo came in looking low.

"He sido rechazado," he said. "I take the shots for my legs so I can walk in como un hombre de acción. I tell them mi historia, mi servicio como capitán de los patrulleros. No, viejo, they say to me. We are not so desperate yet."

"Estás loco," said Felix. "They have to attack over the beach or fall from the air. It is a job of the young."

"Soy cubano," shrugged Mambo.

The men in La Perla saluted Mambo for his gallantry then, cigars passing hands, toasts offered. Felix began to feel uneasy as he poured the drinks. This would be the one that counted, the one that was written on the final page, and he would be left behind. Not on the wrong side this time, but only as a spectator, a cook, a profiteer.

"They're going to come in by sea," said some of the men, with the assurance of insiders. "Atacando a las playas como *Los Sands of Iwo Jima.*"

"Exactamente lo que Fidel is expecting," said others, just as sure. "Every inch of the beaches has mines under it, even Varadero. They're going to fall from the sky con los paratroopers. Fidel has shit for aviones and his pilots are on our side. They're going to come in by air."

If it was by air that would be one thing, Felix thought. Falling out of airplanes was a young man's game, and there would be no dishonor in staying behind. But if it was by sea and you were a marinero with experience in the navy and with good health, what reason could you have for not at least volunteering to go?

"Sería los dos," said a third group, exasperated by the military ignorance of the others. "You strike the beach to draw his forces to the coast, then drop la infantería from planes into the interior. Y pues la gente, los cubanos, raise arms to join them everywhere."

"Esta vez es la última," they all agreed. "This time we do it right."

At Scipio's house the Invasion was more than a rumor. Once a month he would have Felix over for Sunday dinner in a grudging admission that they were still family. Always there would be a speech about the tragedy of the island, with special scorn for those who had been fooled into helping the izquierdistas steal it away. Felix would continue to eat Lourdes's cooking, which was improving month by month, but Blas would end up pushing his plate away and leaving the table in angry silence.

This Sunday Scipio was perched at the head of the table carving carne asada with a knife he had borrowed from the butchers, moist, thin slices folding away with a fragrant breath of steam. Lourdes was looking more worried than usual, like she might have been crying, and Felix had noticed fresh flowers around her little shrine to La Virgen del Cobre as he entered the apartment. Blas was more relaxed than he remembered seeing him since the years before, not chain smoking or pacing the tiny rooms like an animal in a circus cage. Ambrosio seemed older, more sure of himself maybe, and strange little Marta had the glow in her eyes she got on religious holidays or when receiving the Host.

Marta said a shorter blessing than usual and then Lourdes shot out of her chair to begin serving. She barely ate at meals, Lourdes, but hovered like a short-winged bird, filling glasses and plates. Felix tried to skip lunch on the days of his visits so he wouldn't deal her the insult of a less than wolflike appetite.

"We have good news, hermano," said Scipio. He lifted the platter of cut meat without looking and Lourdes took it from over his shoulder and began to serve it around the table.

"My sons are going."

On Calle Ocho at that time if a man said his sons were going everyone knew where and what for. But there was something like a challenge in the way Scipio announced it, something like a reprimand.

"Dónde?" said Felix, trying to seem innocent.

"Para la Invasión. Para recapturar nuestra tierra."

Felix looked to the boys. Blas was already eating, looking more like his father every day. Ambrosio blushed. Felix was proud as an uncle was proud, then had a stab of worry. The battle would not care that these were his nephews, that they were supposed to grow kind and wise and have children and outlive him. Good people were killed. People you loved were gone from your life forever.

"Cuándo?" asked Felix. "Con qué grupo?"

"You will read about it en los periódicos," said Scipio, stabbing a forkful of papas and hefting it onto his plate. "You and the other collaborators."

Blas sat back and glared at his father, then looked to Felix. He spoke softly.

"No puedo decirte, Tío. Top secret."

Felix smiled. "Everybody but Fidel himself has come into La Perla talking about it. No es tan secreto."

"Those are men of talk," Scipio sneered, jabbing with his fork for emphasis. "Son los hombres de acción who go to fight."

Felix felt the point of this as if the fork were pressing into his skin. He looked to Ambrosio, pretty, sensitive Ambrosio who always wanted to throw the fish back in, who cried when they slaughtered a bull, the one he read *Treasure Island* to when the boy was sick with the measles. Tío, the boy had said, some day I'll be a writer like Robert Louis Stevenson. Or a poet like Guillén.

"Ahora. You're going to be a guerrero."

"I'm going to try, Tío."

"Y tus poemas? Tus libros?"

Ambrosio straightened, looking noble and impossibly young. "We write in blood now, Tío."

Felix wanted to cry. He tried to remember which text of Martí that was from, which glorious, doomed poem of revolt.

"May God protect you both," he said then, and rose to give each an abrazo, Lourdes dropping the platter on the table to run weeping from the room, Scipio glowing righteously at the head of the table and little Marta following it all with greedy, shining eyes.

The next day the boys left for the secret place the yanquis had arranged.

Rumors grew wilder in La Perla Perdida. The factions separated into areas of the room that stayed constant day after day. In the rear by the cash register were the derechistas, men who had supported Batista at least in spirit or who felt his only fault lay in his corruption or his inefficiency or in the inefficiency of his corruption. These men talked a hard line of military control and restoring property and order and punishing los culpables in a direct and brutal fashion.

By the west wall under the mural of Cuban history and culture sat the centristas, men who had opposed Batista on moral grounds but had been powerless or too fatalistic or too frightened to fight him, men who still supported Prío and the Auténticos or one of the other opposition parties from the years before. These men talked much of the Constitution of 1940 and the importance of restoring property and order and of keeping the yanquis at a respectful distance in rebuilding the nation.

Near the door when there were tables left and the suspicious looks and dark whispering of the other groups did not drive them into the street, sat the izquierdistas, or what passed for leftists on Calle Ocho in those heated days. Men who had fought against Batista or supported the rebels in the fight, many of them younger men who had been turned down by the yanquis because of their past. These men talked about the true spirit of revolution and the fair distribution of wealth and the danger of ending up with the same shit and different flies. They spoke more softly and seemed to know fewer rumors from the camps.

"They're in the Dominican already," went one rumor. "Learning to be frogmen. Submarines will take them to the coast and they'll sneak in from there."

"Our boys are just a diversion," went another. "They'll land on the north coast, and then all the yanquis in the world will come over the wire at Guantánamo."

"They're holding them in the swamps," went the darkest, most suspicious rumor. "Pretending to train them but really just keeping our boys penned in. Kennedy made a deal with Fidel and he's afraid we'll screw it up."

Felix stood under the giant green sea turtle, following it all with an increasing sense of anxiety. A frente was formed, with leaders from the different factions joining and being allowed to go visit the camps. There was a rumor of trouble among the troops and political fighting and then one week many of the younger men who sat by the door were gone.

"We've lost," moaned the derechistas. "They've sold the Invasion to traitors. Fairies and traitors."

"It's only fair," said the centristas. "That's what the Frente is supposed to be. All united for victory, and we sort the rest out later."

"Finalmente," said the men who were left who sat near the door, louder now that their boys had been accepted. "Kennedy isn't going to sell us back to the same bandidos. Sabe que todos somos patriotas."

It was March on a rainy late afternoon when Omar from Las Tunas came in for a celebration drink. Omar had been in the mutiny at Santiago in the last days of the time before and was older, over forty like Felix. He said he had been accepted for the Invasion.

"They're building a second force," he said, grinning over the tall glass of rum and Coke Felix had supplied on the house. Felix had a license only for beer and wine but kept a private stock for the special occasions that seemed to crop up almost every other day.

"I met a yanqui named Bob in the lobby at the Eden Roc," said Omar, who had risen to capitán of the bellboys at the hotel, "and I knew from the list of his phone calls at the desk that he was un importante. I see him in the lobby one night and he is a little borracho and happy from the bar and he says to me, 'Gaspar'— this Bob is not so good for the names—'Gaspar, I think maybe you are going home soon. How are those apples?' And I tell him 'Señor Bob'—they eat that shit up with a spoon, Señor this, Señor that— 'Señor Bob,' I say, 'the only manner I wish to go home is with a rifle in my arms.' He laughs, and when I tell him my history in the navy he says this thing can maybe be arranged and whispers to me about the second force."

"Y cuándo viene?"

"Mañana. En alguna parte del estado de Louisiana, pero es un secreto."

The half-dozen men who he had shared his secret with slapped his back then and Felix stood them all to free drinks to celebrate and somebody put the national anthem, the one from the days before, on the jukebox and tears were wept.

When Mambo came in with the crowd who wanted coffee and talk after dinner, Felix told him the story.

"We were both in the stupid, shit-eating navy," said Mambo, weighing the possibilities.

"We are both as old and as useless as Omar," said Felix.

"And as stupid."

"More stupid. Estupidísimo."

"It makes one think," said Mambo.

They left it at that and had many glasses of rum without Coke as the night progressed and the rumor of a second force passed through the men in La Perla like a flu. They drank rum for thinking, not for celebrating, and Mambo limped to the jukebox and back to the counter all night, playing the greatest hits of René Touzot and Tito Rodríguez and Benny More, swaying dreamily on his stool, sometimes singing softly along with a chorus. Felix felt the floor begin to move beneath him, rolling gently like a friendly sea, and once or twice caught the men in the mural on the west wall, Columbus and Minnie Minoso and especially José Martí, looking directly at him.

At the end of the night there was only Mambo on the stool and Felix behind the counter.

Mambo sighed. "Ahora, viejo," he said, looking to Felix with eyes that cut through rum, that cut through time and memory. "Qué dices?"

"I think we are too old and too stupid not to do this thing. I think we are lost, Mambo."

Mambo nodded. "Then may God have mercy on us."

Omar arranged for them to meet with Señor Bob. He had a face like red leather and a big smile and smoked American cigars that smelled like the mold under lawn chairs.

"You boys married?" he asked after hearing their stories.

"No, Señor Bob," said Felix.

"I am wedded only to the sea," said Mambo, drinking heavily since the night at La Perla and shot full of painkillers for his knees. It was a line he had used for seducing tourist ladies in his dancing days. "To the sea and to la Cuba libre, tierra de mi corazón."

"I love you people," said Bob, clapping Mambo on the back. "I wish we had more like you on our side."

On the ride to New Orleans Felix could think only of La Perla Perdida, locked, closed for business. CERRADO HASTA LA LIBERTAD said the sign he'd left on the door. He could think only of the talk it would cause, the rumors, the toasts that would be raised to him. And Scipio, stopped on his way to work by some acquaintance and congratulated on the bravery of his brother, his fat collaborator of a brother. Scipio left behind to wait and chop cows into pieces. It was stupid and vain, he knew, and not the way a grown man facing war should be thinking. But it was better than thinking about what would happen next.

"I know you," said the man across the aisle.

Felix didn't recognize him. "De Cuba?"

"Sí. You gave me a ride in your boat."

"La pesca?"

"No," said the man. "La Resistencia. You picked me up on an island and brought me to the coast in a storm."

It was the guerrilla Nidia had sent him to get.

"And now you're here."

"Things change."

"Are you going where I'm going?"

"I hope so."

Felix nodded. He remembered the night, the fatigues, the rain, but the man's face would not come to him.

"I didn't recognize you."

The man shrugged. "I had a beard."

"So they finally sent us a cook," said the boy sitting on the bunk when he saw Felix walk in. Then Mambo limped in behind and some of the others who had come on the bus from New Orleans.

"Muchos cocineros," said the boy's friend on the upper bunk.

A man who carried himself like an officer came in from the back then and watched the new people filling up the room, plopping their suitcases down to sit on them.

"Qué pasa?" he said, frowning.

"Llegamos," said Mambo.

"I can see you're here. But who the fuck are you?"

"Fighters," said Mambo. "Reinforcements."

The man who walked like an officer snorted and stomped out past them, muttering curses. More boys in green fatigue pants and white T-shirts came out from the back, spreading among the bunks to stare at the newcomers.

"De dónde son ustedes?" asked the first boy.

Mambo shrugged, looked at the men around him. Most he only knew from the bus ride. "Miami, Tampa, New Orleans, New Jersey—y ustedes?"

"Oriente," said the boy. "We're all from Oriente. We're with Nino Díaz."

"What are they training you for?"

"Amphibious landing. Infiltration."

Felix began to feel better. He could run a landing craft, could smuggle small teams ashore. They could use him here.

"Are you observers?" asked the boy in the top bunk.

"We came to fight," said a man behind Felix.

"Es el pelotón de los Senior Citizen," said the boy and the others from Oriente laughed. A man who seemed to be about thirty came forward through them, smiling, and offered his hand to Mambo.

"Welcome to the Counterrevolution," he said.

"Está el encargado aquí?"

The man laughed. "If anybody is in charge they won't admit it. We drill a lot and try to get them to tell us when we're going. If you've just been in Miami you probably know more than we do."

"We can run boats," said Felix, putting his hand on Mambo's shoulder. "De cualquier clase. If it floats we can run it."

"Viejo, if they don't send us soon we'll steal a boat and you can drive us to Cuba," said the boy on the top bunk.

"Any spot on the coast, we can put you there."

"We're going back to Oriente. To finish what we started."

The man who walked like an officer stomped back in looking like he'd just lost an argument, followed by a tall yanqui with thinning blond hair. The yanqui wore civilian clothes with a pistol strapped on his hip.

"I'm Ray," he said to the new men. "We'll get you squared away in a minute. Chow is at eighteen hundred, followed by orientation for you new people."

"Esos no vienen con nosotros," said the first boy. "We don't need them."

"You fellas want to move your bunks back, make some room for our new people. We'll have more beds coming in a minute."

"Ray," said the first boy, louder. "These viejos aren't coming with us, are they?"

"We have people working on the best use of personnel, Jorge. You don't have to concern yourself with that."

"Mierda," grumbled the man who walked like an officer. He waved his hand to the boys from Oriente. "Síganme, compañeros," he said and walked into the back. The boys followed, shooting annoyed looks back at the newcomers.

"Another caucus," sighed Ray. He turned to the new men. "You want to push these bunks tighter to the wall, make room for the new beds."

"When are we going?" asked the man behind Felix.

"They'll tell me when they tell you," said Ray. "Tomorrow wouldn't be early enough."

They trained on the lake. There were exercises and lots of running and wading through the water carrying packs and a little rifle training.

"I have a better rifle than this at home," said Mambo. "If I'd known I would have brought it."

"They'll give us our real weapons when we go," said the smiling man, who turned out to be an arms instructor.

"Cómo sabe esto?"

"Because they want us to win. Why wouldn't they give us their best?"

"Porque somos cubanos y they are yanquis."

"They're not like that," said the smiling man. "We're doing a job for them. If they sent their own men down to kick Fidel's ass— *kaboom!* La guerra atómica." He held the rifle Felix was aiming by the barrel and gently pushed till it was pointing to the ground. "What have you ever shot at, compadre?"

"Sharks," said Felix. "Gaviotas. Fuí marinero."

"You must have killed a lot of them." He took the rifle and handed it to Gato who had been a railroad engineer in Cuba and a Bible salesman in West Palm Beach. "You don't need to practice shooting anymore. Go catch those men I sent running."

The running was the worst for Felix. Whenever the instructors didn't know what else to do with the fighters they would load them up with heavy packs and have them run down the dirt roads from the barracks to the lake and back. That or long marches through swampland. Felix had walked in a swamp before but it was a long, long time since he'd run anywhere. Felix and the men who were nearly his age would make little grunts after a while, faces turning color with the effort, struggling to keep up.

"If this were a combat situation," the yanqui instructors would say, "you people would be in serious trouble."

"I am in serious trouble," Felix said to Mambo, coughing and dizzy at the end of a run. "They're going to burst my heart before the fidelistas can shoot me."

Mambo sat massaging his knees. The man who smiled worked it so Mambo never had to run, but his knees hurt anyway. "That would be a great loss. If the fidelistas shoot you I'll see to it that you are celebrated as a martyr to freedom. Mothers will say to their sons, 'Miho, you must eat too many plátanos and drink too much rum so you may grow up to be like Felix de la Pena.' "

"El Mártir de la Última Cruzada."

"I will have them name a burdel for you in Manzanillo. Men will say, 'I am going to Felix de la Pena tonight to be laid.' "

Felix flopped onto his back, blood still pounding in his skull. "Los orientales dicen que infiltraremos como Fidel. Que vamos a ser guerrillas en el monte."

"If we are going to be guerrillas in the monte," said Mambo, "I am going to need a horse."

The ones from Oriente who had been there for months, the ones with Nino Díaz, made it clear they didn't want the new men with them when the Invasion started. They stood in groups, glaring and speculating, they pushed up to the front of the mess line and tried to show the new men up in training. Felix thought that getting shot at was nothing to be selfish about, but the food was not bad and there was lots of singing and joking and at dusk he could watch the herons gliding over Lake Pontchartrain. Something big was happening and he was part of it.

In the morning the man who smiled was blown apart while demonstrating the use of the hand grenade. Felix had straggled behind to throw up in the woods after a run and there was an explosion and he was surprised to find that he could run again immediately. When he got to the range people were running and there were parts of the man who smiled loose on the sand. Some of the ones who always sat close by the instructor were hit and writhing in the dirt. Mambo sat holding his ragged left arm across his knees, staring at it. Most of his elbow was gone.

"I won't be going home," he said when Felix knelt by him.

"Esta vez, no, viejo. But soon. Can you move your fingers?"

"No sé. I can't feel them."

Mambo breathed deep, trying not to pass out. "See that the beer is good and cold for me when I come," he said, face draining as the feeling seared back into his arm. "They say that under Fidel the beer is always warm."

"For this he must die."

"For this," said Mambo, "he deserves to teach Cubans to drive automobiles. Para la eternidad."

Felix had been in training for a week and a half when the Invasion started. Ray spoke to the men before they were loaded onto the trucks that would take them to the ship.

"It's your ballgame now, fellas," he said. "Go make us proud."

The first thing Felix noticed about *La Playa* was that it had no radar. The ship looked more fit for hauling bananas than for spearheading the first wave of la Cruzada de Libertad.

"Security," said the yanqui who shipped out with them from Key West, the one they called Curly.

"Seguridad de quién?" asked Felix. "If I was Fidel I would be very secure that my enemy attacks with no radar."

"We'll have plenty of air support. That's the word from the top."

"Air support for a secret infiltration?" said the man who carried himself like an officer.

"Secret is not so important anymore," said Curly. "The orders I have just say we go ashore and slug it out. Like the others."

"Qué otros?"

Curly was uneasy. "The rest of the invasion force. Fellas, we're just one part of the operation. Other people are coming ashore at other places."

This was the first any of them had heard that they weren't the advance guard, the core group filtering into Oriente the way Fidel had done on the *Granma*.

"Dónde?"

"Cuándo?"

"Cuántas?"

"Fellas, fellas, we're just role players here. I'm just as ignorant of the big picture as you are."

"We accept your ignorance," said the man who carried himself like an officer. "What we cannot accept is your command."

Curly gave them an unpleasant smile. "Who do you think footed the bill for this tub?"

"Los mismos pendejos who did not equip it with radar."

"This operation is supposed to look Cuban."

The man who carried himself like an officer turned to the other men who had circled around Curly. "If it will look Cuban," he said, "it will *be* Cuban. We will not be turned from our purpose."

The argument smoldered on the *La Playa* as they eased past the Bahamas and pointed toward Haiti. Felix stood on deck and watched the stars and told the men who'd never been to sea where he thought they were. It was a beautiful, clear night and it kept him from dwelling on how fucked up everything seemed to be. The ones from Oriente were all complaining out loud that the old men were going to be an anchor around their legs when they reached the mountains and Felix had not been checked out on the launch he was supposed to pilot and this Curly did not seem to have been told much of anything. If the other forces were scheduled to land before them the coast would be alive with patrols and they were chugging in with no radar like a freightload of sheep to be slaughtered.

If he had to run it would be bad.

"Eso es El Cazador," he said, pointing into the night sky. "El que los yanquis llaman O'Ryan, la constelación irlandesa. There is his belt, his shield—"

He could hear the man who carried himself like an officer and the other importantes from Oriente speaking in heated voices with the yanqui.

"Y eso es Polaris, la Estrella del Norte."

"Are we close?" asked one of the boys, one who was so excited or scared that he kept flopping face down onto the deck to do push-ups.

"Chico, we were close when we were in Key West."

"I think I can smell it," said another.

"That's just Jorge shitting his pants," said the boy who did push-ups.

There was a loud slap on deck then and several of the boys jumped. Felix found a flashlight and they searched till they saw a flying fish writhing on the stern.

"Our air support is here," said Jorge.

"Cristo, how did he get up so high?"

Felix held the fish up by the tail and watched it, wide-eyed and glistening in the flashlight beam.

"Quieres ir a Cuba con nosotros?" he asked. The fish twitched its wings and Felix tossed it overboard.

"Qué cobarde," said the boy who did push-ups. "A brave fish would have joined us."

Very early in the morning on Saturday Felix sensed land. They'd been running with lights off for a couple hours and there was the slightest promise of a sun on the horizon to the east.

"Estamos cerca de Guantánamo," he whispered, straining to make out the details of the coast. "Thirty, forty miles east. Es el Río Mocambo."

The order came down to put the launches in and Felix scrambled into his the moment it hit water, checking the motor as best he could in the morning dark, getting the feel of the way it rolled. When he realized he'd forgotten his rifle men were climbing in and it was too late to go back on board.

Nobody spoke. They sat with their rifles across their knees, faces set for whatever came next. The plan had been that the man who smiled was to lead a group of ten ashore to scout and mark the landing but now he had been blown apart and many of his team wounded. Instead a rubber raft took off with a party led by an old navy hand. Felix could have told them the mouth of the Río Mocambo was all rocks and hell on small boats, but he figured they had eyes.

The sun tipped over the horizon and he heard a gasp from the other boats bobbing in the water alongside as the island took shape and color. You could swim the distance to shore.

He was ready. They would do this thing and there would be no turning back. The part on the launch was fine, he could bring the men in, as many loads as it took. But then on land, if they were waiting, if he had to run? There was a scene in his head, a scene he had tortured himself with a hundred times, running uphill without a rifle, lungs hot and pressing up into his throat, falling, too exhausted to rise, rolling onto his back to see a man with a beard standing over him, a pistol, hot metal, pressed hard against his eye. The fear at that moment was like a small animal in his stomach, panicked and clawing to get out.

They waited, launches bobbing in the water, nobody speaking. The sighs he heard from men were like those he heard as a boy, waiting in the pews at La Soledad church to enter the booth for his confession.

Dios mío, estoy muy desconsolado para ofenderle—Felix had always thought God was more angered than pleased by the prayers of the unfaithful and he cut the words off in his head.

This would be a good place to jig for pargo, he thought. The yanquis, the ones who knew nothing about fishing, loved that. It gave them something to do with the rod. He thought about the fish underneath them, then thought of the way the big ones crowded around the shrimpers at sea when they'd dump their nets of trash fish, the way they'd hit anything that went into the water then, and he wondered if they were spotted without the radar how many the sharks would get and how many would drown, pulled under by the heavy boots the yanquis had bought them.

They waited.

Felix was beginning to worry about the noises his stomach was making when the rubber raft came back and the scouts went on board. The men in the water began to curse and talk out loud. It was a half hour before they were told to pull up the launches. When everybody was on board the *La Playa* motored away from the coast.

Curly was arguing with the importantes from Oriente, more like a prisoner now than a commander or comrade. Felix saw the radio man being marched away from the controls and into his quarters by a pair of fighters carrying their rifles.

"The conditions are not correct for an infiltration," said the man who carried himself like an officer. "Tomorrow at the same time we will complete our mission as originally planned."

It was a long day and night at sea, fear and frustration hanging over the men like a bad smell. Felix went below to help with the cooking, the familiar rituals calming his nerves a bit. But then he caught himself thinking the thoughts of a condemned man—this will be the last galleta that I eat on this earth—and had to push his mind even further. He planned the expansion of La Perla Perdida back home, bigger kitchen, more tables, a new front window, till he realized if they were successful back home would be Nuevitas and not Miami.

The next morning they were back off Río Mocambo and again the launches were lowered and a motorboat was sent ahead to scout. This time Felix remembered his rifle. It seemed heavier than in training, too heavy to even think about running with.

The motorboat came back and again the launches were pulled up and they sailed away from the island.

When they were about four miles out they saw yanqui ships, destroyers, charging in toward Guantánamo. The men crowded the side to watch.

"Es la Invasión," cursed Jorge. "They're going in without us."

"Es solamente una diversión," guessed the boy who did push-ups. "The destroyers are just there to make Fidel nervous."

"Whatever it is," said Gato, "those are not Cubans."

When the word came in on the radio finally it was not good. There had been a landing, a big one, in the south in the Bahía de Cochinos. The fighting was not going well and the troops were pleading for air support. The *La Playa* was ordered to set course for Puerto Rico. The purpose of their mission had been lost when they didn't land the first day.

The yanqui they called Curly and the man who carried himself like an officer sat at opposite ends of the ship, not speaking. Every now and then a handful of men would call for a mutiny, asking for support to turn the ship around and head to Playa Girón, but the will of the force was broken. When they pulled into the harbor on Vieques Island there were yanqui Marines with rifles waiting to take them into custody.

When Felix got back to the Perla Perdida even the coffee seemed bitter. Most of the main force was in prison on the island, ridiculed in public trials. Men with sons dead or captured sat at the tables in La Perla without ordering, stunned, angry, breaking into sudden tears. Their conversation was an acid hissing of confusion and regret, a single word spoken again and again.

Betrayal.

Betrayal.

Betrayal.

"Qué pasó?" asked the men who knew Felix had gone, who wondered why he was back behind the counter whole and healthy.

"We were betrayed," he would tell them, and at first that simple incantation explained all. The men would nod their heads sadly and walk away, repeating. "We were betrayed."

But in time as information came in the mood changed. Felix had been with the ones who didn't land, the force that was supposed to create a diversion to draw Fidel's troops from the south but remained untouched off the coast, the ship of cowards.

Men began to draw the routes of invasion on the green map of Cuba printed on the placemats Felix had designed, arrows thrusting upward from the Playa Girón met by red-inked blocks of resistance. But no arrows were drawn knifing in from the Río Mocambo, only question marks and circles of confusion and the occasional epithet, underlined and in capitals—

COBARDES.

"Qué pasó?" the men said to Felix, only now it wasn't a question but an accusation. Lunch business dwindled, the factions all finding a lonchería with only their own kind to eat in. Toward the end there were days when only Mambo came, Mambo with his arm gone at the elbow.

"At least we tried," he would say, the canciones from the jukebox sounding hollow in the near-empty room.

"We?" Felix would say, eating his own lunch from the other side of the counter. "Hombre, you lost your arm for freedom. Eres un mártir por la patria. I'm the one who didn't try, who didn't get his feet wet."

"People will forget."

"I won't forget. Ni mi familia ni los otros Brigadistas. Los cubanos nunca olvidarán."

"Eres estúpido, hombre. You would have fought if they gave you the chance."

"Men are stupid creatures," said Felix. "More stupid than the fish in the seas. I can not stop the way I feel. Soy un cobarde."

"A coward would have never volunteered. At your age—"

"I could have tried to turn the ship. Pudiera haber dicho algo, done something. Instead I listen to the yanquis, to the ones who carry themselves as jefes. No, Mambo. Soy un cobarde."

They were silent for a long while after that, Mambo listening to the music, Felix pushing his food around his plate. He watched the shadow of the giant sea turtle, swaying gently with the breeze from the open door to Calle Ocho. When Mambo spoke again there was longing in his voice, the longing that came when he spoke of his dancing days.

"So how did it look?" said Mambo. "La isla?"

Felix thought of the moment the sun tipped over the sea and the outlines of the land hardened in his sight.

"Green. Green and beautiful."

"This place," says Tío Felix, "used to be good for the marlin, for the tunas and sailfish. We fly kites over the bait, hook onto the big ones. Now is all gone."

Marta looks around, sea in every direction, and tries to conceive of where they are drifting as a place.

"There is groupers underneath us," says Tío Felix. "And the tilefish, very deep. But the marlin doesn't run here anymore."

It was a spot where Felix would stop and drift when he bought the new boat, in the years when he was fishing again, in the years when he was transporting men to the island in the secret war. First for the yanquis till they proved they were not to be trusted, and then for whichever splinter group would approach him with a plan and a passion. He had been within sight of the dark coast a half-dozen times but never stepped ashore. None of the men he left off survived.

"This place belongs to nobody," says Tío Felix to his niece. "Ni a los Estados Unidos ni a Cuba ni a nadie. In this place there is no countries."

Marta watches Tío Felix standing relaxed in his cockpit, breathing deeply, a peaceful smile settling on his face. The boat rises and falls on long, rolling swells. She thinks of the big fish underneath, of the violent strength needed to tear them up into the air and still can only imagine her uncle in his kitchen, shaking a pan of sizzling mariscos.

"You won't betray us, Tío?"

Her words are thin and strange to her ears, lost over the empty water.

He looks at her as if he doesn't understand the question at first, as if human language does not apply to him. Then Marta sees the hurt on his face and wishes she could reel the words back in, yank them out of the air.

"I would have fought if they let me," he says quietly. "I was ready to die."

He looks away from her in the direction of the island, then turns the engine on, and swings the *Nidia* around toward home.

TWENTY-THREE

➤ "WHEN I WAS YOUNG I had the seed for sons."

Salvador el viejo is thin and ghostly on the dark road. "Juan, Pedro, Pablo, Tomás—en este orden." The old man carries his rifle in one hand, like a piece of wood. "Y después María, Elena y Anselma. But I was older then and had lost some of my force."

The boy walks in front, rifle held away from his body, alert. He takes several steps, then pauses, listening. Practicing.

"How far are we from the beach?" asks the old man.

Diosdado stops, cocks his head, and runs a hand over his coarse bush of hair. He looks into the sky.

"The stars can't tell you that," says Salvador. "What good is it to patrol if you don't know where you are?"

The boy gives up. "A qué distancia?"

"Ten minutes' walk. Less for a young one like you."

"I can't hear the waves."

"Bueno. Open your nose."

Diosdado breathes deeply through his nose, turns, breathes in again.

"The swamp is behind us."

"Y el mar?"

"The sea—just a taste—in this direction."

The old man nods. "And Iburrí is making charcoal, keeping his oven alive. Just to the west. When all the carboneros were still working, day and night, it was more difficult to smell."

"And it is cloudy tonight, with no moon—"

"No hay de qué, niño. Before la Revolución, when I was younger, we would hunt for caiman with only our senses. Not a flashlight, nothing. If you made a wrong step they would bite your leg off."

"Nunca he visto un caimán," said Diosdado. "Not in the wild."

"They were all arrested, after la Revolución," says Salvador. "They were taken to the farm to breed."

The old man and the boy step off the pressed-dirt road, easing through a break in the wall of thorny marabú bush, finding a narrow path through the trees. It is darker in here, the boy more cautious in his movements.

"That would not be a bad life," he says. "Taken to a farm to lie in the sun and to breed. I hear they eat chicken every day. Not a bad life at all."

Salvador nods. "Until they kill you and tear your skin off."

They walk in silence for a while, the boy stepping ahead, ducking branches, crouched low, rifle ready.

"There is a story they tell about Liborio," says the old man finally. "In this one he is a carbonero, here on the peninsula."

The boy sighs, wishing the old man would be quiet so he could concentrate on his stalking.

"Liborio hears of the jewels at the bottom of the Laguna de Tesoro," Salvador continues. "Jewels the Taíno threw there when the Spanish first came to make them Christians and murder them. Liborio is a poor man, his family always hungry, living on snails and spring water with sugar in it. Sometimes there is no sugar."

It is quiet for a long moment and Diosdado realizes he can no longer see the old man. He turns back and searches till he finds Salvador leaning with one hand against a tree, his face grim, lost in a thought.

"Estás cansado, viejo?"

"You don't know that sound," says the old man. "Your children crying with hunger. Your soul ripped from inside you with each sound. On the beach, above you, las gaviotas y las cagaleches mocking you, screaming their cries. You are no man, your children are starving and you can't feed them."

Diosdado lowers his rifle. "Y Liborio?"

Salvador looks at him as if he had suddenly appeared. "Liborio? One day Liborio is cutting mangrove to burn, chopping branches at the edge of the swamp, when the misery of his life as a carbonero overwhelms him and he decides he will find these famous jewels of the indios or die trying. He leaves that moment, taking neither food nor water for his journey. As he crosses the swamp the mosquitos are like flocks of birds, like a curtain of anger that he cuts a pathway through with his machete. Snakes coil around his ankles, briars tear at his skin, the troganes in the branches above caw his name, laughing at him. But finally he reaches the Laguna de Tesoro. Liborio lays his machete down, takes off his clothes and dives into the water."

Salvador begins to walk again as he tells the story. Diosdado stays at his side, rifle loose in his hands.

"Under the water he meets El Tarpón, swimming near the surface. 'Señor Tarpón,' he says, 'you live in these waters. Can you tell me where to find the famous jewels of the indios?' El Tarpón swims around him in circles, looking at him first with one fishy eye, then the other. 'Jewels cannot float, my friend,' he says. 'You must go deeper.'

"So Liborio swims down and down until he reaches the green plants that grow like trees from the bottom of the laguna. There he meets El Manjuarí, who is half fish and half lizard. 'Señor Manjuarí,' he asks, 'can you help me find the famous jewels of the indios?'

"El Manjuarí peeks out from behind a frond of green plant. 'I have been here a long time,' he says. 'I remember the days of Guamá, jefe de los indios. I remember the day they threw things into the water, things that sank like stones to the bottom. If that is what you are after, you will have to go deeper.'

"So Liborio swims all the way to the bottom, where you sink to your waist in loose muck and the water is thick with decay, and there he meets El Caimán.

" 'Señor Caimán,' he says, 'you have lived here since before there were men. Can you help me find the famous jewels of the indios?'

"El Caimán smiles, showing his long row of sharp teeth, and looks Liborio up and down. 'Come with me, my friend,' he says. 'I think I know what you are looking for.'

"Liborio follows El Caimán, slithering along the bottom of the laguna, crawling through rotten logs, through things that are green and slippery, till they come to a nest made of reeds. In the center of the nest are three stones, perfectly round, polished smooth.

" 'Here,' says El Caimán. 'Here are the treasures left by el jefe de los indios. I have guarded them all these years.'

"Liborio takes them in his hands. 'But they are only stones!' he cries.

" 'I don't know what stones mean to men these days,' says El Caimán. 'But to the indios these were precious.'

"Liborio is sick in his heart. He thinks of his wife and children at home, worrying, hungry, thinks of the long journey back through the swamp. 'I will have to return empty-handed,' he sighs.

"El Caimán smiles again. 'I'm afraid you can't leave, my friend. My children are hungry too. You have to stay here so we can eat you.'

"Liborio is terrified, his mind swimming with gruesome thoughts. 'But the water is full of fish and lizards!' he cries. 'Why not feed them to your children?'

" 'Why should I chase after them,' says El Caimán, smiling, 'when every week they send me a new carbonero?' "

Diosdado frowns. "Es el fin?"

"Sí. La historia termina allá."

"It's a bad story."

"It is a story without hope," says the old man. "A story from before la Revolución."

They step through a tangle of guao trees onto another pressed road. The sliver of moon breaks through the clouds for a moment.

"Before la Revolución there was no médico here, no hospital, nada. Once a year the médico for La Compañía would come to the Central Australia to cure the cutters of their worms. The rest of the time women had to wait days for a boat to Cienfuegos with their babies sick in their arms. Each time this happened to our baby, the mother's milk running through the poor thing como una cagaleche, vomiting, crying day and night. Juan, Pedro, Pablo, y Tomás," he says. "María, Elena, y Anselma. None of them were alive when the boat came to Cienfuegos. None of them lived a full year."

"Siete?"

"Seven babies. Cada uno la misma historia."

Diosdado nods sadly, straining to see the old man's face in the weak moonlight. "Y Jesús?"

Salvador smiles. "When la Revolución was triumphant, a time of hope followed. Like after Machado."

"I don't remember Machado."

"Niño, you don't even remember Batista."

"I wasn't born."

"In a time of hope, the sap rises in the trees. The blood rises in men. In this time Jesús was born. La Revolución había triunfado, I was a man once more and could father a son. But this time, when the sickness came, there was Fidel. Fidel had brought us la clínica in Cayo Ramona. We walked there with Jesús and the médico cured him with a pill. Because of Fidel, my name will not die."

Diosdado rests his rifle on his shoulder. "Have you heard from Jesús? A letter?"

The old man shrugs. "Yo soy analfabeto. When Fidel brought the reading, I was too old. And Africa," he says, "I think Africa is very far from here."

"In two years I will be there."

"Africa?"

"En Angola, como Jesús. I will quit this milicia de mierda where nothing ever happens and travel the world. It is not a bad life, the Army."

Salvador nods. "Until they kill you and tear your skin off."

"They do that in Angola?"

"I have heard stories. It is a savage place."

"Do you worry about Jesús?"

Salvador shakes his head. "I have already given seven. God can not be so cruel."

Diosdado grips his rifle firmly and begins to stalk again. "What I really want to do is to build bridges. I understand how they stay in the air, how the pieces work together to be strong. I can put them together, piece by piece, in my mind when my eyes are closed. But at school they say the State has enough ingenieros, enough bridges, that I should stay here and study to work in the tourism."

The old man shakes his head. "Turismo. Los turistas vendrán cuando los mosquitos se hayan ido. And the mosquitos are going nowhere."

"There are turistas who come to the village of Guamá to live in huts like the indios."

"Pero los indios nunca tuvieron restaurantes."

"Sin embargo, viejo, yo me voy a Angola," says the boy. "I can't breathe here anymore. Sometimes, in the army, when the enemy is on the other side of the river, they need somebody to build a bridge. And there I will be."

"There are rivers in Angola?"

"Creo que sí."

"I hope so," says Salvador, frowning. "It would be too bad to go there and find it was a desert."

Diosdado stops, breathing deeply, alert. "I think I can smell it now. I think I can smell the ocean."

"Es posible. Do you know what this place is?"

The boy looks around. "The road to Girón?"

"In this place, at this spot in the road, a battalion was lost."

The boy shakes his head. "Ahora lo recuerdo. They took our class here when I was little. There were speeches. Always there are speeches."

Salvador looks at the ground as if searching for something very small. "I was not in the milicia then," he says. "But when we heard the shooting, a group of us, carboneros y pescadores, volunteered. They gave us rifles and a canvas bag with bullets in it and sent us along with the regular troops. It was in the middle of the day, very hot. We were standing in the back of a truck, squeezed together, the sweat of our bodies soaking through our clothes. It was a long line on the road, camiones, tanques, more men than I had ever seen together in my life. The smell of gasoline. Noise. All of us scared, knowing only rumors, que los mercenarios y posiblemente los yanquis habían atacado. Racing to meet them at the beach, to fight them. I had shot a rifle at a caiman, at a bird, but never at a man. I pictured thousands of yanquis, tall as palm trees, coming ashore with cannons in their arms. Fidel had warned us that this would come. And then there was a buzzing overhead and we saw our aviones, our bombers, flying low. The men sent up a cheer. I can't tell you how my heart soared. The throb of their engines sent blood through my body, I was no longer a scared pescador with bare feet and an ancient rifle, I was a cubano, a warrior. Everyone was standing, cheering, the camiones y tanques stopped in the road, even the tanquistas standing up in their metal holes, waving their arms. Then the bombs came."

"No fueron nuestros aviones?"

"They had been painted to fool us. We stayed on the road to cheer." Salvador turns in a circle. Diosdado follows his eyes.

"Aquí," he says, "aquí fué el Infierno. They dropped fire on us, a fire that sticks to the skin like tar. Men in the back of the truck with me were burned to charcoal. Los carboneros cambiaron a carbón."

"Pero tú?"

"I was one of the few untouched. God put me there to witness Hell. Los tanques, los camiones, los soldados—todos quemados. More than a thousand men."

Diosdado looks into the dark as if for bodies. "I will fight them in Africa."

"Niño, in Africa you will fight Africans. The men on the beach were cubanos—"

"Gusanos! Desgraciados—"

"Cubanos, sin embargo. Some of them died to attack us. This I will never understand."

"I will try to remember this place."

"It should not be difficult."

The boy sighs. "It was before I was born."

"But now I have told you—"

"You were there. It isn't the same."

Salvador nods sadly. "Tienes razón. You will have your own hell. An African hell. Tú y Jesús."

After a minute of walking the old man and the boy stop to pee alongside the road, one on each side. Diosdado carefully lays his rifle in the dirt. Salvador calls over his shoulder.

"Hay otra historia de Liborio," he calls. "In this one he is a zafrista, a poor cane-cutter, in the days just after la Guerra de Independencia. One afternoon he is alone in the field, still cutting as the others eat their meager lunch, and he chops through a row of cane to discover God, sitting in an expensive white suit on a little stool, the type the colonos used when they stopped to survey their property.

" 'Buenos días, Liborio,' says God. 'I have come to see how my cubanos are doing.'

"Liborio stands with his clothes soaked with sweat, his hands cracked and bleeding, his feet bare and filthy. He sticks his machete into the ground, spits out the piece of cane he has been chewing on, and thinks for a long time about what he should say to God.

" 'First of all, Señor,' he says, 'we are no longer subjects of the King of Spain. We are free men.'

" 'I can see that,' says God, looking at Liborio from head to foot. 'The difference is astounding.'

" 'But I wonder sometimes,' Liborio continues, 'why life is still so hard.'

"God smiles at him. 'My son, nothing on this earth can be perfect, or nobody would want to go to Heaven. Sugar is sweet, but man has to labor to take it from the ground. The ocean is wide and bountiful, but it has sudden storms and dangerous currents to pull you under and drown you. This Cuba is so beautiful, the pearl of all my Creations, so I had to make the pests, los mosquitos, the sea urchin, the thorn of the marabú, all so life here would be less than Paradise. Nothing can be perfect in this world.'

"Liborio ponders this, trying to fathom the wisdom of God's ways. 'But nothing can mar the beauty of freedom,' he says finally. 'Surely freedom is perfect?'

"God smiles again. 'For that,' he says, 'I created los yanquis.' ''

The old man bends and shakes the last drops away before tucking himself in and joining the boy in the center of the road.

"Nunca he visto a un yanqui. Not a living one," says Diosdado.

"Ni yo tampoco. I have seen only pictures of them. A few were killed near here, pilotos de los aviones, the bombers, who were shot down. They looked like any dead man. When they peeled away the avión, all the hot metal, there was only a man inside, quemado como mis amigos."

Salvador begins to sing, his voice deep and surprisingly strong for an old man—

> *Si dicen que del joyero*
> *Tome la joya mejor,*
> *Tomo a un amigo sincero*
> *Y pongo a un lado el amor—*

A dog begins to bark in the distance.

"Por qué cantas, viejo? They will hear us."

"Quién?"

"Los enemigos. Los yanquis."

Salvador laughs. "Niño, nobody is coming back here to invade. Nunca. Not here."

"Then why do you volunteer to make the patrol?"

"For the same reason I always sing when I reach this part of the road. To be above suspicion."

"No entiendo."

"Oyes este perro? That dog belongs to Roa and his bruja of a wife. They are the jefes of the Committee."

"Y pues?"

"They have their hands in everybody's soup, up to the wrist. If they don't like you or want something that you have, they bring you in front of the Committee for discipline."

"This is well known. But why do you wake their dog?"

"At first they accused me of lacking the fervor of la Revolución.

So I volunteered to walk the patrol, to guard the coast while every-body else sleeps. Then they accused me of sleeping on the beach during my watch instead of walking the route. This is very old business between me and Roa, it goes back further than I can remember. So now, each time I pass I sing, which wakes their dog, who wakes them and their neighbors, and they can all be sure I am not sleeping on the beach but out scaring the yanquis from our shores, patrolling the road to Girón."

"But your singing would warn an enemy you were coming. It is stupid—"

"I am known as a stupid old man. But an old man above sus-picion."

"The Committee for the Defense is our voice—"

"Niño, es una organización política. As with all such things, the ones with the longest beaks get to the water first. Roa has a beak that stretches all the way to La Habana."

A voice cuts the night, cursing the barking dog.

"Now everyone is awake."

Salvador smiles. "Eternal vigilance. The price we pay for free-dom."

The old man moves down the road, Diosdado walking backward next to him as if to cover his retreat.

"Hay otra historia de Liborio," says Salvador. "In this one he is a poor obrero, a worker in a tobacco warehouse in the years before la Revolución. He works hard all day, this Liborio, and at night he trudges home to his tiny room in an apartment building and falls into bed, exhausted."

"Is this going to be another sad story?"

"Óigame, niño. Liborio is a good man, a hard worker, but he is innocent of the ways of the world. On Election Day he just sleeps, too exhausted to go out and sell his vote. One night he comes back from work and opens his door and there is this tipo, a big man with scars on his face, a real gangster, standing there.

" 'Qué pasa?' says Liborio, surprised and frightened. 'Esta es mi sala.'

" 'Now it is mine,' says the tipo, and closes the door in his face.

"Liborio runs down to the man who takes his rent money and tells him what has happened. The man shrugs.

" 'You have to ask the landlord,' he says. 'I'm just the manager here.'

"So he gets the address of the landlord and he knocks on his door and explains what has happened. 'I always paid my rent on time,' he says. 'Why have you given my room away?'

" 'I am only a landlord,' he says. 'And this is a criminal matter. I suggest you go to la policía.'

"Liborio goes to the station of the policía and finds the jefe there. He explains his problem. But the jefe de policía just shakes his head.

" 'No puedo hacer nada,' he says. 'This tipo, this gangster, is connected to the políticos. If you want your room back you will have to talk to them.'

"So Liborio goes first to the headquarters of the Ortodoxos and finds the jefe de políticos for the party. 'A gangster has taken my room and I am told he is the friend of politicians,' he says.

" 'This sounds like the work of the Auténticos,' says the jefe of the Ortodoxos. 'They are very corrupt people. What can you give us?'

"Liborio has not thought about payment, as he is a very poor man. 'If you help me, I will vote for you in the next election,' he says.

"The jefe de los Ortodoxos laughs at him. 'A single vote is a very small thing. I'm afraid there is nothing we can do for you.'

"Liborio is disappointed, but as he has nowhere to sleep at night, he goes to the headquarters of the Auténticos and finds the jefe there. He explains his problem to the man.

" 'This sounds like the work of the Ortodoxos,' says the jefe. 'They are very corrupt people. What can you give us?'

" 'If you help me,' says Liborio, 'I will vote for you in the next election. Twice. As many times as they will let me in the door.'

"The jefe of the Auténticos laughs at him. 'Votes are such seasonal gifts,' he says. 'They are only useful on Election Day. I'm afraid we can't help you.'

"That night, as he tries to fall to sleep in an alley under a roof of cardboard, Liborio offers a prayer to God.

" 'Señor,' he prays, 'please make this tipo go away from my room. If you help me I will give you my devotion.'

"A voice, deep and mysterious, echoes in the dark alley.

" 'Hijo mío,' it says, 'there will always be a room waiting for you in the Kingdom of Heaven.'

"Only that and nothing more. So in the morning when Liborio rises, joints aching, coughing from the damp night, he goes to find

El Diablo. Liborio stands in the graveyard holding a black cat by the tail, swinging it one, two, three times over his head, then spitting over each shoulder. The ground opens at his feet and there is a staircase leading down. Liborio is scared, but he will die if he must sleep in the open another night. He goes down the stairs, and at the bottom there is a man dressed in black, with an account book in his hands.

" 'Señor Diablo?'

" 'Liborio,' says El Diablo, 'what are you doing down here?'

" 'If you will get a certain person to give me my room back,' says Liborio, 'I will sell you my soul.'

"El Diablo sighs and claps Liborio on the shoulder. 'Life must be very hard when a good man like you comes to me. Let's take the tour.'

" 'What tour?'

" 'If you are going to sell me your soul and dwell here for eternity,' says El Diablo, 'you have to know what the accommodations are. It is only fair.'

"So El Diablo leads Liborio around Hell and it is a pretty miserable place. In room after room people are swimming in vats of liquid fire, smoke like acid burning their lungs, screaming in despair. Near the end of the tour Liborio spots the door of a room that no screams are coming from. When El Diablo is not looking, he goes to it and opens it a crack to peek in. A gust of cool air hits him in the face. There, sitting around a table under a big ceiling fan, are the gangster and the jefe de policía and the jefe de los Ortodoxos and the jefe de los Auténticos, all laughing and smoking cigars and drinking cold beer and playing cards as putas in slinky underwear rub up against them. Liborio is shocked. He turns to El Diablo.

" 'Can they be dead?' he cries. 'I saw them up above only yesterday!'

" 'They're not dead,' says El Diablo, shutting the door and pulling Liborio close to whisper. 'In fact, those are my landlords. I am only the manager here.' "

The boy pauses to shake a stone loose from his shoe. "So he is fucked again, Liborio."

"Siempre jodido. A man without luck."

"I'm glad I was not born yet for these politicians. For these Ortodoxos y Auténticos."

The old man shrugs. "Today we have the Committee."

"The Committee is different. We can join the Committee."

"We *must* join the Committee. To be above suspicion. To be there each meeting when the criticism is done. To accuse our neighbors when they accuse us."

They have reached the Playa Girón. A few patches are lit by the empty tourist bungalows. The rest falls off into darkness. The sea is gentle tonight, rolling, the waves hissing lazily as they break over the sand. Tiny ghost crabs dart from hole to hole, a faint, frenzied patter that precedes the old man and the boy as they tromp across the beach.

"In the old days the políticos were bandits, they were liars and thieves. But down here, in the asshole of the world, there was nothing for them to steal. They were only a bad rumor to us, a foul smell that blew from the cities once in a great while."

"Before la Revolución."

"Sí. Before the roads, la electricidad, la clínica, todo. Before Fidel."

"Y ahora? Después de Fidel?"

"Y ahora, niño," says Salvador el viejo, looking out over the dark and peaceful sea, sighing the deep sigh of an old man, "now he has made politicians of us all."

TWENTY-FOUR

Diario
7 de Septiembre, 1960

➤ EN ESTE LUGAR todo se pudre en vida.

(There are stains on these pages, stiff islands of brown and yellow, purple smears where ink has run from sweat.)

In this place everything rots while still alive.

I have not been dry since the day we arrived. The door of the airplane was opened and we were embraced in a wet heat, a heat that sears in the open and smothers under the green jungle canopy. A heat that slides its arms around you and sucks the breath from your lungs with a hot, wet kiss of decay. This jungle is a woman, I think, and fertile, so fertile she threatens to smother us in the vines and shoots and runners that snake out from her loins, to drown us in her lusciousness.

We are high in the steaming green mountains, living in a wound on the wet skin of the jungle. The evidence tells us we are in Guatemala, but that is only a name and everything that surrounds us seems beyond naming.

In this place the plants are fleshy and damp. If you watch they will grow before your eyes, grasping for life, sucking in the hot mist. We slash through vines thick as men's arms, the severed parts bleeding milky green sap, seething rotten gas. We stretch fences to keep them back, but in days our perimeter is overgrown, sharp wire swallowed by ropes of green.

In this place the insects are monsters. Orange and red and jewel green, horned and armored and swivel-eyed. I've seen them carry small frogs off in their jaws, seen them strip a tree of hand-sized leaves in minutes.

In this place the people rot as they grow. The indios are starved, liquid-eyed and brown-toothed, one step up from the mud they are covered with. Insects swarm around their faces, burrow under their skin. They came to the side of the road to watch us pass on our drive up here, our men staring out, sweat-soaked, hammered senseless over the ruts and holes as the truck climbed, old engine moaning with the steepness and the weight, the indios staring in, scratching, ribs hollow and bellies taut with gas. Hunger on two legs.

In this place, in this decaying green Hell, our nation is being reborn. The jungle is a woman, I think, and fertile.

There are six of us to a room, two bunk beds of three tiers. Below me is Segura, a gambler from La Habana they call Sure Thing. Above me is Serafín, called El Ángel Negro. Across from us are the cousins from La Esperanza, known as Flaco y Más Flaco because they are so skinny, cousins who whisper in their own private language after lights out. Above them a real hidalgo, an Andaluz who never smiles who we have named Don Curro. His people came to Cuba when he was a boy and he believes this fight is the noble thing to do. I am called El Poeta.

Blas is not here yet. I wonder if he is with another part of the force, chosen to lead because of his experience.

Our trainer is a little Filipino, a jungle fighter the men call El Chino Vallejo. He is a rooster, strutting the length of the compound, battle-scarred, itching to fight. He tells us the jungle is our mother, that we must turn to her for protection, for nourishment. With him there are some kind of Russians, men thick and solid as gray stone walls. Each command is translated from their language to English to Spanish and then we are cursed for obeying so slowly. We hike in khaki fatigues and black baseball caps, half civilian and half soldier, crawl through mud, climb high into the rain-choked mountains. I have fired the recoilless rifle, the submachine gun, the .45 pistol, weapons they lock away from us at the end of each day. My body is hardening like a scar, slowly and with pain.

A boy I didn't know fell from a cliff in the jungle and was killed. We have named ourselves from his recruitment number—la Brigada 2506. There are just over three hundred of us here, but we think they must be training others in another place.

This morning a boy was bit by a poisonous snake and sent away. We are surrounded by the jungle, prisoners trapped within its steaming thickness. I would feel better if we were closer to the sea. Here we are at the mercy of people we have never seen, people we can only imagine exist. We are a sword sharpened every day for battle, but with no idea how or when we will be put to use. No news of the world penetrates here, only rumor seeping into our barracks at night. At night we are free to doubt, to ask questions. This doubt is a disease that rots the spirit.

We speak of the human soul. Only Segura thinks that it may not exist. We may all have to kill a man, many men. Is this murder?

"Where the cause is just," says Don Curro, "there is no murder. We are on a Crusade, with the blessing of God. When the Christian fought the Moor, he had the blessing of God. When he fights the Communist, the atheist, it is the same."

"But Christians kill Christians in war," says Sure Thing. "What then?"

"There are men, patriots, who will be executed if we don't win," says Serafin. "We will be saving their lives. Maybe a killing that saves a life is no murder."

"They are all murders," Flaco announces.

"All murders," repeats Más Flaco.

"But on the Day of Judgment some murders are forgiven. This is all we can hope for."

"Our only hope."

The Flacos were in the underground when they were students. Maybe they have already killed.

"It's all a matter of odds," says Sure Thing. "You train and you learn to be a good soldier, but when the bullets fly they have no mind. No training, no honor, no soul—only a path. And if you and the bullet are on the path at the same moment—"

He snaps his fingers.

"There is no murder," he says. "Only physics."

"But God guides the hand of the righteous," says Don Curro.

"If He exists."

"We have been given hands and hearts," says Andaluz, "and eyes to see. With these miracles how can there not be God?"

"And our barracks?" smiles Sure Thing. "Our uniforms, our rifles, our mortars, todos? These are from God as well?"

"We are His soldiers."

"We are soldiers of the yanquis," says Flaco.

"The yanquis," Más Flaco repeats.

"But do the yanquis really exist?" Sure Thing is enjoying the talk, a man who believes devoutly in himself. "Maybe there will be an invasion and maybe there won't. Maybe there is a paradise, maybe not. Maybe the yanquis will appear out of the sky at the end of the day. Maybe," he says, "this is just a test of our faith."

"As life is of our souls," says Don Curro.

They ask me what I feel. I tell them we must always believe in God, but never rely on Him.

The same applies to the yanquis.

Diario
25 de Noviembre, 1960

Hoy llegó Blas.

(The handwriting is different here, less flowing, bitten deeper into the paper with caution.)

Today Blas arrived.

He came with a small group of others who were put into the Third Battalion. I was not able to talk to him till dinner, when there is disappointing food on filthy trays. Blas does not know why he was delayed, only that the yanqui recruiters accepted him, then rejected him, then called him again just after the Election.

Politics.

Blas at once became friends with the ones called watermelons, Army green outside, red inside. Los fidelistas sin Fidel. Men who fought in the mountains and in the underground, who risked their lives to bring the General down. They sit apart from the casquitos, who wore the yellow of Batista, who are proud to have opposed the Revolution, claiming that liberty has always burned in their hearts. Some were involved in Barquín's coup, others left the island still loyal to the General. Between them are the civilians, men like Serafín who watched what went before from a distance, and the young, innocent of the past.

Blas is my brother. Don Curro and Sure Thing stop talking whenever I first enter the room.

Politics.

There has been a change in our training. El Chino Vallejo is gone, replaced by Colonel Frank, a tall and noisy yanqui. The jungle is no longer to be our mother. Instead of a guerrilla infiltration we are being trained for a frontal invasion, the kind we have seen in the movies of John Wayne. Open air, a beach, airplanes, cannons from ships offshore. Colonel Frank says to think of ourselves as small, efficient cogs in a great machine of war, single drops of water in the tidal wave that will cleanse our nation.

We train for this grand assault but still the jungle surrounds us, mocking us. At times I fear we are only here to carry the flag, to give a Cuban face to actions the yanquis will engage on their own.

Every evening the rifles are collected and counted. With Colonel Frank there are more yanquis, the trainers of the Special Forces, men with eyes like swords and bodies taut with violence. They teach us to kill with our feet, with our hands. At night Sure Thing goes to his card game, Don Curro escapes into his literature, the Flacos tell their private jokes to each other, bursting into laughter before the words are done. Other men gather around the glow of flashlights, reddish and ghostly under their chins, arguing in whispers, each group tending a private garden of mistrust. Serafín and I walk across the base, from guard post to guard post, mostly in silence. I have never been so close to a negro before, and this Serafín is a moody one, with eyes that take everything in and give nothing away. When we are in action he is the steadiest, the most serene in movement, firing his weapon as if he can see the arc of each bullet, a thoughtful student of what must be done. He does not read well and I am teaching him what I can.

Young girls climb to the base at night and come by the fence, opening themselves and hissing for our attention. Some of them are already pregnant, looking not much older than Marta. The indios look like children and then they are old, nothing in between. The men pay them cautiously, pressing a quetzal or two in the girl's palm then clutching her wrist till they are done, one on either side of the razor wire, touching only where they must to complete the act. The men complain how dirty they are.

If we are not allowed to fight soon the Devil will take us all.

Diario
2 de Diciembre, 1960

Dos patrias tengo yo: Cuba y la selva.

(The hand lightens with the poetry, words slanting, bent forward like skaters on a pond. The words have been fought over somewhere else, nothing is crossed out or written over.)

> *I have two countries: Cuba and the jungle.*
> *Or are they one?*
> *Cuba, grieving widow*
> *Of a thousand black nights,*
> *Mourning a lover betrayed.*
> *The jungle, Mother,*
> *Nursemaid to revolutions,*
> *Bottomless womb of a million bloody births.*
>
> *The Mother holds me*
> *In binding embrace, hot breath*
> *On my face, pulling me back*
> *To what is bright and wet and sure.*
> *The widow, calling,*
> *Voice echoing over deep water,*
> *Seducing with ancient words of glory.*
>
> *Now is the time to begin to die.*
> *The screaming flag,*
> *The red call of battle*
> *Quickening the heart's hot will to ripen.*
> *The thoughtless jungle*
> *More eloquent than man.*
> *The widow's night more thrilling*
> *Than the sun.*

Ambrosio de la Pena Cruz

Diario
13 de Enero, 1961

"Tienen miedo de la verdad," dice Blas.

(The writing is disjointed now, the letters slanting one way then the other. The words run off the page a few times, as if written in the dark.)

"They are afraid of the truth," says Blas. "They don't trust me because I was in the monte when they were home hiding between their mother's tetas."

They walk among us like wolves among house dogs, Blas and the others who just arrived, the barbudos who have shaved their beards, the underground bombers who will fight in the open this time. They carry themselves apart, speaking less, following the commands of the instructors efficiently but without the quick snap of obedience. Their eyes judge everyone, everything, but they hold their opinions like clenched fists.

"Spies," say the casquitos, the conservatives, the secret Batistianos. "The Kennedy people have sent us spies."

"They have to be watched," say the centristas, men who measure their trust in you by the date you left the island. "If they support the Constitution of 1940, maybe they can be tolerated."

Blas left a little more than a year ago, when Matos and Agramonte were arrested, but his heart is truly in this fight.

"I have paid, chico," he tells me. "I have paid in weeks without sleep, in months without hope, paid in hunger, in blood, in the deaths of my close friends. What did I pay for? Not for what El Caballo is doing in La Habana, and not for a return to those blood-sucking old men in Miami. Not for what is in the pockets of yanquis and their pet casquitos. When you have paid what I have you can never settle for less than everything you fought for. I understand this and Fidel understands this, and that is why he is most afraid of the men who fought at his side. It is why Matos rots in prison, why hundreds of good men are put to the wall and shot. Fidel wants the world to think there are no men like me, that only Batistianos oppose him, the rich and the corrupt. And these fucking yanquis are going to make that the truth. They will make a hero out of him."

I remember when Blas visited the first time, after the soldiers had come out to look for him. Thin and weary and hard. The beard was what angered Father the most, the symbol of everything he did not like and did not trust about what was happening. Damn student politics, he called it, and blamed it on Reds and foreigners among the faculty. Blas wouldn't argue with him, just staring with a face that was a challenge, speaking softly as if to a child. He had aged so much, Blas, he was a man now and I was more of a boy than ever. He was kinder to me than when he left for university, but distant, as if part of him was still in the mountains. When Father stormed away and Marta had fallen asleep on his lap, I told him I wanted to join.

"Ay, chico," he said. "There is nothing good about it. It is only an ugly thing that has to be done once, properly, and then never repeated. For Cubans to fight each other is a sin, a sin I hope you will never commit."

His face is smooth now, the men here scolding even the hint of a beard, but he still has the eyes that are a challenge, still thin, still weary, still hard. Blas is one of the leaders, one who causes questions to be raised, one who brings us face to face with our keepers. His power is not from charm or the cleverness of political argument or fame or rank, but from the force inside him, the knowledge you have standing near him that his words will be backed with actions, that his actions will cut to the bone. Neither of us has made much in public of being brothers, but since he came here my weight has increased in the world, I have enemies and allies and eyes watching me always. Even when I try to stay apart from the barracks debates men pull me in to ask what I think, hoping to define one extreme of the argument. I am the brother of Blas de la Pena and this is a mountain I will have to conquer, a mountain I struggle up every day. He is the spot on my soul, the original sin that makes me mortal. I had hoped we could all start clean here in the jungle, Cubans reborn from the ashes of the past, but now I see the past is like this clinging jungle, no sharp boundaries, no clear path, just an endless grappling for air.

This morning most of the Second and Third Battalions resigned. They stayed in their barracks, sending word that they would not take orders from Batistiano officers, that they were not American citizens and could not be ruled by yanquis in civilian clothes sitting on top of the hill.

There were shouting matches and fistfights, rumors of buried pistols. I was sick with shame at us all, men who would be liberators squabbling over useless scraps of history, over the ridiculous alphabet of political factions. Men were making deals for the future, forming coalitions, appointing cabinets before a shot had been fired for freedom.

Colonel Frank was gone and the one we call Sitting Bull was in charge. San Román offered to step down as commander and become a common soldier again, but it was too late. Most of the men respect him as a soldier but he is the favored boy of the yanquis and they are keeping us all tame with lies.

They finally got us all mustered into formation and Sitting Bull climbed the wooden platform to face us. We felt the special forces yanquis slipping behind us and to our sides. We stood at parade rest, soldiers without guns.

Sitting Bull did not take long. He said he was boss. He said San Román was still our commander. He said anyone who had a problem with this would be sent back to Miami.

San Román climbed the platform then and called for unity. We were all Cubans, all brothers. He called for those men with a will to fight and to forget about political things to step to the right and form ranks.

I moved without thinking, as did the men around me in the First. Phrased in such a way, who could refuse? We turned and moved to the right several yards and formed ranks, shoulders square, eyes front, and it was very still. It felt like the jungle stopped growing around us, if only for that instant. I waited for the cheer that would signal we had all moved together, but it didn't come. I let my eyes slide over to see.

There were only a hundred left of those who resigned, standing at attention to our left, faces grim. Blas was in the first row. San Román asked them to reconsider, but I knew if they were men like Blas there was no bending their will. Blas was only a few feet from me, I could see the details of his face, and I thought of what Sure Thing said about the path and the bullet and I saw there was no way I could walk across that space and survive. The special forces yanquis moved around them then, their pistols drawn, a few with rifles, and marched them down to the tents the tanquistas had been using.

Sure Thing is taking bets now that they will be gone when the sun rises. Whenever I pass a group of men their voices lower and I hear the word, brother, brother, and I force myself to act as if it is nothing to me. I don't know if I have betrayed someone or been betrayed, I am proud and embarrassed at once. I am afraid they will call me out tomorrow and send me home as well. I am afraid for the soul of our Brigade without Blas and his friends. I am afraid this jungle will swallow us all forever.

I am not afraid of the truth. To whoever wants to know, I am the brother of Blas de la Pena, a hero of the Cuban people. He is a peak that I stand on, a light I can follow every day.

Soy el hermano de Blas de la Pena Cruz, patriota y guerrero. Viva la libertad!

TWENTY-FIVE

THE LIMOUSINE IS the safest place he's ever been. The seats, soft leather, purr into position at the touch of a finger. The air temperature is under control, the tinted glass takes the edge off the bright world outside and offers a blue mystery to anyone on the street. There is a glass panel you can slide up between driver and back-seat passenger, soundproof, and behind there is a liquor cabinet with a place for ice and a small TV and enough room for two tall men to sit facing each other and stretch their legs. The inside smells new, though it isn't, smells like a place immune to earthly time.

It is the quiet that Serafín notices the most, the soft solid response of the engine to his foot, the city noises outside muffled, unthreatening. Most of the business is to and from the airport, and even the rumble of the big jets overhead is dulled. If a client wants he'll play the radio, but Serafín prefers to listen to the silent weight of the car, gliding tight as a torpedo through the city.

The hard afternoon shower is somebody else's problem. Serafín eases the limo over empty downtown streets in a kind of dreamy slow waltz, Marta sitting beside him in her white nurse's uniform, smelling like soap and starch, her cap held in two hands on her lap. Serafín has an awe for the uniform, even Luz seems more serious a person when she wears it. The rain is a distant hiss on the pavement. Marta has never asked Serafín for a ride before.

"Es cómodo."

"You should sit in the back for true comfort."

"Do you sit there?"

"Sometimes when I'm waiting. It's like a small apartment. Mi casa de cuatro ruedas."

With her he feels self-conscious in his own uniform, darker-skinned. He has left only the gloves off.

"You like this work?" she asks.

"It pays well. It's quiet."

"Quiet."

"Sí. Tranquilo."

Something is going to be said. Serafín feels it, as though the air in the limo has changed suddenly. There are things that he wants to have happen, words he wants to say and hear, but he knows not to hope for them. He tries to relax his mind and be ready. Something is going to be said and nothing will be the same.

"Why did you go?" she asks.

"Dónde?"

"Back then. Con la Brigada."

He shifts in the driver's seat, considering, signals a right turn.

"Why did Ambrosio go?" he says. "Y los otros?"

"There is no way Ambrosio could be of our family and not go. We had lost so much. But you—negro y pobre—"

Serafín smiles. Papi used to talk about the poor, about the responsibilities of kindness and charity. Papi had a job as a busboy at the Hotel Nacional and every day breathed the same air as the grandes Señores of the world. Black, of course, black from a line of emancipados that stretched back to the beginning of the nation, but never poor.

"It was a kind of fever," he says. "You know what a fever does."

Marta frowns, studying his face. "You wish you hadn't gone?"

He shrugs. "Good men were killed."

"And how do we honor the dead?"

Serafín smiles again and Marta looks away into the rain, pouting.

"I'm sorry," he says. "You make me think of Ambrosio. At the camp he was always asking these questions. Qué es el honor? Qué es la justicia? Existen o son solamente ideas abstractas? Vale la vida sin reflexión?" Serafín coasts the limo through a flooded intersection, watching the wake it cuts curl off the fender. "I didn't have any answers then, either."

Marta speaks softly. "But these are not bad things."

"Son importantes. Ambrosio was many things that I would like

to be. He had a sense of what is right, and that gave me strength.
It gave me hope. But I was only a small fish, carried by the wave
of the moment."

"Si tuvieras la oportunidad," says Marta, "if there was another
invasion, planned only by Cubans, would you go?"

So it is this. Serafín turns the air up a notch.

"An invasion?"

"An action. A blow against the Communists."

"There have been actions for years. Nothing has been won."

"Every time there is a successful action people remember the
Brigade. They remember that the war is not finished."

Serafín looks out as they cross the Causeway, rain slanting hard
onto the waves, bending the palms that line the road. The sky is
lightening to the north.

"Are you planning an invasion?"

He hopes that she will hear it as a joke, a way to slip the question,
but her silence gives him a chill.

"If I were a man saying this to you," she asks, "would you feel
the same?"

He has seen other men try for her over the years, some drawn
only by her beauty, others caught in the challenge of unlocking her
secrets. He has heard lies die half spoken in the mouths of smooth
talkers, seen proud men discover their own vanity under her gaze.
I'll thaw her out, they say, I'll make a woman of her, then walk
away huffing like beaten roosters, muttering insults.

Serafín looks in her eyes and feels what it is she wants, sees the
deep cool water and knows he could have her and what a thrilling
thing that would be but only if he surrenders to it completely, diving
down and down and forgetting everything else. This is something
he's wanted, being alone with her, in the quiet, close, but there is
nothing safe in her eyes. It is hard to breathe and for a moment he
considers buzzing down the tinted windows to swallow the wet air
outside.

"Marta, if you were a man," he says, "I wouldn't have listened
even this far."

Marta puts her nurse's cap on, carefully, pinning it into her hair.
Fifth Street is deserted as they enter the Beach and Serafín turns
left up Euclid.

"You have to want to do it for yourself," she says finally. "For
Cuba. Not for me."

Serafín feels a sinking rush of what must be jealousy. She is involved with somebody, a group, a man. She is beyond him now. He sees her jaw tighten, muscles braced against his arguments, his warnings.

"I'm sorry," he says.

The rain has let up and there are pools of standing water in the nursing home lot. Marta steps out and straightens her uniform.

"Gracias, Serafín," she says. "Eres un amigo."

"Es un sendero peligroso," he calls to her. "Be careful."

Serafín watches her pick her way around the puddles. She waves and goes inside. He pulls out of the lot, tires swishing hub-deep in water, and heads toward South Beach. At the cross streets he catches a glimpse of ocean, gray and choppy. He thinks of Marta surrounded by sea, thinks of her facing the sharp rocks of the coast, thinks of her, lost.

He sees the Cadillac parked outside Joe's Stone Crab and stops across the street. Soto will be inside, at a table with women and politicians and other drogueros. Big León, the bodyguard, will be alone at a small table nearby, a bowl of conch chowder in front of him, jacket open, watching the entrance. Serafín sees the boy who took his place as driver sitting in the front of the Cadillac, head bobbing to radio music.

In a moment Serafín will go in and sit by León and ask permission to speak to the jefe, to see if he can get in touch with Blas de la Pena. But now he sits waiting for the last of the noon shower, quiet and dry, in the safest place in all of Miami.

TWENTY-SIX

Villas always starts with the coffee. His own small sacrament—the waiter placing a cortado in front of him, the miracle of the sugar, the heat of the cup on his fingers, bringing it close to his face to breathe in the aroma. His eyes close with that first deep breath of coffee, the pure animal pleasure of it, the familiar bite at the back of his throat. He draws it over his tongue with a single lazy kiss, chewing on the thickness of it, café cubano, spreading through his body rich and warm and sweet.

The waiters at the Versailles know him now and relax their efficient noontime rush. Villas has a small table against the wall, the first customer in for lunch and the last to leave, holding each bite of food in his mouth as if trying to remember its name.

"To eat without tasting," he says almost every day to Orestes, the busboy, "is to live without thought."

Villas performs the rite again, sighing as he puts the cup down, concentrating on the taste, holding on to it, feeling the same thrill as the first one he drank here, the one he waited twenty years for.

The men in the galeras at La Cabana wore army uniforms from the days before, with a large P stenciled on the back. Some had been jailed there in the time before, for other crimes against a different state, and said it had never been so crowded. The bunks and the cots that had been pulled in were filled and men argued over the best spots on the floor for sleeping. They stepped over and around each other, debated the latest rumors, grilled each newcomer for news of the outside. It was noisy and temporary, like a train station crammed with hundreds of passengers stranded by some natural disaster, some act of God. The Revolution was young and the rhythm of prison life still uncertain. Only the executions were routine.

They fired the cannon over the harbor at nine and then it was dark and it was quiet and you listened and counted. Sometimes they'd do a dozen in a night. The gates would open and the van carrying the firing squad rolled across the yard. Villas slept on a patch of floor near the barred opening that looked out toward the castle and the lighthouse. He could feel the breeze come in over the water to the north, could hear the footsteps of the condemned as they passed from the isolation cells. The common criminals downstairs would jeer and pound the iron bars of their cells as each of the condemned was led by, then the bark of the jefe of executions and a dozen boots hurrying down the stone stairway into the moat. There were prayers in the galera then, men around him whispering in unison, and Villas would move his lips to the words he hadn't thought of since he was a boy.

Again the jefe of executions cut the night, shouting orders. Arms ready. Aim. . . . Then a tiny moment of balance between one word and the next, a breath's pause separating life and death and sometimes Villas would recognize the voice calling out, details of a face flickering behind his shut eyelids.

"Viva Cristo Rey!" they would call.

"Abajo el comunismo!"

"Viva Cuba Libre!"

Then the moment would tumble, the crack of the rifles below echoing across the old stone fortress. A silence, breeze wafting through the vaulted opening, the smell of the sea. Waiting, dreading the inevitable. The smell of the sea. And finally, like breath suddenly expelled, the muffled pop of the tiro de gracia into the ear of the condemned. Before La Cabana, when he was a free man, Villas had falling dreams, drowning dreams, dreams where he stared down the barrel of a loaded rifle. He always woke just in time, shaken but intact, before the final moment. In La Cabana his dreams were fatal.

"I am guilty of having a skill," says Figueroa as they stand with their backs against the wall of the galera, Villas and Figueroa and Alzado, watching the restless crowd of prisoners struggle through another day of boredom at the brink of death.

Figueroa was in the air force in the days before, a pilot of transport planes who was arrested and tried with the others from his base shortly after the Triumph. The case drew attention, people arguing it in the cafés and on the streets, following the trial each day till all the men were acquitted by the tribunal. The Revolution is merciful, the people said, the Revolution punishes only the guilty. But then it was decided from above that a terrible mistake had been made, that bourgeois notions of legality had interfered with the proceedings, that the people had been cheated of true revolutionary justice. The acquittal was overthrown. Figueroa was sentenced to thirty years in prison.

"If I had carried the same supplies for the army in a truck," says Figueroa, "I wouldn't be here. Fidel is not afraid of being run over by a truck. Pero un piloto con coraje y habilidad es un hombre peligroso. Twenty pilots with balls could take this country."

"And I," Alzado says, "am guilty of having balls."

Alzado was a barbudo, a hero of the Revolution, a comandante wounded twice fighting in the Escambray, a bounty placed on his head by Batista. Within six months of the Triumph he was back in the Escambray leading a group of men who swore they would finish what had been betrayed.

"They have circles within circles," says Alzado. "Contra Batista, in the time before, there was only a line, a single sweep that was easy to hide from or break through. Pero contra Fidel es otra historia. Fidel era guerrillero, and he knows how thin the soil of revolt is, he knows what hurts. Against him we would be surrounded and break through the circle, but there was another circle outside that, closing in, then another. The guerrilla can not fight every day. He needs to hide, to rest, to lick his wounds and find new compañeros. Fidel sabe esto. Este hijo de puta sabe luchar en el monte," says Alzado. "This is why he will not be killed by a simple pendejo with balls like me."

"This is why a bomb must fall on his head," says Figueroa.

"If I were a pilot," says Alzado, "none of us would be here."

There is a bullet still in Alzado's thigh from when he was captured. He walks close to the wall or from bunk to bunk, grabbing for support, dragging his leg behind him. But when the requisas start, guards screaming into the galera beating anyone within reach, kicking whoever falls, driving the men down the stairs into the yard, Alzado can move as quickly as anybody.

"If they're going to kill me," he says, "I want them to look me in the eye."

In the afternoons before what is called lunch, when the men wander stunned and hang listlessly on the bars over the openings at each end of the galera, Villas lectures on the French Revolution, his specialty from the days before. Men gather in a circle, some out of true interest, looking for parallels to the present situation, most just for an hour of refuge from their own thoughts.

"A class revolution," he tells them, "is a wild animal in a cage. While the cage exists, while the rules of society pen it in, the animal knows who its enemy is."

"His enemy is the pincho who locked him in," calls one of the men.

"Exactamente. But once he escapes, once he is loose in the world, there are no rules. In every direction there is only the unknown. Resultado? Fear. And when an animal fears, he strikes out in every direction, *every*one is his enemy. Conspiracies, denunciations, coups and pogroms, ancient grudges, all settled in blood. Now is the Jacobin period of our Revolution, when it begins to eat itself in fear. And we, los infelices adentro, are the victims of this phase."

"Soy víctima de Fidel Castro," says a man who was a bank clerk. "De nadie más."

"Es solamente un oportunista, Fidel," says Villas. Villas had been a star at the University, young and popular with the students, political enough to gain their respect but able to keep their debates from spilling into violence.

"He takes advantage of what the animal does, he drives it this way or that, but the Revolution is the force. Its power is in its wildness, in the fury it has built up in captivity."

"Pues, Maestro," calls an old campesino, "aun los animales salvajes viven por reglas."

"Bueno. The wild animal finds its own rules, it settles into habit. And then, as in France, there will be fewer killings."

"By then," says Alzado, "all of us will be pasado por armas. There are more executions every night. Somebody is in a hurry."

"Dígame, Maestro," asks the little man they call El Topo, the one who sighs all day. "Por fin qué pasó en Francia? How was the slaughter ended there?"

"Con caudillo," Villas tells him. "With Napoleón. Of course then he led them into war against the rest of the world."

"That would be better than this," says Alzado.

"So we wait for a Napoleón to save us?" says El Topo.

Villas smiles sadly. "I'm afraid we already have our Napoleón. What we need is a Wellington to come save us from *him*."

"Pues, estamos fritos," sighs El Topo. "Then we are fucked for sure."

At night in the galera men pray as other men are tied to a stake in the moat below and executed. At night in the galera it is so crowded on the floor that the rats have to crawl through a maze of bodies to find each other. At night in the galera Villas shivers on the cold stone by the opening nearest the sea, trying to concentrate on history so mathematics can be held at bay.

History tells him that the regime might fall, that the Colossus of the North will not tolerate opposition. History tells him that governments in Cuba are houses built on sand. History tells him that each Revolution hardens into something else, hot blood growing sluggish, ideals decaying into practicalities. History happens to other people.

Villas knows what is happening. He understands the logic of the executions, the brilliance of their inconsistency. One man attempting an assassination gets off with ten years, another is shot for a rumor of conspiracy. No one is safe. There are no fixed sentences, only the whim of raw and unyielding power. He understands the logic of the executions as the voice of the jefe barks out, as the rifles crack, as a chill from the north creeps up the back of his neck.

At night in the galera Villas shivers on the cold stone floor and contemplates Revolution so mathematics can be held at bay.

Who is not with the Revolution is against it. The Revolution is a weapon, the Revolution is a wild animal held on a short leash. The Revolution needs enemies like fire needs fuel. The Revolution needs Narciso Villas. To create the New Man there must be the old one to compare him with. Villas is an exhibit in the museum of the Revolution, a fossil from the days before. He is a subject in the laboratory of the Revolution, its most extreme ideas, its darkest experiments, will be tried first on him. The Revolution is a rational one, a movement of concepts and logic. Behind each act of terror, each screaming rush of guards, spit flying, curses flying, bayonets jabbing and slashing, behind each body torn by bullets, there is a plan, an intelligence, a purpose. Life has meaning.

A man sobs in the moat below.

"Madre!" he calls. "Perdóneme, Madre!"

The jefe of the executions answers, unforgiving.

At night in the galera Villas lies shivering on his patch of stone floor and tries to think himself out of his body, into the dry and distant realm of philosophy, into a Zen acceptance of each moment as its own wonder. Insects crawl over his body. His asshole burns from shitting thin acid liquid all week and his teeth are loose and sore in his jaw. The wound on his back, infected and crusty, throbs no matter what position he curls in. There is a floating pain behind his eyes that he recognizes now as simple hunger and his balls are swollen and tender and no matter how hard he tries to drift away into pure thought his body, traitor, pulls him back into the galera. The Revolution has infected his bowels, has dug its long claws into his stomach, the Revolution owns his body like a pest that grows bigger as its host wastes away. He shivers and thinks that when it is done, when all of the old Villas has fallen away, there won't be a New Man in his place but a parasite, a great hungry worm that is half belly and half mouth.

The lawyer he was given looked like he hadn't slept since Machado was in power.

"Try not to make them angry," he said as they walked in to face the tribunal. "You're getting twenty years."

The weight of the number fell on Villas, pressing the air from his lungs. "We haven't had the trial yet."

"The Revolution is merciful," said the lawyer with no hint of irony. "They've spared you the anxiety of suspense."

There were five men on the tribunal. A barbudo in charge who drew pictures on a pad the whole time, who sometimes propped his feet up on the table and looked at his watch with annoyance, three campesinos, new at the game, sitting stiffly as if at a holy ceremony, trying to appear to understand what was being said, and Morales. Morales was young and good-looking, his uniform ironed sharp, his eyes bright and probing. He could have been one of Villas's students. Morales held the file, Morales did all the questioning, the light of the true believer shining on his face, taking a Jesuit's sharp pleasure in the clarity of his arguments.

"You are accused of taking part in acts of counterrevolution."

"I have taken no action. I regret to say this, but I have taken no action."

"You organized clandestine meetings—"

"I invited men to talk—"

"At these clandestine meetings—"

"There was nothing clandestine about them."

"They were held in secret."

"If they were held in secret, how does this tribunal know about them? A group of Cuban citizens came together to discuss—"

"To *plot*—"

"To discuss the direction the Revolution has been taking. We published resolutions. We signed them. Is this clandestine?"

"They were published in newspapers that have been closed. Newspapers that betrayed the Revolution."

"They were in business at the time. I don't claim to be a prophet, only a patriot. The resolutions were sent to the government's newspaper. They didn't print them."

The campesinos looked to Morales, confused. The barbudo in charge yawned, scratching something out on his drawing pad.

"We asked for a voice in the government," said Villas. "Our Revolution was fought for freedom, for the right of the people to share in the planning of their own destiny. It is not only the right but the duty of the people to be heard."

"The people?" Morales gave his little smile, his little Jesuit debating-society grin of triumph. "And what do you know about the people, Professor Villas?"

"We were all human beings at these meetings, lo juro. People."

"Reactionaries, adventurists, enemies of the State—"

"Cuban citizens. Enemies of tyranny, whatever form it takes."

"Do you deny there were men present who were hoarding arms for counterrevolution?"

Villas almost smiled but thought better of it. "Armas, para qué?"

Morales frowned. "Do you deny this?"

"Arms were not present at the meetings. Arms were not discussed at the meetings. We were seeking a government built on laws and understandings, a government able to encompass different points of view."

"The pluralist fallacy."

The campesinos looked to Morales, then to the barbudo. No one explained. They looked to Villas again, wary, wondering what this new crime could be.

Villas continued. "If the Revolution truly belongs to the Cuban people and the Revolution truly must criticize itself to stay alive, then we were only doing our duty. We were discussing ways to improve what belongs to us."

"Men who were at these meetings have been jailed for possession of arms. You were an influence on these men."

"And men who were with Fidel in the monte, men he knew as comrades, who followed his every thought, have been executed for treason. Has Fidel faced a tribunal for these associations?"

Morales smiled bitterly. "You should have been a lawyer, Villas."

"Of that my conscience is clear."

The sleepless lawyer was impassive beside him, immune to sarcasm, mutely playing his part in the ritual.

"A professor, a historian, a man with influence over young minds. And you spread poison—"

"I spread *truth*—"

"The truth of the oppressor. History written by imperialists. You say you have committed no acts. A thought is an act. A word is an act. A silence is an act. Why do you fight the Revolution?"

"I fight *for* the Revolution. For its principles, for its soul—"

The barbudo cleared his throat and looked up from his pad. He leaned forward and stared at Villas for the first time. The campesinos looked relieved. Maybe something they could understand would happen now.

"Maestro," said the barbudo, "do you accept the workings of logic?"

"I do."

"And you say you are with the Revolution?"

"Absolutely."

"Then you will accept its verdict. Twenty years."

The barbudo went back to his drawing. Soldiers came to escort Villas away. Morales sighed and tossed the file aside, disappointed, eager to prove his points before handing down the sentence. The campesinos were relieved, pleased with the decisive round number, flattered to be part of the weighty process. The lawyer who never slept was unmoved, following Villas out of the room.

"Have you ever won a case?" Villas asked, head held up, trying on the role of the noble victim.

"Every day I keep myself out of prison," said the lawyer, "is a victory."

*   *   *

At night in the galera Villas weakens and mathematics chill him to the bone. Twenty years. Thirty-two plus twenty is fifty-two. Cisneros, the mulatto who was a veterinarian, is fifty-two. A gray man with breasts and a look of hopelessness in his eye. Twenty years. He knows it in months, weeks, days, minutes. Twenty years of nights that won't end.

When sleep comes it is no comfort, only a surrender to cold and painful exhaustion. Villas falls into a dark hole twenty years deep, cold black space rushing past, falling, falling, and the only thing more terrible than the falling is the thought of the impact when he hits bottom.

"The only thing I truly fear," says Alzado in the daytime, looking out over the prison yard, "is that the women in my life will meet each other."

At least in the daytime there are no executions. At least in the daytime there are others to talk to, there is some escape from the grim cage of your own thoughts.

"I've never been tied down in one place like this before," says Alzado. "I could always say, 'Adiós, mi vida, I have to go. I can't tell you where. I can't tell you when I'm coming back. But I will hold you in my thoughts.' Then we would make love like it was the last time, because they knew I might die. When I returned there were no questions, no suspicions, only joy. We would make love like it was the first time."

"War is good for keeping women in line," agrees Figueroa. "Sudden orders, the whims of generals, these are wonderful excuses."

"Raquel would wait for me in the city," says Alzado, "while I went off to see Crecencia in the quimbambas. When I felt Raquel might be getting itchy for a man, duty would call me back to the city, and Crecencia would pray for my safety."

"And how was there time for fighting?"

Alzado scowls. "The fighting was bad. Bad food, no women, people trying to kill you. If it wasn't for the fighting, war would be paradise."

"Do they send you letters, sus mujeres?"

"The last time we were allowed, there were three from each.

They both want to go comfort my mother. Luckily my mother is dead."

"They say we're having a visit."

Alzado shakes his head. "They only allow us things so they can take them away. This visit will never happen."

"Then you have nothing to worry about."

"Se equivoca, hombre. These are both women of great character. Each of them will try to get in to see me, they will try again and again. My terror is that they will be there together in the office of petitions, waiting for the huevón who has this function, and they will begin to talk. They will be great friends, mi Raquel y mi Crecencia, there will be sympathy between them at once.

" 'Cómo se llama su comandante?' Raquel will ask, because she is the one who is more forward. 'Alzado,' Crecencia will answer. 'Felipe Alzado.' There will be a moment of silence then, she has control of her emotions, mi cielita Raquel, and then she will curse and say, 'Ay, Señorita, what the barbudos have done to Cuba, Felipe Alzado has done to us.'

"Crecencia will cry at first, she is an old-fashioned girl, and then she will become like steel and say, 'Pues, qué debemos hacer?' They are orgullosas, both of them, proud women who eat no shit, and they will agree on what must be done and go in to el huevón of visits and permissions and tell him they have an accusation to bring against a prisoner in La Cabana, a certain Alzado, known for his treachery."

Alzado shakes his head, half serious. He is a thick man with curly black hair. His hands look like he could crush iron.

"That same night I will be shot, another brave cubano betrayed by his pinga."

"Qué lástima." He has Villas and Figueroa laughing, a strange kind of laughter knowing that Alzado has not been sentenced yet, that there is still the possibility he really will be executed.

"The only pity is for the women," he says. "They are going to shoot me, one way or the other, and all my women will have of me is the memory of our time together. I know what a gift this would be, the romance of having a dead hero for a lover without putting up with his foul language, his bad odors and muddy boots. It is a pity to have that destroyed."

"You shouldn't talk that way," says Villas. "You haven't been condemned."

"They are waiting for me to begin to have hope. Then they can kill me. They only allow things so they can take them away."

After what is called lunch the men stay apart for a while, as if mourning the sorry excuse for food they have been presented. Villas thinks about Lupe. He wonders if he is dead in her heart. They were both married once before, both cautious at first, both willing to throw all their hopes and terrors into the hot struggling nights of sex. She has wide shoulders, Lupe, heavy breasts that feel solid and tight in your hand when you lift them from below, beautiful white teeth that show when she laughs or smiles or bites hard into your skin. Her left eye runs with tears when she makes love, she likes to sit on him and bend over brushing the ends of her long hair, cool and silky on his bare chest, then sit up straight arching her back, never taking her eyes off his and all the things they were afraid to ask from each other came out then, all the heat and desperate need they were afraid to offer in words turned into pulling wet muscle, into breath held and hissed out, into a thrilling drive to push past caution and sadness and rational thought. She was a believer, Lupe. At the time he was taken the Revolution was still a god for her and he was only a man. He had hoped in time that would change, but the Revolution owned time now and it was too late for him with Lupe.

His body turns traitor again, thinking of Lupe making him hard for the first time in months. He has the wild thought that he should announce the fact to the galera, should stick the evidence through the bars and wave it at the guards up in the garitas, should let them know there is something the Revolution doesn't own yet. There are men in the galera who talk of sex constantly, others who talk of food or liquor or brag of the killings they'll do once they're released, stroking their fury in public. But Villas keeps it for himself, rolling on his side on an unoccupied cot, hugging his erection between his thighs and trying to keep the moment alive, picturing her eyes her lips her tongue her wetness her breath, the noises she makes, the tears streaming down her left cheek, the noises, the noises, and he's crying, it's gone, only the lack of her is there, only the promise of never again. He thinks of the words he could have said that would have kept him alive for her, even now. But he was cautious. He was holding back, for what, for what possible reason? I have committed no acts. I regret to say this, but I have committed no acts.

Bodies move past him. The men in the galera are numb to each other's anger, to each other's blood and shit and urine, they've been pressed together inside a ring of bayonets, naked belly to naked butt, they've moved dead men aside to make room for the living, but they still respect the privacy of a man who is weeping.

In the mornings at La Cabana the meal is warm cane syrup made from the waste sugar used to feed cattle. Villas looks at his portion in his metal cup, slightly greenish, flecks of chaff floating on the surface.

"It only reminds me that I am hungry."

"Then why do you drink it, Villas?" Alzado has his shoe off, watching the foot on his injured leg, trying to will the toes to move.

"I need my cup empty in case they give us water."

Figueroa laughs. "I'll drink it for you."

Villas considers, swirling it this way and that in his cup. "It helps keep me alive."

"Then why do you drink it?" Alzado repeats.

"I haven't lost hope."

"Shhhh," whispers Alzado. "Don't let them hear that, they'll come with the bayonets."

"You haven't lost it either. Look at you—if you didn't have hope you wouldn't care about your foot."

"This isn't hope, it's only an experiment. All my life they tell me that faith can move mountains. Bueno. I have faith in my own body, always. But it isn't moving these fucking toes."

"That is the definition of faith, hermano," says Figueroa. "Something that we believe in even though it doesn't work."

"Eres un cínico."

"If it worked, it would be science."

Villas drinks the sugar water down. The pain that floats behind his eyes wakes up. His tongue seems to swell back into his throat. "You have to believe in something."

"Bueno, Villas. En qué crees?"

He turns away from Alzado's foot. It isn't a good color and the toes aren't moving at all.

"Truth," he says. "History."

"La Historia?" Alzado scowls. "Es una puta, la Historia. I was shot twice fighting in the Escambray contra Batista, no?"

"You have told us this."

"If one of those cabrones had been a better shot I would have been killed. And now I would be remembered as a national hero. A martyr."

Villas nods. "Y pues?"

"So it is a lie. Nothing changed in my heart between then and now. History will call me a traitor because some comemierdas couldn't shoot straight."

"It depends on who writes the history."

"Or rewrites it," says Figueroa.

"Then History is a puta." Alzado slowly pulls what's left of his sock over his lump of a foot. "What she says depends on which guy is up her bollo."

"No importa," says Figueroa. "Everything is forgotten in time."

"I only worry about my sons."

"You never told us you were a father."

"Están embarazadas, mis mujeres."

"Las dos?"

"Both of them. That was in the letters. Raquel is six months along and Crecencia is seven. Both say they are carrying low, they feel they are having sons. Cómo no? They were conceived in a time when men were dying. Nature knows to replace itself."

"Tienes suerte. You will leave something behind."

"I only worry what their mothers will tell them of me."

"Su padre era un patriota cubano," says Villas.

"Con pinga gigante," says Figueroa.

"Posiblemente. But what will they learn of me in school? Que era gusano, un enemigo de la Revolucíon, tirado a La Cabana por sus crímenes. A traitor."

"It depends on who is writing the history." Villas feels his stomach arguing with the sugar water, resisting, then relaxing into a queasy surrender.

"If my women keep their faith, then my sons will know who their father was," says Alzado, pulling himself to his feet. "That would be history enough for me."

The smell hits them like a fist.

Rice boiling, black beans stewing, a salty whiff of pork frying below.

"Es una nueva tortura," says Figueroa. Men are crowded around the barred opening that looks over the yard, trying to see what they can smell. "The guards are going to have a feast and make us watch."

"It's not a good sign," says Alzado. "They'll use it to make us fight each other."

But the food comes up steaming in metal drums and there is enough for everybody. The steam collects in drops of water rolling off the faces of the common criminals who jealously dole it out, guards shadowing them to make sure nothing gets taken back downstairs. The men in the galera eat silently at first, nervously watching the gate for the sudden rush of soldiers with bayonets, certain this is some trick. El Topo has tears streaming down his face as he eats in a fever, his sides trembling with anxiety and relief.

"There's going to be an amnesty," says one man, gulping his food down. "They want to get us healthy so it doesn't look so bad for them when we're released."

"There is a new jefe of prisons," says another. "A man of science. He wants to make us strong so we can work in the zafra."

"They're fattening us up for the kill, como cochinos," says Alzado. "They're feeding us hope so they can yank it from our mouths. Don't get used to this kind of food."

Villas tries to eat slowly, as if it's just another meal, but his hands shake and he can't seem to chew anything long enough before he swallows it. When there is only one bite left he looks at it for a long moment, considers leaving it, just to show somebody something, then tilts his plate and it disappears down his throat. He looks at the other men, some running their fingers over their plates and licking them clean, others sitting with vacant faces, a bit out of breath. A few look angry and maybe feeling the slight prick of shame that Villas does. To be manipulated like that by people you hate, to be led by your stomach.

The soldiers come in then, more restrained than usual, pushing the men down the stairs and out into the yard with a minimum of kicks and curses, a slight look of confusion on their faces. The men are lined up in their formations and counted. Guards weave about them constantly, making sure no one speaks. They stand and wait. The afternoon sun burns on the tops of their heads, sweat soaks through the backs and armpits of their uniforms. A few of the sick ones, men with TB mostly, begin to shake and finally slump to their knees. The guards don't kick them today. Villas has to smile at the wait. First the food, something out of the ordinary, unannounced, now this standing in wait of what comes next. Prisoners take strength from certainty, with routine they can build up their defenses like masons laying brick. But if you can replace reflection with panic, thought with fear, if you can use time itself as your weapon? Villas smiles and sweats and shifts his weight from leg to leg and tries not to imagine what will come next. He thinks about the succession of the French kings and at some point Alzado, swaying on his one good leg, puts his hand on Villas's shoulder to steady himself and the guards don't kick them today. A small man in sharply pressed fatigues walks in front to speak to them. Villas recognizes the man.

"I'm sorry to keep you waiting," says Morales in a relaxed voice, as if addressing his class on the first day of school.

"Many things have been happening in a short period of time," he says. "When history takes a great leap forward there is confusion. Mistakes are made."

It seems like he is speaking directly to Villas. Villas tries to look through him, through the guards behind him, through the walls of La Cabana all the way to the shore.

"Mistakes are made," repeats Morales. "The Revolution recognizes this fact. The Revolution knows that a man's life is nothing to be wasted. Ideological confusion," he says, "is no reason to throw the life of a man away. The Revolution is willing to forgive the mistakes of a man who truly desires to build a new Cuba. But there must be mutual trust. There must be education. We are providing this opportunity—a program of political rehabilitation. We know that most of you are true patriots, confused by the lies of the previous order, lost in the rush of history. We will not leave you behind. Any man who desires to take advantage of this program, to join his fellow Cubans in the march of progress, should stay below after the morning count. I understand that there have been some excesses here in the past, that there is resentment. The opportunity to accept the Doctrine, to enter the program, will always be open. All we need from you is a word. The restrictions placed on those joining will, of course, be less stringent. Sentences may be reduced substantially. No other government in history has acted with this generosity, this understanding. I hope you will all take advantage of it."

Morales begins to turn away, pauses, then faces the men again.

"There will be a visit allowed tomorrow," he says. "Political rehabilitation will begin the day after."

Morales turns, and on that cue the guards are on them like a pack of dogs, screaming insults as they herd the men back up the stairs, their normal viciousness surprising once again after the political director's reasonable words and soft tone. Cisneros falls on the stairs and is trampled by prisoners, then kicked and spat on by the guards, dragged feet first his head banging on each stair up to the open gate of the galera and tossed in, barely conscious. Villas tries his usual dodge of keeping other prisoners' bodies between him and the guards but this time he is thrown off balance in the rush and trapped against the wall to the side of the stairway by a trio of guards who stomp down on the tops of his feet screaming "Run, faggot! Run, faggot!" so close to his face he has to squint his eyes against their hot breath, and finally they slap him sideways into the doorway so he can scramble up the stairs on all fours, slipping on blood and taking a boot in his ribs just before he sprawls through the gate.

"Anybody who signs up for this new shit," shouts Calderón, black and wiry, "I kill them when I get out!"

But Calderón is doing thirty years and his voice is swallowed in the roar of opinion and argument that fills the galera once the gate is slammed shut. Men wave their arms, faces turning red, fists pounding down on bedframes as they emphasize their allegiances, the men arguing for compliance with the program or at least a show of it just as vehement as the ones planted against it. Villas finds a patch of wall to lean against and hopes nobody will pull him into the fight, knowing that Morales has time for a weapon, that this moment's fury couldn't fuel most men for a week, much less twenty years. A few of the men valiantly call for quiet, call for an orderly debate on what must be done.

"Estamos juntos," says Prieto, an organizer on the docks in Santiago in the days before, a man with graying hair and a body shaped like an oil drum. "We must stay together. If they separate one of us, we all suffer. We have to make a group decision."

"Communist bullshit!" calls one of the casquitos, a man who had been an officer at La Cabana in the days before. "That's the same thing they tell you in their fucking doctrine, everybody is together. I say we each make our own decision and live with it in our own way, like men."

"What good is it to rot for twenty years if you can tell a few lies and be free in two?" calls another.

"Free? Free from what?" Pardo, half dead with tuberculosis, hangs on to the rails of a bunk bed, eyes dark and frightening. "Cuba no es más que una prisión grande. You pass beyond these walls and what is there? More bastards with guns, telling you what to do, what to say. We have to take a stand somewhere, let's take it here!"

"Qué podemos hacer?"

"We can tell them to shove their fucking visit," says Alzado. "We can stay upstairs tomorrow and send their food back and tell them that until we are treated like men we are willing to die. All of us."

It is quiet for a moment then, the meaning of Alzado's words coming clear to the men. Villas looks at their faces. They aren't ready for that yet. He isn't ready for it yet though he knows it's the only way. Alzado, certain he is a dead man, is ready. Alzado has been ready from the first time he walked into the monte with a gun on his shoulder.

"And what do you think they will do?" asks Figueroa. "What will they do in return?"

"They'll send the families home first," says Alzado. "And then they'll come in with their rifles and their bayonets and we fight them till we die."

He wants this badly, Alzado, to die fighting, to take some of the enemy with him, to go out from the unseen blow in the heat of battle.

"We all die one day," sighs El Topo, looking around at the faces of the men, hoping they aren't taking this idea seriously. "Why be in a hurry?"

The debate loses control then, factions forming, raging loud then splitting up into small brushfires of contention, men arguing halfway through the night. Villas and Figueroa and Alzado give up and lie down near each other, turning it over in their minds, shivering against the ocean breeze. It feels like there might be a storm and the air is cold and liquid.

"The visit is only to soften us all up," says Alzado in the dark, almost to himself. "The families will come in with all kinds of promises they've heard about the program. Mothers will be crying. It's only another kick in the balls."

"At least you'll see your women," says Figueroa. "You can put things square with them, hermano. We have to take advantage of what life sends us."

Alzado rolls over and faces the wall.

They come for him in the last hour of darkness. Four guards, swift and quiet as they can manage, one holding a towel over Alzado's face while another yanks a pillowcase over his head, the other two twisting his arm behind his back and dragging him across the floor and out the gate, his good leg kicking viciously at nothing.

Most of the men wake. There are whispered conversations. They listen. Villas and Figueroa wrap themselves up in their thin blankets and go to the barred opening that faces north. There is a hard wind now, with drops of moisture in it, and it's difficult to hear the gate in the yard open and the truck rumble through, difficult to catch the bark of the jefe of executions. The common criminals, bored with killing by now, don't bother to rouse themselves to jeer. It's so hard to hear, and always before a man scheduled to be shot was transferred to the little cells downstairs first, so he could sweat it out with the other condemned, wondering with each set of approaching footsteps if his name had come up. Maybe it's for a beating or an interrogation, maybe a secret transfer, something else, it's so hard to hear, to be sure it isn't only your imagination and the memory of all the nights before.

"Armas listas!"

The voice of the jefe of executions, cutting the night like a snap of lightning.

"Apunten!"

A moment hanging, enough to pull in one breath and let it go.

"Raquel!" cries the condemned man. "Crecencia!"

"Fuego!"

Villas thinks he can feel the rifle reports in the palms of his hands, gripped tightly around the bars of the opening facing the moat. He turns his face aside as fine droplets of rain begin to whip into the galera.

If you listen hard there is something like a pop, muffled, from the moat below. Villas thinks that if someone tries to take Alzado's bunk tonight he'll kill them.

"Maestro," Figueroa says softly. "I'm going for the program."

Villas realizes that he wants Alzado's bunk for himself. The floor will be wet soon.

"Por qué no?" says Figueroa. "I'll play their game while they're in charge and live to spit on their corpses. You understand, Maestro? I was only a pilot."

*   *   *

When the gate to the yard is opened there is a stampede of emotion, mothers crying before they lay eyes on their sons, children confused, exhausted by the long wait, wives and girlfriends trying to look their best in wrinkled dresses and sweat-streaked makeup. Villas stands to the side and searches among the faces. His parents are on the other side of the island, in Santiago, and he doesn't really expect them to be able to make the journey. Lupe hasn't come either. He has been readying himself for half a day, telling himself she won't come, she won't come, forget it, but when he makes his third sweep of all the visitors and her face is still absent he feels dizzy and has to sit.

Then he sees the women, both of them with their hands folded over their bellies, standing close to each other in the group of people who haven't been told that their men have been transferred or executed. One of them has a movie star's lips and hair dyed blond. The other is a girl still in her teens, no stockings, with shoes that have had several owners. Both scan the faces of the prisoners around them, trying to hold on to some little bit of hope. Villas stands. In ignorance there is hope. Figueroa lays a hand on his shoulder, also watching the two pregnant women.

"No viene su esposa?"

"She's gone to Miami," Figueroa says, face a blank. "Cepeda's girlfriend is her cousin. She just told me."

"She'll be safer there."

Figueroa shrugs, disappointment gnawing inside, and indicates the two women.

"We have to move them apart, Maestro. It's the least we can do."

Villas takes the guajira.

"Crecencia?"

Her eyes swing to him, wide and full of fear. There is no way to make it softer.

"Alzado ha sido pasado por armas. Lo siento mucho."

"Cuándo?"

"Anoche."

She nods. Tears come to her eyes but don't fall. Villas can hear the blond woman, Raquel, weeping behind him.

"He called your name at the moment of his death," says Villas. "You were in his thoughts constantly."

The tears come down then, slowly, the girl standing with her sturdy legs held apart, hands open protectively on her belly.

"Gracias, Señor," she says politely. "Es usted muy amable."

She nods a goodbye and moves to a seat on the opposite side of the yard from where Raquel is sitting, holding her head in her hands, body still shaking. Figueroa comes to stand by Villas.

"I told her he cried her name out at the end," says Figueroa. Por qué no? Es la verdad."

"Dije lo mismo."

"Fucking Alzado," says Figueroa. "Gets himself shot just so he won't have to face his women."

They laugh then, and Villas feels no pain for a long moment. No hunger, no fear, no sadness. A moment that does not belong to the Revolution.

"When you go in for the Doctrine, hermano," he says to Figueroa, "you have to study hard. Learn what they want to hear and let them hear it. Get yourself out and find a way to go be with your wife in Miami. But don't believe what they teach you. And never, never betray a friend for them."

The pilot's face hardens, looking Villas in the eye. "With the wrong luck," he says, "I could have killed Alzado in the time before. Or he could have killed me. This life is a puta, no?"

That night the food was hot and good and plentiful again. The men in the galera buzzed with the news from outside, were charged with the energy of the visit, could hardly stop talking to eat. But they fell quiet when Morales wandered in with only two guards at his side. He walked among the prisoners, making small talk, nodding sympathetically, stating his hope to see them all in the program tomorrow. He came to stand over Villas.

"Buenas noches, Profesor," he said pleasantly. "We meet again."

Villas nodded to him, sitting on Alzado's old bunk, his bowl of food warm on his lap.

"I was very sorry about your friend. That was not my department. There was nothing I could do."

The men around them were silent now, watching.

"So what do you say, Maestro? We need good minds in the program. We need good minds to build the new Cuba. Or are you too proud to be a student again?"

Villas looked at his food, barely touched. His body longed for it, his insides knotted with desire, the warm smell of it drifting up from the bowl and caressing his face. He looked to the men, Figueroa, the others, watching him.

"Villas?" Morales was smiling at him now. Smiling. "Qué dice?"

A silence is an action.

A word is an action.

A thought is an action.

Villas stood and locked eyes with Morales. He held his bowl away from his body and turned it over, hot beans splattering on Morales's brilliantly shined boots. A blur of movement rushing at him, white light pops between his eyes, the cold stone floor of the galera slamming the back of his head. He felt sick to his stomach.

Roast pork.

Villas presses on the meat with the back of his fork, beads of sweet fat oozing between the tines. Fat is life, thinks Villas, smiling. Grease is wealth.

The lunch crowd is arriving now, noisy, laughing. He puts a small piece of the pork in his mouth, juicy and hot, and settles around it. The noise from the others fades. He can sense the hot food melting into him, becoming part of his body. There are still nights when he wakes sweating, hurting, and pads out to the kitchen of his small apartment. The white surprise of the refrigerator light reassures him, reminds him of where he is and where he is not. And the food inside, inert under cool cellophane, innocent of panic, solid and available. He'll hold an orange in his hand, bring a plate of leftovers close to his face, think about the tortilla he'll make for breakfast, eggs and sausage and potatoes and cheese and his body will relax, the image of the food carrying him back to bed warm and safe.

Salt on the tip and side edges of the tongue, sweet in the front center, and comfort, the warm solid comfort of food in the rear just as it squeezes down his throat. A faint nip of charcoal, between briny and bitter, at the edges of the meat where the fire is trapped into it. He wonders if there is any pleasure in the gorging of wild carnivores, if taste is a factor at all or if there is nothing conscious between the labor of tearing at flesh from the bone and the stomach desperate to be bloated.

"No somos animales," he says to Orestes, who has drifted over to see if everything is cooked to order.

"Somos seres humanos."

"Sí, Señor Villas," says the boy, confused but eager to be agreeable. He speaks Spanish like a tourist, this Orestes, like a tourist with many years of language study and a bad ear.

"Cuándo nació usted?" asks Villas.

"Sixty-one." And then, translating the numbers in his head, "Sesenta y uno. En Miami."

Twenty years old. Villas tries to picture himseslf at twenty but it won't happen, his link back to that young man has been cut. Instead the years of his imprisonment come to him in a sudden hollowness, a sense of falling. He sighs.

"Nineteen sixty-one," says Villas. "The year we slept on dynamite."

There was new meat in the dining hall at Modelo. Two boys, rough ignorant brothers from around Guantánamo, charged with stealing dynamite from a road construction site. Villas and Zuñiga and Puig were chosen to be the greeting party.

"Bienvenidos," says Zuñiga, sitting across the table from the boys as Villas and Puig take the chairs on either side of them. "Qué les parece la Isla?"

"We just got here," says the older brother.

"We don't know yet," says the younger.

"En qué Circular les han puesto?"

"Circular número tres," says the older.

"Ah. That's where we are." Villas is always the friendly one, the ally. Zuñiga, once a lawyer, is the prosecutor, full of questions and challenges, and Puig, with his scarred, impassive face, is the silent judge.

"It's not so bad," says Villas. They are both scared, as scared of their new cellmates as of their jailers. "We try to work together. Not like in the square buildings where it's every man for himself."

"Have they talked to you about the political rehabilitation yet?" says Zuñiga, suspicious.

"¿Qué?"

"El Adoctrinamiento. The classes. If you go and you promise to say what they want and betray your friends you get better treatment."

"We just got here," says the older one.

"They will offer it to you."

The older one shrugs, scowls down at his food.

"If they offer it to you, what will you do?" Zuñiga won't let him go. Zuñiga's eyes are dark, relentless.

"¿Quién sabe?" The older one is trying to be tough, to pretend Puig staring at him inches from his face means nothing.

"If they promised to let you out tomorrow, would you suck on the Director's pinga?"

The older one tenses to rise but Puig has his shoulder in an iron grip.

"Don't be offended," says Villas. "We have to know who you are. They send spies in among us all the time."

"No somos chivatos," says the younger one, pushing his tin of greasy soup away in disgust. "We wouldn't lift a finger for those pendejos."

"Bueno. Maybe you can sleep on our tier. We can't be certain there are no spies among us, but we can make sure that if there are they are treated as badly as we are. On our tier in Circular Three there are only those who refuse the rehabilitation. Los plantados."

Something in the younger boy's eyes tells them he has been warned about the plantados. Zuñiga smiles his wolflike smile.

"¿No tienes hambre, chico?" he says, indicating the younger one's soup.

"Tiene gusanos."

"¿Cómo no?" Zuñiga produces his spoon and skims a clot of tiny yellowish worms from the surface and pops it into his mouth. "Es la sola cosa que vale la pena comer."

Both of the brothers make a face.

"Están muertos," says Villas, reassuringly. "They die when the water is boiled."

"Estás equivocado," says Zuñiga, fishing for more in the watery soup. "They are stuck here on the Isle of Pines, trying to survive on the same diet we do, starving. They give in to despair and decide to drown themselves in this poor excuse for soup. Here even the worms have no meat on them."

"Tier seven, all the way on the top," says Villas. "We have the best view, the best communications, the best literature."

"No podemos leer," says the older, more as a challenge than a confession. "We never learned."

Villas doesn't have much hope for them. He doesn't have much hope for himself, either, but still he goes ahead.

"You don't have to be able to read for our books," he says. "You only have to listen."

> *Let not our babbling dreams affright our souls;*
> *Conscience is but a word that cowards use,*
> *Devised at first to keep the strong in awe:*
> *Our strong arms be our conscience, swords our law!*

Sosa pauses, eyes to the sky, searching. In the evenings on the seventh tier the men who have read books take turns trying to remember them out loud. Once there was a book, a translation of *Michael Kohlhaas* by Heinrich von Kleist, but it was discovered in one of the requisas and taken by the guards.

Villas looks to the brothers.

"We understand that part," says the older.

The circular echoes with voices, the voices of a thousand men, calling from floor to floor, calling across the inside balconies, calling to the free sky overhead. Restless men walk around and around their tier, the ones training for escape or just for the sake of training go up and down the stairways between the tiers. It is like being in an aviary with birds that can't fly, in a hive with bees that can't sting, a huge cylinder packed to the top with men who have nowhere to go but in circles.

Sosa begins to move his hand in time with some internal rhythm as the words of the play come back for him.

> *Remember who you are to cope withal—*
> *A sort of vagabonds, rascals and runaways,*
> *A scum of Britains and base lackey peasants,*
> *Who their oercloyed country vomits forth*
> *To desperate adventures and assured destruction.*

Sosa smiles, pleased with himself.

"This is Fidel," says Zuñiga, "giving the comandante instructions before he sent him here."

The book listeners laugh. Sosa shakes his head.

"There are gaps," he says. "There are words missing."

"No importa," Villas tells him.

"And I remember only my role."

"But it's the most important one. The king."

"How does the battle come out?" asks Puig. Puig takes all the stories seriously, as solemn as if he were hearing a friend's misfortunes.

" 'A horse! My kingdom for a horse!' "

"Falta su caballo El Rey," whispers the younger brother to the older. "Está perdida la batalla."

" 'Slave,' continues Sosa,

> *I have set my life upon a cast,*
> *And I will stand the hazard of the die....*
> *A horse! A horse! My kingdom for a horse!*

Someone on the tier below is singing, something sad about a young woman dying of a fever. Villas looks to the brothers.

"He has set his mind," says the older. "He will take his chances."

"Bueno. Entienden todos."

"And then I had a long fight with swords with Richmond and he killed me. Then he says he will marry Elizabeth and make the kingdom whole again, but I don't remember so well because I was trying to hold my breath."

"He got what he deserved," says Puig, satisfied.

"Bien hecho, Eusebio," says Villas to Sosa. "I wish we could have seen you play it."

"The limp was the worst of it. Even after the play I couldn't get rid of it. I'd trained my hip to be deformed."

"You have to be careful what you pretend to be," says Zuñiga, his wolf eyes fixing on the brothers from near Guantánamo. "Sometimes there is no road back."

There are four of the circulars in Modelo, the shorter round dining hall placed in the center of them. There are two large rectangular buildings also full of prisoners and the hospital and the chapel and the cement-block guardhouse and the soldiers' garrison at the rear, all surrounded by walls and wire and layers of checkpoints and then the island itself, full of troops on practice maneuvers, troops testing artillery, and then the ocean.

Villas and Zuñiga sleep on canvas cots that hang out from the side of the wall on chains, folding up in the daytime. Villas and Zuñiga sleep in cell 45 with four other men on standing cots and on the floor, next door to the only toilets on the tier. The toilets are usually clogged and Villas spends his night breathing shit and urine, wakes to the sound of men being violently ill. For the morning and evening head counts he stays standing in front of the cell with Zuñiga while the other men run down into the circular yard on the bottom floor. Lights play on the outside windows of the cells all night. Guards walk around the circulars with dogs, looking up at the windows, each cell numbered clearly on the outside. A thousand men do not sleep quietly. Villas breathes shit air and listens to their cries, their arguments, their snoring and wheezing. The tuberculars never stop, hacking until dawn. Zuñiga calls them prison crickets. Sometimes there is artillery practice nearby at night and men who were soldiers once watch the tracer rounds through the outside windows. Villas lies on his cot listening, a man in a uniform that doesn't fit with a P on the back and one on each thigh, a man with his skeleton poking out from his body.

In his dreams he is a man locked in prison with other men. In his dreams there isn't enough to eat. In his dreams he is too hot or too cold, he is itching with lice. In his dreams soldiers rush in with bayonets.

Soldiers rush in with bayonets. On the seventh tier there is more warning, the cry coming from Circular 4 the moment the soldiers run out from their barracks. But on the seventh tier there are more stairs to get down without being stabbed or kicked or beaten, on the seventh tier there is time for the soldiers on the ground floor to work into a murderous frenzy waiting for you to run out, on the seventh tier the fall is a killer if you go over the rail. Soldiers rush in with bayonets, Villas can hear them shouting below, and he rolls out of his cot and slams it in against the wall, darting instantly wide awake through the men on the floor trying to hide their few items of contraband, running down the big marble stairs even as he hears the riot of the soldiers rising up toward him.

"Vayan!" He screams to the brothers, frozen in confusion in the middle of the stairs, and he is by them, all senses alert, feet flying as he careens around and down, around and down, finally into it— curses, sticks whipping, rubberized chains lashing out, screams, Zuñiga down, sliding forward with his arms stretched straight in front of him then tumbling, rolling, and lying still as soldiers run over him clambering upward and prisoners trample him fleeing down. Villas fights not to be swept past by bodies, manages to squat and protect Zuñiga's bloodied head with his shoulder. A man tumbles over his back, bounces, finds his feet and keeps running. Someone clamps a stick over his throat from behind, yanking him off Zuñiga and he kicks out blindly, gravity swinging them around and down and he is sliding down the stairs on top of a soldier holding a stick across his throat till they hit the landing and then he is pounded as if by a huge wave, his body a rag kicked and thrown and slammed down again and again.

The punishment cell is bare of furniture. Cold cement floor, an open pipe at the back to shit and piss down, a tiny hole at the base of one side of the sealed metal door where they can slide in food and liquid. Villas is naked. If he lies on the floor he can just barely stretch his legs out. Above him there is a grid where guards can walk and watch him at all times. None of his teeth seems to be broken, though his jaw is swollen and the first time he urinates it is tinged with red. It is not too cold so far, in the daytime. He wonders how Zuñiga is. When he calls the only response is from one of the ones above, telling him to shut the fuck up. When he keeps calling a guard comes overhead to poke him with a long pole and threaten him.

It will be cold when night comes.

There is no explanation of the punishment. There is no length given to the sentence. Only the walls, floor, grid overhead. A pipe over the shithole meant to be a shower but no faucets to turn it on. The lights inside the building are up above the grid, dim and constant. Food twice a day, cornmeal mush, rubbery bread, globs of overcooked macaroni. Warm water in a tin can along with it.

If I can put myself in a prison of routine, he thinks, then I am my own prisoner, not theirs.

Villas names the four corners of the cell. Northeast, northwest, southeast, southwest. Gibara, La Habana, Santiago, Isla de Pinos.

The shithole is in the Isle of Pines. Lunch is eaten in La Habana, dinner in Santiago. Nothing much ever happens in Gibara and Villas spends most of his days and nights there, as far from the Isle of Pines as he can get.

In the universe of his cell the sun has no effect on time. At first there is only the sound of the artillery practice outside and the changing temperature in the room. Night is cold. Gradually he learns to distinguish the comings and goings of the ones above. Four shifts, which must mean six hours each. He calls the first change of guard six in the morning and bases his day on that. The period between first change and lunch is morning, between lunch and dinner is afternoon, between dinner and third change is evening, between the third change and six in the morning is night.

Morning.

Stretching exercises, slow, getting the feeling back into hands and feet from the cold night. Body search. Thorough, meditative search of himself from toes up, ending with a careful finger-walk through the hair on his face and head, hunting lice and bedbugs and the occasional cockroach. The captives are executed with the thumbnail of his left hand, splayed out in the insect mortuary on the wall between La Habana and Isla de Pinos.

Morning call.

"Buenos días. Hay otros plantados adentro?"

Silence.

"Hay alguien?"

No answer, or a curse from the ones above.

Patriotic dedication. Villas stands, sings "Al Combate Corred Bayameses" in the strongest voice he can muster. Sometimes one of those above will hum along quietly.

Morning lecture—Paradox in History.

"Students, we must always be aware of the disharmony between the popular perception of government and its actual practice. The ideals of a political movement and the methods used to obtain those ideals are often at odds. In France the concepts of liberty, equality, and fraternity became a sort of drug, inducing a delirium of murder and social fragmentation. In North America the development of popular democracy was fueled by a prosperity built on slave labor and exploitation of newcomers. With any society in transition, paradox is the norm rather than the exception.

"Let us examine the Cuban model."

(The students rapt, silent in their attention, keen minds hanging on his every word. Villas pacing, connections sparking in his mind, new ideas taking shape even as he speaks.)

"The Revolution aims to set us free but must imprison many.

"The Revolution exists to spread power among the people but first must centralize it.

"The Revolution must protect true freedom of speech with censorship.

"The Revolution strives to create a New Man but is guided by the Old ones.

"Within the Revolution the individual must surrender himself to the will of the Masses, though that will is interpreted by a handful of individuals.

"The Revolution promises change but first must create order.

"Students, we are beings of spirit and we are beings of intellect and we are animals. Rarely are these three natures in harmony. The tension this creates in man we call personality. The tension it creates in groups of men we call society, we call government, we call culture.

"Comments or questions?"

Villas takes the part of the students then, arguing, elaborating, delving into specifics. Sometimes the student is Zuñiga, cynical and combative, sometimes it is Alzado, yearning for practical applications, sometimes it is Villas himself as a young man, torn between the sage passivity of the long view and the necessity to act.

Sometimes the student is Morales.

"Maestro," he asks, eyes sparkling with the thrill of the trap about to be set, "what you call paradox seems to me to be nothing but reactionary slander. Your interpretation of events is relativist"— his voice soft, condescending, lecturing the professor now—"your analysis is unscientific. What you see as a constant is really just a phase, a period when errors are made by men in transition from one form of society to another. History is not a word game, Maestro, it is not an amusing puzzle to be played by academics. History is action. History is in the lives of the people. You think you are above history, Professor Villas, that you can keep yourself apart from it. This is a dream."

The arguments with Morales remain civil. Villas tries not to raise his voice. When class is over he is exhausted and has to sit.

Construction.

He closes his eyes to choose the materials. His father always laid the materials out first, wood, stone, cement, tools. You have to see the job before you can do it, he always said.

Villas builds a beach house in Gibara. A wooden frame house on stilts with a balcony overlooking the water, with big side windows with shutters that fasten back and a roof of clay tile painted blue. He can see the house completed, but that is only a mirage, just a dream that he has to work to make real.

He starts with the stilts, twelve-foot posts of cypress. Laying them out on the hot rocks, brushing creosote onto the lower half. Waves. Seagulls. Smell of the creosote burning in his nose and throat, the sticky liquid burning the backs of his hands where it splashes, the wood staining dark and red, drinking it in.

Walking off the foundation with stakes and string and the metal right angle his father used to own. Sinking the auger for the first hole into the harder ground just up from the sand, twisting, feeling it bite into earth, spreading his legs for leverage and twisting, twisting the handles—

Lunch.

Wet warm cornmeal with a bitter bean mashed into it, on a plate with no spoon. The cup of water. He moves to La Habana, sits cross-legged. He tilts the plate to his mouth and pushes a bit in with the fingers of his right hand. It tastes like something fermented, with a tinge of bitterness. He holds it in his mouth a long time, chewing what little substance there is to chew, letting the fuel in it seep into his body. It feels good just to hold something edible in his mouth.

In La Habana there is an enormous choice of restaurants and cafés, most of them in the Vedado not far from the University. He chooses the outdoor café on a corner in La Rampa that serves mariscos at lunch, little white tables under red-and-white beach umbrellas. Taste of salt and lemon, tomato and pepper. Cold beer. Women passing, the sun bouncing up from white stone, a hint of a breeze coming over the Malecón blocks away. Women passing, the way they walk. Mero a la parilla, tender and white under the sauce. Thick round galletas, a whole bowl full of them to dip into the cocktail sauce when the fish are eaten, to toss in the air for the gulls on your walk afterward. A scoop of mango ice cream in a smooth silver bowl, melting slightly at the edges in the midday heat. Women passing in colors like tropical birds, all lips and hips, skin cocoa and mango and cream. Coffee. Coffee like a jolt of sweet fresh blood in your veins to keep you from swooning into the afternoon of La Habana, into the nuzzling surrender to sun and food and breeze and naptime dreams of women, passing.

Villas saves a half inch of the water. He returns to the Isla de Pinos, squatting over the shithole, relaxing and concentrating at the same time. Defecation first, then wiping himself with the fingers of the left. Then urination, first on the fingers of the left hand, the guajiro way, and then as forcefully as possible onto the mire of his own shit already clogging the hole in the floor. Strafing practice. If they won't give him water to flush with he'll use his body's. He rinses the fingers of the left with the last of his drinking water, then wipes them dry on the wall.

The plate and cup go back out through the slot under the welded-shut door.

Afternoon.

Forced march. Three paces from Santiago to Gibara, three from Gibara to La Habana, four diagonally across, back to Santiago. Counterclockwise in the triangle for a hundred laps, then a hundred clockwise, then fifty counter again, slow ones with his eyes closed. Snapping his turns at each corner, counting the laps in a kind of meditation, keeping his pace steady, mechanical, self-discipline the only discipline worth having.

History, second session—Perspective in History.

This one sitting in Gibara, knees drawn up, imagining the event, filling in the details, then finding his way into the mind of each of the players. Their worldview, beliefs, their fears and prejudices, their dreams.

Martí, hollow-eyed and humorless, the Apostle in exile.

A soldier in the Spanish garrison, hot, bored, syphilitic, longing for his Asturia, determined not to die in this pesthole fighting mosquitos and murderous peasants.

A Dahoman chained below deck in the middle passage, yanked out of his tribal life and into this damp hell, calling on gods who no longer answer.

The Portuguese trader above, helming the ship, reading his future in the force of the wind, the color of the sky, calculating the loss in gold with each slave gone blind and thrown to the trailing sharks.

Men in power. Men at war. Men in prison.

Men in prison.

It always ends with that. Brothers across the centuries. Villas feels his sense of history shrinking, the complex layers of culture and economics and ideology stripped down to a hard kernel of those behind the doors and those who hold the keys. Of men with guns and men without. Those are the constants, those brothers and sisters in chains. He wonders who is to be admired, the Taína who poisoned herself and her children rather than give over to the Spaniard, the black slave leaping overboard, lungs exploding, his chains dragging him to the bottom, or the ones who bore the whippings and the privations and the soul-crushing labor and lived to pass their blood on, lived to pass on their memories and their strange twisted remnants of culture and the red coal of their hatred, glowing secret and vital throughout the generations till it burst forth in the fire of revolt. The ones who survived at any cost. They had their plantados and their integrados, the Indians, the slaves, had their rebellious mambís and their abject collaborators. Naked in his hard corner it seemed to survive or to perish in denial were equal triumphs, were two fronts in a long battle. It was only when it came down to the individual, to Narciso Villas in a punishment cell in the Modelo Prison on the Isla de Pinos, that the decision became difficult.

I believe in free will. I believe it exists because I can prove it exists. I can prove it exists by saying no.

Perspective in History ends with his hands tightened into fists, teeth clamped hard together, breathing agitated. He looks to see if the ones above are watching. If there is a guard he will stand and look the man in the eye, unafraid, daring him to send his long pole down. But they are somewhere else, blessed with the sense to be absent during his fleeting moments of courage.

I am not waiting for my life to begin again. This is my life. This will be the rest of my life.

There are monks who live this simply. Men who choose this solitude. For them it has meaning. If the unexamined life is not worth living, he thinks, what of the life that is only examination, the life with no action that can touch a human soul?

He wishes he had made a child with Lupe.

After history comes art.

Villas has a piece of metal the size of a thumbnail that looks like it has been twisted off a metal plate. The first thing he scrapes onto the wall is his name—

NARCISO IGNACIO VILLAS DELGADO

He owns the cell now. Several times a day he looks to that

collection of letters that signify a man, that bring forth images of a life. He feels less alone.

The rest of the drawing goes slowly. To draw it, first you have to see it. A parrot. He works to push everything from his mind but parrots, parrots flying, sitting on a branch, fluffing their feathers, parrots stripped now of their color, the line of parrot separated from everything that isn't parrot. He fixes on a bird just landing, wings spread, feathers fanned wide as it hovers down onto a perch. He tries to see it on the wall. The work of concentrating swallows huge gulps of time and when he hears the scrape under the door he has scratched only a tiny double circle of an eye on the wall and begun to imagine how his idealized bird can fit around this suddenly tangible beginning.

Dinner.

A plate of macaroni cooked into a gluey knot, soft, slippery plastic on his tongue. He chews every bite fifty times. No color, no taste, no smell. His jaw is still sore.

Defecation. Urination. Ablution.

Evening.

Evening starts with the singing. He finds that he knows parts of hundreds of songs, knows dozens all the way through. He sings twenty each evening, going back over them till they sound right, making up verses to fill out the ones incomplete in his memory. His voice is worse than ever, but here only the emotion is important, the rhythm, the feel of the words vibrating in his chest and throat. He stands with a palm flat on each wall in La Habana, bouncing his voice into the corner, letting it resonate against the stone. He tries to hear the orchestra playing, conga drums rapping out an introduction, then sings along with the beat, swaying slightly. If none of the ones above are there he will dance a bit, dance with small steps and his left hand across his chest, something he never dared in public.

Ay mi cielito lindo,

he sings—

Vives tú pa darme mal.
Has querido destruirme
Del principio al final.

When he has finished the twenty he sits in Gibara, always the warmest, and tries to figure out how he has come to be here. The turning point in his life, the moment when—if he had gone left instead of right, said yes instead of no, thought something different, done something different—the walls around him would disappear and he would walk free into the world.

The meetings in his apartment were not the cause of anything. Morales was right, there were men hiding guns who came to talk there, it was easy to guess which ones. Eventually he would have helped them as he had helped his students against Batista in the time before. If he wasn't guilty of the charges it was only because the Revolution had taken him too soon. The turning point had to be earlier than that.

When he was a student he had worked for Eddy Chibás and burned with the righteous light of reform. The old men in power and the political gangsters who snapped at their heels sickened him. In Santiago they were the ones who controlled the jobs, the ones who winked and pinched your cheek and collected their dues, who grinned and said such is life, who paid for the funerals of men they had broken, who left big tips but were rarely charged for a meal. Cuba is a feast, they said. If you help me get fat I'll make sure you never starve. Cuba is a whorehouse, they said, the most elegant and pleasant to work in in the world. We are Latins, they said, the only order we can abide is the natural order of the strong ruling the weak. Cuba is a paradise of corruption, they said. Even the priests have surrendered here.

When he was a student at the University he believed history could be a science. If you cut away the lies and puffery, the baroque delusions left by the Spanish, it was sharp and cold and cut like a sword. You could see a succession of men exploiting other men from the first Indian Columbus laid eyes on to the mustard-yellow shacks of the workers for United Fruit. Economics and law and culture were one, and religion only a tool that had been wrested from the poor by the rich and was now used to keep them in line. If Cuba was a being it had passed through its infancy, broken with its parent Spain, and was now in a late, troubled adolescence. It waited for Villas and his generation to bring it into the rational light of adulthood. The myth of the Latin temperament would be buried, the beauty of the past preserved, while its cynicism and violence were torn out at the root. When he was a student at the University he worked for Eddy Chibás and thought the island would be cleansed by the sheer heat of their anger and rectitude. Then Eddy Chibás shot himself in the stomach over the radio, shot himself in a messy, almost accidental way, and died.

After that he was certain about nothing. He dove into the comforting relativist waters of history, made professor younger than anyone before him and adopted the pose of the wise man on the sidelines. What would happen would happen, the forces were enormous, all you could do was gauge which way the earth was shifting and try not to be crushed. There was the moral obligation to your friends, of course, the need to add your puny weight to the push toward progress. He was younger even than some of the students who stayed on year after year to politick and organize but were rarely seen to enter a classroom. His favorites were not the academics, constantly displaying their litanies of remembered detail for his admiration, but the zealots, the ones who discussed Machiavelli with a gleam in their eye, the ones who followed his discourse on Robespierre as a practical guide, as useful as auto mechanics. These would be the razor edge of the final sword and he would be their teacher. Chibás had been premature, had been too high-strung, nearly alone in the vanguard. But now the old men were tired and lazy, the yanquis were busy with Russia, the Communists fat and stagnant in their labor unions. Youth would do it. Youth would sweep over the island like a tidal wave and leave the new Cuba, the adult clear-seeing Cuba of his dreams.

When the assault on the Moncada barracks occurred he saw it only as a sign. If even Fidel, big, hotheaded, long-winded Fidel could be moved to such an action, such a bold near-success, think what the better minds, the calmer heads of their generation could do.

Was that the moment? That underestimation? Or when the first reports came in of the disaster with the *Granma,* Fidel again, reported captured and killed at the landing with the rest and him thinking ay, Fidel, you've found your calling. To be a martyr, to be remembered for your courage instead of your recklessness, your scattered attention, your loudest voice in every room. But it couldn't be that, not misjudging a single man. This was history he was caught up in, not the melodrama of some political actor, even Fidel would tell you so in his speeches.

Villas sits in Gibara, hugging himself, fighting the cold now, and works back through time to the moment of his doom.

A hot day in Santiago de Cuba, as only days in Santiago can be hot. A heat that comes from every side, that wants to cook you into the pavement. The air you breathe singes your lungs like hot steam, the glare off the naked sides of buildings hurts the backs of your eyes. Narciso and his father and his mother and his sister Adrianita climbing Padre Pico up to the old city. His father with their picnic in a box he used to keep his tools in and his mother with Adrianita in her arms, stopping to rest every so many steps, looking back over the city and the bay. Narciso hauled himself up the steps, exhausted and happy, in the new used shoes that didn't quite fit, the string on the left dyed black to match the shoelace on the right. He kept quiet about the raw patch growing on the back of his heel, afraid to break the spell of the day together. Old men were laughing over dominoes at a table set up on the street corners. A pair of black men in straw hats perched above them, cradling guitars, playing and singing a trova about a woman happy to hear her cruel husband has been lost at sea. His father's guayabera stuck to his back with sweat, forming a wet island whose shape was constantly changing.

The family stopped three quarters of the way up and sat to one side of the steps. His father was breathing heavily as he pointed.

"Allá, a la derecha, está nuestra casa."

Narciso followed his gaze and imagined that he could see the roof of the tiny house they lived in, could see the yard where the neighbors tied their goats, could see the naked posts out front waiting on the rumor of electricity.

"Y allá, a la izquierda"—he pointed—"está el lugar donde llegaban los esclavos."

His father had taken him to this place, run-down and briny-smelling, and told him the stories of the slave trading. There was nothing left from those days but a few rotted pilings sticking up in the water, but Narciso had the feeling it was an evil place, a place the santeros in town would pass and make one of their secret signs for protection.

"Todos tus antepasados eran marineros," his father told him. "On your mother's side Portuguese, Isleño on mine. If you were a sailor out of Santiago in those days, you worked for the negreros.

De Africa a Hispaniola o Haití, y a veces a Cuba. After the revolution in Haiti the sugar took over here and those were the golden days of the negrero.

"Men passed in one end and sugar came out the other. Most of the slaves were spoken for when the ships came in, they were taken straight off the boat and herded into wagons bound for the gran centrales. Al central in those days once the furnace was fired they never let it cool till the season was ended, boiling molasses day and night. The slaves fed the huge roaring mouth with fuel, fed the bubbling vats with cane, fed their bodies to the central. They breathed chaff and sweated blood, the sun cooked them outside in the fields and at the pressing mills and the furnace cooked them when they worked the boilers and they ate standing at their jobs and slept four hours out of twenty-four. The central was a huge roaring mouth fed with black souls till it shat out sugar and the ships kept coming with more, more bodies, more hands to work, more human beings to replace the ones who died or killed themselves or were murdered by their masters. The central was a furnace that burned you to ash or tempered you like hard steel. The central gave birth to the Maceo brothers, eleven bronze giants, gave birth to the ones who followed Céspedes, gave birth to the ones who resisted and survived."

His father told him these things slowly, carefully, making sure Narciso understood the way he did when he explained how to use a tool or choose a piece of wood.

"When your grandfather was a boy," his father told him, "he saw the last of the public selling. The slaves would be led onto platforms in groups of four and five, shackled together at the ankle. Hatless in the midday sun, barefoot, sweat pouring down their bodies, stripped to show the buyers what they were bidding for. The sales agent carried a little rod that he used to roll their eyelids up so the buyers could look into them for signs of disease, he wore a glove on one hand and peeled down their lips to show off their teeth. There was a doctor, a veterinarian who lived in town who was hired by the buyers for the gran centrales to examine the Africans for signs of weakness, for illnesses that would keep them from working. Some of the free blacks who worked on the docks would come around and watch, silent on the edges of the crowd. When he was a young boy your age, your grandfather helped his father, who had quit the sea to work in metal. His father was the one who repaired the shackles the negreros used to bind their captives with, hand to hand, ankle to ankle. He had been on the ships before but had lost an eye to the sea and was afraid of going completely blind. When he was a boy your age, your grandfather helped to unshackle the slaves."

His father told him these things quietly, not like he was telling a story but as if he was giving instructions, directions on how to behave in the world.

"At night before the public selling the slavers kept their captives staked out by the docks, pinning them down around a huge bonfire meant to keep them warm and visible to their guards. Sometimes the free blacks or some of the slaves working in the city would camp nearby and they'd have a drum and they'd begin to beat the drum and sing and the men in chains would sing an answer to their song and stand up around the bonfire to dance, ankles shackled together and staked to the ground, dance with their heads and shoulders and arms and hips, dance in one spot all night long barely moving their weighted knees up and down, sing and dance to the beat of the drum carrying over the water. When he was a boy your age, your grandfather would sneak out at night to watch the slaves who were about to be sold dance though they were staked to the ground and he would help his father unbolt and pry open the metal, crusted with blood and bits of skin, peeling the irons loose from the wrists and ankles and necks of the slaves once they were sold, a tangle of stinking manacles thrown over his shoulder ready to go back to the ships of the negreros. And more than once he found himself kneeling, positioning the small anvil his father carried, fear thick in his nostrils from the sweating men around him, and he'd look up into the eyes of a boy only a few years older than he was and the eyes were like his, eyes of a boy wishing only what he wished, to be able to run away, eyes asking what will become of me now? He would look to his father, one eye dead, the other impassive, swinging his mallet with the mute skill of a craftsman, his thick hand steady on the black boy's trembling leg as if it were a piece of wood and he'd start to shake inside, this boy, your grandfather, shake because he knew there were terrible evils in the world and because now that he'd let those eyes look into his he would have to fight against it, shake because he had some idea of the furnace he would be riding into. Your grandfather looked into the eyes of men taken as slaves. And when the Maceo brothers rose up in Santiago your grandfather, son of negreros, white and poor and without any school, your grand-father was at their side with a machete in his hands."

His father told him these things after he had been able to drink a little rum, days when they sat and watched the sea together and then walked home and his father went to sleep because he was tired and there was no work for him. On those days the streets of Santiago were alive to Narciso, alive with history and the dark blood of his ancestors. He would run down the block and find his friend Pascal, who the others called Medianoche because he was so black and they would attack the tall weeds by the packing shed with sticks cut to be machetes and Pascal would be Maceo and he would be his grandfather, barefoot hero of the War of Independence.

Narciso sat looking toward the spot his father pointed to and thought about his grandfather, ancient and hard, a wrinkled nut of a man, trying to imagine him as a small boy. Then he heard some-thing snorting and looked up the steps to see Don Feo huffing down toward them in a white suit.

Narciso's father saw him and stood. Don Feo was the jefe of all the building on the docks, the man who told you if you worked or not. He had a man who drove him around in his car and a man who carried his work ledger and a man who stood behind him wearing sunglasses and looking mean. Today he was alone and walking on his own two little feet and Narciso was amazed he didn't fall forward and roll down the steps. His father called the jefe Don Orfeo or Señor, but he was so ugly, so pockmarked and pig-nosed, his two bristling eyebrows growing into one angry ridge, that every-one else called him Don Feo behind his back.

Narciso's father stepped up to meet Don Feo.

"Señor," he said softly, with a slight bow.

"Villas," said Don Feo between gasps. "I'm glad I saw you down here."

"En qué puedo servirle?"

Narciso watched his father, his father looking up at Don Feo, clutching his hat in his callused hands. The fat man had not ac-knowledged his mother, also standing now. Don Feo took out an enormous handkerchief to mop his face with.

"You know Benítez, the cabinetmaker?"

"Sí, Señor."

"My wife has bought a guardarropa from him, but his boy didn't show up today and there is no way he can lift it onto the truck alone."

Narciso watched his father. He saw anger run up his father's spine, then dissolve at the shoulders and trickle back down. If you weren't so fat you could lift it yourself, he thought, or you could wait till tomorrow when the boy will be there or you could open your eyes and see this man's family with him. His father only looked down at his feet.

"Señor Benítez is still at his shop?" his father said.

"Seguramente. And you know where I live?"

"Sí, Don Orfeo. At the very top."

"Bueno."

Narciso's father gave his little bow again, put his hat on his head, and without a word to his wife and children, trying, in fact, not to meet their eyes, the son of the man who fought beside the Maceo brothers hurried down the long slope of Padre Pico as fast as he could.

Don Feo watched him for a long moment, then turned to nod to Narciso's mother.

"Buenas tardes, Señora," he said, then began to labor back up the steps.

It wouldn't be spoken of. Whenever his father joined them again his mother would pretend that was the plan all along, the name of the jefe of the waterfront never mentioned. And when he was able to drink a little rum Narciso's father would tell him carefully the stories about the slavery days, or tell him how only the needs of his family kept him from going to Spain to fight against the tyrant Franco.

"Vámonos," said his mother quietly. "No sense in waiting. We'll eat when we get to the top."

Narciso pulled his shoes off and tied them together, slinging them over his shoulder. He started up, eyes staring a target onto Don Feo's massive backside laboring above him, thinking Some day, jefe, some day you will get yours. He wasn't hungry anymore.

He isn't hungry anymore. Not in the usual way, the dull ache in his stomach, the pain behind the backs of his eyes. Now it's more like every cell of his body is crying, needing. Villas hugs himself against the cold, aware of his nakedness, his skin grayish and loose on his bones, joints aching. He tries to think away the dread rising up in him like black cold water, tries to think heat, light, to think anything, anywhere but naked here in this cell.

Night.

Night is when they have you. The lights dim and constant, the floor cold, alive with insects, the ones above watching. Watching. Sleep comes like a slow wave of nausea, his body giving up to weariness, eyes rolling back in his head, mind reeling, drifting, thoughts melting half formed one into another then jolted! Struck! Hard pain jammed into the ribs just under his arm crying out with eyes shot open twitching away from the pole, the pole, following the jabbing long pole up to the grid and past it to the face of the one above, silent, smiling.

Villas sits up, back to the wall, eyes locked on the one above. The one above smiles, draws the pole up hand over hand, and walks out of sight. No sleep. Wait. Even the ones above sleep sometimes. Eyes open. Watch. No sleep. None. If you build your own cage of discipline they don't control you. Gray walls. Gray walls, gray walls, gray—jolted. Again. In the groin, pinned to the wall, twisting away, the pole following, probing, don't grab onto it or they come in and beat you. Cat and mouse. The pole draws away.

How long did I sleep? A minute? An hour? Feels more like a minute. Sore in the ribs, bruised, still throbbing just below the kidney from the second time. Lying on his back now, watching, waiting for the ones above, watching the grid. The grid. Squares and rectangles floating, hardening, lowering slowly to slice him into squares and rectangles, no blood left in him only gristle and bone and the pole! The pole jabbing in the soft hollow of his stomach, straight down on him and he cries out in surprise and no sleep, no, don't let them catch you, fighting every cell against sleep, every cell fighting and the pole! again if only he could sleep through the jolt the pain thoughts melting half-formed the POLE, the POLE, rolling away, eyes shot open the grid almost on top of him now, I won't cry out, never, climbing those steps, endless, leading up away from the harbor and the POLE, jolting, I've read this book you bastards I won't be your insect, sleep, no sleep, fighting every cell, every cell fighting, the cell, the cell. I am the cell and they fuck me with this fucking pole this POLE, rolling, insects scattering, laugh from the one above the cell, the cell, little slit of a mouth for food, toilet pipe bunghole, grayish walls, the ones above thinking, the ones above making law, ego, superego, id, fucked by the POLE, fucked squirming away, fighting, every cell hungry for sleep, every cell dancing, dancing in place, dancing staked to the ground, dancing black silhouette before the fire, flying home, legs pinned, dreading, dreading the POLE, jolting, ribs burning and the smile from the one above and the sudden smile from Villas as he realizes. The smile from Villas.

I am the insect.

I am the parasite.

Eating out the body. Eating through the brain.

Never kill the host, hurt him, suck him dry, sap him, never let him rest. Never. Never rest.

Every ounce I consume saps the host.

Every effort they make to fight me.

Every minute they spend to punish me.

Every thought.

Every doubt.

Torturing the ones above, keeping them awake. Every time I close my eyes—the POLE. Take that, bastard.

Sleep, will you? Just close my eyes—

The POLE. Poor bastards. Puppets on a string.

Villas giggling, drunk with power.

Feed me, bastards. Build my shelter. Watch over me day and night. Slaves. Slaves to the parasite.

The parasite burrowing deep into the brain of the host, the unclean host, its lies, betrayals, secret murders hardening into a bad thought, hardening further into an original sin, a spot on the soul that sprouts small legs and an enormous mouth and sucks the host dry from within, no getting rid of me. The host afraid to cut himself open, afraid of the burning light of truth, using only the POLE, the fucking POLE, losing sleep, losing time in paranoid worry, losing energy, poisoning his own body to kill the parasite but it's part of him now, we live together, together, both ends connected to the POLE, jolting, somebody screaming, stop that, somebody covered with shit and insects screaming walking aimless circles and somebody has written a name on the wall, on the wall, the screaming wall watched by a bird's eye, no escape, together, joined together eating yellow mucus on a metal plate, sapping its strength, burrowing through the brain, the parasite, one of thousands, hundreds of thousands, every cell fighting, fighting every cell, no sleep, no waking, no day no night no night thoughts melting into the screaming bird's eye watching for the ones above never sleeping, slaves, dancing, dancing pinned to the floor by the POLE, the POLE, order, discipline, screaming hay otros adentro? nobody, alone in the host in the cell time melted trapped with a screaming pile of filth and there are letters scratched on the wall and shit a foot high piled in the Isle of Pines and in La Habana so many places to eat the women passing mango and cocoa and cream breezes flowing over the Malecón to eat to eat sapping the host every ounce of protein each cell fighting fighting each cell every moment of no sleep every doubt every doubt I am the doubt the parasite screaming through the brain melting into the screaming wall's eye watching above the ones jolted! awake with its long beak pecking away no sleep pecking smiling never-blinking bird above eating the parasite fighting through the body up the steps the endless steps to the never-blinking eye above.

When they bring Villas out after three months the men in the circular peel a membrane of filth away from his skin. Zuñiga, limping with a half-healed crater in his buttocks, feeds him and borrows a razor someone has hidden and shaves the thick greasy beard off and chops the hair on his head short and does the best he can with the army of lice living on his scalp. Villas sleeps for three days straight.

"Está oscuro," he blurts on the third night, sitting up in bed. "The light is gone."

"It's night," says Zuñiga from the bed above him.

"They still allow night here?"

"Yes," says Zuñiga. "It doesn't cost the Revolution a thing and the men seem to like it."

"How long does it last?"

"Not long. Till morning."

"Have I been dreaming?"

Zuñiga doesn't answer for a moment. "You were gone," he says after a while. "Now you're back."

"On the Isle of Pines?"

"On the Isle of Pines."

The next morning Villas manages to stand for head count and he is taken away by guards. Morales is waiting for him in the office of the director.

"Bienvenido a Modelo," says Villas, sitting in the chair offered before his shaky legs can betray him. "What have you done to be sent here?"

"I'm your new political rehabilitation director."

"Congratulations. I was worried when I saw you," says Villas. "You look pale."

Morales looks older, tired. He's grown a beard.

"I was in Poland," he says. "Training."

"Ah. New methods." Villas feels light-headed, not totally certain this conversation is really taking place.

"You were in the punishment cells for a long time," says Morales. "Since before I arrived. I'm worried about your health. And I'm concerned about your family—your mother is not well."

Villas swallows a flash of anger. "The Revolution has made such strides in medicine," he says tightly. "I'm certain she will be well cared for."

Morales leans back, sighing, and looks Villas over from head to toe.

"I admire your stubbornness. Most of the ones who choose the Doctrine are not worth the effort. Their re-education can root only so deep because they are shallow men. Men like you, however, could be of real use to the nation."

Morales lifts a cigar from his shirt pocket and lights it, puffing hard. The smoke makes Villas dizzy.

"I'm sorry," says the political comandante. "Would you like one?"

"I've given it up," says Villas.

"Bueno. As I said, there is a certain admiration, but it has no effect. It does no good. You and the other counterrevolutionaries have been forgotten, you might as well be monks in a tower, worshipping some god who has died long ago. To resist further is an empty gesture."

Villas breathes in smoke. H. Upmann. Exhales. A silence is an action. He stares at Morales. Stares.

Morales scowls, leans forward. "You want to remain a parasite?"

Villas smiles. The image is a familiar one, comforting somehow.

"Precisamente," he says. "We are doomed to feed each other, you and I."

"I understand that I feed you, Maestro, that the Revolution is burdened with your support. But how do you feed me?"

"If I did not exist, what would you be?"

"I would be free to perform more important work for the Revolution."

"You would be free?" Villas smiles, sighs. "Lo siento mucho, Comandante, but I can not grant you your freedom."

Morales is on his feet then, standing over Villas, hands shaking. Villas tenses, ready to be hit. But the new comandante of political rehabilitation only signals with his cigar and the prisoner is taken back to his circular.

That night Villas sits up in his bed again.

"Have I been dreaming?" he says.

"Yes," says Zuñiga from the bed above him. "You've been dreaming that you're in prison. Nothing could be further from the truth. Go back to sleep."

In the morning there was an air battle outside before first count. Men crowded to the windows, standing on their toes, on their drinking cans, on each other to see out the window as a large bomber floated through black clouds of flak to bomb a boat moving near the mouth of the river. The plane was silver, flashing beautiful and calm in the morning light. Machine guns stuttered in the distance.

"Somebody is attacking!"

"This is the end! This is the war!"

"They're trying to bomb us!"

"No, pendejo, son nuestros amigos. El barco es el enemigo."

"He hit her! Coño, mira esto!"

And then the guards began to blast into the windows with their own machine guns, rounds singing and clanging and ricocheting overhead as the men scrambled to the floor.

By noon the secret radio had been assembled and word began to spread.

"Hay una invasíon," said Puig. "A cado lado del país. North, south, east, west, Fidel is surrounded."

"Fidel has flown to Russia," said Flores. "Stuffed a trunk full of yanqui dollars and hopped on a plane with Raúl."

"It's only Cubans so far," said Bécquer. "But the marines are on their way."

Men shouted and embraced each other and dared to steal a peek out the windows every now and then. After the time when what was called lunch was usually served they saw the truck.

"They're unloading boxes."

"Finally the Red Cross."

"Estúpido. That's dynamite in those boxes."

"They're bringing it underneath. Into the tunnel below us."

"Para seguridad," said Zuñiga uneasily. "They know the yanquis won't bomb here because of us. They don't want their stockpile blown up."

"When the yanquis come we'll grab the guards and shove it down their throats."

The news was relayed from the radio all day, bits and snatches that the men considered and debated and interpreted according to their natures. Villas sat on his bed listening, willing to wait and see. Nobody slept the entire night, hanging on the edge of rumor, waiting for news or a bombardment or the executions the most pessimistic of them expected. The reports were confusing, each side claiming a crushing victory. A man on the second tier started to weep at the top of his lungs, unstrung by the suspense.

The jackhammers started at dawn.

"Los oye?"

"There's a lot of them. At least one of them right under us."

"It's a strange time to be making repairs."

"They're digging escape routes for the garrison. For when the marines attack."

"Escape to where, hombre? Esto es la Isla de Pinos. If you don't have wings you're fucked."

"They're drilling holes," said Zuñiga, limping back and forth, already sweating with the break of day. "They're packing the dynamite they brought into the holes. Under every circular."

The men grew silent, listening to the chatter of the jackhammers.

"Por qué?" said someone, but they all knew why.

"When the marines come to liberate us—"

"But why do they need so much?"

"No survivors, niño. Nada. Just dust."

"We'll be the first Cubans in space," said Sosa, and some of the men laughed.

By noon the rumors from the radio had hardened into one story.

"They're losing," said Puig. "Son solamente cubanos de Miami, no yanquis, nadie más. And they're losing."

"What about their air force?"

"Maybe we saw it this morning."

"They're losing on all fronts?"

"Solamente hay un frente. En la Península de Zapata, cerca de Girón."

"Imposible. Es un engaño de Fidel. What Cuban would start a battle there?"

"If they're losing, at least they won't be coming here," said Sosa. "And nobody will have to light the fuse."

Villas smiled, drifting off on his bed hung from the wall. "They're just as worried as we are. With that much explosive the Director, the political comandante, the guards, all the soldiers in the garrison, todos, we all go up together. Todos estamos jodidos."

Zuñiga sat on the edge of his bed, legs hanging down, tense, listening for some warning sound as if there might be a way to save his own life while others perished.

"They stuffed tons of that shit underneath us," he said over and over. "Tons of it. We're sleeping on dynamite."

Villas rolled onto his stomach. "They can pack my ass with it for all I care." His eyes began to swim back, thoughts melting into one another. "As long as nobody sticks me with that fucking pole."

Orestes brings the dessert Villas has ordered. Dulce de leche— a small can of sweetened condensed milk boiled unopened till it solidifies, then coaxed out in a perfect cylinder on a plate. Villas imagines the fat he has been able to put on looks like this, smooth, creamy, slightly sticky caramel-colored fat, sweet Cuban fat. He tucks a spoonful way back on the roof of his mouth and holds it there, the caramel dissolving slowly, sweetly, seeping into his blood and brain, a warm smiling rush that makes him drowsy and buzzed at the same time.

He looks at his watch. The woman said she'd be there at one. He has lots of time. You have to eat the caramel slowly, pace yourself, drinking cold water in between attacks to fight the headache an overload will bring. Each thick spoonful makes you need another, the secret of sugar.

The spoon pulls a rounded mouthful away from the mass on the plate with a little sucking sound, carving a concave scallop in the caramel cylinder. Villas turns the spoon upside down and slides it in, smooth on his tongue. The thickness of it, the richness, still hard to believe. He looks at the plate. There is enough. There is more than enough and time to eat it. It's going to be all right.

*   *   *

Sugar.

In the mornings they were given hot water with raw sugar in it and a piece of tasteless bread. The sun was not quite up as they assembled in their work block, fifty minus the ones sick or hurt enough to be allowed to sweat in their hammocks all day or the ones who had accepted the Doctrine overnight and been spirited away in the political officer's jeep. The transports rattled into the yard and the men readied themselves, dull morning eyes focusing slightly. Getting on and off the trucks was the hardest part of the day.

"Muévanse!" shrieks Paredes, charging from one side.

"Comemierdas! Maricones! Gusanos!" screams Verdugo from the other, bayonet slicing the air as he runs. "Arriba, arriba, pendejos!"

The men with the practiced panic of sheep, bodies flying and faces blank, herded this way and that by the jabbing circle of guards, hurried with kicks and curses, desperate to keep a few bodies between them and the nearest bayonet, leaping and climbing and crawling onto the open-backed truck and crowding together standing up till they are packed so tight it is possible to faint away and never fall, possible sometimes to approach a state of sleep on the bone-jarring ride to the day's labor. Villas runs with them, keeping an eye out for Zuñiga staggering along, trying to get on the truck first and reach back to help his friend up without Paredes and Verdugo, their supply of fury inexhaustible, taking special offense.

Once on the truck there is a kind of peace for a while. Only the road assaults them, smashing up through the rusted bottom of the truck to rattle their hunger-loosened teeth. Villas lets his mind flop back into thoughtlessness, barely aware of the bony ghosts around him. Somebody pinned against the sideboards moans as the weight of twenty crush him barreling around a corner. Villas opens his eyes only when they slow a bit, then feels his stomach drop when the truck takes the left fork to the canefields.

He hates the cane worst of all. Worse than spreading manure or cutting hay or planting pangola grass or weeding around the poor fucked mango trees that never bear fruit, worse even than the rock quarry when he was on the Isle of Pines. They can keep track of your work in the cane, Verdugo and Paredes up your ass all day, setting impossible quotas and beating you when you can't make them.

The truck skids to a halt and the wash of dust that has been following them all the way catches up, billowing around obscuring everything but the man mashed up against his face, a walking corpse named Moret who prays to himself constantly when the guards aren't too close.

"Santa María, Virgen del Cobre," he mutters, his breath hot against Villas's face, "hágame la merced de otro día."

The dust thins, settling on the coughing prisoners, and Villas catches sight of the green hell awaiting them.

"Bajen!" shrieks Paredes. "Gusanos perezosos! Vayan!"

"Corran, mierda! Parásitos de mierda!" screams Verdugo.

This time Verdugo times it better than Villas, kicking him just as he hops down off the back of the truck, sending him sprawling forward against the other running men and onto the ground. Villas scrambles hand and foot to keep moving, getting to his knees before Zuñiga catches him under the arm and helps him stumble out of range.

There is no hurry. They are lined up and counted again, one of a dozen odd times they will be counted during the day. Then they stand in ragged formation while Paredes and Verdugo and the other guards and drivers drink coffee from a metal tureen, calm and disinterested as lions after a feeding. The violence getting on and off the truck is only a ritual, an opening in the day's boredom when all their dull hatred can be let loose.

The machetes and files are piled and waiting. Villas takes his and walks to the row Verdugo indicates with a wave of his bayonet. The sun is three thick fingers over the horizon now, already scorching the air, and green cane stretches before him as far as he can see.

"A trabajar!" calls Paredes.

The cutting begins.

Step—*chak, chak*. Step—*chak, chak*. Villas hugs his own rhythm tight as a heartbeat, concentrating, while beyond it he can hear the steady swishing thud and snap of the work block advancing through the cane, an antlike assault of ghosts with blank faces. He keeps pace with Zuñiga in the next row, cane to the right, tops and leaves to the left, step—*chak, chak*. Ahead to the right Villas catches a glint of metal, something blue moving, bits of moving blue peeking between the tall cane. It is the backs and arms of common prisoners, cordoned off from the infectious plantados by a half-dozen guards in olive green. Colors. Step—*chak, chak*. What would men do without them? Step—*chak, chak*. Geometric shapes, badges, tattoos, facial hair—men would find a way to separate themselves. Geniuses at discrimination. Step—*chak, chak*. Breathing raw cane chaff, scalp and skin itching with the fiber, already thirsty to the bone, letting the weight of the machete do all it can without anger or joy, only the intense focus to chop clean, away from your feet your body and keep Verdugo's bayonet out of your asshole. Cane falling as cane has always fallen on the island, cut by hand in the murderous sun. The work is hard enough but there is also the endless horizon of swaying green, the knowing that it will be there tomorrow and tomorrow and so will you be there, no end to it till there is an end to rain and sun and earth.

Villas knows some things now.

Step—*chak, chak*.

Villas knows about the quiet joy that must come along with the aimlessness of the tiempo muerto, the relief that seasons must bring to the people who live their lives in cane. He knows something about their minds now, minds made of time and sweat and the painful wrestling of muscle against earth as well as of thoughts, of emotions.

Step—*chak, chak*.

Step—*chak, chak*.

He knows what it must mean that enough rum to make you drunk can cost three days in the fields and a pair of real shoes three weeks in the fields and a woman to have for your own and the children she bears three months, three years, your life in the fields.

Step—*chak, chak*.

The knowledge brings him no comfort or strength. If only the cane he cut would buy him enough rum to be drunk or, better yet, enough cold water to drink himself full and wash himself clean, a lake of cold fresh water all the way to the horizon. But he cuts only to keep moving, moves only to keep living, lives only to cut more cane for the Revolution.

He knows what it is like to be hopeless.

Step—*chak, chak*.

A long carpet of green stalks lies out behind Villas, trail of his wasted days, his wasted life. He knows some things now. He knows that sugar is the sin.

Sugar is the siren. Standing wild on the island, beckoning. And the men, desperate to be what they could never imagine at home, restless in paradise. Sugar beckoning, the drug the whole world aches for, and the men scraping the top off the island to plant cane, more and more, sucking the earth dry and moving on, dragging other men in chains to die for sugar, locking free men in bondage for sugar, building a thin, grand façade of wealth on sugar and broken bodies.

That was what the new wind was supposed to blow away, that addiction, that culture of blood driving money, and here is Villas, step—*chak, chak,* step—*chak, chak,* one of thousands obeying the tyranny of the cane, grinding his life into sugar.

For who? For Cubans? One grain in a hundred. The drug still shipped away to buy a thin, not-so-grand façade of material progress built on sugar and capital and lies.

Step—*chak, chak.* Step—*chak, chak.*

Villas breathing raw cane chaff and sweating out the little water left in his body, struggling through a green sea of cane, the cutting edge of a commune of counterrevolutionaries working as one arm to produce capital for a socialist revolution.

Step—*chak, chak.*

Villas doesn't smile at irony anymore. He is dying of irony. He is unimpressed by ideas as the sun cooks the back of his neck, as his tongue sticks dryly to the roof of his mouth, thoughts piling up useless behind him in a long carpet of green.

Step—*chak, chak.*

Conscious thought is slowly baked out of him, lulled out, drained out step by step through the green field leaning over his head till he has a twinge of consciousness and finds himself stumbling back over this morning's stubble toward the promise of water and midday break.

The guards take turns sitting in the meager shade of the transport trucks. Villas joins the other ghosts chewing hard-kerneled rice with sour peas mashed into it. When they finish most of the men lie back on the patch of ground by the irrigation ditch, covering their faces with their arms, motionless. Vultures collect overhead, circling, cruising low now and then to check the ghosts out. Villas moves the last of his water around his mouth and swallows. Carreras has his cutting hand lying palm up in his lap, trying to squeeze a cramp out of it. Tacón, half blind in the eye he's sliced on a cane leaf, lies with his knees tucked to his chest, rolling slowly from side to side to ease the pain in his back. Zuñiga sharpens the blade of his machete with his file, concentrating on each stroke in a kind of meditation. Nobody jokes or laughs or tells stories except Maldonado the lunatic, Maldonado of the too-bright eyes who claims to have cut his first ton of cane on his eighth birthday. Maldonado is a brown frog of a man, short and thick and bowlegged, with skin like chapped leather. He is the only one of them still on his feet.

"Este cañaveral lo han jodido bien," he says. "Look at this shit. Somebody has been through here to fuck it all up."

"They bring school kids and factory workers out on the weekends," says Zuñiga, eyes fixed on the blade and the file. "They bring extranjeros to work, the ones who love to kiss Fidel's ass. They do as bad a job as we do."

"But we're *try*ing to fuck it up," says Maldonado. "Look at how this shit is leaning every whichway. Whoever harvested last year cut it knee high, they left all the sugar in the stubbles. Then the new stalk comes up all spindly, it can't stand on its own."

"Like the Revolutionary Youth," says Zuñiga. "Fidel's new crop is going to be shit."

Villas massages his calf with his thumbs. "The joke is on us, though. We're the ones who have to chop through it."

"When I worked for La United we got a higher rate for this kind of shit," brags Maldonado. "Era el número uno cuando tenía quince años. And when I turned sixteen the cabrones came to take me, the number-one cutter in the batey, and put me in the army. Who knows what wonders I would have performed if I had stayed in the cane."

"The only wonder for me is to survive a day without cutting my toes off."

"I was cutting three rows a day. Fifteen, sixteen tons. One for every year of my life. It was the same with children. Once I began with women the children began to spring up everywhere."

"Did they look like you?"

"Sin duda."

"Qué lástima. A whole batey full of ugly children."

"And all this with such a little stub of a pinga."

"Hombre, it's not the length, but the thickness that means potency," says Maldonado. "Como la caña."

"And most of the sugar is left in the stub," says Zuñiga, holding his blade up to the sun to peer at it. "Como la caña."

A slight breeze kicks up and they hear the knocking of the stand of bamboo that towers over the side of the access road. With the breeze comes the stench of roasting vegetables.

"Mira," says Maldonado, craning his neck to look back into the fields. "Están quemando."

Black smoke rises from the block on the far side of the one they've been working. The sound hits them then, the rumble and pop of a small war as the breeze takes the sheet of flame across the field, the tops catching, leaves curling and crackling, twisting free to float up into the swirl of heat over the stalks as the fire gathers power, roaring through the cane.

A smile grows on Maldonado's froggy face. The others watch blankly. It means only extra heat and the smoke and maybe more vermin scurrying into their block. The plantados only get the fields that won't burn or won't stand up or that are full of snakes and rats, the ones that have to be cut the fastest under the worst conditions. The common criminals will get this block once the tops and leaves are burned away.

"Somebody knows what they're doing," says Maldonado. "That is a beautiful fire. Mira!" He points to the sky. "Vienen las aves!"

Small birds swarm in a shifting cloud over the burning field, swooping low to catch the hoppers that shoot up through the smoke like rockets. Above them a layer of hawks drift, watching for whatever runs out for the ditches around the block, and higher up a dozen vultures soar, waiting. Hot lunch today.

"I hope it kills everything in there," says Acosta. Acosta was bitten by a rat last week and has braided scraps of cloth and leather around his shins.

"No hay nada como un buen fuego." Maldonado smiles his lunatic smile and then the political officer pulls up in his jeep, covering them with dust.

The guards surround them wearily and the ghosts rise to their feet. The political officer, the one they call Popeye because of his squint, stands on the back of the jeep to address them.

"You men," he begins, "have been given every benefit of the Revolution."

Villas looks around him. Ghosts. Men in rags with dead eyes, barely conscious as Popeye's words wash over them. The political officer rattles on about the wonderful opportunity of rehabilitation. Villas sees ten, maybe a dozen who will take the opportunity soon.

Good men, all of them, but men reaching their personal limit, men with families they haven't seen in too long, men who will die if they resist anymore. Maldonado won't go because he is too crazy and Zuñiga won't go because he is nothing but anger now and Villas won't go because—he doesn't know why exactly. He looks past Popeye waving his arms on the back of the jeep, out to the black smoke, to the birds frantic above the air-bending heat. Villas won't go because to resist is his nature now, no thought or history left in it, only the pure will of habit. The birds will eat until they are bloated, Verdugo and Paredes will be furious when it's time to get on the trucks, new cane will grow where they've cut the old and Villas, unblinking, will live whatever life he has left outside of the Revolution.

"I have offered you these opportunities, and you have chosen not to take advantage of them. Bueno. The Revolution has only so much patience, only so much understanding."

The ghosts begin to tune in to what Popeye is saying now, sensing that something is about to change.

"The man who will be taking my place is very hard. He is more interested in obedience, in the work force meeting its quota, than in providing opportunities of reform for counterrevolutionaries. If you will not be integrated you will at least be useful to society. Adiós, compañeros. You will wish you had me back again."

The men stand mutely, waiting, but Popeye is finished. Change is the one thing left that can frighten them. Popeye is a prick, but a prick whose moods and habits are known. He steps down and walks away to confer with the guards. The men lie down again.

"We're getting a new one."

"No importa. What more can they do to us? They feed us nothing, we work whenever the sun is in the sky, we have no shoes, no contact with our families—"

"There is always something worse," says Villas. "Life has no bottom."

Zuñiga snorts. "Excuse me, Professor Villas, but we don't need to hear that kind of shit. Keep your philosophy to yourself."

"I heard of a camp where you stand in shitwater and clear a sewage drain with your hands," says Acosta. "Rats swim in it."

"Is the water cold? How do I get there?"

Zuñiga rises, his wolf's eyes fixed on the ground a few feet away. He steps quickly and lunges, coming up with a black snake as long as his arm. He brings it back, holding it just behind the head, the snake clenching its body into one shape after another as if trying to spell a word.

"Another counterrevolutionary," says Zuñiga. "They're everywhere."

"Rat snake." Maldonado steps close and bends to grin inches from the snake's darting tongue. "Hola, Culebra! Qué tal? Mira esta cara." He flicks his tongue out at the snake and laughs. "We kept one of these in our house when I was a boy. Never had a problem with rats."

"Pero tenías una gran culebra en tu casa."

Maldonado shrugs. "It has no smell, La Culebra. It doesn't bark or leave hair in your food. Ours would slide halfway up the wall to catch a lizard."

Zuñiga looks to the guard left watching them, Knocknees, and back toward the political officer's jeep. Knocknees is watching the fire.

"To me he looks like a perfect candidate for political rehabilitation," says Zuñiga. He turns and tosses the snake like a limp horseshoe, landing it perfectly in the front seat of the jeep.

"Qué es una culebra sino un gusano grande?" says Tacón.

"A gusano with teeth, hombre."

"Como nosotros."

"Nosotros?" Zuñiga sniffs. "What good do our teeth do us? We don't chew, we don't bite. If we were men with teeth we'd take our machetes and start cutting these bastards till they shot us dead."

They are quiet for a moment. The thought has occurred to them all.

"When I was fifteen years old," says Maldonado, breaking the silence, "I had thirty-two teeth in my head. Who knows how many I might have had if they didn't take me for the fucking army."

Popeye gets in his jeep, starts it, and guns away, kicking dust onto them. The guards close in to push them back to work.

"Pobrecita Culebra," says Maldonado. "Va a ser Comunista."

Walking back into the cane Villas feels dizzy. The cane is suddenly too green, the sun is smack in his face and he has a panicked moment where he doesn't know who he is or how he got here, only that he belongs to the cane, the cane rising up over his head, early-season green and tangled, a jungle of hard stalks and there is Paredes behind him with his bayonet and his stream of curses and it comes to him. He's the one who cuts the cane. Concentrate on that, bend to it, give yourself up to it, motion by motion, deliberate step by step—*chak, chak.* Step—*chak, chak.* The shadows of vultures ripple on the too-bright ground beside him.

When Villas is called out of his hammock he wonders how long he has been there, staring slack-mouthed at a pair of flies copulating on the ceiling, without a thought in his head. Verdugo kicks him twice on the way across the yard to the administration shed. Verdugo is an artist of the kick, landing the toe of his boot sharp on the sensitive bone just above the asshole, time after time. A kick that lifts men off their feet. The only thing to do is to hit the ground stumbling forward, not running, never running, and try to reach wherever you're going before he can land too many more.

Morales is in the shed sitting at a metal desk. There is no other chair. He studies the file open in front of him before looking up.

"Villas."

"So you're the new one."

Morales doesn't look new. There are flecks of gray in his beard, a beard that grows in patchily as an old bull's hide. His olive greens haven't seen a crease in years. He smokes a cigar and takes it out of his mouth to cough. He has the dull glaze of failure in his eyes.

"I'm the new one. They send me where the toughest cases are."

"Congratulations. They must have great confidence in you."

"There aren't too many of your type left, Villas."

"You've done your job well, then."

Morales takes his cigar out of his mouth, coughs. "Your mother is dead."

Villas nods. He has imagined it a dozen times.

"Cuándo?"

"Hace un año. You should have been notified. Bureaucratic error."

Morales speaks in a flat, disinterested tone. He looks at Villas, shakes his head.

"All of you must be insane. To live like this. It's a disease of the mind."

Villas, thoughts drifting, comes back to something that occurred to him that day.

"It's not our fault," he says.

"Qué?"

"None of it is our fault. Not yours, not mine."

"Totalmente loco—"

"It's the sugar."

"Qué tiene que ver el azúcar?"

"The original sin. The sugar is the original sin."

Morales scowls. "Original sin. The Jesuits used to debate with us about that for days."

Villas smiles. "I knew it," he says. "Jesuits."

"You have some theory about sugar, Villas?"

"It would be good for you to cut cane, jefe," says Villas, knowing it's true but empty of arguments, reasons, historical precedents. "I think it might restore your faith." Morales glares at him. "In the Revolution."

"I'm tired of you," says Morales, and motions Verdugo to take him away.

On the way Villas sat up front between Paredes and Verdugo, their breath smelling of foul meat, their thighs and shoulders pinning him in.

"You have a history with this new guy?" asked Verdugo. "He didn't seem pissed off when he gave the order."

"We've been in the same place before."

Paredes laughed. "He hasn't been where you're going now. There isn't room."

"You're our first tenant," said Verdugo. "We just built this place to store shit and you're the first load."

"After the tapiada," said Paredes, still laughing, "we'll move you around in a shovel."

The tapiada turned out to be a kind of drawer built into the side of a hill, a cement bunker five feet wide and only two deep, with a slit in the front for air. Once the guards had peeled the remnants of his clothes off and shut him inside, Villas found he could neither stand up fully or lie down without doubling his legs up. He squatted, fingers hooked into the front opening to take some pressure off his knees. There was a hole to shit in in the corner. The cell was nothing but corner. Villas wondered if he could will himself to die.

He closed his eyes. Green fields swayed in the wind.

Tomorrow they'd be cutting cane without him.

*   *   *

The Versailles is only a quarter full when the woman finds Villas at his table. The woman is young and good-looking, with bright, probing eyes.

"Señor Villas."

He stands and helps her into the extra chair he has asked Orestes for. He moves the remains of his dessert from between them. Villas likes to leave a bit uneaten, pleased by the luxury of it, fighting his impulse to lick the bowl clean and scout the other tables for leftovers. He doesn't feel full.

"Gracias por darme la cita," says the young woman. "Es un honor."

The light of the true believer shines on her face. Villas has a twinge of fear. This is what the fish feels like, he thinks, when the hook sets in its mouth.

"You have been a great inspiration to us all," says the young woman.

"That was not my purpose, Señorita. En qué puedo servirle?"

She looks around them. Nobody is at the tables nearby. Orestes leans with his back against the wall across the room, scanning the floor.

"We are planning an action, contra la dictadura. We would be honored if you would join us."

Swimming peacefully in one direction, he thinks, then stopped suddenly, suddenly fighting, drawn by invisible forces, the surface looming brightly above—

"I am not a soldier."

"We are none of us soldiers, only patriots. We wish to fight Communism."

"To fight Communism. 'The fault is not in our stars, but in ourselves, that we are human.' "

She looks at him blankly.

"*Julius Caesar.*"

The eyes, implacable, shining. "If you came it would lend a great prestige to our action."

Fighting, straining back toward the cold water at the bottom—

"I would be an inspiration?"

"Sí. Y se vengará por lo que le han hecho."

Villas smiles sadly. "I have already had my revenge on them. It hurts too much to do it again."

The woman looks into his eyes, confused. He feels the line between them break. Free.

"You were trained by Jesuits?" he asks.

"My confessor, when I was young—"

"The new stalk rises from the old. I can tell that you are very brave, Señorita, very determined—"

"Pero no se va unir a nosotros?"

Villas shakes his head no. "May God protect you."

When she is out the door Orestes comes to clear plates.

"A beautiful girl, Señor Villas. She looks like you a bit. Your daughter?"

Villas smiles. Do I look that old? He wonders what he'll have for dinner tonight.

"In a way," he says.

TWENTY-SEVEN

ROOSEVELT LOOKS LIKE he's watching a snake.

"See?"

"How long has he been like that?"

Roosevelt, head lowered, eyes fixed, frozen in the doorway. "Since I come in. Since I try to come in. I take one step an he outs with this sound. I'm not goin in there. Sound wasn't natural."

"Go get the nurses."

"Man, Wilson, you go get the fuckin nurses. I'm not turning my back on the man. He lay a curse on me."

"You already ugly, you already stupid, what more can the man do you?"

"How he *breathing*. Like a locomotive climbin upgrade. An I never seen a man that color."

"You're that color."

"Fuck you, Wilson."

Wilson steps into the room, steps in front of DuPre's bed to look at Scipio. DuPre is on his side, head propped on a hand, watching.

"He's going."

"You ring the buzzer, DuPre?"

"He's been doing this for an hour. Is his daughter on?"

"Not her shift."

"You'd better call her."

Wilson leans on the old Cuban's bedrail and speaks softly. "Calm down, man. You gonna pop your string for sure, you keep that up. Breathe easy. Easy."

The old man is a blackish-red color, the color of dried blood. His eyes bulge from dark sockets. He huffs in air through his nose, his thick chest swelling, then forces the lungful out through his teeth with a look of fury, staring at something invisible only inches from his eyes.

"Man, Skip look like that bull," says Roosevelt from the door.

"What bull?"

"Bull in the cartoons? One that's fixing to charge at the skinny bullfighter, he be tearing up the ground like that, breathing fire out his nose and steam out his ears—"

"Yeah. I guess he does. Imonna get the nurses."

"He's going," says DuPre. "Call the daughter. Get them to call Marta." He calls across to the old man. "Cálmate, viejo. Suave. Respira suave. Espera con nosotros. Espera a su hija."

"You talk that?" says Roosevelt, making room for Wilson to pass into the hallway.

"Espera un rato," croons DuPre. "No hay prisa. Espera a Marta, viejo. No quiera estar solo. No quiera morir sin tu hija."

"Man, lookit him," says Roosevelt, cautiously coming in a few steps. "Sweatin buckets, all buggy-eyed, an chuggin up that hill like a old steam engine. Damn. Look like he almost to the top."

Pressing. Squeezing him again. Air pressing, blood pressing, bodies pressing. A man keeps them away. A man of power. Blood pressing. Pressing blood out into the woman. Vessel. Bearer. A man pressing blood out, surviving in blood, immortal in blood. A man of power. Driving blood sweet through the root into the vessel, exploding, power exploding in the blood in the vessel a man pressing back, pushing away. Even breath a struggle. Too many bodies. Bodies pressing, clawing, climbing each other for air, for survival, pressing blood exploding into sons strong and weak and the girl, the girl a curse, blood curse, bad blood, a man losing power. Squeezing. Squeezing, blood spraying, teeth flying into smiles, into grimaces, blood spreading, drying, ending. No more. No good. Black blood exploding, nothing, no good, no use, no calves. Blas. Ambrosio. The girl. Blood pressing back in, backed up, no power, no calves, no good. Bodies pressing the fight for air, to go on, clawing to call their name into the air. Squeezing, exploding, teeth cursing, flying, spreading out across the day the blood spraying hot and losing pressure, drying. Fight it. What you can fight you can understand. Squeezing back. A man. A man of power, exploding to survive in blood, clawing, pressing back to call his name in blood. A man of power. A man. Pressing back. Fighting, squeezing back,

clawing, blood climbing, blood pushing hard into the root the chest the arms
strong to fight, the head pressing out, no more, calling—
Scipio. Scipio de la Pena.
Exploding.

When Marta comes in in her street clothes the orderlies are doing
inventory. Roosevelt puts the items in the bag and Wilson writes.

"One cross on a chain."

"Religious medal. One."

"Pictures."

"How many?"

"Seven."

"Photographs. Seven."

"Comb."

"Plastic comb. One."

The drapes have been drawn around his bed. DuPre has been
cranked up to a sitting position. He watches Marta.

"He said his name," DuPre tells her. "I told him to wait for
you, but he said his name and he went."

"Slippers."

"Slippers, hospital issue. One pair."

"Watch."

"Watch. Metal band—"

"One a them Twisto-flex—"

"One."

Marta steps inside the drapes. Somebody, Wilson probably, has
put a chair for her next to the bed. The rails are down. There is a
sheet pulled over her father's face. She pulls it off.

Marta looks away. She sits, finds her father's arm under the
linens. The muscle in it has spread out, loose. She thinks of the arm,
the muscle in it alive, flexing with power even when he slept.

"Padre," she says very softly, so the others can't hear. "Nos
iremos. Te prometo que volveremos a Cuba en su nombre y en el
nombre de Ambrosio. No te olvidaré, nunca. Te honraré, Padre."

She can hear the orderlies droning on the other side of the drapes,
can hear each item thunk into the plastic inventory bag. She stands
and replaces the sheet.

"You will be proud of me."

Marta steps out into the room, crossing herself.

"Was there a priest?"

"There wasn't time," says DuPre. "I'm sorry. He wasn't scared. That much I could tell."

"He was mad at something," says Wilson. "Tough old guy. Sorry."

"Radio."

"Portable radio, plug-in. One."

"Toothbrush."

"Plastic toothbrush. One."

"You have a big family?" asks DuPre.

"No. Me and a brother. My mother." Marta is staring at the closed drapes, working something in her mind.

"Grandchildren?"

"No," says Marta. She stares at the bulging plastic bag Wilson holds out for her. "We never gave him that."

TWENTY-EIGHT

▄▄▄▄▶ THEY PARK ON a little knoll overlooking the fresh-dug section of the cemetery. Duckworth pulls his binoculars out of the case in the driver's seat.

"Should I go out and mingle?" asks Rivkin. "I can eavesdrop in Spanish."

"Don't want to spook them for nothing."

"What, spook them. I could be anybody. Friend of the family, anybody."

"Sure. You could be some Anglo cop messing up their service. We can spot him from here." Duckworth adjusts the focus ring.

"But they might say something—"

"The Old Boy was clean as far as we know. No reason to get people upset."

Duckworth picks out what must be the wife and daughter, together in black. The daughter maybe thirty, tall and pretty, American-looking. No makeup. They usually wore makeup. The wife weeping into a handkerchief. Standard issue. Born to be a widow.

"You think he'll show?" asks Rivkin.

"Mostly I like this cemetery. Good shade to park in."

"I'm serious."

"So am I. Once I had a dog explode on me, left him in the car in the open sun, forgot to crack the windows."

"Explode."

"They suffocate first, then the gases build up—"

"What kind of upholstery?"

"That velour kinda stuff. Maroon."

"Whew."

"Yeah."

"You had a maroon car."

"So?"

Rivkin shrugs.

"It had a black top."

They are silent for a moment. Not much of a turnout. An older guy, thick, in sunglasses. A thin black one, younger. Those two handling the Cuban flag.

"Ought to be a law against that. On American soil."

"Against what?"

"The flag," says Duckworth. "They want to go do that back home, fine."

"It's just a piece of cloth."

"Don't tell them that, buddy."

The men spread the flag over the top of the coffin.

"This belong to the Vatican?"

"What?"

Duckworth puts the binoculars down. "This land doesn't belong to the Vatican, does it? I mean it's a Catholic cemetery."

"So?"

"I just thought of it. The Church belongs to the Vatican, right, so maybe the land does too."

"It's hallowed ground."

"What's that mean?"

"If you get booted from the Church, divorced or something, they can't bury you here. But I don't think it can belong to the Vatican. They're a foreign power."

"Like Israel."

Rivkin gives him a look. "I don't think the Vatican has an air force."

Rivkin looks troubled by something, squints his eyes toward the little funeral party.

"You think he might come, though?"

"They take their family serious."

Rivkin nods. "Family can be hell. I've got a brother, every time he sees me, some gathering, wedding or whatever, he says, 'How much do they pay you people?' Like he thinks it's a public scandal we're underpaid, but really so he can say, 'Damn, first-year guy out of school gets that much in my game.' Republican. Only thing we can talk about in a civil tone is football."

"My brother follows the Gators," says Duckworth, "and I'm a Hurricanes man. We don't talk at all anymore."

The one who looks like a priest but doesn't have a collar steps up to speak first. The one with the collar who doesn't look like a priest stands behind him, staring at his feet.

"I think you people got it beat," says Duckworth. "Put 'em in the ground right away, keep it simple. Spend your money on the living."

"Different strokes."

"My folks used to go in for those open-casket jobs. Uncle Earl all made up and waxy-looking, some big ole Baptist windbag wheezing on about the Valley of the Shadow, all the piney-woods aunts and cousins shouting amens. Liked the singing, though."

"The singing is nice, whoever does it. Though the organ is not my favorite."

There are a dozen altogether. The family, the black kid and a young black woman, the priests, a handful of old-timers. No Blas so far. Duckworth swings the glasses to the side.

"We got a watcher."

"Where?"

Duckworth points. A young man, dressed sharp in a dark suit, sunglasses on, waits on the pathway below, watching the service.

"That him?"

"No. Too young. Me and Blas go back some. That isn't him."

"What do we do if he does show?"

"Put some people on him, see what he's up to. There's gonna be a war down here we should have a good seat."

"I was at the morgue yesterday—they've rented a refrigerator truck from Burger King to keep the overflow on ice. We got a waiting list for autopsies."

"It has been lively."

"Somebody said we're heading for a new record."

"They had a pretty good crop during the Prohibition. My Daddy was out chasing rumrunners in the Keys, he had some stories."

"That was crazy. Tell people they couldn't drink."

"Somebody thought it was a good idea."

"Religious fanatics."

Duckworth shrugs. "Don't know what the big deal is now with this cocaine. Easy enough to tie one on legal."

"You never tried it?"

Duckworth puts the glasses down, turns to stare at Rivkin.

"You have?"

"You know—before. In college. I experimented."

"Experimented."

"Yeah."

"And how did the experiment turn out?"

"It takes a few tries to get a proper idea of what you're dealing with."

"Uh-huh."

"You get lots of energy."

"Like Cheerios."

"Incredible energy. Very speedy. I'd get this feeling in the bridge of my nose, this buzz, like the top of my skull was floating off."

"That's good?"

"It felt good at the time. Doesn't last long. Kind of like sex."

"Speak for yourself."

"I mean like the orgasm part. Very intense, very short-lived."

"So people cut each other up and leave the remains locked in trunks of automobiles so they can have quick sex in their nose." Duckworth shakes his head.

"It doesn't make you crazy or anything. It's just a drug."

"It's just a drug."

"I feel like I have better insight into what we're up against."

"I know what we're up against," says Duckworth. "But I don't go stickin it up my nose."

Rivkin shrugs, squints again. "I wish I knew what they're saying."

"They're saying the Old Boy was a good family man. Good provider. Cuban patriot. Respected by all. They're big on that, the respect."

"Isn't everybody?"

"I went down there, I was a kid. Seemed pretty easy to put somebody's nose outa joint. Whole damn island had a chip on its shoulder."

"You were there?"

"Sure. Before the beardos come in. My brother took me down to get laid."

"Really?"

"That was the place to do it."

"What was it like?"

Duckworth sighs. "It felt good at the time. Didn't last long. Kind of like sex."

Rivkin makes a face. "I never did that. Paid."

"Anyhow, I mostly remember not feeling too welcome. Lots of colored around, Chinese. Hard guys. Like if you looked at em the wrong way they'd cut you up."

"You could catch a disease."

"What the hell, it was their country. But this is *ours*."

The mourners walk away from the site. The stocky one and the daughter are supporting the mother, none of them nodding when they reach the young man watching. The black woman stops by him, seems surprised. They rejoin the party, arm in arm.

"He's not gonna show, is he?"

"Good. Keep his business out of my yard. All of em. Colombians, Dominicans, Haitians, Ricans, Cubans. Send it all back. All of it."

Rivkin smiles. "That's a tall order. What about these people, with Fidel at the wheel down there?"

Duckworth shrugs. "Tampa would be far enough."

T W E N T Y - N I N E

➤ THE BALL CRACKS off the fronton wall and whizzes back toward the players. A man in a red jersey catches it underhand in his curved cesta, makes a perfect backward windmill with his arm then snaps it sizzling at the wall.

El Halcón blocks the light on the betting form.

"A qué juegas?"

"Trifecta."

"Es una locura apostar el jai alai."

Walt studies the sheet. "The thing is, I don't follow this, don't know the names of the players even, so I don't have any prejudices. You only bet hunches, even if they do dump a game you can't be suckered."

El Halcón sits. "If you only bet a hunch," he says, "they don't have to sucker you."

A player in yellow dives for a lag shot and misses, the match ending to polite applause. The men return to the players' bench and begin to peel off their outer jerseys.

"Qué hay de nuevo?" asks Walt.

"Her father died."

"I saw that in the *Diario*. She still with the program?"

"Más que nunca."

"New recruits?"

"Nadie. She has the boat, the guns, as many people as she wants. Solamente esperando por los explosivos."

"You told her no more people, no boom-boom from our side?"

"I told her. She is trying but I don't think it happens."

"No wonder. Crazy-assed operation."

"Tienes razón," says El Halcón. "What kind of idiots would plan to attack in a swamp with only two roads leading through it?"

Walt gives him a look. The Basque anthem plays over the PA system, the tape warbly with use. The players, sorted into their new teams, line up and face the crowd through the metal screen. The anthem ends and they give a desultory wave with their cestas.

"Son duros, los vascos," says Walt. "I knew some of them in Spain. They took shit from nobody."

El Halcón yawns. "But Franco fucked them just the same. Fucked them from the air, fucked them from the sea, fucked them on land. It isn't enough, being tough."

"No."

"You have to be smart. Like these ones. Every game, a different team. Win or lose, they get paid the same. Como tú."

"What do you mean, like me?"

"Como tus jefes. Como la CIA. It looks like you don't have a winner, you switch horses."

"Politicians. If the Agency had its way—"

"If the Agency had its way Cuba would be Puerto Rico."

"I can think of worse things."

"Seguro." El Halcón looks out onto the fronton. "It doesn't work, you know. They have them switch teams to stop the cheating, but the ones who want to still find a way."

Walt puts the betting form down. The match starts, the players punishing the wall, the crowd cheering. Ahead of them a half-dozen Mexicans, pickers out on the town, count off and chug their huge containers of beer in unison. One of the blues makes a spectacular backhand to keep the ball in play, leaping and twisting.

"I don't think I can swing the explosives without two or three more in the pot," Walt says under the shouts of appreciation.

"So lie to them."

"And when they pull the boat? No way."

"Pues. Estamos terminados."

"Maybe we could dummy something up, get some boxes marked—"

"She'll test it. Está loca, pero no es estúpida."

Walt's stomach kicks in. He pushes his fist against the part the doctors tell him is his ileocecal. Every time the ball smacks the wall it's like a rabbit punch.

"I know where you can score some," he says.

"Yo?"

"You don't have to be there. Set it up for her and her people. They get caught, fine, we move in and take some credit. If they don't even better, there's juice on the boat when we finally blow the whistle. They'll love it, pulling in something they didn't provide in the first place."

El Halcón gives a twisted smile. "Is a funny game you play, compa."

"Vayan azules!" call the Mexicans, cupping their hands around their mouths to shout. "Kick some ass out there!"

"Damn good athletes," says Walt. "But people only come for the action."

"Who are you backing in this one?"

Walt studies his Trifecta ticket. "Hard to tell," he says. "They all look the same after a while."

THIRTY

When Walt got down to Camp Trax they put him on the pussy detail. He had been working out of Homestead, recruiting for Operation Mongoose until the day of the Inauguration when the door slammed shut. No use letting the new tenants monkey with a good thing. The Kennedy people talked a tough line but had soft ideas about who should be invited to the party.

Walt counted fifty-six different exile groups elbowing for control of the secret Invasion, which was so secret that Cuban women stepped aside at the supermarket checkout line in respect for him, old men stopped him in the street to clasp his hand and thank him for what he was doing and young men ran after him calling lies about their age and military experience.

"No soy lo que piensan," he would say to them, smiling. "Soy hombre de negocios, nada más."

But if he was only a businessman it was a business everybody wanted a piece of, and he basked in the excitement of the moment, was drunk with the spirit of the Cubans. History was going to be made, a door would open and things would never be the same and Walt was one of the men who held the key. Then Kennedy became the new tenant and the dozens of applicants who had been rejected when Walt wrote "premature anti-Batistiano" or "fidelista sin Fidel" on their charts were joining the hundreds of others turned down elsewhere in politicking with the administration to get in on the action.

The Agency closed his shop in Homestead and sent him off hunting for putas.

Bobby Alejos had donated a section of his coffee finca for the training base. A Guatemalan soldier who didn't shave yet pressed the gas pedal of a new jeep to the floor and held it there till they had nearly killed every burro and Indian walking the muddy road between the airstrip and the Camp. A beefy Austrian in cowboy boots greeted Walt at the perimeter checkpoint.

"About time they send somebody down," he said as Walt staggered out of the jeep. "If my boys are not getting laid we maybe haf mutiny."

Walt had been told he was being transferred to act as liaison with the Guatemalans. Davies, the station chief, put him straight.

"We've got a clap epidemic brewing. These local Indian gals back their asses up to the fence, our boys slip them a quetzal or two and they go at it. Then the next one takes his turn. A few isolated cases turn into a hundred real fast."

"We can't afford rubbers?"

"These are Cuban boys, Walt. They think only a pansy would wear an overcoat. We keep passing them out and they keep filling them with water and using them for target practice."

Walt felt his high spirits about the operation sinking. "Why not go out and clean the girls up?"

"This camp is already causing our hosts a certain amount of embarrassment. If we start officially involving the locals in a brothel—"

"Es un insulto a la pureza guatemalteca."

Davies nodded. "You've dealt with these people before, dealt with this kind of situation before. When you were with the Fruit Company—"

"We brought them in from Honduras," said Walt, trying to mask his disappointment. "We set up a house near the men's barracks. They called it the Company Store—"

"Have it done in two weeks." Davies was already reaching for his phone, the meeting over.

"The local women won't be too happy about it. Freezing them out of the trade."

"They're Indians," shrugged Davies. "They're not part of the conversation here."

*   *   *

They owed him better than this. With his contacts in Guatemala, his history in the coup, they owed him. He'd almost died for the fucking country.

Walt was working for the Fruit Company out of Quetzaltenango, shaping the local profile and cleaning up after the American personnel, when he was contacted by the Agency. They had his OSS file, of course, and his rep from the Sugar Company to go on. Pick up a few extra dollars, they said, help your country fight the Reds. No conflict of interest. It wouldn't be that different from what he was already doing.

He liked what he was already doing. There was a fraternity in the Fruit Company and it had welcomed him. The publicity sell was relatively easy, as the Company's housing and wages were well above what the home-grown ladinos were offering and it was all just bananas to the people back home. The only drawback was the country itself, the thickness of it, the poisonous greenness of the mountains, the unsettling fecundity. He found the fruit obscene, the way it grew jutting point-up on the bunch, the bunches hanging heavy in unbelievable numbers, it was too much. Whatever comes easy comes cheap, he always thought on his field trips into the bush. He found the Indians impenetrable, the food inedible and the women unpleasant. Early on his first tour of the Company holdings he got a dose of malaria that laid him up for a week.

"Bienvenido a Guatemala, hermano," laughed Big Mike, his immediate superior. "You've picked up your first souvenir."

So it was the health benefits that finally swayed him when the Agency came knocking.

Arbenz was in power then, with his pinko wife and fellow-traveler friends, making the usual spread-the-wealth noises that made the ladinos so nervous. He had the Indians riled up and support from the factions in the Army who hadn't gone into exile and the rest of Central America was watching. The Fruit Company held all the face cards, of course, owning the power company and the telephone system and the railroad and controlling Puerto Barrios, the only Atlantic port. And when Arbenz started yanking untilled land from them they hollered all the way to Washington.

"You look at a map," said the Agency man who recruited Walt, "and what stands between us and Bananaland here?"

"Mexico?" said Walt. He wondered if it was a trick question. "And who's running the store there?"

"Mexicans?"

"My point exactly."

At first Walt was mostly just a host, helping Bernays and the other PR honchos run their fact-finding junkets, rehearsing the workers and overseers they'd be exposed to, glad-handing the strange mix of lobbyists who'd been collected for the effort. Sometimes he'd even pose as a local manager when the Fruit Company's man was a little too redneck for the liberal press. The men brought down to ride herd on the harvesting were mostly Southerners, good old boys who'd give you the shirt off their backs but were at a loss to describe the workers as anything but "the local monkeys" or just "our niggers." There was quite a rush, and though Big Mike was impressed by Walt's sudden access to pols and journalists, he was itchy for the real action to start.

"In the old days we would have done it ourselves," he said. "Back in Honduras once, the Banana Man got wind that the monkeys in charge were about to make a deal with a competitor. He found himself an unemployed strongman named Bonilla hanging out in the States, gave him a ship, some guns, and snuck him out of New Orleans. Wham, bam, alacazam we got a new head monkey running the country and old Sam has got him in his pocket."

"This won't be so different," Walt told him. "We just have to sell the idea a bit first."

The Dulles brothers were behind it, which gave you State and the Agency, Ike was in, which delivered the rest of the executive, and it turned out even Lodge at the UN owned stock in the Fruit Company. The American public were eating up stories about the new Red Menace in the glossy magazines and the ladinos, the people who really counted in Guatemala, knew whatever Arbenz had planned for the Fruit Company would go double against them. The stage was set for the Liberator, the beacon of freedom and democracy shining in this heart of darkness, and the only job left was to choose him.

The Fruit Company wanted their former legal counsel, languishing in Mexico City. The Agency sent Hunt to meet with him but the man was in poor health and what they were after was a military type, someone who could keep the Indians in line. It boiled down to a General and a Colonel.

Walt was in on both the meetings, representing the Fruit Company's interests. The General, gathering dust in El Salvador, was a regular don, real sixteenth-century stuff. He heard the terms of his future presidency and haughtily shot back terms of his own.

"What's your impression?" asked the Agency man as they left.

"He thinks we need him," said Walt.

"He's wrong."

The Colonel was a vain little chihuahua of a man, immaculately dressed, cooling his heels in Honduras. He had joined Arbenz in the coup that finally put the old crowd out but he had gotten the short end of the stick. He seemed more interested in the military campaign than the political deal.

"We'll take care of all that," the Agency man told him. "Your job is to act as a magnet for the freedom fighters."

The Agency man asked Walt what he thought.

"Not a bright light."

"That isn't what we need."

"He looks more like a regular Joe. Bit of Indian blood, maybe. That could be a plus."

"That damn Arbenz has got all the looks."

"Claro. Like Alan Ladd with height."

"Who's the Spanish Rock Hudson? Maybe we should just hire an actor."

"The General's an actor. But he only knows one role."

"So how about this guy, Walt? You think he'll do what he's told?"

"If we explain it *very care*fully."

It was never much of an invasion force. A couple hundred Guatemalan exiles, the usual soldiers of fortune and Latin American adventurers. The Fruit Company put its railroad and its network of employees and its Great White Fleet at the disposal of the Agency, building a fifth column in key areas, and Walt used a few old friends in the Dominican to draw a generous contribution from the Caudillo. A few planes were bought, pilots recruited. Important officers in the government Army, known to be disaffected or just greedy, were offered cash incentives to sit out the impending conflict. The Fruit Company controlled all communication in the country except for the radio, and the Agency was setting up its own station equipped to broadcast and to jam the competition. All through this time Walt felt an enormous sense of well-being, of belonging to a larger something. No conflict of interest. No serious hitches or troubling second thoughts. Big things were about to go down and he was as far inside as you could get.

The Colonel finally met his loyal followers in Tegucigalpa, two days before the kick-off. Walt was shaky, suffering a relapse of the malaria but determined to take the whole ride.

"I want to be in on the kill," he told the Agency people. "I've come so far with this thing."

"Officially you're a civilian—"

"Protecting Company property."

"Right. Well, the way these things go, the safest place is probably with the Colonel. You can help hold his hand while we cook the goose."

They were only twenty-five miles in from the Honduras border when the end came. It was June, clear skies, and the Agency had its tiny air force against Arbenz without a single plane. He had tried to buy some months earlier but the Agency had secretly blocked the sale. The biggest problem was finding anybody to surrender to.

And Walt had a terrible case of the shits.

Whenever the column would stop in some dusty village he'd have to excuse himself and find a private place to let go. The urgency of the call surpassed his considerable fear of snipers. He was consumed by the idea of dying with his pants down around his ankles.

When he'd come back the Colonel would be waiting for him with eager eyes.

"Cómo vamos?" he would ask. The Colonel was disappointed by the relative lack of interest the Indians were showing in his triumphant march to the capital, puzzled by the absence of any serious resistance from the government. He thought Walt's sudden disappearances were some quirk of yanqui tradecraft, a rendezvous with privileged and up-to-date information. Walt hated to disappoint him further.

"We're doing fine," Walt would tell him. "The eyes of the nation are upon us."

They had a radio, of course, but it was receiving only the Agency's rebel station. Walt had read most of the dispatches a week before, helping, in fact, to translate and punch up the rhetoric.

"I've heard of rewriting the history books," said Chucky, the kid the Agency had sent to turn out copy, "but this is the ultimate."

"It should sound Guatemalan," said Walt.

"How would you put 'Casualties were minimal'?"

"When is this for?"

"D-Day plus three. Outskirts of the capital."

" 'Poquísima.' You can lay the diminutives on. 'Las sagradas fuerzas de la democracia encontraron poquísima resistencia mientras ganaban hoy otra victoria en la gran lucha por el alma de nuestro país.' "

"The soul of our country? Bit florid, isn't it?"

"This is Guatemala, kid," Walt told him. "Metaphors run wild down here."

The real task was to keep the Colonel from wandering too far inland and revealing just what an illusion the whole invasion was.

"You have only to rest your feet on Guatemalan soil," Walt told him, "and the people will rally around you."

"Hay un otro golpe?" asked the villagers as they passed through. "How long will the fighting last?"

Walt told them it would be a swift and decisive victory.

"Bueno," they said, regarding the force with uneasy smiles. "Win or lose, as long as it is swift."

At the end Walt was delirious. His fever rolled into camp at the base of his neck, sending alternate chills and hot flashes shuddering down his spine, sweat pouring off his face and rolling into his ears as he lay curled on his back in the rear of the second-in-command's jeep.

"The Army has deserted him!" somebody shouted, the American voice cutting through a dream troubled by bright parrots and green bananas. "It's over!"

Walt thought they were talking about the Colonel. That the force had bolted, that he was on the wrong side, sick, stranded, about to be dragged before a firing squad of dark greasy men wearing bandoliers. Visions of Indians holding machetes in their thin, strong arms crackled through his head, visions of men with faces implacable as stone gods. He started to cry.

"I should have stuck with sugar," he said.

"Walt, we won! It's over! Arbenz bought the whole show, he's packing his bags."

"I should have stuck with sugar," Walt sobbed, opening his eyes to a blazing sky. "The banana game is too rich for me."

The Fruit Company doctor said it was nip and tuck for a while, that Walt had been ranting in Spanish about ghosts and baseball. He had almost died for the fucking country.

And now they were sending him off to hunt putas.

The Agency assigned Dr. Amoros, a nervous little Cuban gynecologist who had been working in a car wash in Hialeah, to accompany Walt on the talent scout. They recruited in San Salvador, in Tegucigalpa, in Managua and Bluefields, in San José in Costa Rica. They concentrated on girls who worked near military bases, girls used to seeing a rush of men during a few hours of leave, girls used to rough handling and low pay. Davies had given Walt a chunk of money out of the medical appropriation to pay for the girls, who were to be listed as "health care workers." After Dr. Amoros had passed them through the blood tests, Walt interviewed them. There were only three questions.

"Quién es el presidente de su país?"

Many of the girls didn't know who their president was and were passed without being asked anything more.

"Qué piensa de su presidente?"

Almost all of the girls who knew who their president was professed great admiration and respect. One even claimed to have had relations with her president, performing for free out of a sense of patriotic duty.

"Qué piensa de Fidel Castro?"

Most of the girls knew what the game was and how to play it. There were a lot of disapproving comments about his beard. There was one, though, a Costa Rican girl with dyed blond hair and a classy, gallega air who seemed to think the whole thing was a joke.

"Es cierto que sé quién es mi presidente," she said, smiling pleasantly at Walt. "Es el presidente Kennedy. Es presidente de todo el mundo libre."

He wasn't sure if she was trying to be provocative or just to suck up to him.

"Y qué piensa de él?" he asked.

"Es muy guapo, el Señor Kennedy," she said, staring boldly at Walt, "but is hard to know a man till you have fuck him."

Walt felt himself flush but managed to scribble on the personnel form. "Bueno, habla inglés?"

"Cómo no? We are all yanquis now."

"And what do you think of Fidel Castro?"

The girl, Carmen, considered for a moment. "He has outlaw las putas en Cuba," she said. "Yo soy puta. So we can only be enemy, no?"

Walt told himself it would be good to have one among them who spoke some English. He told himself that the girls would be kept under wraps, no contact with the outside till after the Invasion was launched. He told himself that a fresh mouth was not the same as a security risk.

"You understand," he said to her, "that if you take this job you do what I say."

It was the hardest thing to get the recruits, the Cuban boys, to understand. If the Agency was going to back them with its power and prestige they were going to have to play by certain rules. There was no free ride being offered.

Carmen smiled a lazy smile. "A sus órdenes, mi comandante. Qué quieres?"

It was a tiny office on the second floor. Walt had ordered that there be no interruptions while he was interviewing. His desk and chair were the only furniture, leaving them to stand in the open where he could see their body language as he put the questions to them. There was a fan on the windowsill that scattered the papers on his desk if he didn't lay something on top of them. When he touched her hair he could see the roots growing out, dark brown, almost black.

When they were done Carmen arranged herself and helped him pick up the papers that had blown onto the floor.

"I have this job?" she asked.

Walt sweated a stain onto the personnel report as he signed his name. When the door closed behind her he moved his chair over by the fan. His neck tingled where the sweat evaporated. A mistake. Very unprofessional. He smelled something, something like flowers rotting, and realized it was her perfume on him. Having her down there would be good, would be a test of his will.

The girls they recruited were flown immediately to Guatemala City, then held in quarantine a few miles from the Camp while a barracks was constructed for them on the other side of the fence from the men. When Walt returned he had the girls transferred to the barracks and hired locals for the cooking and the laundry. He set up a system of two shifts a day, one for men with red coupons, one for men with green. The trainers were able to use the issue of coupons as a behavior incentive, and nobody got a coupon till Dr. Amoros had given them medical clearance. During the shifts Walt sat downstairs with his feet up on a desk, shooting the shit with the kids who waited their turn. The Cuban boys were friendly and homesick and called him Señor Alcahuete, but not in a nasty way.

"Señor Alcahuete," they would tease, "you must be hombre muy fuerte to have so many daughters."

"And I give them all to you," he would answer. "Por la patria."

The boys who were finished would stop on their way out and clap him on the shoulder or salute. "Por la patria," they would say.

Some of the kids would pump him for information, information he had not been made a party to.

"No sé nada de los planes," he would tell them. "Soy commandante de las nalgas, nada más. El gran pimp por la libertad."

The boys would laugh then and talk about all the beautiful asses they were going to liberate.

"You're doing a bang-up job," said Davies when Walt asked to be moved to something more vital to the operation. "We need you where you are."

"There are hundreds of pimps in this country. Can't you hire one of them to take over?"

"You're medical and morale here, Walt," said Davies. "We've got to keep these boys motivated. You just run your shop the way you've been doing. We'll take care of the military end."

In the early afternoons when the girls got up, Walt would sit in the mess and listen to them complain as they ate their morning meal. They called him Papi, but not in a nice way. They were homesick and bored and nobody had told them they were going to be held as prisoners in the middle of the fucking jungle till the job was done. The Cuban boys were so stuck up, they said, so vanidosos, they were almost as bad as yanquis. Even the girls who had never been with a yanqui said this.

"When will this fucking Invasion happen," they asked Walt, "so we can go home?"

"You are being paid well."

"There is nothing to buy here. De qué vale el dinero?"

"You're being fed and housed for free."

"The food is shit," they said. "We live in a barracón."

"But what you're doing is very important. Son amigas de la libertad."

"If you believe so much in libertad," they said, "why can't we leave?"

The Agency had decided that once the girls had contact with the Brigade they were a security risk and had to be held till after the Invasion. The girls were homesick and irritable, but they were surrounded by men with guns and miles of mountain jungle. They turned their two shifts a night and came to Walt with handfuls of green and red coupons for tallying. He had set up a piecework system like they had used in the Fruit Company for the pickers. Walt kept records of how much each girl had earned in American dollars and subtracted anything she ordered from the men's PX. No cash was issued. Dr. Amoros examined the girls twice a week and held lectures on personal hygiene. When he finished Walt would give a motivational seminar.

He had given similar talks to the sales force at the Sugar Company and the Fruit Company. It was important to build rapport, to make the employees understand they were all part of a vast team effort.

"In life," Walt would start, "we can't always choose what role we come to play. For instance, I did not choose to be an alcahuete."

Some of the girls snickered. Walt sought their eyes, speaking sincerely, trying to draw them in.

"Once we have been assigned our mission, however, we can only make up our minds to be the best at it."

"Si la misión es chupar la verga," said the little one with the husky voice they called Zorilla, "yo soy la campeona."

The girls laughed and catcalled as Zorilla mimed her specialty. Walt remained calm.

"There is nothing wrong with being proud of your work," he said. "But these boys need more than physical release. They need to feel important, they need to feel wanted. I know it's difficult, but you have to make each boy feel like he's the only one you've been waiting for, the one you always want to see."

"Papi," said the Indian from Tegucigalpa they called Mamacona, "it sounds like you have experience."

There was more laughing and catcalling. Walt waited them out.

"Soy hombre," he said quietly. "And as a man I know what would make me feel good, would make me feel wanted. I think you know the truth of what is being planned on the other side of the fence. For many of these boys, you will be the last woman they ever touch, the last woman they ever see. For many of these boys you will be their only love."

This shut them up. It was what he loved about the Latins, the heart they had, the sentiment.

"We have no way of knowing when the great battle will begin. Each time you are with one of those boys, remember that he might have only hours to live. That when he makes the ultimate sacrifice, the last name that passes his lips may be yours."

At that point some of the girls were crying. Walt stepped forward and laid his hand on the shoulder of one of the guajiras from Salvador.

"May God bless you in this work."

It was a performance he enjoyed, the only drawback being Carmen. Carmen would sit right in front of him and smile through the whole speech, not reacting, just looking at every part of his body as if judging livestock at a county fair. It made Walt sweat. He spent much of his day playing mind control games in order not to think of her, but she made it so hard. On the days when Dr. Amoros checked the girls out, between the medical exam and the first shift from the Camp, he would order her to report to his bungalow across the yard from the puta barracks.

He had tried to dwell on the details of her nights with the Cubans, to look at her entry in the ledger book, counting coupons, to curdle the idea of her body. But knowing she was there, that he could have her any time, made him sick with lust for her. He grew impatient with the waiting in between and tried to convince Amoros to add another VD exam to the week. He lay in his bed under the mosquito netting and thought he could smell her on the occasional breeze that wandered through the yard into his bungalow.

Carmen would sit on his lap, the netting draped around them, and hold him close like they were dancing, whispering hot words in his ear. She would tell him all the things she was going to do in the filthiest Spanish he had ever heard, her breath on his neck like the blistering winds the Indians said were evil and that always gave him a sinking, frightened thrill. The way she touched him was desperate and violent and left him uneasy for days after. He swooned into daydreams of her, longing like an addict, and kept a record of each boy who drew her token on the recreation shifts.

Walt had set up a blind draw system to discourage the Cuban

boys from developing favorites and fighting over the girls. Each girl was assigned a plastic poker chip with a number on it. The discs were stacked in a tray and the boys drew them in order as they came in for their shift. Trading was forbidden.

Carmen was number 13.

"Tu eres el único, Papi," she would hiss into his ear when he was in her. "You are the best."

Walt knew it was a lie but it sent a chill through him every time. He knew the boys all schemed and bargained to get Carmen's token after they were upstairs and that she always had more coupons than the other girls when the night was over. He wondered how many of them were dreaming of her as they drilled for the Invasion.

"I die por la patria," said the kid they called El Bicho as he came downstairs one night, "pero vivo para Carmen."

The first sores appeared after the revolt at the Camp had been dealt with. Walt had had rashes before, had survived a half-dozen different strains of jungle rot and exotic fungus, but nothing like these sores that didn't hurt. He knew what they had to be, had seen Dr. Amoros's slides and heard his lectures, but couldn't accept that he, Walt, could have such a thing. Each morning he would pull the sheet down and look at himself and there they'd be, bigger and redder than the day before.

"La sífilis," said Dr. Amoros after a moment of poking and sighing. "No hay duda."

Walt stood with his pants around his ankles. "Cómo?" he asked. "Solamente voy con Carmen, inmediatamente después de sus exámenes."

Amoros seemed to shrink before him. "Es posible hacer un error."

"A mistake? This is supposed to be your specialty."

The Cuban looked away and began to pull at the tips of his sterile gloves, stretching the rubber out and letting it snap back.

"It *isn't* your specialty?"

Amoros began to rub a pair of wooden tongue depressors together, as if figuring out if he could make fire with them.

"En Cuba no era médico," he said shyly. "Solamente enfermero."

"An *or*derly?"

"I am not a young man. I want so much to be here, in this Invasion. Por la patria."

Walt pulled his pants up and zipped them. He slid off the exam table and kicked a wastebasket across the room.

"I work in a clínica en La Habana," said Amoros. "I see everything they do. La sífilis a hundred, a thousand time. I do the blood test for them."

"She's infected the whole damn Camp."

"No, Señor Walt. Todos los otros usan gomas."

"Cubans won't wear rubbers, Amoros—"

"If they want to fuck with Carmen they do. She makes them or no bollo."

Walt felt like he couldn't breathe. "How do you know?"

"She tells me this. And she is always making me use it when I go with her."

Walt sat back on the exam table. He wanted to strangle Amoros but the little man looked too pitiful. "When you go with her?"

Amoros hung his head. "I am a shame," he said. "I try, but I can not help myself. When it is time para el exámen, we are fucking instead."

Walt thought of the way she held him, the way she would nip at his face and neck, the intensity of her attack and suddenly was frightened. "I'm the only one. The bitch did it on purpose."

"No sé por qué ella nunca le dijo," said Amoros. "She is a strange woman. Una bruja."

There was plenty of penicillin for the Camp. Walt agreed to keep Amoros's professional status a secret and Amoros invented a bacterial rash for Walt's service record. He also agreed to list Carmen's affliction as a form of mountain leprosy that required quarantine. Walt supervised the building of a tiny shed at the edge of the perimeter, across from the Camp stockade. They were holding the mutineers there a few days before they shipped them out. Carmen was locked inside for treatment. The shed was mostly tin, with a small grated window facing the jungle. Amoros tacked a patch of mosquito netting across the window after the first week. Walt controlled everything that went inside the shed. Late at night she would call for him, her voice eerie and disconnected wafting across the dark yard, calling vicious words of love.

"Papi, muero por ti," she would call. "I die for your love. My soul is starving for you. Papi. Ven a mí, Papi. Por favor. Por favor."

"Everything running smooth in your shop?" asked Davies when he called Walt in.

"Smooth enough. It's routine by now."

"Good. We'll put one of the Guats on it. We're sticking you back in your recruiting shoes."

"We've got enough girls. They're all trained—"

"This isn't girls." Davies had an old, battered Coke machine in his office that buzzed and rattled but delivered the goods if you fed it coins. It made Walt long for home. "This is a black operation. There are some people in the Invasion force who we would rather not include in the new government that will be declared on the beach. Undesirable elements."

"I thought we purged all of them after the revolt?"

Davies fed the machine and pulled out two Cokes, dripping with a cold sweat in the afternoon heat. He opened them on the hook and gave one to Walt.

"Some of them didn't show their hand. And Kennedy's people are on the warpath again, all this 'broad spectrum' shit. So if we can't make these people disappear *before* the Invasion—well. The heat of battle, bullets flying everywhere—anybody could get killed."

Walt drained the soda in a long gulp. Finally, this was something real, something important. "How many targets?"

"We're calling it Operation Forty."

"Shooters?"

"Ten or twelve. We've got a couple dozen prospects staked out for you. Most of them worked for Batista in the old days. They've scattered around—a couple in the Dominican, some working for Tacho in Nicaragua, men in Panama City, Buenos Aires, Tampa, a bunch you can reach out of Homestead. It's good pay and a chance for these characters to settle an old score."

"You think our kids will let them in? Some of those tigres aren't too popular."

"We'll be stowing a few of them away with each of the units. Once they hit the beach nobody's going to be checking credentials."

"Except Fidel."

Davies smiled. "Fidel," he said, "is not part of the conversation here."

Walt met El Halcón in the Dade County jail, busted under suspicion of torching a bowling alley in North Miami. It was a favor for a couple mob guys who owned it and needed the insurance cash to cover expansion in other markets. The DA's office was not thrilled at the visit but Walt was operational and that was the highest card you could hold in Miami in '61.

"Está seguro que puede hacerlo?" Walt asked when they were alone in the room the lawyers used. "You positive you can kill somebody if we get you out of here?"

"If it would get me out of here," shrugged El Halcón, "I would kill *you*, así." He snapped his fingers.

The men Walt had been meeting were older than the kids at Camp Trax. They had been schooled in counterinsurgency Latin style, pounding terror into the population, killing when they had to or when they couldn't help it or when they just got bored or lazy. They had nombres de guerra like Perrito, León, Tigre Gordo, Cabezón, La Cobra, El Halcón. Most of them asked about the money first, then about the details of the job and whatever amnesty and position would follow. They wanted to know what weapons they would be issued.

"A quién voy a matar?"

"Does it matter?" said Walt. "Besides, I don't know any of the names. Those will be handed to you just before you go. All I can tell you is you'll have three targets and once you're done with them you just blend in with the Brigade and try to stay alive."

El Halcón gave him a long, chilling stare. "If this thing is fucked up," he said, "I come and find you. No es amenaza, es promesa. Soy hombre de acción."

"Sure," said Walt. "All you guys are men of action."

El Halcón was released in Walt's custody.

The men Walt found who were interested and still capable of staying sober were sent to Puerto Cabezas in Nicaragua to wait for the embarkation. Three men from the Agency who specialized in black teams took charge of them there, keeping them out of trouble and drilling them in the infiltration procedure. Walt was transferred back to the puta barracks.

Business was booming as the Invasion was clearly about to happen. The boys could tell from the amount of live ammo they were being issued on the range that the day was near. The chaplain and the puta barracks were swamped. As he watched the Cuban boys come downstairs Walt wondered which ones might be targets.

It was a strange kind of power. He didn't have all the information but he was at least closer to the source than these boys who would be throwing their bodies on the line. He thought of all the money, all the planning and power driving the Invasion, the logistical bulk of it, concentrated into one pinpoint of pressure, one bullet aimed at a spot between somebody's eyes. Castro was the main target, yes, and he had to know that, had to lie awake nights thinking about it. But some of these boys here, laughing and slapping him on the back, some of them were on a list only Walt and a few others knew existed. Walt felt a sudden comfort in the orderly chain of events that would lead to those executions, in this world where death was not random. Information was his power, his weapon and shield, and the farther up he could move in that hierarchy of knowing the less chance that he would find himself on the sharp end of events, that any murderous thing would be speeding toward a spot between his eyes.

The day after they shipped the Brigade to Puerto Cabezas Walt let Carmen return to the barracks with the other girls. It was a shock to see her. She was so pale her veins showed blue through her skin. Her hair had grown out, dark roots several inches long and the whole thing matted like a sick dog's. She had lost all her roundness, her bones jutting sharp, her eyes bugging from their sockets, all the juice in her used up. Her smile twisted into a hateful sneer when she caught sight of Walt standing by his bungalow as the sentries led her across the yard.

"Mira," she croaked in a voice that hadn't been used in too long. "El Papi. La jiña que anda."

She pulled herself loose from the sentries, walking unsteadily on her own, and came to Walt. He was frozen to the spot, amazed that a single order, a few words that he spoke in anger could do this to a human being. Carmen reached him and put her hands on his shoulders, brought her face close to his. She brought her pelvis up tight against him and it was like a strong hand gripping as she held him close like they were dancing and smiled and hissed into his ear, her breath hot and sharp.

"Te doy mi vida," she whispered. "Por la patria."

She bit him then, a vicious animal bite clamping his cheekbone between her teeth, blood washing down his neck immediately and Walt panicking as the woman held on, dug harder with her jaws, the sentries rushing to try to pull her away and Walt screaming, hitting her with his fists, pulling at her hair but she just ground in deeper till his knees went and they fell, Carmen on top and the sentries hitting her with their gun butts while Zorilla came out and saw and started shrieking for the others who poured down into the yard, murder in their eyes, slapping and kicking at the sentries as Walt methodically smashed his fists against the crazy woman's head, his arms tiring, Carmen bleeding from the ears. Dr. Amoros rushed out and somehow got through to give her a shot in the buttocks and she slowly eased the pressure from her jaws till Amoros could pry them apart and she lolled into unconsciousness on top of Walt, still hugging him cold as a corpse.

The doctor who put Walt's face together back in Miami said he was already so full of penicillin there could be no chance of infection from the bite. He was held for three days in the skin-trauma ward under the false name the Agency had registered when they had him admitted. When he tried to phone his contact numbers they had all been disconnected. His only bridge to the outside world was a radio in the day room, lorded over by a burn patient from Fort Lauderdale who sat with his fingers glued to the dial, spinning it constantly through the band as if searching for a station or a song he could never quite find. His head and neck were wrapped with bandages, eyes covered over, his skin oozing through the gauze. Nobody in the day room was going to challenge his control of the airwaves. Walt listened desperately, catching only a few tantalizing words before they were jerked from the air by the restless man from Lauderdale. Walt couldn't get a picture of what was happening, only that the Invasion had begun.

"Have you heard the news from Cuba?" he blurted finally. "Has there been a report?"

The man held the dial at a point that only brought forth whining static and tilted his head as if trying to guess where Walt was standing. "Cuba?"

"Cuba."

"You mean the invasion thing."

"Yes. How is it going?"

The man from Lauderdale shrugged and continued his search through the radio waves. "Sorry, pal," he said. "I'm just as much in the dark as you are."

THIRTY-ONE

➤ ENVIAMOS DINERO A PUERTO RICO
says the sign out on the sidewalk,
 Y A LA REPÚBLICA DOMINICANA, MEXICO, GUATEMALA,
 EL SALVADOR, NICARAGUA, HONDURAS, COSTA RICA,
 PANAMÁ, COLOMBIA, VENEZUELA, Y ARGENTINA.
Victor leans against the doorsill next to the sign, smoking, watching the come-and-go on Calle Ocho. Slow day. Things were always slow unless it was the first or the fifteenth or payday. Then there'd be a line out onto the street and down the walk, a regular little United Nations of people wiring money home. It kept up the front. There was even a little profit in it, the legal part. Victor looks at his watch. At one the woman with the wonderful thighs who works at the travel agency across the street comes out to walk to lunch. Victor never misses it. She always seems about to burst out of her tight dress and it never fails to restore his spirits. I put enough aside, find una hembra como ella—

A taxi pulls up and Blas de la Pena steps out.

Victor chokes on his lungful of smoke.

Hombre, pendejo, this is it. You have really fucked yourself now.

Blas hands a bill to the driver and quickly steps past Victor into the office. Victor tosses his cigarette down, grinds it on the pavement, looks up the street. If I run, where do I run to? If I ran in to the woman at the travel agency—ay chica, they're going to kill me—what would she do?

Maybe it will just be a warning. Maybe they don't know.

He takes a deep breath and steps inside.

Blas is sitting at the desk, neither angry nor friendly. He pushes the phone toward Victor.

"Llame a Cocheros Reales," he says. "Tell them to send Serafín Cordero whenever he's free, drop me off at 37th north of Flagler. Give them your name."

Victor makes the call to the limo service. He wonders if it's a code. If he'll be taking the ride as well.

"They say a half hour." He hangs up the phone.

"Bueno."

Blas leans back in the chair. He's a hard one to read. Victor has heard stories though, and now with the problems with the Colombians there is blood in the air. Just last week Soto came by and told him to be sure his piece was clean and ready, that no part of the operation was safe from now on. He thinks of the .44, smelling of gun oil, sitting in the drawer right in front of Blas.

Victor reaches for another cigarette, then catches himself. No way I can light it. Breathe deep. Nothing is wrong till it's wrong.

"I'm not here," says Blas. "Nobody on the outside knows, nobody on the inside knows. Entiende?"

"Claro."

"Necesito dinero. Two grand."

Victor nods, goes to the safe. Is this a test?

"I'll have to cover it," he says. "If I'm not supposed to say you've been here—"

"Le doy un cheque."

Victor opens the safe and counts out the money. He feels Blas watching the back of his head. So much. So much goes through the place, between the front business and the laundering, a river of cash rushing through. And he has taken so little. A sip. Really so little when you consider the amounts. How could they know?

Blas is holding a signed check when Victor turns with the money. *Union City, New Jersey. Santos Montalvo.*

"Classy name," says Victor.

"This will clear in a week, no problem. You figure out the rest."

Clear in a week. A week. Victor relaxes a little. He puts the check in the safe, closes it. Or is he just playing with me? Victor sits in the chair next to the desk, glances at his watch. The woman with the wonderful thighs is gone.

"Ahora," says Blas de la Pena, swiveling to face him. "How's business?"

* * *

Serafín eases up Calle Ocho, timing the lights, wondering who it is who asked for him personally. Sometimes it's the older women, the ones who are afraid of anything new, and sometimes it's the business guys with their mistresses, trying to keep the number of those in the know to a minimum, and sometimes it's the out-of-town drogueros who remember him from when he drove for Soto. It looks like it might be hot outside again, the sun-blasted streets brownish-yellow through tinted glass. A few of the walkers peer into the back, squinting to penetrate the dark window and see whatever big shot might be in there. Privacy is wealth, he thinks. He slows to let a woman carrying her laundry in a plastic garbage bag cross the street. Even the rich could be miserable and lonely, but they at least didn't have to do it in front of everybody else.

Serafín drifts up to the curb by the El Mercurio sign. Before he has the limo in gear Blas is sliding into the front seat beside him.

"Nos vamos," he says.

Serafín swings the car out onto the street.

"Está en casa?"

"No sé. I haven't seen her in a week. Desde el funeral."

Blas nods.

"Siento lo de su padre."

Blas looks out the window. "He was old. We only fought when we were together. Esta generación—" He shrugs. "They were hard ones, the ones from '33. They had to eat a lot of shit."

"Es verdad."

"But then who hasn't?"

Serafín turns right on Douglas.

"She's serious about this," he says. "I think she's pretty far into it."

"Guns?"

"Creo que sí. No tengo evidencia, pero creo que sí."

"Y con quién? Any names?"

"No. Her only friend I know of is Luz, and Luz doesn't know anything about it. You know how Marta is."

"Are you fucking her?"

Serafín grips the wheel, his eyes straight ahead.

"Hombre, no soy un hermano celoso. She's a grown woman, who she's with is her business."

"Nothing has happened between us."

"Too bad. She should get some pleasure out of life. And there is nobody else?"

"No. Luz would know that."

They ride in silence a moment. Blas scowls when they cross onto his old block.

"I never liked Havana much back on the island," he says. "I like it even less here."

It seems like there is more dust now. Lourdes dips the cloth in the bucket, twists it tighter and tighter to wring it out. She climbs onto the chair and begins to wipe the top of the living room wall. Before she always had to wait till He was out of the house to do it because He didn't believe that dust could settle on a wall. It went against the laws of gravity, He said, and besides I've never seen any dust on our walls. She thought of telling Him that was because she wiped it off every day while He was gone but didn't want to make Him mad. Lourdes doesn't remember there being dust like this back in Camagüey. Dirt-dust yes, brown and sandy, blowing across the yard, carried in on the clothes of the men, trapped in piles under Esperanza's broom. But not this gray layer of fuzz. She keeps all the doors and windows closed but it doesn't seem to help. And now even with Him gone she waits for the hours when He used to be away working before she attacks the dust.

Lourdes climbs down and moves the chair, then climbs up and wipes some more and then Blas is in the room.

It takes her a long moment to realize he's really there, in the flesh, and not like the times she thinks she hears Him in the next room or sees Him for a fleeting moment in the chair she won't go near because it holds the smell of His cigar smoke.

"Has vuelto," she says.

"Sí."

"El funeral fué el viernes pasado."

"Lo sé. I didn't hear in time. I was planning to come down anyway."

Blas seems like a strange man, a man she doesn't know. She remembers the little boy who lived in their house in the other world. The one who pushed away, who was drinking warm milk from a pan in the barn when he was three months, weaned already, strug-

gling to stand, to walk, squirming off her lap to go find out what
the men were doing. Who worshipped his Father till he went away
to La Habana and fell into the politics.

The man, Blas, stands in the middle of the room looking around
uneasily.

"Todo el mundo asistió al funeral," she tells him. "Tu Padre
era un hombre de respeto."

"Mami," he says, softly, "come down off the chair."

She steps down and automatically heads for the kitchen. When
Blas catches up with her she is pulling cans of food from the cabinets.

"Está Marta en el trabajo?"

"No sé. She stays away longer and longer. She comes in sometimes when I'm already asleep. This is not right for a young girl.
Si tu Padre viviera todavía—"

"She's not such a young girl."

"Todavía no está casada."

"Lots of people aren't married, hoy en día. It doesn't mean so
much." He looks at the cans. "I'm not staying for lunch, Mami."

There is a layer of dust on top of each of the cans, a few of them
starting to rust. When the man leaves she'll wipe them clean then
go over them with the steel wool.

"There's so much food."

"You and Marta will eat it. Do you need any money?"

"Tu Padre proveyó de todo."

Blas crosses and tries to open the window over the sink. It is
stuck shut.

"Van a sofocar en esta casa," he says. "Do you go out?"

"Al cemeterio. No está tan lejos."

"Bueno. You should go out every day. Get some air."

Sopa mondongo.

In the last years He still liked it but it was so much trouble to
make she started buying in cans. He never noticed the difference or
never mentioned it if He did. Now Marta wouldn't touch it and
there were so many cans. So much food.

"I don't know where I'll be staying tonight. Tell Marta I want
to see her before I have to leave."

Blas pushing away, out of the house without breakfast to be with
the men, up on a horse before he was in school, scaring her to death,
out on the ranch following his Father till it was dark, picking up
language from the monteros, walking as if he had boots on even

when he was barefoot. Blas pushing away, out with the men and Marta silent in her room, in her own strange world of frightening moods, leaving her with Ambrosio. Her son Ambrosio. Her baby. Lourdes can still feel his arms and legs wrapped around her, his baby breath on her neck, still feel the weight of him on her hip. Ambrosio whose hair stayed curly, Ambrosio smiling, crawling on the floor nearby while she played canasta with Tilda Hernández and the others, Ambrosio happier to draw a picture of a cow for her than to ride on top of one, her baby, her heart. The one they took away.

"I'll try to come by again," says the man, Blas, and starts out the door.

"Tu Padre," she says, "tu Padre era gran hombre."

"Lo sé, Mami. I'm sorry for you."

The bills that he has left on the table look brand new, crisp and clean and folded only once, sharply, exactly in the middle. Lourdes doesn't touch them. Maybe Marta can use them when she ever comes home. Lourdes stares at the new bills for a moment, bringing her face close. They seem to have collected a thin layer of dust.

"Is it a beauty or what?"

Rivkin sits in a deck chair by the old woman and the old man on the Jewish side of the veranda. The old woman leans over to clutch his knee as she speaks, digging in with bony fingers.

"It's very nice," he says. "A piece of history."

"I knew you'd appreciate. From your walk of life."

"Pardon?"

"Mr. Building Inspector. A professional eye."

"Right. It's a beauty."

Duckworth is back in the car, just across Ocean, resting his legs. They said they were from the city, checking fire exits, and climbed to Piñiero's room. Not in. Duckworth went back down before Rivkin screwed the door to take a look. No curiosity, Duckworth. No sense of adventure.

The old woman turns to shout at her husband sitting next to her.

"He loves the place, Sy. I told you."

Thirty years ago there had been a nautical theme, the front painted white with blue trim, the veranda floor a lighter blue with

white seahorses stenciled in a pattern. White lifesavers hung over
the front rail. The bellhops were dressed as ship's stewards and
there was a deep-diving suit standing in the lobby, the burnished
brass helmet always shiny. His parents would walk down the beach
with him then help him hotfoot across the street to the lobby to wait
for his Aunt Selma to come down. He hated wearing shoes. He'd
have a Creamsicle from the beach sticky in his hands and his feet
swishing in the basin they kept to rinse sand off and then his Aunt
kissing with all her powder and lipstick. A New York smell, intact
even here. The people on the veranda would call him over and ask
his name and how old he was and say what a smart fella. There
were no sides to the veranda then unless it was men and women
sometimes. At night there were pinochle games and he'd lie back
on one of the lifesavers and listen to the dark waves across the street
and the voices of the players, loud and edgy and funny and to the
same voices in Yiddish from next door where the older people stayed
and fall asleep in the ring dreaming it really was an ocean liner they
were on, steaming off to who knows where.

"How long have you lived here?"

"How long are we here, he asks," she shouts to her husband.
The old man is brown and leathery, a Jewish turtle, his bald head
covered with freckles. He stares across the street, working hard at
breathing, and doesn't acknowledge his wife.

"Twenty years this August," she says. "We tried a community
at first but it was all golfing. Sy doesn't golf."

Piñiero's room was small and depressing. No air-conditioning,
a sagging single bed, 50's Formica table with aluminum legs, a
hotplate on the dresser, girlie mags scattered on the floor. Spanish
girlie mags. He realizes they never went up to Aunt Selma's room,
that it was about the veranda, about the beach and the nightclubs
and the room was where you changed clothes and slept and his
single Aunt Selma didn't have much money and even less real glam-
our to anybody older than six. The lifesavers were long gone now,
the front chipped and peeling, the lobby thick with mildew and
disinfectant.

"These were palaces in their time."

The old woman squeezes his knee again. She could crush steel.

"This was our dream. To live here."

Rivkin sighs. "Well. You made it."

Three young men in sport shirts and polyester pants chatter

away on the cha-cha side of the veranda. Rivkin can only pick up a stray word or two. Definitely not marielitos, they look more Indian than anything. Guats, maybe, or Hondurans. They were getting all kinds. A teenage boy in a white uniform runs past, making little grunts every couple strides. The three Indians chatter and point and the old woman shakes her head.

"Always running, that one. Everywhere he runs. To live a long life you shouldn't hurry."

She puts her hand on her husband's shoulder.

"Eighty-eight years old. Would you believe it?"

Rivkin would believe a hundred.

"Amazing," he says.

The sign over the desk said fifty dollars weekly and you couldn't find that in any white neighborhood across the Causeway. He was glad his parents were in Bal Harbour now, everything below the Fontainebleau had gone to shit.

"It was rayon," says the old woman.

"Oh?"

"Before, with the natural fibers, we couldn't make a payroll. But when he jumped on the synthetics—*shoo!* Like a rocket to the moon. Rayon *made* Sy."

Piñiero comes bouncing up the walk then, about to turn in to the veranda when he spots Rivkin and keeps moving, a little quicker now, down toward 5th.

"Hello, Mr. Piñiero!" shouts the old woman. "They're inspecting us!"

By the time Rivkin hits the sidewalk Duckworth has already cut into Piñiero. Truly amazing. Playing possum in the car.

"You remember our old pal Hymie."

The way Duckworth says it makes him cringe.

"Hola, Jaime," he says. "Qué tal?"

Piñiero keeps his head pointed down. "You two are crazy, coming after me in broad daylight. You want to get me killed?"

"We missed you, Hyme. Lost touch. Didn't even know you'd moved to the Beach."

Rivkin moves to the ocean side of him, rubbing shoulders as they walk. "You could have sent a postcard. Our feelings were hurt."

"What do you want?"

"Hear you quit your job, Hyme."

"What do you want?"

"That's parole violation Number One—"

"And you've got a hotplate in your room."

Duckworth and Piñiero both give him a look. He shrugs.

"It's against house rules. There are old people living there, no elevators—"

"We want what we had before," says Duckworth.

"A relationship," says Rivkin.

"You talk, we listen."

"About what?"

"We got Justo Camejo's ride sitting with a trunkload of fiambres, right?" says Rivkin. "Colombian coldcuts. Kind of thing that provokes rumors."

"Somebody doesn't like Colombians," says Piñiero. "Somebody also doesn't like Camejo. Narrows it down to a couple thousand."

"You dealing again, Hymie?"

Piñiero looks Duckworth square in the eye. "If I was dealing would I be living in that shithole?"

"So you don't know anything."

"Nada. I don't see any of those people."

"No special activity, nobody making moves?"

Piñiero frowns, thinking.

"I got a socio at the airport, trying to get me on with the baggage. I call him this morning he says Blas de la Pena just came off the nonstop from Newark."

Duckworth and Rivkin trade a look. "And to what do we owe the pleasure?"

"Maybe he came down for the sun. How do I know?" Piñiero slows as they near 5th. "There's people up here who shouldn't see me with you."

"That's enough for now," says Duckworth. "If you're serious about that airport job and you need a reference, let me know."

They leave him and cross Ocean then, Rivkin flashing on the smell of the beach when he was a boy. The smell of Coke in green bottles, hot sand, ocean spray, Coppertone. He did most of his swimming in the pools behind the hotels, hair bleached near-blond with chlorine, a white band of untanned skin across his nose where the rubber plug went. In the afternoons his father would take him over to see the Marlins play minor league ball and they'd have a squad of trusties from the county farm under guard in the right-field stands, waiting to hustle the tarp over the infield when the noon shower hit. He brought his glove and prayed for foul balls.

The Marlins were gone now and the verandas along the beach were empty or filled with dead-end geriatrics and refugees and people were flying to Mexico or the Bahamas to find the sun. If there was a fire alarm and if it worked he hoped the old woman was a light sleeper. Sy was past hearing anything.

"That was nice of you," he says as they get into the car. "Offering to be a reference."

"Lots of shit running through that airport." Duckworth pops the air-conditioning on full blast. "Old Hymie could do us some good there."

They turn and head south along the beach. Rivkin watches the old places slide by.

"This neighborhood used to be magic."

Duckworth shrugs. "If you like hotels."

When Tío Felix sees Hong out on the floor he thinks the worst. When they quit because they're ready to start their own place you get notice, you get a week or two to find a new one. But if it's a mood or a grudge they walk out in the middle of the lunch rush screaming Cantonese threats and you're good and fucked. Tío Felix puts a platter of chicken and rice down and turns to face the cook.

"Hay un hombre en la cocina esperando por usted," says Hong. "He look like trouble."

There is a man named Guante who collects for the old boys, the ones who still run missions down to the island every once in a while. If you don't make a contribution it is bad for business. Felix walks to the kitchen and tries to think if Hong has ever met Guante before. There is enough cash in the safe if that's what it is.

Blas stands in the shadow of the seafood freezer. He looks thinner but still strong as he gives his uncle an abrazo.

"Tío," he says. "Ha pasado mucho tiempo."

"Two years."

"I'm sorry I missed the service."

Felix shrugs. "Funerals are all the same. And Scipio was gone from us when he had the first stroke."

Blas indicates Hong, back over the burners, noisily shifting pots. "You're doing well?"

"Nothing to complain about."

Blas nods. He has his father's way of keeping you in suspense, waiting for a judgment.

"Is Marta using your boat for something?"

Blas was always the toughest to sneak something past. Scipio was too sure of himself to pay much attention and Ambrosio was a romantic and could be distracted by fun. But Blas, even as a boy, cut through it all.

"Why don't you have a job, Tío?" he would ask.

"This is a job. I take people out on my boat."

"That's only for fun. You're always laughing and drinking."

"They pay me for that."

"Pay you to laugh and drink? Like the putas do?"

"I may be a puta," Felix would tell him, "but I am also my own boss."

And Blas would understand.

"If my boat goes somewhere," Felix says to him, lowering his voice and keeping an eye on Hong, "I go with it."

"So you're in on this?"

"No sé nada de nada. You know your sister. She weaves mysteries out of thin air."

"Do you know who she's mixed up with?"

Felix feels himself sinking. Marta is the one who visits him, who talks to him, his link to family. And here is Blas out of nowhere, hiding from the police, absent from his father's funeral, acting like the jefe de familia. Felix sighs.

"She asked about a man named Nuñez," he says. "She maybe has met with this man."

"Dónde puedo encontrar a ese Nuñez?"

"El Motel Cockpit, en LeJeune. Es el gerente allí."

"Bueno. Gracias, Tío."

Blas starts for the back door.

"Ya nuestra Marta es una mujer madura," says Tío Felix. "She has a right to be fucking up her own life."

Blas shakes his head and gives his uncle a grim smile.

"Not while she has family left to fuck it up for her."

DuPre is reading when the hard guy comes in. Strolls in like he owns the joint and stands staring at the empty bed. There is something obscene about them cranked up high and stripped of linen, something that insults death. DuPre hits his call button under the top sheet.

"You're looking for somebody?"

The hard guy ignores him, frowning at the empty bed.

"If it's a patient here, give me a try. When there's business on this floor I've got my nose in it."

The hard guy stonewalls, pretending not to speak English the way they do when they don't want to deal with you. If you use your Spanish on them they'll act insulted.

Luz steps in and makes a face like she's seen a ghost.

"Blas."

"Era su cama?" He nods toward the bed.

"Sí. Ahí se murió su padre."

"Sufrió mucho?"

"No más que en vida."

The hard guy considers this for a moment. "Bueno. Está Marta hoy?"

"It's a day off," says DuPre, unable to hold still any longer. "She takes Thursdays and Fridays."

Blas scowls. "Quién es?" he asks Luz.

"Un amigo de su hermana," says DuPre. "El vecino de su padre en sus últimas horas."

Blas turns his back on him. "You know where I can find her?"

"At home, in church," says Luz. "Since the funeral she's been missing work. She won't talk. I worry about her."

"Bueno. Si la ves, dile que la estoy buscando." Blas gives the empty bed a last hard look and is gone.

"The brother," says DuPre to Luz.

"Sí. That's why you called?"

"He looked like he was going to break something."

"Like the father. If you had known the father before his stroke, you would understand."

"Huevos duros."

Luz laughs and cranks the empty bed down. "I hate it when they leave them like this. We have to get you a new roommate."

"I'd like a blonde," says DuPre. "Twenty-five, maybe thirty. Some nice girl with a waterskiing injury."

"You like blondies now. My feelings are hurt."

"Marta won't be coming in much anymore," says DuPre. "Maybe she'll quit."

Luz puts her hand on the old man's shoulder. It's hard for her to separate his sadness from her own. "I'll make sure she gets this room."

DuPre tries hard not to cry. Pitiful, that it means this much to me. Senile old bastard, they should put me down like a horse.

"So what does he do, this Blas? This brother?"

"Nothing good," she says. "Nothing good anymore."

Rufo is waiting for Luz in the parking lot when he sees him. At first just some tipo, expensive clothes and a strange walk, as if he's wearing boots instead of the shiny alligator jobs he's got on. The features take shape as he walks across the lot and passes in front of Rufo sitting on the hood of his car smoking. The face clicks in— photos in the *Herald,* the few times he came in when Rufo was still waiting table at The Forge. Blas de la Pena. El Tiburón, back in town.

The men will want to know.

THIRTY-TWO

"CANDLES," says the Swamp Demon, and pulls the lid off the cooler.

They don't look like candles, at least not the way he thought they would. They are shorter and square-edged, with a twist of wire at the end. Padre Martín looks to Marta who looks to the Swamp Demon, the little one who squats by the cooler.

"Show me," she says and digs under to take a stick from the bottom.

This is not happening.

Marta follows the little one through the sawgrass to the trees.

This is not happening. We are not in this wilderness dealing with these people.

And then, breathing deeply to quiet his hammering pulse, he remembers that Jesus dealt with men like these. One of the Demons, the fat one with the red beard, says that they aren't angels.

"None of us are," says Padre Martín, smiling politely.

"We're not *Ang*els, man," says the other, the one in the leather vest. "People see a dude on a bike, they think Angels. Bullshit. We see an Angel, we fuck him up good."

Padre Martín nods. Marta and the little one are kneeling by a tree at the edge of the little oasis of trees, the little one digging at the base of the trunk with his knife.

"Spider knows his demo," says the red-bearded one. "Used to blow up slants in the marines."

"Marines eat that shit up," says the other. "Eat it for breakfast."

They look like the illustrations of pirates in the books he read when he was little. The one in the leather vest has a drooping black mustache and a gold earring and a thick scar across the bridge of his nose. The one with the red beard and the hairy gut bulging out under his T-shirt has tattoos, mostly of women and snakes, covering both his arms.

"She got tight lips?" The one in the leather vest.

"Pardon?"

"Your bitch. You're into something you don't want a bitch got loose lips. Bring the heat down, she gets on the rag behind something."

"She can keep a secret."

"We had a bitch riding with us, rode with this guy Ponymouth, she was always getting loaded and telling the world. Ponymouth did *time* behind that shit."

"Bad scene," says Red Beard.

Padre Martín nods sympathetically. He wonders if they might just take the money and leave them out here. Or worse.

"Stapled her to a tree," says the one in the leather vest.

"Fuckin A. Like this—" Red Beard spreads his arms as if crucified.

"I'd of stuck an egg in her mouth," says Leather Vest. "Rotten egg, really vile. Then sew her lips together. Make the punishment fit the crime."

"Fuckin A."

Nobody would find them till there were buzzards. Padre Martín feels the lump the money makes in his pocket.

"You-all are gonna off old Fidel, right?"

Red Beard is squinting at him, grinning with his crooked gray teeth.

"We have a mission."

"Fuckin A. All you cubanos want to off the sucker. Don't blame you."

"People see a guy on a bike, they think scumbag, they think weasel. Bullshit. Demons are patriots, man."

Padre Martín smiles and nods and starts across toward the trees. "I should see this," he says.

Spider is crimping a wire to the explosives he has wedged under a hollow he's dug beneath the tree trunk.

"You got four leads from this box," he says. "You can juice four separate charges from it, one at a time or all at once. I brought you plenty of wire."

He pushes the charge deeper into the hollow, then packs a bit of loose dirt around it.

"You want your stuff under the weight if you can. Give it something to push against."

They stand and walk back toward the other two, Spider rolling wire off a plastic spool.

"You get real slick, you do this by radio. But for homemade, this'll do you fine."

"How far away do you have to be?" asks Marta.

"Just use all your wire and keep your head down." He turns to walk backward for a moment. "Imonna have to charge you for this one too, you know."

"We understand."

When they reach the others Marta kneels with Spider to watch him cut the wire, strip it, and attach it to the detonator box.

"Rigged this up myself," he says. "Works off this big ole flashlight battery. You want to carry you a spare."

Padre Martín wipes a palmful of oily sweat from his forehead. He feels queasy. A half-dozen cattle egrets, shockingly white, are scattered standing erect in the green sawgrass, poised as if listening for something. The tattoo on Red Beard's shoulder closest to him is of a woman with enormous bare breasts and a panther's whiskered face. There is a tangy smell in the air. The Demons sit on the ground.

"You wanna get low, buddy," says Leather Vest. "Them splinters'll cut you in two."

Padre Martín prostrates himself on his stomach, facing the trees. "If I cast out devils by Beelzebub," Christ said, "by whom does Beelzebub cast them out?" Christ knew men like these. Christ saved men like these. Leather Vest has a cross around his neck, a thick iron cross on a silver chain, bumping against his bare chest when he moves.

"Do you believe in God?" says Padre Martín suddenly.

Only Marta doesn't turn to look at him. Red Beard laughs.

"It's a *rule*, buddy. You don't believe in God, you can't be no Demon."

Spider hands Marta the box. "Be my guest."

Mostly there is dust. When Padre Martín opens his eyes there is dust all around them and thicker dust obscuring the treeline and then—*wham!*—the tree trunk startles them smashing to earth only twenty yards away, and cattle egrets skim low over their heads.

"Only *you* can prevent forests," says Red Beard in a deep voice and his hairy belly wobbles as he laughs.

"That gonna do it for you?" Spider asks Padre Martín. He looks to Marta and she nods.

"We'll take it all."

Spider says thank you as he accepts the wad and re-counts the amount twice on his lap.

"The cooler is just to throw the highway bulls off while we had it on the bike," he says. "You want to keep it nice and warm."

Marta transfers the explosives and the wire and the box into a laundry sack. Padre Martín's knees are liquid when he stands.

"You buy from Angels, man, you never know." Leather Vest has his arm around Padre Martín's shoulder. "Sumbitches'll burn you. But we give you the real goods there. Light up some Commie ass with that shit."

The Swamp Demons get on their bikes and rev up, leaving Marta and Padre Martín to walk back to the road. He looks to the blasted spot in the earth where the tree was, at the raw wood exposed on the trunks around it. The egrets cruise back in and land almost exactly where they were before.

"Thank you," Marta says to the bikers over the sound of the engines. "This will bring justice to our people."

"Fuckin A," says Red Beard.

THIRTY-THREE

AT NIGHT THE INSURGENTS control the terrain.

Dewey listens, breathing shallow with his mouth wide open. His eyes have adjusted to the dark by now and he lies on his stomach watching the infiltration routes.

You always hear them before you see them.

The Old Woman is snoring very lightly. Outside a few cars cruise by the beach, the tail end of a drunken shout swallowed in the gentle wash of surf across the street. The oscillating fan thrums in the corner, cooling the sweat on his face then retreating, letting the hot dead air in the pullmanette close around him. Dewey listens hard to cut through the sounds. The pistol seems insubstantial in his hands, flimsy as plastic. It's so hot for April and the Old Woman only lets him open the window a crack. Dewey pours baby powder on his neck and crotch and pits to keep from sticking to himself, wadding the single thin sheet between his thighs, laying one of the soap-smelling hotel towels over the pillowcase to absorb some of his moisture.

He rests the gun on the edge of the bed, arm relaxed.

If you don't have a shot you don't pull the trigger. If you do, there will be time enough to ease into position.

The key to counterinsurgency is to assume the thought pattern of the enemy. What does he see, what are his objectives, what does he fear? The raids so far have been simple probes, recon and foraging coupled with the psy-ops effects. Sleep deprivation. The warrior who doesn't sleep loses his edge, makes judgments based on fatigue rather than relying on his training and a cool assessment of the combat variables. Since the raids started Dewey hasn't gotten more than an hour or two of sleep a night, with the day taken up by his med duties and the Old Woman. At night there is only vigilance.

Dewey hears the first one.

Low, maybe nine o'clock, just past the Old Woman's bed. The gnawing. It must be at the dresser, under the legs, the only wood in that sector. Not a clear shot unless he comes down off the bed, and forget that. The floor is a minefield. The idea of stepping on one. Or of being overrun—

Dewey raises the pistol and sights on the Old Woman.

He moves up from her mouth, open, snoring softly, to a point just above the eye, a point slightly obscured by her pillow.

Feathers.

At this range even the pitiful little belly-gun, this toy you'd rob a gas station with, will get cloth and feathers and the soft part of the temple and lodge in the brain. Killshot. Dewey imagines the feathers, some stuck bloody to the sheet, others floating, up in the air, wafting down like little angels around her.

Dewey opens his eyes wider, fighting a sneeze. Just the thought of it. He has to have foam rubber because of the rash he gets and the Old Woman clucks her tongue and says I don't know how you can sleep on that.

Dewey doesn't sleep.

He watches, waits, deadly in the night. I am a cobra, cold-blooded, poised to strike.

Dewey lowers the gun and rests it on the edge of the bed.

The gnawing. On and off, the insurgent stopping to listen every few seconds, scanning for movement in his sector like any good point man.

Conventional warfare has no place in suppressing the guerrilla. You make patrols, the guerrilla waits them out. You set traps, the guerrilla loses a few at first, then becomes even more wary. The guerrilla is a cancer, slow and sure, an opportunistic disease that you can rout again and again without ever wiping it out.

Counterinsurgency is the only way. Stealth, secrecy, patience. Dewey stifles a yawn.

Another one, almost straight ahead at twelve o'clock, in the kitchen galley. The sound of paper. Rustling.

If you know their minds, you know their needs.

If you know their needs you know where to find them, know how to lure them out into the open. The rustling stops. Dewey holds his breath. It should be picking up the scent now, hungry but cautious, all its senses wired in.

Come to Poppa.

Dewey steadies the pistol, using the edge of the bed for support. He wishes he'd had time to check the weapon out. The guy at the taxi stand said he shot gulls with the exact same model, blew them out of the air. Dewey thinks about the feathers, left floating after the body drops like a stone. An effective short-range killer. The ammo, tiny and hard-pointed, glossy in the fresh-smelling box. A thrilling smell. Turned down in three stores before the sleepy-eyed clerk with the boil on his neck who never spoke slid the boxes across the counter and rang up double the price. The profiteers always come out on top. Their day will come, though, and Dewey will be the messenger.

Hey, pal, I came to bring you your bullets back. Where do you want it?

Patience.

Whenever he asks her when they're going she says soon. Have patience. She hasn't been to work for a few days, maybe a good sign, a sign she is making the final preparations for the mission. He thinks of what he has hidden in the cardboard box up in the little closet where the Old Woman can't reach anymore. Thinks about how it will feel to hold when he puts it back together. Thinks about what it can do.

A sound, movement, halfway across the floor from the kitchen. He's taken the bait. Soon.

Dewey tightens his finger around the trigger.

Squeeze that baby. Imagine your round piercing straight into the heart of the enemy, a deadly laser from your eye. Take a deep breath. Squeeeeeze—

Patience.

The antidote for terrorism is counterterrorism. Make them fear *you*. Make *them* lose sleep.

Become the guerrilla.

Gray movement. A body taking shape. Cautious. Move—freeze. Move—freeze. The gnawing stops in the other sector.

Dewey takes aim.

It has to be done. Just a minor nuisance, say the people, the appeasers, the faint of heart. Just a little disturbance in the hills, in the outlying villages, don't overreact or you'll make it worse. But when the shit hits the fan and they're crawling all over the place who is the first to point fingers? Who is the first to ask how could you let this happen?

I see you. Locked on and ready to rip.

Dewey makes a click with his tongue, the one that freezes them in their tracks. Head up, nose twitching nervously—

It is more of a crack than a pop, like the sound his belt makes when he whips it against the bedpost in the morning.

I didn't blink. I didn't blink but I didn't see it either and then the Old Woman is up and there is noise in the hallway, geriatrics shouting to each other behind locked doors and he's stuffing the piece between the mattress and the springs and tucking under so that when the light blasts on he can rub his eyes and look up at his grandmother with the betrayed look of someone yanked unjustly from sleep.

"What's the matter?" he says, squinting into the light.

"There was a shot," she says. Wild-haired and shaky in her nightgown. "In this room. There was a shot."

"Something fell, Gramma. Or you're dreaming."

She looks around the room. Dewey checks the floor as she turns her back. No dead mouse, no blood. Not even a wound. Just a little gouge, a slanting nail hole.

"What's this on the floor?" she says.

"Where?"

"I've got it on my feet. What did you do?"

"I haven't done anything."

"Don't think I don't know."

"You're dreaming, Gramma. Go back to sleep."

She bends as much as she can to look at the floor by the kitchen. She comes back by his bed.

"Peanut butter." She spits it out like an accusation.

"You're dreaming."

"There's peanut butter on the floor."

Dewey groans, closes his eyes. "I make my lunch there. It must have spilled."

"Peanut butter *spreads*. It doesn't *spill*."

She gives him a long look and he opens his eyes to try to stare her down. If he'd just put it under the pillow, he could pull it out now. Let her stare at that. Go to bed, bitch. *Now*.

Feathers, floating down like little angels around her.

She turns away. None of the ones moving around in the hall now will do anything. Scared of their own shadows, scared to stick their noses out of their own building. A way he'll never be.

The Old Woman flicks the light off, climbs back into her bed.

"It *spreads*," she calls as a parting shot. "Don't think I don't know."

It was a mistake. A miscalculation.

Dewey rolls onto his back and tries to ease his pulse down. Sleep. The perimeter is secure for the night. But they'll be back, tomorrow night and the night after that and he'll need to be sharp. This, tonight, was a tactical error. The sniper is a limited weapon, good mainly as a psychological factor, a stopgap, a simple calling card to the enemy.

The struggle has escalated. Stronger measures are called for. Dewey begins the long march toward sleep, smiling, secure that he's got the solution resting high up in the little closet where the Old Woman can't reach, that he's got the answer to everything.

Firepower.

THIRTY-FOUR

THE HEAT MAKES him smile as he steps onto blacktop in the lot of the Cockpit Motel. Right now the weather is shit in Union City. The people are there and the music is there and the food and the clothes but the sky is never the right color in New Jersey, the air smells gray and the sun is a stranger. The only thing fucking Miami has going for it.

Blas checks out the few cars in the lot and steps into the office. A man with a face like stucco pocked by bullets is slouched over the desk reading a comic book.

"Hay habitaciones?"

"Forty for the night," he says without looking up. "Fifteen an hour."

Blas lays six twenties on the counter. The man looks at him.

"Three nights."

The man scoops the money in and pushes a register toward Blas. He signs as Simón Bolívar and makes up an address in Tampa.

"Carro?"

"No car. I just came off the plane."

"Equipaje?"

"No luggage." When he gets back into town they'll tell him where they've moved his clothes, where the safe house is.

The man pulls a key on a plastic tab off a hook behind him and lays it in front of Blas. Blas looks into his eyes.

"Nuñez," he says.

"Qué quieres con él?"

He didn't think this could be the one. Too much of a flunky. "Is he in?"

"No. Later maybe. Lo conoces?"

"Tell him Mr. Bolívar wants to talk to him."

Blas crosses the lot to unit Nine. An airplane roars above him, wheels out to land. A Cadillac is parked in front of unit Eleven, with a rag hanging over the rear license plate. Blas turns to breathe in the heat for another moment, then unlocks his door.

Mirror on the ceiling. One door, front window. Glass blocks set in the shower at the rear. Only one way in.

Blas turns the TV on. Women together on a rug. Turns it off.

There is a chain on the front door that would give with a hard kick. Lots of towels. A room for fucking.

Blas kneels on the far side of the bed, sighting toward the door.

Somebody may get fucked in this room, thinks Blas, but it won't be me.

Between the political meetings and the nightclubs and the arrests and tortures there was very little time to go to class. Blas was in his second year, studying architecture at the University, when they killed the head of Military Intelligence.

"Su padre es gran ranchero en Camagüey," said his discussion leader in the Federación Estudiantil after Blas complained about their lack of action. "Muy rico, muy influyente—"

"I am not my father," Blas told him.

"Bueno. But it will take us some time to discover your character. Hasta luego, debe estudiar y tener paciencia."

"How can I pay attention to the idiocy in a classroom when the country is coming apart around me?"

"Study the people," said his discussion leader. "The people will guide you."

The discussion leader didn't say exactly which people he meant. If he meant hired men Blas had studied plenty of them, had worked his father's cattle at their side, gotten drunk with them, considered some of them his friends. If he meant the cane cutters or the cigar makers that was more difficult, but he suspected it was even more abstract than that. So much of what was shouted about at the student meetings was made of air, the constant din of it made his head hurt. The Ortodoxos argued with the Guiteras crowd who argued with the Communists who argued with the Trotskistas. At least when he wandered into his architecture classes to rest it was about something concrete. Buildings. Laws of physics and strength of materials. But these factions were arguing poetry, they were debating dialectics and inevitable processes and the nature of the spirit. If he didn't know damn well that within the FEU was Echeverría and his Directorio and that they were planning something big he would have chucked the whole thing and gone back home. Or maybe tried to join with that crazy Fidel stumbling around in the Sierra.

"I am an excellent shot," Blas told the discussion leader, who he knew was tight with Echeverría and Chomón and the other big wheels of the inner circle. "I can drive a truck. I can go three days without sleep."

"Otro vaquero," said the discussion leader, smiling. "In time we may need cowboys, lots of them. We will keep you in mind."

Mostly the student politics seemed like a perverted game. The students would organize a protest, start a demonstration. The sbirris would rush through the campus and crack heads, drag people off to their headquarters or to the SIM and they'd be beaten to a pulp, sometimes worse, grilled about who the leaders were. If they were well connected, the families of the students would ransom them away from Intelligence with money or promises. Then there would be another demonstration to protest the brutality of the police. It was too old a story, already old in the days of the Spaniard, and sometimes running through the streets and hiding in toilets and classrooms Blas felt ridiculous playing at it. It was time for real action, the kind of action his father's generation had brought against Machado. But the inner circle was a tight one and he had wandered in from Camagüey with cowshit on his shoes and he couldn't blame them for being wary.

"You haven't been arrested yet," said his discussion leader. "It's hard for us to trust a virgin."

"You haven't been laid yet," said his friend Ramiro. "This is a crime in Havana."

Ramiro was his key to the night, a boy who would be a student for years and years and then one day become the owner of a large company without ever having to open a book or lift a heavy object. Ramiro had longish hair that fell off to one side of his forehead as if it were tired and an expensive rumpled jacket that he wore every day and a cigarette always lit in his mouth. He had attached himself to Blas because he was bored with the friends he had grown up with who were also students who never went to their classes at the University but then he was bored with most everything. Ramiro was never awake before two in the afternoon and knew the best cheap places to drink or eat Chinese food though money was never the point as he always paid with fistfuls of tired bills, limp and wadded from the pockets of his jacket. In Camagüey people would have taken him for a maricón except he liked to go to the putas.

"Esta es Concepción," he said introducing a grown woman with red hair that wasn't dyed to Blas in the parlor. "She is the woman for you."

Concepción did everything Blas had ever dreamed that a woman might do with him, did it with her eyes slightly closed and a wicked smile on her face that told him it was meant to be fun, that there was nothing to be proved. In between times on the first night he heard Ramiro with another girl in the next room, still talking though you could tell he was in her.

"I should take you home to meet my father," he was saying. "He's crazy about blondes."

When they left the dueña was sorting a pile of damp, wadded bills and the three girls waiting were sharing a red Popsicle from the freezer.

"It isn't manly," said Blas the first time.

"Al contrario. Fucking with Concepción is the most manly act I can think of. Your virility has increased by a hundred percent in only one visit."

"I mean having you pay."

"You're a Catholic, no?"

"My family is."

"Bueno. Then you understand the concepts of sin and atonement. When I spend money it is an act of penitence. Surely you would not rob me of that?"

"Penitencia para qué?"

Ramiro sighed and gave his twisted little smile. "Para seguir siendo Ramiro."

The life in the clubs was like a dream. The luxury, the people, the shows. Beautiful women in spangles who thrust their bare breasts at you were not common in Camagüey and in his first months at the University Blas went as often as Ramiro invited him. They would go with a few of the other boys Ramiro had grown up with and drink and talk and watch the women and then usually go to the putas afterward. Blas tried different ones but Ramiro was right, Concepción was his favorite, and sometimes when he could afford it he went to the house where she worked without Ramiro. He didn't like the other boys that much but at least they didn't talk philosophy and he was always the best drinker, the one who could still stand at the end of the night.

The night was thrilling and wide open and full of people like Ramiro who barely existed in the light of day and it was as removed from the life of the cattle ranch as he could imagine. If he could have been a little more blind or a little more drunk he could have let it all swallow him up.

"What is this guy, a priest?" one of the friends would say when Blas would make a comment about something that struck him wrong in the club.

"He's a Communist," Ramiro would say.

"Same thing."

"I was just wondering where they get all their money to throw away," Blas said.

"Un regalo de Dios," Ramiro would say. "A gift from God to tempt the weak."

"Another priest."

"And because I don't wish to be tempted," Ramiro would say, "I'm wasting mine as fast as I can."

The clubs were full of yanquis, some with their wives and sometimes just men and sometimes college boys his age and it was clear they had come down for something they wouldn't allow at home, for something cheap and exotic. A place to wipe their feet. And with them were the Cubans from the police and the military and the corrupt politicians and the businessmen who owned the right to work, grinning oily fat fucks who hadn't lifted a finger in years except to take a payoff and no matter how much he drank Blas couldn't help but see the makeup on the women now, thick crusts of it, grainy under the hot lights, cracking with the strain of their smiles and now there was something desperate in the beat of the music. The music. The beat, the congas, the claves, there was a secret message in it, a code, like in the slave days when they signaled from plantation to plantation with their drums and if you listened and you knew you could read it. It was the wild heart of the island, the part that never gave in and here in the clubs it was shackled, plastered over with rouge, drowned in rum and yanqui dollars with the musicians playing by rote, smiling dead smiles, unaware of the bomb sizzling in their hands.

"Mi amigo Blas no es ni cura ni comunista," Ramiro would say to the others, catching Blas with a scowl on his face as he watched the crowd around them. "Es un tiburón. When the capitán has deserted ship and we all are diving overboard, he is the shark who will finish us off."

During the school holidays Blas wrote home that he had to stay in Havana and study. He spent his days walking around the city, watching the people, seeing how things worked. He spent his nights with Concepción. One day he saw his discussion leader from the FEU in the little park near the palace, concentrating on the traffic. Blas stood by him for a long moment before speaking.

"Is something going to happen?" he asked finally.

"When it happens you will know." It was clear that the discussion leader didn't want Blas to stay by him. "Cuando pase, todo el mundo lo sabrá."

They'd been back from holidays a few months when Ramiro talked Blas into going out in the Vedado one more time. The Montmartre wasn't his favorite and he didn't have the money Ramiro had to gamble but things were happening on the island and he couldn't get to the center of them and he hadn't been truly drunk in too long a time.

"Mira este grupo," said Ramiro as they stepped in. "Half the biggest thieves in the country, all in one room."

It was the same sharp tongue and twisted little smile as always but Blas knew now that Ramiro was lost, that these were his people and he'd never have the strength to escape them. He was not so different from his father, the immaculately dressed charmer with feathers of white at his temples and a different young woman, usually blond, at his side whenever they'd run into him at one of the clubs.

"The old dog is still sniffing," Ramiro would say as they retreated from his father's dazzling smile.

Tonight it was the usual sprinkling of yanquis with sunburned noses and their leathery wives and some Havana politicians and men who owned things like Ramiro's father and one singer they'd heard at another club with her boyfriend who looked like a gangster and a table of colonels with their wives.

"Ese es el jefe del SIM," muttered Ramiro as they passed the table of colonels and wives. "Sentado a la derecha."

Blas glanced over and saw nothing special, a smiling man in his mid-thirties, out with friends. He didn't look like a torturer. And then he almost stepped on Concepción. She was packed into an evening gown, something he'd never seen before, dripping with jewels, smiling. She looked like any one of the colonels' wives. She was with a red-faced yanqui businessman introducing her to a bunch of other yanqui men who could have been his brothers.

"This is Connie," he twanged. "Connie's a real hot ticket. Aintcha babe?"

Concepción saw Blas in the corner of her eye as she smiled and spoke to the men in passable English. He felt betrayed in a way he never had before, even waiting for her to finish with another client at the casa. The whole fucking country is a whore, he thought, and swerved toward the bar.

"Qué hembra tan linda!" cracked Ramiro and Blas nearly hit him.

They were in time for the last floor show, and as he watched Blas pondered whether he should get completely drunk or save himself to betray Concepción with another puta later on. He could do both, of course, but it took the edge off being with the woman and the edge was what it was all about for him. Ramiro kept ordering rum and Cokes for them, four at a time, and pretty soon there was no choice.

It was very late when they went to the tables and Ramiro surrendered himself to chance, wearing the same twisted smile as he won, then lost, then lost, then lost, the croupier nudging his weary bills into a damp pile with his stick as if they were infected. Blas was drunk enough for the moment and wandered through the casino watching the action, watching the women who all looked like Concepción to him now whether wives or mistresses or prostitutes with their breasts peeking out and the jewelry hanging on them and maybe it wasn't their fault but he hated them. He was to the point where it all began to separate, the sound over in one corner of his consciousness not quite in sync with the people moving their mouths, talking and laughing with a sharp edge around them as if they were two-dimensional the women barking sharply the men's eyes bright as jewels with an uneasy hunger like well-fed stock penned before slaughter and the room spun around like the roulette wheel with Blas the tiny ball the most separate of all outside even his own body thinking what can I do to make these people shit their pants and here's more rum and seeing himself, seeing this university boy who could be one of them in a couple years if he played his cards right out on a drunk reeling through the casino and he understood perfectly what fueled Ramiro's little smile and the room was emptying out.

It was very late, maybe four in the morning, and Blas was still floating on rum and Ramiro was passed out sleeping in a chair next to the baccarat table. Blas tried to rouse him but his head just flopped from one side to the other and he mumbled something about his father being good for the money. Blas never understood the attraction of the gambling, as crazy as believing in a politician, lots of promise and then your pockets were empty. He went out to the foyer hoping there would be some taxis left and the driver could help him carry Ramiro. He wasn't so steady himself.

The screams started just before the hammering of the machine-guns.

Two students who were big wheels in the Directorio blew past him as they ran back into the casino. Blas stepped into the foyer and there was the screaming still and one of the wives, bleeding, ran into the wall of mirrors thinking it was the way out, cracking her head and the mirror, pearls scattering on the floor with the empty machine-gun shells. Two of the colonels were on the floor, one wounded and the one who was supposed to be the head of Military Intelligence dead, blasted apart. The wives were hysterical, screaming, and Blas stood staring in a kind of rum-heavy shock till the police yanked him off his feet and dragged him into the patrol wagon.

More than anything he wanted to be unconscious.

If they hit him just right and hard enough under the jaw it made the other blows go dull for a while, but that wasn't the same thing. The worst was when they hit him anywhere in the center of his face now that the nose was broken and he couldn't tell where it began and where it ended. It was only pain there now and the tall one kept snapping the back of his fist against it, shooting a white flash shrieking back through his eyes to the rear of his skull, and he felt sick, swallowing blood, stomach muscles wrenched from puking out the rum and the Chinese food and something hot and yellow he was sure was supposed to stay inside. His arms were tied behind the back of the chair and his feet were tied together and he was naked with his vomit drying sticky in his lap. The short one had something hard twisted in a wet towel and he whipped it across Blas's face, jerking his neck sideways, and the tall one kicked him again and again below the knee with the stiff toe of his boot. Blas gasped for breath between the shots to his head, sucking air and blood down his throat then bracing his tongue behind his teeth so they wouldn't crack when the next blow came. There was only one thing they wanted to know.

"Quiénes fueron?"

"I don't know them."

Smack.

"Quiénes fueron?"

"There were two. That's all I saw."

Smack. Smack.

"Quiénes fueron?"

"I didn't recognize them."

Smack. Kick.

"Quiénes fueron?"

They didn't want to know that he was Blas de la Pena. They didn't want to know who his father was or where he was living or how his studies were going or whether he was an advocate of Bolivarism or a dialectical materialist. They kept hitting him and sometimes pushed the chair over onto the wet concrete floor. The situation was bad but not complicated. They were going to kill him or they weren't. The wives had seen the students and the other officers had seen the students and if they didn't know the names of their enemy it wasn't Blas's job to help them out. If they were going to kill him he would die like a man. All he could do was to not be afraid of the pain that would come next, to concentrate on the pain he already owned.

If he lived they would never catch him again without a weapon.

Smack.

If he lived he would make them eat shit with hair in it.

Smack.

If he lived he would make them die.

The fury rose up in him then and he could hear somebody

bellowing in the next room, barely human, till the short one shoved the towel into his face and he realized it was his own voice, roaring wordlessly. The tall one took the telephone book he'd used before and turned it so the hard spine was out stepping closer to Blas and swinging it with all his might at what had been the bridge of his nose.

At some point he was partly conscious again and they jammed a hose from the sink into his ear and turned the water on full blast.

They didn't let him out of the infirmary till the bruises on his face had faded some. They set his nose and cleaned his ear out. He was photographed and fingerprinted. The day he was released the discussion leader was waiting across the street.

"You should stay out of nightclubs," he said. "It's an unhealthy life."

"I didn't tell them anything." Blas still couldn't hear much on his left side. The traffic sounded very distant though he could see it just a few feet away.

"When you're feeling better there are some things you can do for us," said the discussion leader.

Blas was on the suspect list now but not wanted for anything. He could carry information, carry leaflets, carry weapons, and suddenly he'd stepped into a new universe. Havana was divided into the resistance and the police and the mass of people who were sleepwalking through their lives while the Day was creeping up on them. In any crowd he could pick out who was who without badges or uniforms to guide him. There was a power in secrecy, a thrill in greeting a comrade on the street with the usual careless jokes knowing all the while that each of you was likely to be on a mission, each part of the same dangerous society, watched closely by an enemy just as dangerous. The Directorio gave him small jobs at first, courier work, then brought him in closer and closer to the inner circle. It was a game not so unlike the one the students played at the University, but at the end of this there was the promise of the Day.

"After the Day," they would announce in their small group meetings, in their secret cellars and lofts, "after the Day we have to be ruthless."

"Claro."

"Murderers cannot be pardoned."

"The people will insist."

"After the Day we must be deaf to the songs of the politicians."

"The Ortodoxos are finished."

"The old men must go."

"And the 26th of July?"

"They should be our allies."

"They will be with us."

"We'll let them know at the last moment."

"And Fidel?"

"Christ, Fidel—"

"He breathes up all the air in the room—"

"The man cannot listen—"

"Fidel is in the Sierra."

"But he has weapons."

"Fidel will tame the Oriente for us. With the head gone—"

"The body will follow."

"And the Communists?"

"Fuck the Communists. What have they done?"

"Licking Batista's ass—"

"But Fidel—"

"On the Day, when he hears, he'll shit his pants."

"We'll bring the Constitution back."

"But better. We'll make it work."

"This time we'll do it right."

They were mostly middle-class boys, students, many of them Catholic, with a few older men who had fought against Franco in Spain. The plan was simple and direct and if it worked everything would be different afterward.

"The only way to fight a dragon," said the discussion leader, "is to jump down his throat."

On the Day Blas was crammed into the rear of a delivery truck with forty other men, struggling to breathe, an M-1 pressed tight against his chest and a .45 in his belt. It was totally dark and sweaty and all they could tell was that the traffic was bad. A few of the men joked nervously but most were like Blas, quiet, steeling themselves for the sudden rush at what came next.

There was firing outside and then the truck jerked to a stop sending them crushing into each other and then Mora opened the rear and they were jumping out. The street was insane with bullets and Blas took three steps toward the palace before he was on the pavement with something wrong, his leg, he couldn't stand and his carbine was too far to reach and the others around him were stalled crowding around the truck firing up at the top floor. His leg felt wet. The afternoon was frantic with machine-guns, men a few feet from each other screaming over the noise, and they were pinned down taking fire from above, from the third floor of the palace and the top of Santo Angel church, a hard rain of bullets beating the pavement, blistering the metal of the truck. Some of the others ran forward and some ran backward and some fell dead or wounded there at the entrance. There was more fire, from behind them now, soldiers and police closing in to trap them and some of the ones in the first car were running out of the palace now, shot from behind, falling. Blas found himself on his feet running, a lop-sided run dragging his wounded leg stiff to the side, lurching across to the little park, slipping on spent bullets, live rounds screaming past all around him chipping the concrete off the fountain, blasting bark from the trees and he ran no more than three yards from a policeman advancing toward the palace and was past before thinking that he still had the .45.

Two blocks away it was a new world, like falling from a fire into cool water. On Cuarteles Street people had stopped their cars and stood on the pavement exchanging rumors. They stared at Blas limping toward them like he was a fish with legs. A small man standing by his taxi called out as he dragged past.

"Se murió Batista?"

"No sé," Blas said. His right thigh was an angry hole of pain, he nearly fainted each time he put weight on it. The pants leg was black with blood.

"Oí en la radio que Batista había muerto."

"No sé," he repeated. "I didn't reach the palace."

"I've never been inside myself," mused the taxi driver. "They say it's a wonderful building."

It seems like night inside the restaurant. The soft neon wash, the samba whispering over the sound system, the air-conditioning cool and intangible around him. The bar is filling up already, a half-dozen men and a very beautiful prostitute at the plush stools. Blas sits where people can see him and orders a whiskey.

He recognizes three of the men at the bar. Minor players, waiting for whatever happens next. When Rubén used to have the El Tropical he called that part of the bar the bullpen.

"Strictly the short relievers," he'd say. "Hungry boys with big ganas to make the majors. I let them run a tab so I can keep my eye on them."

The El Tropical had been the place in the 70's until the tourists discovered it and started coming in to watch the tipos on their home turf. Then Rubén had a going-out-of-business party for the people in the outfit and the night after there was the fire.

The very beautiful prostitute gives Blas a look. He shakes his head. Why waste her time?

"Mira qué basura nos está visitando de Nueva Jersey." Rubén slides onto the stool next to him.

"Rubén. Qué tal?"

"You picked a nice week to come down," says Rubén. "What's the problem?"

"No hay problema. Negocios personales."

"I heard you were in town, compa, and if I heard, other people heard as well. This is not good."

"Por qué?"

"We got a bad case of the Medellín flu running around town. We got Justo Camejo on the rag, we got these jodidos Marielitos up the culo and we got Jamaicans. You got them up there?"

"Not so much."

"Locos. Locos with Uzis now. I'm afraid to walk the streets."

"I won't be here long."

"The vice cops sniff you out you'll get a steel apartment in Atlanta."

"Conoces a un hombre llamado Nuñez? Es patrón del motel Cockpit, cerca del aeropuerto?"

Rubén thinks for a moment. "Qué quieres con él?"

"Lo conoces o no?"

Rubén nods. "El Halcón. Nuñez is bullshit. I forget his real name."

"I forget my own real name sometimes," says Blas.

"He's pretty bad news, este hombre."

"There was one called El Halcón back in Havana," says Blas. "A real rompecojones. When I was a student we were always going to kill him."

"Same guy. We've done business with him."

"Drogas?"

"Asesino profesional."

Blas frowns, swirls his drink. "Como en Cuba."

"Only now he doesn't wear the uniform and business is not so good. Too much competition. But he's got his motel and he sells dirty magazines and he's connected with the yanquis."

"Mierda."

Rubén shrugs. "Everybody else is, why not him?"

"I'm not. I got nothing to do with them."

"Chico, don't kid yourself. If the yanquis weren't on our side we'd be hiding behind this bar with Bogotá cowboys coming in through the windows. It's a business, you got to have an edge."

Blas scowls and turns to look across to the dining room. "Nice," he says. "This is nice. You got taste, Rubén."

"I got ulcers, compa, that's what I got. This fucking town, this fucking business. There's too much money floating around, it makes people crazy." He puts his hand on Blas's arm. "This thing, cualquiera tienes con Nuñez, this isn't crazy shit, is it? We got enough troubles down here without you. No offense, Blas, but I get a pain in my stomach when I see you."

It is very pleasant in the bar. There are people around him whose biggest worry is what to order, whether to have a cocktail before dinner or along with it. He thinks they may have used the restaurant for a scene on a TV show.

"There are some things I need you to do for me," says Blas and turns back to his drink.

On his first day in the Sierra Escambray Blas helped to hang a man.

He still didn't walk right. The doctor who had come to the burdel was the abortionist the putas called when they were pregnant by a client or a boyfriend and didn't want to stop working, the man they recommended when the yanqui tourists asked for someone to fix their girlfriends or daughters. Concepción told him that Blas had been shot in an argument with another client but it was clear he didn't believe it even before he took the pieces of machine-gun shell out of Blas's thigh and tried to set the shattered bone. They were in a room with a beaded curtain and a tiger-skin rug and Concepción held his head in her lap, twisting a handkerchief soaked in rum and stretching it for him to bite on as the abortador probed, Concepción crooning "Chico, chico, vamos a salvarte, chico—" and the room spinning and in the same moment Blas knew he was in love with her and that she was calling him chico because she didn't remember his name. There was the dueña coming in to say you have to get him out of here, maybe only once but it seemed like a dozen times and the abortador talking as he probed and pulled about the crazy students trying to shoot their way in to kill the Dictator looking for the stairs to the third floor when everybody knew there was only a single elevator up. Most of Blas was in the leg then, as if it were bigger than he was, a huge ravine of anguish that had widened with each step as he crossed half of Old Havana to get to the burdel. At some point he heard the doctor say he'd lost too much blood to live and needed to be taken to a hospital and threatened to shoot the man with his .45 though he had lost track of it some time back and instead he caught hold of Concepción's wrist as if he would stay alive as long as he didn't let her go. At some point he wasn't conscious anymore and never saw her again.

He still didn't walk right. By the time the network had found him and smuggled him back home to Camagüey he could take a few steps without crutches but only once or twice a day. He knew if he worked at it this would improve, but for the moment it meant there was no escape from his family.

"You have to rest," his mother would say, sitting by his bedside every morning when he woke.

"Sí Mami."

"Do you want anything to eat?"

"No Mami. I can't eat in the morning if I'm not going to work."

"Rest, then."

"Sí Mami."

She would sit and watch him rest then, silent, Blas closing his eyes and pretending to doze till it was unbearable and then making the noise he made when he had to urinate and she'd leave and send in Ambrosio.

"Puedo orinar solo," he would say to his little brother.

"Bueno. Cómo te sientes?"

"They're going to suffocate me. A thousand bullets didn't hit me, a hundred police agents drove past me in the street, but these people will drive me insane in a week."

"They're worse since when you left. I can't wait to get away."

"Don't hurry. The University isn't what you think."

Ambrosio would shrug and smile his trusting smile. "There's

nothing for me here. I try to have a conversation about a book, about an idea—blank stares. This place makes men into cattle. It's either the University or join the guerrillas in the Sierra."

Blas laughed. "Tú? A la Sierra?"

"Por qué no?"

"Hermano, you can't even shoot a cow when its leg is broken. What would you do in the Sierra?"

Ambrosio would wear his hurt look then. "If you had made it to the third floor of the palace," he asked, "and there was the Dictator, all alone, unarmed—what would you have done?"

Blas made a pistol with his fingers and pressed it against Ambrosio's forehead between the eyes.

"Boom," he said. "Un golpe para la democracia."

"Have you killed anyone?"

The way he asked it made Ambrosio seem even younger than he was. Blas braced himself on the headboard of the bed and slowly pushed to his feet. "In the Resistance you learn not to ask questions like that."

He had been hit before he could take a single blind shot at the palace. But he had killed men in his heart, dozens of them, and would kill more in the flesh once he got to the mountains.

"Do you think it's a sin?"

Ambrosio said things like that out loud, unembarrassed, Ambrosio wrote secret verses and wore his most tender feelings on the open book of his face. Blas hoped it would all be settled before his brother could be drawn in.

"Once you commit to action," he said, "the only sin is to betray your comrades." Blas stepped across the room, stiff, trying not to limp. "The rest is survival."

"You're walking better."

"Bueno," he would say. "Go tell Mami I have urinated successfully."

One day he came back to his room to find Marta inside on his crutches, her feet wedged in to use them like stilts. She hopped down and placed them carefully on the bed. She was a strange little girl, as likely to talk to the chickens in the yard or Mami's plaster Virgin as to a person, with eyes that seemed to judge as well as see. There was no teasing her, and when she fell into a dark mood only Ambrosio of all the family could coax her out.

"Has ido a la montaña?" she asked shyly.

"What mountain?"

"The one they talk about."

"Talk about in church?"

"The one Ambrosio and his friends talk about. Siempre están hablando del monte. Del monte y del llano."

"You mean the Sierra. I haven't been there. I've been fighting in Havana, in the plain."

"Will you go to the Sierra?"

"Yes."

"And be part of the Struggle?"

"As soon as my leg is well."

"I'll pray for you," she said.

"Gracias, Martita."

"And if you die you'll be a saint."

With his father it was two roosters circling, spreading their wings in display.

"Tontería," his father would say suddenly, walking through the room, in the middle of a meal, out on the property once Blas was well enough to ride with him. There was no need to ask what he meant.

"If we had been successful," Blas said quietly, "the world would be singing our names."

His father scoffed. "The names of assassins."

"It was not a knife in the back. We met them in daylight, man to man."

He knew his father gave money in private to certain men, local politicians, for their consideration in matters of business.

"Pests," his father would say. "Like ticks on healthy cattle. They'll always be with us."

The old men, the men who fought during the Machadato, often spoke this way. As if the failure of their own revolt meant that all resistance was useless, was only a passing phase of youth. A game. And Camagüey was a backward place, a place where dust and cowshit were manufactured, an empty plain as far from the intrigues and sabotage of Havana as from the guerrilla war in Oriente.

"They'll be with us always only if nobody has the balls to fight them."

"Comunistas," his father would sputter then. "De qué vale luchar si el país lo van a los comunistas?"

"When you made war on Machado," said Blas, "what did they

call you? We are no more comunista than you were. The men in the Sierra—"

"Son bandidos—"

"—are no more bandidos than the mambís were when they fought the Spaniard. Padre, you can't be afraid of losing what you have. We can never go forward with that kind of thinking."

The conversation would end there and his father's speech begin, on his feet, red-faced from shouting, reminding his thankless son just who he was talking to and comparing the dwarfs in the mountains now to the giants who had walked the earth in his day. Blas could feel his leg throbbing then, the blood in it tight and angry, concentrating on an image as his father's words became mere noises and time slowed down. Sometimes the image was a woman with red hair that wasn't dyed. Other times it was of a room with a chair and a sink and a wet cement floor. There was silence between them when his father ran out of steam, and if there was any pride or worry mixed with the old man's disapproval it was never spoken aloud.

One day when he was using the steps on the front porch to work his leg, Ambrosio galloped into the yard.

"Pozo just told me the rurales are coming!" he shouted. "You'd better hide."

Blas was wearing the pistol Ambrosio had bought for him in town but he knew this wasn't the place to make a stand.

"Cuándo?"

"Three minutes behind."

He didn't want them to catch him in the house and he couldn't run yet and he'd be easy to spot out on horseback.

"Ayúdame."

Ambrosio gave him a leg up and he eased himself over the lip of one of the huge tinajones that sat in front of the house. There was rainwater in the jar, up over his shins, and he crouched with the pistol out and ready. A moment later he heard the jeeps pull in.

"Buenos días."

It was Guzmán, the colonel in charge of the rurales.

"Buenos." Ambrosio.

"Buscamos a su hermano."

"No sé donde está. No le hemos visto hasta casi un año. Está al Universidad."

Footsteps of men getting out of the second jeep. The click of something hard against the side of the tinajón.

The colonel spoke casually, as if this arrest were not a life-or-death matter for him. "Sabemos que él está aquí. Alguien le ha visto."

"Su informante ha visto un fantasma. Mi hermano está en La IIabana."

The door opening then. His father's voice—

"Coronel, qué es esto? Soldados a mi casa?"

The tone he used to command, sure of himself, the gran vaquero. And the colonel back, politely—

"Lo siento, Señor de la Pena, pero debemos buscar a su hijo Blas. Órdenes."

Blas knew the expression his father had on his face now, a mixture of rising anger and surprise that anybody might resist his will.

"Mi hijo está en la Universidad, estudiando arquitectura."

It was the first time Blas had heard his father say the word "architecture" without scorn in his voice. The colonel was persistent.

"Bueno. Con su permiso, debemos buscarle en casa."

"Duda de mi palabra?"

A pause. Then—

"No, Señor."

It was easy to hear that the colonel doubted his father's word a great deal, but that he was not eager to press the issue. In Camagüey his father's word had the weight of land and time and tradition behind it. Blas could hear the men begin to move back toward the second jeep, not even waiting for the order from their jefe.

"If you should see your son Blas," said the colonel, retreating, "please tell him we would like to speak with him."

The jeeps drove away and Blas relaxed the pistol but stayed crouched in the jar. He didn't want to climb out from hiding while his father was still there.

"Blas está seguro?" asked his father when the soldiers were gone.

"Sí Papi," said Ambrosio. "He smelled them coming. Es un guerrillero verdadero, Blas."

"The rebels have been seen in Camagüey. Trying to cross from Oriente to the Escambray. Tontería."

"Sí Papi. Pero son muy bravos."

Blas could imagine his father's scowl and then heard the front door close. When he let his breath out the sigh echoed in the damp tinajón.

At dinner that night the visit of the Guardia was not mentioned, not by Blas, not by his father, not by Ambrosio. The next day Blas set out for the Escambray.

He still couldn't walk right.

He took the roan horse his father had given him when he was fifteen, and canvas sacks of supplies Ambrosio had put together with Esperanza, the old cook, and a compass and a pistol and the little Remington he shot birds with. He got up before first light and rode west across the plain.

The leg didn't hurt when he rode but when he stopped and tried to walk it was either on fire or asleep. Small planes buzzed over him a few times during the first day and he waved up at them. Blas rode the horse across the plain at a canter, crossing the ranchlands of his father's friends and enemies, cutting south of Guáimaro away from the central highway. He was the only human in sight for hours at a time and it made him feel small. When he did see men they seemed as placid as the livestock they tended, men made of leather and dust who noted his passing without turning their heads. Camagüey might have given the nation Ignacio Agramonte but in the open spaces of the province the flame of revolution was cold. If the men who watched him failed to suspect his intentions it was only through their lack of imagination.

Blas walked the horse through the wooded areas, flies pestering its ears and tail, lather drying on its neck. When the sun was directly overhead he found shade by a river, holding the roan back until it was rested enough to drink, lying on the ground with his bad leg stretched out trying to get some feeling back in the toes.

Blas crossed cattle lands and pineapple fields, orchards and rice plantations, cutting wire to get through in some places and tying it back in place behind him, following the banks of the rivers till he found the best place to swim the roan across. He lived on dried beef and cold rice and water and whatever fruit he found along the way and the time it rained he kept riding till it got too dark to see. That night he took his boots off, not caring that his feet might swell too much to get them back on.

Blas never spoke to the horse, but they were aware of each other's moods and by the second day they found a rhythm together. Blas wondered what it could be thinking, heading steadily westward into new territory, grazing on strange pasture, sleeping without a fire when there was no way to shelter it from sight. He wondered if horses had any sense of a future they couldn't see, smell or hear, any sense of dread. The idea of the Sierra and what would happen next was growing inside him and only his fierce will kept it from turning him around. If death waited to the west, that was the direction you headed.

There were hawks overhead every day, almost motionless high in the sky, rabbits flushed scrambling from the roan's hooves and snakes startled awake to whisper through the grass. Blas noticed the tiny lizards only when he got down to walk a bit every evening, to walk evenly without a limp, covering any hint of pain. The only way to handle pain or fear was to go forward, to meet it face to face.

Blas held grimly to the animal's back in the wet chill of early morning, through stands of thorn trees, across dust-choked arroyos, mile after mile till they forded the Río Jatibonico with the bluish sierras of Las Villas ahead in the distance. There were swamps to pick through then, canefields to skirt, an army guard post he walked past at night. On the last morning he almost lost the horse swimming the Zaza. On the far bank Blas sprawled on his back, the roan beside him with its head held low, sides heaving.

Blas thought about the country he had crossed and felt as if he owned it all now, an ownership that had nothing to do with fences or borderlines. He thought about the ranch and the things he loved about it, thought about his family, thought about everything but the mountains and what waited in them. He got back on the horse and headed up.

They found him sitting at the edge of a patch of tobacco on the last hillside before the real climb began. Blas had the feeling he was being watched, so he dismounted and shifted the pistol into the top of his boot and waited. There were three of them, two guajiros and a tall one who sounded like he was from Santiago. The tall one walked directly toward him, smiling, as the others drifted in from the sides.

"Who sent you?" he asked.

"Nadie," said Blas. "I came on my own."

One of the guajiros stepped behind the roan. Blas couldn't see his hands.

"Cómo se llama?"

"Blas de la Pena. De Camagüey."

"Y qué hace aquí?"

Blas looked at him directly. Among the stories that came down from the mountains where those of the spies and chivatos who tricked men into showing their sympathies. In Havana he would have had an introduction, a code word.

"What the fuck do you think I'm doing here?"

"Mountain climbing?" said the tall one, smiling.

Blas was sitting with his arms over his knees, right hand dangling near the boot with the gun. He could take the tall one standing over him and the guajiro squatting to his left, but the one on the other side of the horse was a problem. He couldn't see the man's hands.

"Es peligroso, escalar estas montañas," said the tall one.

Blas nodded. "Lo he oído. Puede darme direcciones?"

"Direcciónes? A dónde?"

He fixed the positions of the men. If he started he would have to look the bullets through each of them without flinching, to will them dead before they could react.

"I want to find the Second Front of the Escambray."

"Un turista—"

"I want to fight."

If it was going to happen quickly it would be now. The tall one kept smiling. "Who do you know who is with this group?"

The one on the far side of the horse was going through his saddlebags now.

"I know men who I should not name to strangers."

The tall one nodded. "We'll need to take your horse."

The squatting guajiro stood to take the saddlebags and the rifle, hefting it in one hand.

"We'll give it to the local people in payment for food. Do you have shells for that rifle?"

"I brought five hundred."

"Coño. The man is an army."

"It isn't much unless you're shooting birds."

"We take what we can get." He signaled the guajiro on the other side of the horse. The man stepped up to take hold of the reins. He had a heavy-looking revolver in his free hand. He hopped onto the roan's back and wrestled it around to head downhill.

"Vámonos," said the tall one. "We should move out of sight."

Blas stood and followed the tall one, at their mercy for the moment, hearing the other guajiro on foot several yards behind him.

As they came out of the tobacco field the mountain seemed to tilt suddenly, the muscles in his bad thigh raw as he strained upward. It was getting dark.

"Dicen que Che Guevara va a venir con tropas," called the tall one, moving easily up the slope. "Every day we come down to meet him. Today we find only you."

Blas was already too winded to respond. He leaned into the mountain, using his hands now and then as he fell forward. If he breathed through his nose he didn't sound so out of condition, but it didn't give him enough oxygen. The tall one was moving so fast. Blas surrendered himself to the climb, horselike, looking only at the ground immediately ahead, punishing his legs, one-two, one-two, as if pain was the point of it all, pushing himself to exhaustion and past it as he labored up and up. His hands were bleeding and he could tell his feet were too inside the boots and his lungs and heart were hammering against each other. Go out and meet it. He would stomp this fucking mountain down, tramp it as flat as the plains of Camagüey.

When the tall one stopped for a break Blas struggled on past him.

"Dónde vas, compañero?" the man called.

Blas didn't have the strength to turn. "When I get to the top I'll wait for you," he said.

The men in the camp looked almost as weary as he was.

Bearded, gaunt, a half dozen of them sat around an iron pot waiting for water to boil. Blas stood with his legs spread apart so the shaking wasn't so noticeable. He wanted to fall forward and sink into the earth. The one who seemed to be the leader, a man with a big nose and a savage bush of hair, stood to face him.

"Qué tenemos aquí?"

"It followed me back," said the tall one. "Every time I thought I had lost it I would turn and there he'd be, right on my tail, unshakable. Como un tiburón en el mar."

"And what is it called?"

"Señor Blas de la Pena."

"I know him." The one closest to the fire, not much more than a boy, spoke. He had tiny patches of fuzz on his chin that passed for a beard and Blas didn't recognize him. "He was with the Directorio," said the boy. "He was at the palace."

The leader stepped closer to look at Blas in the pale firelight.

"You've got the right mountains, compañero, but the wrong guerrillas," he said. "Somos del 26 de Julio."

Blas shrugged. "The Directorio is fighting the same war, no?"

"Maybe. Cubelas is being reasonable, but Gutiérrez Menoyo and his group are off on their own adventure."

"I came up here to fight the casquitos" said Blas. "If that's what you're doing I want to join."

The leader snorted and motioned for Blas to follow him. "In that case, compa, you're just in time for the execution."

The young man who knew him stayed to tend the fire as the others dragged themselves to their feet. Blas couldn't tell if they were totally demoralized or just exhausted.

"They had the trial while I was gone today," said the tall one as he fell into step beside Blas. "This chivato led us into an ambush and we lost two men. Up here justice is swift."

"I heard that you set the enemy free when you capture them."

"As soon as we can."

"And when they catch one of us?"

"Shot immediately. Or questioned and then shot."

"So the safest thing to be in these mountains is a soldier for Batista."

"If you want to be a guerrilla," smiled the tall one, "you need a sense of irony."

The informer was another guajiro, a short, curly-haired man with huge liquid eyes and a noose resting lax on his shoulders. His hands were tied behind his back with wire. A pair of guerrillas leaned against trees nearby, smoking, watching him. When the leader's flashlight beam caught him between the eyes he pissed in his pants.

"Aurelio," the leader said to the chivato, almost gently, "es la hora."

One of the men guarding him tightened the rope snug around his neck as the man began to mutter a prayer, starting it again and again but unable to get past "hallowed be Thy name." It took several tries to loop the weighted end of the rope over the high branch that had been chosen.

"That knot won't break his neck," said Blas. It was the knot they used on the ranch to hang a slaughtered calf up to bleed.

"We can't risk a shot here," said the leader, "and we can't build a platform to drop him from. It's the best we can do."

"He could hang there a long time before he dies."

"Bueno. You're going to help him."

There wasn't a signal. Two of the men grabbed the rope hanging over and began to yank it down hand over hand, the fiber singing against the tree bark, till it took the weight of the informer, then hauling like deckhands raising a sail they ran him up till his head was nearly touching the branch. The leader nudged Blas forward.

"Pull on him," he said.

It was a test. The others circled around, watching, one flashlight beam on Blas, the other playing on the feet of the hanging man. Blas felt like his body was lead. Go out and meet it. He stepped forward and jumped as high as he could manage catching the man around the thighs, hugging tight, the smell of urine sharp in his nose and swinging himself now, the soles of his boots at least an inch off the ground.

It felt good to take the load off his legs.

The very beautiful prostitute passes close on her way to the ladies' room, her perfume nearly knocking him off his stool. Blas waves his hand in front of his face. She is beautiful enough not to have to advertise. Blas watches the fish in the wall-sized tank behind the bar. A school striped like zebras drifts by. Bubbles stream up from the helmets of little plastic deep-sea divers. The woman comes back past him, her eyes alive, holding her head at the angle they do when they don't want to sniff in public. The shit is everywhere now.

"It makes me sad," Blas says out of nowhere to the bartender, a little Dominican-looking guy with a mustache. "Me hace rico, pero me pone triste."

He should have known it was over when the yanquis brought him back from the jungle. One day a guard stepped in past the wire and dumped a sackful of shoes out onto the ground. Blas and the others sullenly matched the rights to the lefts and tried them on till each found a pair that sort of fit, tossing away the thin slippers they'd been forced to wear after the march to the prison.

"We could use some laces," Blas called to the guard, but he was already on the other side of the wire.

They were shipped out on a navy transport, still under guard, from Puerto Cabezas. The two who had malaria went into the infirmary. The other dozen sat on bunks, isolated from the crew. A few hours from port a steward brought them lunch.

"What happened to Cuba?" asked Rubén, who spoke the best English.

The steward looked at him blankly.

"The war? The invasion?"

"Oh. That." The steward was ladling out bowls of soup with rice, the liquid tilting with the roll of the ship. "That's been finished for weeks. They got their butts kicked. Major fuck-up. Barely got off the beach."

It wasn't a surprise exactly, but Blas felt a chill shoot through him. One of the men began to cry angrily.

"And the men?" asked Rubén. "Los soldados?"

"Fidel's got most of em under lock and key. Having a big trial on the television. Real sideshow."

Blas tried not to think about Ambrosio. Whatever it was had already happened.

"That's the strangest damn thing about it," said the steward. "Who'd have thought they had TV down there?"

A man in civilian clothes gave them a speech before they were set loose in Miami.

"First of all, gentlemen, remember that you are guests in this country. This is a privilege that may be revoked at any time. Now there may be certain members of the press who wish to stir things up, make a name for themselves, and they will approach you asking about your experiences in the recent conflict. I have to remind you that your comrades are being held by hostile forces and that our government is engaged in delicate negotiations for their release as we speak. Anything you leak to the press may lessen their will to proceed with these negotiations. I would recommend absolute silence."

"You're saying that we are welcome in your country," said Rubén, "as long as we do not exercise our rights."

The man in civilian clothes did not change expression. "You people keep your noses clean," he said. "You'll be watched."

Nobody in Miami, it turned out, was much interested in Blas's experience in the recent conflict. A sense of failure hung over the Community like the gloom of the rainy season. There were the men in the dungeons to think about and for many there was the realization that they were not going back soon, maybe not ever, and that Miami was now home. Nobody wanted to hear how socialism without Fidel had been subverted by the yanquis. Nobody wanted to hear from a man who had been expelled from the Brigade.

"We were only puppets," Blas complained to his uncle, sitting in the lonchería early in the morning. "And when we pointed out the strings, they had to isolate us, to cut us down."

Tío Felix was sympathetic, with his own story of betrayal that nobody wanted to hear. "Es siempre la misma historia, sobrino," he said with the resigned shrug that seemed to be his permanent expression, "como los griegos y los dioses. What is life and death for us is a sport for them. And whenever we're about to win a victory on our own they fall from the sky to claim the prize."

"But they're not gods, the yanquis, only cabrones with too much money. And this was no victory."

"No," said Tío Felix quietly. "Fidel beat them for once."

As soon as it was said both men were aware of the perverse drop of pride that was mixed with their bitterness.

Tío Felix would listen, but Tío Felix listened to everybody, it was both his nature and his profession. Blas found no comfort in his sympathy. The day of Ambrosio's service his father looked through them both like they were dead.

Rubén got Blas a job delivering soda. Rubén had been trained as a lawyer but his family were restaurant people from Havana who made a place for themselves in the Community the moment they stepped off the plane. Anything that Cubans ate or drank that nobody else in Miami cared for went through their hands. Tío Felix bought from them, as did most every restaurant and grocería on Calle Ocho. Fruit stands, supermercados, farmacias—Rubén's family was a pipeline to them all. Once Tío's old friend Mambo had helped him get his license, Blas was turned loose in a panel truck rattling with cases of Malta Hatuey and Materva watermelon soda.

It got him around Little Havana and the neighborhoods spreading out from it. He saw the people digging in, improving their English, becoming citizens. He heard the talk, sometimes the wild, angry, revengeful talk of men in exile. But more and more it was talk of the yanqui dollar and how to obtain it.

"La Comunidad ha descubierto una droga," he told Rubén, hanging out at one of the family's lunch places. "El dinero."

Rubén laughed. "Compa, they were hooked on that before they got here. Look at who came up, look around you—is this Cuba? Es solamente la crema, no los campesinos."

"Crema? It's the scum that floats to the top."

"Hombre, you won't get by here with that attitude. You sound like a comunista."

"They've forgotten what we're supposed to be doing here. Somos exiliados—"

"And is it a crime for an exile to make money?"

Blas scowled. He realized he'd been talking too loud again, smacking the tabletop, a disease he'd inherited from his father. His father who was beginning to have a successful business.

"I worry that we're becoming yanquis," he said.

"No te molestes," said Rubén, smiling. "So far we aren't invited."

When the ransom was paid and the first planeful of Brigade members returned Blas was not there to meet them. When the president addressed them in the Orange Bowl and the Brigade presented his beautiful wife with their banner, Blas did not attend. But when Rubén told him the war was starting up again, secretly, he was ready to fight.

"I only need to know who is in charge," he asked.

"Nosotros."

"No CIA? No yanquis?"

"Artime has a group that they are training. And there is a unit forming in their army, at Fort Knox—"

"Tontería. These are only to keep us under their control."

"Exactamente. Pero nuestro grupo es independiente. Solamente cubanos."

"Bueno. I have an uncle who owns a boat—"

"Tu tío," said Rubén, "is tied to the others, working for the MRR. I'm surprised you don't know this."

Tío Felix had been going fishing a lot lately. Blas smiled to think of the old guy still struggling, trying one more time.

"I can lead men in the mountains," said Blas. "There are friends in the Escambray, the Tardió brothers, the—"

"The Tardió brothers died fighting. Everybody there is dead or relocated."

"Then we'll have it to ourselves."

Rubén laughed. "You miss being filthy and lousy and hungry. You loved that shit in the mountains."

"We had a purpose."

"We still have a purpose, compa. Only now we do it from long distance."

Cowboy Cuepas had been a mechanic and a cropduster for La United before the revolution. When he was boy in Pinar del Río he had been a reader in a tobacco factory. He wore a Stetson in the cockpit and chewed gum like an American and had never lost his passion for literature.

"Zola was my favorite," he told Blas, driving to their first mission together. "After that, the Russians. The owner taught me always to stop in the middle of an exciting part, so the tabaqueros would be on time for work the next day."

"A qué edad?"

"Eleven. I was a prodigy."

"How much did they pay you?"

"No sé. The money went to my mother. She and my sisters all worked in the factory. For me it was pleasure. Have you read Dickens?"

"My brother was the reader in the family," said Blas. "He's gone now."

They rented the plane at a private strip in Fort Lauderdale from a man named Buddy. He wore a blue baseball cap and circled the little Beechcraft with a clipboard, making notes.

"How long?"

"Two days."

"Have to file your itinerary."

"This has been done."

"Your pal here fly?"

"He's thinking of taking lessons."

"Nothin like it.' Buddy finished writing his notes. "Fellas," he said, squinting at them beneath the bill of his cap, "have a ball."

They hopped down to Homestead and filled up again. Luna, another of the group who Blas knew from Camp Trax, met them with the payload. They took off in the dark.

"*Madame Bovary* was slow, very slow for the workers," Cuepas shouted over the sound of the engine. "But I liked it. They wanted me to skip to the juicy parts."

Blas had never been in a small plane before. "Dónde estamos?"

There was almost no moon and Cuepas had turned the lights off a few minutes after takeoff.

"We're a hundred feet above the ocean," said Cuepas. "Flying south. Dumas, on the other hand, was a huge success with them."

Blas flicked his flashlight on and played it over the instrument panel. "Where does it say how high we are?"

"It doesn't, not this low. I can see the water."

Blas turned the light off and pressed his face against the side window. "No puedo ver nada."

"Usted es el bombardero. Don't worry. You only need to drop the stuff when I say so."

There were jars of fósforo vivo that would ignite on contact. If they were fired at from the ground there were grenades that Blas was to wedge into other jars and pull the pins before he dropped them. When the glass broke they would go off. He hoped they were more reliable than the grenades they'd had in the Directorio, than the ones they'd had in the Sierra.

"*The Count of Monte Cristo,*" said Cuepas. "They came early the week I was reading that."

It would have been safest to turn right around and head back once the load was dropped, but Cuepas buzzed the field low, twice, so they could see what they'd done. The patch of flame spread like a puddle on the black island. Blas was exhilarated at first, but as they gained altitude the fire became a tiny pinpoint of red.

"One canefield."

"We will put one white hair in Fidel's beard," said Cuepas. "And the people who live here will know we haven't given up."

Blas couldn't see the flame at all now as they banked out over the water. "Or maybe they'll just curse the sons of bitches who made their work more difficult."

"That's how it is up here. You can only guess what you left behind." Cuepas was philosophical. "This is why there is great literature about imprisonment, there is great literature about the foot soldier, there is great literature about the sea—but not one great work about flying."

On the way back he quoted Joseph Conrad from memory.

*   *   *

The first time Blas saw the blonde she was stopping traffic in a bar owned by Rubén's father. Blas watched her for ten minutes and then watched the rest of the men in the place watching her.

"La rubia," he said when Rubén came by. "Por qué está sola?"

"She's waiting for her boyfriend."

"He's late."

"Sin duda. He gets out in five years."

The bar was high up on the Beach, a place the Old Havana playboy set and a few American gangster types liked to drink at. It had the biggest aquarium tank Blas had ever seen.

"She must be lonely."

"Her former patrón has eyes watching her. Only a man of great stupidity would go near such a woman."

Blas got to his feet. Straight at it. She had been sitting there being blond and drinking alone like a challenge for a half hour and it bothered him.

Rubén laughed. "A stupid man or my friend El Tiburón."

He expected her to be hard, to cut him with words when he sat down. He was surprised at how young she was now that he was close enough to see. Her hair wasn't dyed, at least not that he could tell.

"Come to stare at the new fish?" she said quietly.

"You are alone. Lo siento. I feel bad for you."

When she looked at him she seemed a bit hurt. He hadn't expected that. "Thank you," she said. "Nothing wrong with a little sympathy."

"What are you drinking?"

"Too many daiquiris. I really don't need another."

"What is your name?"

"Babe."

She wore a black satiny dress with thin straps. She had an even toasted color from the sun, all over, and had green eyes. Blas had seen women like her in the clubs in Havana, sitting close to middle-age yanquis, laughing with their teeth stained red with lipstick. He'd never spoken to one before.

"You are like a jewel in this room."

She smiled then and shook her head. "Don't be too charming," she said. "I get enough of that."

Blas reasoned that she was a woman used to a man being in charge of her, that being in this bar, dressed as she was, meant she was hoping to be taken charge of by the next one. He felt a bit drunk on her perfume, perfume that had its own heat and weight.

"We should go somewhere else," he said, standing.

"I have my car here."

"I'll drive it. I can come back for my own later."

His own was a panel truck with logos of various soda companies on the side. Babe's was a light blue convertible, top left down. She played the radio as Blas drove her across the Causeway, rock and roll, which he didn't much like. When they reached the outskirts of the Community he told her his name.

"Cuban?"

"Yes."

"I was down there a few times. Havana. Wild nights."

"There is more to it than that."

"Sure."

He took her to a club where the music was soft and no yanquis ever came. He could tell she was amused by the looks she drew as she crossed the floor.

"Is this like what you saw in Havana?"

"No." She looked around, smiling slightly. "There were girls with headdresses and lots of spangles. Vegas stuff."

"You Americans will never understand us."

"We don't really need to, do we?"

She was brave with her mouth, this woman. Blas took a moment to look at her carefully. She had beautiful arms, thin with a light blond down on them. Her breasts were small and her hips were narrow. In other clothes she would look boyish, like the ones who wore their white tennis outfits everywhere. He thought about touching her, making her feel something.

"How can a woman like you be alone at night?" he said.

She looked at him with only a hint of irony on her face. "I was waiting for you."

Her apartment was small. There were clothes hanging in the tiny living room, in the bathroom, on the knobs of the doors. In the bedroom there were photographs of the president's beautiful wife.

"You can't buy that," she said, regarding one of the pictures. "Class like that you're born with. And it doesn't happen in Florida."

Babe wore silk underwear and wasn't a puta. She knew how to

do things and didn't pretend not to. She was blond all over. Blas wanted to make her tremble, to beg him for mercy.

"We can do this again, you know," she said finally, breathless but nowhere near trembling. "You don't have to pack it all into one night."

He felt that he could roll away, close his eyes one moment, then look at her and she'd be new to him, he'd be as hard again as if he'd just met her.

"I have to go away sometimes," he said. "For a few days. To do things."

She yawned. "Don't be mysterious," she said. "Just be nice when we're together."

She fell asleep then, curling up in his arms. Now and then he'd raise the sheet to take another look at all of her.

Blas took a second job on weekends, stacking crates of frozen beef by the docks. He took Babe out on the town three or four times a week. It was clear that she didn't exist in any other life, that without the clothes and the clubs and the drinks and the music she wasn't Babe, wasn't the creature he burned for. When he asked how she filled her days she told him she slept a lot.

Sometimes he would come to her apartment and watch her dress for the night and halfway through he would get too excited and they'd make love hard and fast and then she'd finish dressing and they'd go out. On those nights he would always take her last to one of the rougher bars where the men groped her with their eyes until he was hard again and couldn't wait to get her home. More than once they had to stop by the beach and do what they could in the convertible, never thinking to roll the top up. The strength of his desire seemed to be what excited her, the hungrier he was the more she responded. Before long he was borrowing money from his uncle Felix.

"No hay de qué," Tío Felix would say, handing over a folded wad of cash. "Great feeling for a woman is a rare thing. It must be respected."

Blas took Babe to drink at the Eden Roc and watched through the glass wall as girls in bikinis dove deep and arched their backs on the way back up.

"I'm going to be away for a few days," he told her.

She didn't react. Babe never asked him where he went when he was gone on the missions and she never told him about what she did between their times together. From her color he suspected much of it was spent wearing sunglasses next to a pool. Later they were going dancing at one of the Latin clubs. Babe was a good dancer, a little reserved but smooth. She sat out with him when they played the Twist or anything like it.

"My father was always away for a few days," she said, swiveling back and forth in her seat. "Away more than he was home."

"A salesman?"

"He covered the Southeast. He smelled like airplanes. Like plastic and tobacco. He'd bring me those little soaps and shampoos from his hotel rooms like they were hard-to-get presents, or something made with shells that I knew he got from the airport gift shop. He took me to restaurants."

He'd seen her like this a few times before, unable to sit still, talking without focusing on him. It was only a different rhythm, a different mood.

"Just me and him. He'd order a drink and then say, 'Bring my gal here something good.' Which meant ginger ale with a cherry. He liked cars with big fins."

Babe went to the ladies' room and came back even jumpier.

"Nobody understands just how much pressure she's under. Everybody watching her, judging. It's murder on your private life, let me tell you. But somehow she pulls it off. You'd think she'd drink or something, let off a little steam, but no. People think she's lucky, think she's got it all. It must be hell sometimes."

"This is a friend of yours?"

"No. The First Lady. A friend, Jesus."

"It sounded like you knew her."

"I *understand* her. That's different." She stared ahead over her drink. "What if there was a tragedy?"

"Qué?"

"If one drowned. That would be something, wouldn't it? If one of these bimbos swallowed the tank and went deep-six in front of everybody."

A girl in a lime-green bikini was crawling up the glass wall like a snail. Babe was suddenly morose.

"This fucking state," she said. "Bring them a Rembrandt, they'd glue seashells to it."

Blas touched her on the arm, looked deep into her eyes. He could tell. Once or twice he had suspected but now he could tell.

"Estás tomando drogas, no?"

"Don't knock it, baby," she said to him, looking a bit lost. "Whatever gets you through the night."

"You shouldn't need this."

"Why? Because I have you?"

Blas held her eyes. It wasn't an insult, only a question.

"You Cubans," she said. "You practically invented the stuff."

"Only to sell to you yanquis."

She laughed then. "It's just a taste, baby. Don't worry, I can handle it."

"We should go dancing now."

Driving to the dance club she was quiet for a while, thinking. She leaned her head on his shoulder, then spoke softly.

"I have to get out of that apartment. I'm dying there."

"You can stay with me." It wasn't what he wanted but he knew he should say it."

"Don't be silly."

"I'll help you get a new one."

"With what?"

His face burned. She had never mentioned money before, letting him pay for their nights out without seeming to notice.

"I'm sorry," she said.

"Money is not a problem."

"Sure."

They drove in silence another minute.

"It could be easier, you know," she said finally. "For both of us."

"How?"

"You're smart, you're not afraid of things—it would be easy for you."

"How?"

"You take things from one place to another."

He wasn't surprised, not totally. He had been waiting for a warning from the people she was with before but it had never come. And this was part of their business.

"For who?"

"Friends of friends. Hey, it's just an idea."

They pulled into the lot of the club. He smiled, opened the door for her, and kissed her once on the way to the door. On the dance floor she held him like she needed him desperately and allowed the cocaine to wear down a bit. They danced until she felt dizzy and then made love in the passenger seat of her car in the parking lot, Babe sitting on his lap and grinding into him, the muscles in her jaw and neck taut and Blas felt like a question had been raised and not answered and if he came he would have given in so he held on, watching her face till she melted on top of him, voices of the customers leaving the club rising as they crunched past and saw. Blas was still hard in her and had her get off and hold on to it as he drove to her apartment. Inside he fucked her so hard on the living room couch that it walked across the rug and butted against the wall. Afterward she soaked a washcloth in cold water and ran it over his body.

"It will be easy," she said. "The guy you have to see is one of yours."

"One of ours. Where?"

"Tampa. I can give you the address."

"And how much money is there to be made?"

"In one trip you'd make more than in three years delivering soda."

He had never mentioned what he did for a living.

"I'll think about it," he said, running his fingers over the blond down that covered her belly. "When I get back I will tell you."

This time the boat was in a slip behind a private home in Coconut Grove.

"I hate the sea," said Cowboy Cuepas, helping to load the arms aboard. "Conrad is a wonder, and the book of the great whale, but in life I prefer the land or the air."

"If a boat engine fails, you drift," said Blas. "In a plane you crash."

"Sin embargo, no me gusta el mar. El clima, la soledad. A world of things beneath you, waiting."

"I'm not afraid of sharks."

"That's because you *are* one, compa. Is there anything that does frighten you?"

Blas thought for a moment, stowing the ammunition crates Luna passed up to him. They tried to fill every small crack of the boat with something useful.

"Hanging," he said, finally. "A man shouldn't die that way."

It was a simple mission, in and out like the ones before, dropping off a load of weapons at a spot on the coast and hoping the men who had asked for them were still alive. Blas and the other two were dressed in black, their faces sooted. The boat was painted dark blue, a narrow-hulled thirty-footer with a Perkins fitted with a drive adaptor to increase the cruising speed. They seemed to skim along through the night, chopping the tips of the waves, high with the sheer joy of action till all the Coast Guard boats in the world surrounded them off of Old Rhodes Key.

There were spotlights and men shouting over bullhorns and Luna jerking the boat in a tight circle almost tipping them in their own wake. Blas felt ridiculous with his face all black. They were taken aboard one of the patrol boats, their own towed away to be searched.

"No hablemos con ellos," Luna hissed as they sat below deck, surrounded by blue-eyed men with rifles. "Ni una palabra."

They were brought to a Guard station and fingerprinted and allowed to wash the soot off. They were asked questions in English, then in Spanish by a Puerto Rican officer with a hostile attitude. Blas sat with the others under the bright lights, scowling at the cameras as they flashed, not speaking. At one point a man in civilian clothes was brought in to look at them. Blas could tell he knew Luna from somewhere but pretended not to. After that they were left with a pair of guards who probably understood Spanish but pretended not to.

"They find as much as a marijuana cigarette on that boat," said one to the other, "these boys'll do ten. Anything heavier than that, they can kiss the free world goodbye."

They kept at this awhile, trying to provoke the men into talking, then got bored and had a conversation about how to drain a carburetor.

It was morning when they were brought in front of the Federal man.

"Quite an arsenal," he said. They were mute. "Manuel Luna. Ernesto Cuepas. Blas de la Pena. We know all about you. I don't suppose you'd like to tell me where you picked up the weapons?"

Blas thought of Babe. He wondered if she would wait a month before she found a new patron.

"You're lucky it was us who found you. If you got busted in the Bahamas we'd have to make a case."

She never got out of bed before noon, Babe. She never carried more than twenty dollars cash. She drank frozen daiquiris and ate shrimp cocktail with her fingers and changed her perfume after nine o'clock. She was surprisingly strong when they made love, snapping her hips into him, digging her fingers into his flesh. She was blond all over, not dyed, and if he did time he was going to lose her forever.

The Federal man nodded to the guard, who opened the door for them.

"The war's over, fellas," said the Federal man. "Go home."

It was hard not to run when they stepped into the light of day. Rubén was waiting in the lot with his car. Nobody spoke till they crossed the bridge to Key Biscayne.

"Por qué nos liberaron?" asked Cuepas.

"Some of our people know some of their people. There is a faction sympathetic to us. We worked something out."

"I knew the first guy who looked at us," said Luna. "He was on our boat going to Playa Girón."

"So many weapons," said Blas. "And the boat. What a waste."

"So we lay low for a while." Rubén seemed more tired than they were. "The movement is almost broke."

"I know a way to make money. Fast."

They looked at Blas. The drugs were not serious, toys for spoiled Americans, but he knew at some point in the chain there were men he detested.

"We have the training," he said. "We know the routes."

"Drogas."

"Contrabando. It is a means to an end. We pick it up in one place and leave it in another. Muy sencillo."

"If we sold it ourselves," said Rubén, "wouldn't there be more money? For the group?"

"Claro que sí."

"I know people, people who come into the bars that my father owns. They have mentioned these things to me before."

"And if we're caught?" said Cuepas.

"We're trained not to be caught."

"Like tonight," said Luna.

"If we're caught," said Rubén, "our friends in the government can help. Like tonight."

"As long as it is for the group."

"That's right," said Blas. "For the group."

None of them said it but he could feel a shift, each of them making his silent peace with the idea.

"It's going to be a long war," said Rubén. "And in this country the greatest weapon is money."

It was closer to her apartment than to his own, so Blas had Rubén drop him off on her corner. She would want to know his decision, even if he had to wake her. The sun was straight overhead and he felt strange in the black clothes, hoping he'd gotten all the soot off his face.

The man who opened the door had curly dark hair, Italian-looking, and wore a gold cross on a chain around his neck. Blas couldn't see in past him but caught the smell he was familiar with from their nights together, a smell that had its own heat, had its own weight. The man looked at him, scratching the tangle of hair on his bare chest.

"Let me get that, Carlo," called Babe from the next room.

"It's all right, doll," he called back to her. "It's just the night shift."

Blas had killed a man with his hands once, in a raid on an outpost in the Sierra Escambray only a month before the triumph. He felt the same kind of anger surge through his body, but only stepped to the side so she could see him as she came out of the bedroom.

"I'm sorry," she said when she saw it was him, and he could tell she meant it. "In the daytime you have to call first."

A week followed in which Blas drank rum from the bottle and spoke to nobody. He should have known. The apartment, the clothes, the car—something had to keep it all going, keep the eyes shining, keep it blond and toasted all over, there had to be fuel to drive this monster of a country. Blas sat in the loncherías and bars and listened to the pipe dreams of men who thought they were going back to the island of their imaginations, to other men who thought they were yanquis now, with all the rights and respect that was supposed to mean. Fuck them both. The island was gone, it would never be the way it was or the way he had hoped it could be. This was it. This place. There was rum and women and the money it took to get them and whatever harm he might bring these fucking green-eyed liars it served them right.

*   *   *

The address Babe had given him was a Spanish restaurant in
Ybor City, just across the little river from Tampa. The place seemed
out of control, people crying and running into the rear, and it took
a few minutes before someone would carry his message to whoever
"the Doctor" was. He waited alone at a table. The placemats had
a picture of Don Quixote and his servant on horseback, the old man
carrying a lance.

The man who came out to greet him was Ramiro.

"Blas de la Pena," he said with his ironic smile. "I thought you
were still in Cuba with the barbudos."

Ramiro looked ten years older than he was, with hard lines under
his eyes. He had a new jacket that was just as rumpled as always.
But there seemed to be a new energy to him, an edge, as if smuggling
drugs pumped blood into his veins.

"Por qué la conmoción?" said Blas coolly.

"No lo sabes? Somebody shot the president."

"Dead?"

"It appears so."

Blas looked around the restaurant. It made sense now. A waitress
was sitting by the couple she had been serving, all of them in tears.

"Was it a Cuban who shot him?"

"They don't know. I hadn't thought of that."

There were a half-dozen men Blas knew who would have liked
to have done it, or at least had said so. Ramiro called one of the
waiters over and asked him to bring them a bottle of wine.

"Ahora—what brings you to me, amigo? Old times?"

"Business," said Blas, lowering his voice, still thinking about the
president. He wondered if anything would be different. The voices
in the restaurant were disturbing, the emotion on the people's faces
out of place. He had never thought much of the dead president, but
something seemed very wrong, the way you felt standing on something high just before you lost your balance.

"Babe sent me."

"Babe," said Ramiro, his pale face lighting up. "Hombre, she
is the woman for you!"

*   *   *

Blas sits in a stall in the men's room of the restaurant, smoking. Waiting. They pipe the music in here too. Sergio Mendes–type stuff. Classy. Rubén has turned out to be a classy guy.

Someone steps into the stall next door. Blas coughs. The person slides a briefcase under the wall of the stall with his foot, flushes the toilet, exits. Blas opens the case.

The automatic is flat and heavy. Six clips. A cloth holster with Velcro on the straps. Blas hangs his jacket on the hook, rigs himself up, puts the jacket back on. He flushes the cigarette butt down and steps out to the mirrors, standing in profile.

The weight against his ribs is reassuring. The key to the safe house is taped inside the briefcase. With the gun strapped on Blas finally feels like something is going to happen, feels like he is truly in danger. He feels at home.

THIRTY-FIVE

LUZ CLIMBS to her apartment on the outside staircase, humming softly to herself. Her legs are sore. When she gets to the top she finds Marta sitting on the rail, feet resting on a small suitcase and a Styrofoam beer cooler.

"Marta."

"Puedo quedarme contigo esta noche?"

"Cómo no? Pasa—"

Luz opens the door and lets Marta go in first. The place is a mess but what else is new and Marta has seen it like this plenty of times. Marta lays her things by the couch. Luz nods to the cooler.

"I can put that in the fridge if you want."

"It doesn't have to be cold."

"Bueno. Are you all right?"

"I'm fine. Sorry I didn't call before." Marta sits on the couch. She looks tired.

"Your brother came to the hospital. Lo sabías? He wants to see you."

"I don't want to see him. That's why I'm here."

Luz nods, crosses and opens the refrigerator. "Jugo, leche, soda, cerveza, agua—"

"Nada para mí."

She pulls out a can of beer for herself. "We missed you at work the last couple days."

"I've been busy."

Luz kicks the worn footstool into place, flops down next to Marta and puts her feet up. Like always, she thinks, I ask and she doesn't answer. Marta, who will always switch days with you if you need it, who will cover for you and cook for you when you're sick or depressed, who will listen for hours to your stupid problems with your idiot boyfriends—Marta will never answer a direct question with a direct answer.

"You still got funeral things to do?"

"No. That's over."

Luz opens her beer and tilts a long draw down her throat. Her legs feel better already. "He's gonna find you sooner or later, you know. No te puedes escapar a ese tipo. Why not just deal with him and get it over with?"

She notices that Marta has a book in her hand. It's a diary of some kind, the cover stained and warped.

"Marta," says Luz, "you got to get all this family stuff out of your head."

"What has Serafín told you about me?" Marta has her jaw set that way she does when she thinks you're going to criticize her.

"Nada. He doesn't talk to me about you. I think he's embarrassed to. He still likes you but you're not interested, are you? No importa. Pero me parece que estás afligida. Anything you need, anything, I do what I can to help. Sabes esto, no?"

Luz touches Marta's face with the palm of her hand then and feels the burning, something going to happen, something Marta is pushing herself toward. Marta looks at her and Luz has to take her hand away. The father, Scipio, burned like that the last time she touched him before he died. Something she can't reach, something she can't begin to heal.

"Qué pasa, Marta?" she says, frightened. "What's happening with you?"

"You'll know soon enough. Everybody will know."

"You scare me."

Marta lifts the diary in her hand. "I'm going to leave this here. Would you bring it back to my mother?"

"You're going somewhere?"

"For a few days."

"A dónde vas?"

"Out of town," says Marta. "I need a change of scenery."

THIRTY-SIX

Diario
14 de Abril, 1961

 FINALMENTE EMPEZAMOS.

(Once they are on the water the nervousness, the feeling of dread will fade. Once they are on the water there will be no turning back.)

At last we begin.

I am aboard the *Houston* with the rest of the Second, on the east coast of Nicaragua. We have been sweating out here for a while. They took the leaders of the Brigade away from us yesterday to make plans with the yanquis. When they come back we will be on our way.

The *Houston* is to a ship what a burro is to a horse. Its last job was hauling sugar cane and I am sure it has never been painted since it was built. We had all pictured one of those sharp gray troopships from the movies of World War Two and instead we get this mongrel with a few guns bolted on by Nicaraguans who take an hour to decide which way the barrel should point. If we have to fire them I don't want to be anywhere near.

"So this is our invasion fleet," said Sure Thing when we first saw the freighters tied up to the long pier. "Rejects from the Bolivian Navy."

The men are in high spirits though, the long wait and the uncertainty at the Camp finally over. It has been a party since we got on the trucks at the base, men singing the charanga, calling out boasts and promises. If the ones in charge were smart they would use this energy, they would not keep us waiting on this poor excuse for a ship another hour but send us joyfully on our way to battle.

It is only when I have time to think that the fear takes hold of me.

(The only failure will be in falling short. Even death will be an inspiration, a victory. But if it goes well, this will be only the first. The story will spread. Men will hear of it, men on the island and those in exile, men will be moved to action.)

Serafín tells me his only terror is losing his legs, of being paralyzed. Dying in battle, he thinks, will be a surprise too sudden to be frightening.

"Men in my family have gone to sea," he tells me. "Fishing in small boats. Some never came back. To drown, to fight the water for air and know you are going to lose, that would be terrible. A bullet, *snap*—the next thing you either find out you have a soul or you're gone and you don't have to worry about it anymore."

I wonder if time is different when you are dying. If your mind can race to eternity and back in a second. In my nightmare I am hit and there is a falling moment as the blackness wraps around the answer. Nothing. Nothing is waiting for you. The nightmare always wakes me up with a chill and I can't get back to sleep after.

I had a woman, a prostitute, on leave at the base.

I have confessed this to the Padre and he said God would not be hard on me. Sometimes I think they should take the priests away from war, that there should be no comfort for what we are going to do, only the raw actions and then His forgiveness later. Much later.

The woman was kind, and I think a bit insane. She was from Costa Rica and a prostitute so it is hard to say. The act was less important than the fact of it. Not to die a virgin.

Not to die at all.

There are men crowded around me, the Second and the Sixth Battalions, and many of them truly believe they will not be killed. We are all young, it isn't just that, but rather that they are not afflicted by thought the way I am. Now that Blas is gone they feel free to make jokes about me writing poetry again. They make jokes and then they ask me to read it.

(Joan may never have killed an enemy with her own hands, but she was the light that men followed. "If a woman can do this," the men will say, "then how can we do less?" Each action, each fire, each life brought back to the cause will be an alarm waking the slumbering conscience of her people. This time it would be only Cubans and this time they would do it right.)

Balanceándome en el borde,

(It might not be so hard. I might not have to die.)

Balancing on the edge,
The furnace breathing hot words
Of desire.
Shackled.
Bonded to the fire,
A thousand tongues licking,
Luring.
Thirsty.
Diving to the bottom,
The fiery heart yearning
To feed.
Burning.
Blistering into ash
Or through the furnace passing
Into steel.
Enduring.

I have a special mission. They didn't tell me till I got on board. Sure Thing says the yanquis have so many secrets because they are afraid of themselves. I have told Serafín the secret, which I was not supposed to do, and I am giving him this diary, which I was not supposed to write. The yanquis can keep their secrets and I will pass mine on to you. If I die there will only be my story, my only child. Vanity is what separates us from the beasts, and I have collected mine in this book.

A launch is coming toward us with the officers on board. The men are cheering.

Para mi padre, Scipio de la Pena,

(For my father, Scipio. For my mother,
Lourdes—)

Para mi hermano, Blas, héroe del pueblo cubano,

(—For my brother, Blas. For my martyred
brother, Ambrosio—)

Para mi hermana Marta,

(—For the name of the de la Penas,
for my country, for my God—)

Para mi patria y mi Dios, dedico mi vida a la liberación de la alma humana en mi isla natal.

Con amor y tristeza,

Ambrosio de la Pena Cruz

(Marta sleeps on the couch, the diary held
tight to her heart.)

THIRTY-SEVEN

➤ SOMETHING HAS LEFT a bad taste in El Halcón's mouth. A metallic nip on the underside of the tongue, like fruit gone bad in an aluminum can. It isn't the rum, still burning a dull hole in his gut. The rum comes back sometimes in the mornings, but it doesn't taste like this. It isn't the woman either. He has used the woman before and she doesn't have any special taste. She's not bad, never gives you the feeling she's in a hurry, and lives close by which saves on the taxi fare coming and going.

El Halcón looks in the refrigerator to see if there is something to get rid of the taste with, but the sight of food makes him feel sick.

Gonzalo is reading the sports pages at the desk when El Halcón comes in. Gonzalo reads all day long and is the stupidest man he knows.

"Buen día."

El Halcón nods to him. He looks at the full rack of keys on the wall.

"Vino alguien anoche?"

"Pocos. Two couples around midnight. Kids." It is hard for Gonzalo to keep reading and talk at the same time. "Bolívar get in touch with you?"

"Quién?"

"Bolívar? Su amigo?"

"No conozco a nadie llamado Bolívar."

"He acted like you know him." Gonzalo opens the register, scans it with his finger. "Simón Bolívar?"

"Cómo luce?"

"Grande, pelo oscuro, cubano. Walks funny—como vaquero. Like one of those guys in a rodeo. He asked about you."

El Halcón scowls. "Unless he carried a sword and rode a big white horse this name is bullshit. A dónde fué?"

"He's in Nine."

"There's no car at Nine. There wasn't when I came in last night."

"He comes and goes by taxi. He didn't have bags, neither."

El Halcón grabs the key ring and goes out into the parking lot. The taste is stronger, more bitter. He stops halfway to the unit and wonders if he should get his gun first.

Fuck it.

He knocks first. Waits. Turns the key and pushes. Nine is empty. The bed unslept in, wastebaskets empty, ashtrays clean. He goes into the bathroom. The sanitary band is gone from the toilet seat. Someone has opened the little soap and used it to draw the outline of a shark on the mirror over the sink.

Simón Bolívar my ass.

El Halcón goes back to his unit and pulls his gun out of the drawer. If this is some of Walt's spy bullshit he'll tell him to stuff the whole thing.

If it's something else it could be bad.

There was the one he did in Clearwater two years ago, messy. He never trusted those people. Or the deal with Ventura that went sour. Things come back to haunt you.

El Halcón pours himself a short one from the bottle by his bed and gulps it, then chews down a couple Tums to soften the blow. It's still there. Like holding a fork under your tongue or getting a piece of tin foil in your sandwich. It won't go away. He goes into the bathroom and brushes his teeth. He looks into his own eyes.

A shark.

What the fuck is that?

He straps the gun under his right arm for a left-hand pull. He hates to wear a jacket when it's so hot but there is the deal with Walt and those people and now this fucking Bolívar. It makes him jumpy. El Halcón steps back outside and the girl is there waiting for him.

"Tonight," she says.

"We set it for tomorrow."

"Nos vamos esta noche. A las nueve."

Fucking strange witch-bitch, standing dark as death with her bruja eyes telling him what to do. Giving orders to El Halcón. One good fuck and throw her overboard. But Walt wouldn't go for that.

"Y la dinamita?"

"La tenemos. More than enough."

"Por qué cambió los planes? Cuando tiene un plan, debe de seguirlo exactamente."

"We go tonight," she says, no explanation, nothing. "If you're coming be at the Bayfront docks by eight-thirty. We won't wait for you."

"You need my connections. The Coast Guard—"

She calls over her shoulder as she walks away. "The boat is called the *Nidia*."

He finds Walt out in back of his little house in the Gables, working in the garden. Walt has a white safari helmet on and is pulling snails off plants with a pair of salad tongs.

"Nunca contestas tu jodido teléfono?"

Walt glares up under the rim of the helmet. He has a red plastic beach pail at his feet. He tosses a snail into the pail and then pours salt from a box on top of it. "This is a breach of security."

"Fuck security. I have to talk to you."

"You're not supposed to have my number."

"It's in the fucking book, Walt. You should advertise in the yellow pages. Under 'Flunky—see U.S. Government.' "

Walt sighs. "Sloppy. We're lucky it's only amateurs on the other side this time."

"We're going tonight."

Walt gives the pail a shake, peering in. "No you're not."

"She says we are."

"Tell her no."

"Ella tiene la barca, los explosivos, dos o tres pendejos para acompañarla—por qué me necesita a mí? I say no, she says so long, sucker. It happens tonight."

Walt shakes more salt into the pail, frowns.

"This is supposed to shrivel them right up. I heard it somewhere," he says. "I used to do them with a hammer but it made a mess on the terrace."

"Qué haremos?"

"Tell her you can get her more weapons if she holds to the original plan."

"You still think you can buy everything, don't you? She doesn't want any more. She doesn't need us."

Walt shrugs, puts the salt down. "Then you go with her tonight and I'll get my people in gear. Just make sure they stay on the inside of Key Biscayne going out. We won't let them get far."

"We go at nine."

"We might make the morning edition."

"And if they choose another route?"

Walt squats to examine a wilting plant. "You won't let that happen, will you?" He looks up at El Halcón. "If you're going to show up at my house I wish you wouldn't carry the gun."

"Cuál es la historia del tiburón?"

"Qué?"

"The shark. Simón Bolívar. What is the fucking story?"

"You lost me."

"Some fucking spook checks in at my place, asks for me, no luggage, no car, takes a key and doesn't spend the night."

"Yanqui?"

"Cubano."

"No sé nada de esto, compadre. Probably just the usual pervert. You're getting jumpy in your old age."

The taste is back, moving up his sinuses into his nose. He taps the gun under his jacket.

"We get past the Keys without being stopped," says El Halcón, "I bury the bunch of them at sea."

It would have been simpler just to kill them on the ship and throw them over.

But the yanquis never did anything the simple way, they were always jerking off with one hand and slapping their own wrist with the other. So El Halcón had to sit cramped up in the fucking sweat-box of a storage compartment as they chugged toward the invasion beach. A fucking sardine in a can if anything went wrong.

The head was always crowded with men shitting and being sick so he had to shit and be sick in a metal bucket. One of the others in the operation was being passed off as a crew member, but the geniuses in charge had decided El Halcón would be recognized so there he was with the bucket of waste sliding around his feet as he sweated through his uniform and studied the pictures.

"Learn these faces by heart," the yanqui, Walt, had said. "We don't want you pulling the plug on the wrong boys."

The operation was a bad joke but they had the killing in Tampa for sure and enough on the one for the Italians in New Orleans to mount a good bluff. Twenty to life, they said, unless he was willing to redeem himself with an act of patriotism. The operation was a mess but it was the only way out. Of course if he was caught on the island the Communists would bore him to death with lectures for a week and then shoot him.

The pretty boy was the number-one priority. The one they called the Poet. If he just popped that one for sure he could get his ass back on the boat somehow and claim he'd lost the others in the heat of battle. Maybe they'd get killed by the Communists. If this Walt was any indication of the leadership, the invasion was likely to be a fucking slaughter.

Twelve hours out of Puerto Cabezas he couldn't stand it anymore. He pulled his cap down low over his eyes and went for a walk up top.

Most of them looked like babies. The barbudos would eat them for a snack. He recognized one face from Havana days and did a quick shuffle to avoid the man. The deck was crowded and men were talking and moving around and joking nervously. Somebody had found a pair of tarantulas below and a group was trying to get them to race or fight. He found the Poet alone by the rail.

"De la Pena."

The boy glanced at his sergeant's stripes, straightened slightly. "Sí?"

"We have been watching you."

"Quién?"

"Nosotros. Special operations."

"Sí?"

"We think you are the one we need."

"Para qué?"

"Demolition. I'm taking a few men out of the ranks for the mission. We want you on the team."

It was the way the yanqui, Walt, talked. Special Ops. The team.

Like a fucking Hollywood movie. When he agreed to do the killings, Walt shook his hand and welcomed him to the team.

"I have no training," said the boy.

"We'll handle the explosives. We just need a good soldier along." The boy shrugged, flattered and confused. "Bueno. I tell my squad leader—"

"No diga nada a nadie," he said, putting his hand on the boy's shoulder and moving close. "Es una operación negra. Totalmente secreta. We go to blow up the power supply for the whole area, but nobody is to know this. Entiende?"

The boy nodded gravely. "Sí. A black mission."

"Bueno. When we load into the landing boats, you look for me. If you don't see me, you stay on the beach till I find you. Claro?"

"Sí, Sargento. I won't disappoint you."

He gave the boy's shoulder a little squeeze. What threat the yanquis thought this little maricón could be later was a mystery to him. "Esto es un gran honor, entiende?" he said. "Your parents will be very proud."

On the way back to the storage room he ran into target number three and sold him the same story.

The disembarkation was at night and it was a fucking mess like he knew it would be. El Halcón had the big rifle and the small field pack and there was the netting and the heave of the freighter and other men's boots to deal with and him with no training for this kind of thing, but he managed to hook into his two candidates and get into the landing craft without breaking a leg. There was already firing from the beach and there were lights where there weren't supposed to be lights and men were cursing and the fucking motorboat hit coral fifty yards from the shore and they were in the water. He considered drowning the two but there were others all around and at least no fire was coming out now though he half expected fucking Fidel himself to be waiting on the beach on a big white horse, laughing his head off at them. He had left his rifle on the motorboat but still had the automatic and the backup in his pack. The water was up to his neck and he turned to his boys and beckoned.

"Síganme," he said, pointing. "A la izquierda."

They came out on the beach a little to the left of the others and he ducked low and ran for the trees behind a little bohío and could hear the boys huffing after him, boots on wet sand, and beyond that someone was hollering to come back but he knew nobody was going to chase them. Fucking mother of Christ what a stupid yanqui way of doing something on a beach in a fucking Hollywood movie D-Day invasion. There was only a little firing, sporadic pops from what must be milicianos or the stupid shiteating carboneros getting themselves killed for nothing in this ass-end-of-nowhere swamp that the Communists could keep if they wanted it so fucking bad and there was taste, metallic and bitter under his tongue. He could get shot out here.

A runty little man poked his head out of the bohío as they ran by and El Halcón put the automatic on him. Jammed. Coño.

"Yanquis!" cried the carbonero. "Vienen los yanquis!"

El Halcón ran past him through a patch of marabú, snagging through the sleeve of his uniform to draw blood, stumbling out into a section of tangled swamp where he stopped to catch his breath. A bit of moon peeked through the thick branches overhead. The firing died down to almost nothing in the distance.

"Are we far from the power station?" asked one of the boys.

El Halcón pointed his automatic into the muck at his feet and pulled the trigger. Nothing.

"Hold this," he said, and handed his pack to the boy.

"I kept my rifle dry," said the other.

"Bueno. Give it to me."

El Halcón took the rifle and turned to the one holding the pack and shot him through the mouth.

Something large flapped its wings in the darkness, rushing up and away.

He turned to face the pretty one, the Poet, eyes shining wide in the moonlight.

THIRTY-EIGHT

PADRE MARTÍN SITS in neutral on the MacArthur Causeway, watching the traffic for a sign.

The saints and prophets in the stories were always getting signs, hearing voices, witnessing manifestations of the Supreme Being. In the stories no doubt was ever mentioned, never a thought of did I really see that and if I did what did it mean? How much more difficult, thinks Padre Martín, to act on secondhand evidence, to dare to be a saint or a martyr when there is only silence.

Maybe I'm not up to it.

The traffic crawls forward a few car lengths. Across the divider strip the flow is quick and intermittent from the Beach into the city. Padre Martín checks his watch. The hunting rifle, still wrapped from the shop, burns behind him in the back seat. The box had a picture of an American Dad and Son walking together on a dirt road in autumn, each cradling a rifle, a dewy-eyed stag standing alert in the far distance. Licensed, bought and paid for, it prickles the back of his neck like an occasion for sin. There was a smell of newness, wood and metal newness, when the man slid it out of the box and handed it to Padre Martín. He didn't know which side to hold it on so just hefted it and nodded yes, I'll take it. Maybe the traffic will shift after he picks Dewey up, the lanes to the city hopelessly clogged, and they'll be too late. Or Dewey, absent from work today, will be nowhere to be found.

That would be a sign.

The congestion begins to ease, cars picking up speed. There are pelicans gliding over the water to the right, streamlined, prehistoric-looking. They drop one by one like heavy arrows into the waves, smashing through the surface then coming up empty-billed to float placidly with the evening tide. There are no doves in the sky, no rainbows, no towering waterspouts. The sun sets behind the city, throwing an orange glow on the bare faces of the Beach apartment buildings as he approaches. They do not look like tongues of flame.

The bullets are under the seat. Under the seat in boxes with unbroken seals. It startled him how heavy they were.

He glides off the ramp onto the Beach. It isn't far.

Padre Martín stiffens as he sees a patrol car driving a block ahead. He feels like a criminal already. If there is righteousness in this action it hasn't set in yet. The young woman at the car rental was so suspicious when he said he didn't have a credit card.

"You lost it?"

"No."

"You let it expire?"

"I never had one."

The look, a bit frightened, as if he might lunge over the counter and grab a set of the car keys that hung there.

"How do you *live?*" she said.

Mrs. Aaron next door let him borrow her car, sitting unused in a lot. It smells like cigarettes, the ghost of her dead husband Alex.

"Three packs a day," she said. "Like coffin nails."

If this was one of the stories he would open the glove compartment and there would be a sign. He would turn on the radio and there would be a voice. Scales would fall from his eyes. His consciousness would be pierced with a laser beam of grace.

In the glove compartment there is a brochure for the Monkey Jungle.

"Do you have more than one hundred freckles on your body?" says the man on the call-in show, a dermatologist revealing the warning signs of skin cancer.

"I have spots. Is that the same as freckles?"

"Are any of them raised?"

Padre Martín turns off the radio. He was going to fast today, to reflect. Find a quiet place and hope for some guidance, an inkling, a gut feeling about the rightness of the mission. Then she tells him the plan has been moved up.

How do you *live?*

Dewey has no phone, of course. How does he live without one? What goes on in his mind? And Nuñez, you can feel that Nuñez is a bad man. Then there will be the boat. If it happens, if they go. He still can't quite imagine it. The Bible stories seem more real, the ascensions and transmogrifications, the virgin birth. If it happens, if they go, he hopes the seas will be calm.

If it happens, if they go, he hopes the beach will be abandoned, the moon bright and the path clear.

If they go he hopes they never fire a shot.

The police car turns up Ocean Drive ahead of him. There are a crowd of them parked outside Dewey's hotel and people in the street watching and he holds his breath as he eases past, continuing a few blocks before he parks and walks back. He stands by an old couple, Jewish people, and looks up with them.

"Live and let live, I say," the woman says to him. The old man just shakes his head. "They do a little mischief perhaps, a nibble here, a mess there, but this is no reason for murder."

"What happens here?"

"I feel for the grandmother. A lovely soul. Never did a bit of harm in her life."

Padre Martín realizes that the old man's head shakes all the time. Parkinson's maybe. The wife goes on.

"It sounded like World War Three. At first I was sure it was the newcomers downstairs. You hear gunfire these days, it's mostly those of the Latin persuasion." She gives Padre Martín a careful once-over. "This is not a comment," she says. "Only an observation."

"Somebody was hurt?"

"We had hundreds on the payroll when Sy was still putting out the line," she continues. "An industrious people. Don't get me wrong. Sy was like a father to them."

A pair of men in suits hurry out of a car and the uniformed police clear a path into the lobby for them. Tourists with sunburned noses are starting to take pictures of the hotel front. Padre Martín feels a little dizzy. He hasn't fasted in a long time. He finds himself staring at the tanned, bare scalp of the old man, covered with thousands of freckles.

"I was just getting dinner," says the old woman, seemingly louder, echoing in his ear though she isn't standing close, "opening a can, when I'm hearing machine-guns. A regular gangland symphony, Jimmy Cagney should have been there. At first I think the newcomers downstairs, a prejudice, I admit it, and then it comes to me. The boy. You always hear 'He was the nicest fellow, so quiet.' Not true. Always I could tell there was something off, something missing upstairs. Sy agrees, don't you Sy?"

The old man is looking the other way, out across the street to the beach, to the ocean.

"He shot somebody?"

"You want to kill them, fine, get an exterminator," says the old woman. "Me, I say live and let live."

Rivkin stares at the assault rifle, shocking on the white sheets. There isn't enough circulation in the room. Even with the fan, swinging this way and that, there is only the one little window to the street and there's no flow, all the air has been breathed a dozen times and now the place smells like cops. Rivkin glances to see what Duckworth is doing, then squats and takes a quick peek under the bed. Nothing. There is a poster of a blond woman with nipple bumps showing through her camouflage T-shirt, laden with infantry gear, Scotch-taped to the wall. She's wearing Army-green hot pants and combat boots. Next to it is taped a cartoon of the Ayatollah's face with target rings superimposed over it. Cute kid.

They've cuffed the boy's hands behind his back and planted him on a kitchen chair. One of the local cops stands behind blocking his path to the window. The boy sits stiffly, as if awaiting torture. A towheaded kid with pimples and a Hitler Youth buzz-cut. Rivkin steps over the weights—dumbbells, grip-flexers, chest-springs—the same stuff his own kid has. In the closet hang two pairs of white pants, pressed sharp, and several white cotton shirts. A pair of white shoes is lined up below them, heels pointing out. On the shelf above is an iron and tabletop ironing board. Rivkin checks all the pockets.

"They been through the place," calls Duckworth from where he sits with the old lady. "It aint a bunch of bozos over here."

"Just poking around."

Duckworth sighs and says something softly to the old woman, placing his hand gently on her shoulder. She is still crying, a box of pink Kleenex on her lap. Jagged hunks of the television set litter the floor around her. Craters have been blasted into the stucco over the kitchen sink and there is broken glass and crockery covering the counter. There are smears of something that looks like peanut butter on the floor.

Duckworth steps carefully around them, pulling a chair over to the boy. He sits straddling it backward so he can be right in his face. Rivkin moves to the opposite side, standing just over the boy's shoulder.

"Son," says Duckworth, "you did yourself one helluva mess here."

The boy looks at him without blinking, jaw set firm. Animal crackers. And no wonder, just look at this place. On the old lady's side of the pullmanette everything is the same floral pattern as the Kleenex box. Three days in a trap like this with my Aunt Esther, thinks Rivkin, I'd sign up with the Manson family.

"Know why they called us over here?" says Duckworth. "Boys your age go off the deep end and start popping shots at they grandmamas, they sposed to use little jobs like this here."

He indicates the pistol, the toy-looking Saturday-night special lying where they found it under his pillow. Bagged in plastic now.

"That's normal, that's what your average red-blooded mindfuck will do. But he starts peelin off rounds with this kind of artillery"— Duckworth points to the assault rifle—"and we got to know where he come by such a thing."

The boy gives a tight-lipped little smile, narrows his eyes.

"There was a dozen of these lifted, very professional, inside job, a month ago. We want to know who you got this one from."

"This is a serious offense, you know," says Rivkin.

Duckworth shoots him a look.

"Possession of the—you know—firearm. The other—shooting up—well, it's your own place—it's not *good*, I mean I don't think we can con*done* it or anything, but technically speaking—"

"You his lawyer?"

"No, Chief. Sorry."

Duckworth turns back to the boy. "So you gonna tell us that little thing?"

"Don't hold your breath," says the boy.

"There's gonna be Federal people here any minute. They're not reasonable fellas like us. You don't want to have to talk to them, do you?"

"I don't have to talk to anyone."

Duckworth sighs dramatically, looks back across the room. He lowers his voice to a near-whisper. "You trying to kill that old lady, son?"

The boy's face tightens. "You people never understand," he says. "It's them or us."

"I'll put that on ice for you," says Tío Felix.

Marta holds the Styrofoam cooler in one hand and a bulging cloth laundry bag in the other.

"No hace falta," she says, stowing them next to the bench seat. "It's fine like it is."

Tío Felix is wearing a blue windbreaker and his white cap with the leaping blue marlin on the bill. He is surefooted on the boat, ducking and stepping over and folding and hitching in smooth and continuous motion.

"Puedo ayudarte?"

"Siéntate, Marta. I know where everything goes."

Marta steps down into the cabin to get out of his way. Something good was cooked here not too long ago. She closes the door behind her. Fire extinguisher. Plastic-covered charts. Radio. Wooden box of flares. Cans of food. When Tío Felix steps in from above she has the shotgun open in her hands.

"Para qué tienes esto?"

"Tiburones." Tío Felix takes the gun from her, snaps the breech shut and puts it back on the rack. "You hook the big fishes, you don't want to feed him to the shark."

Marta crosses to look at a chart hung on the wall. So close. A finger away, less. She can believe Rufo's story about the people who swam the whole distance.

Tío Felix sits at the little table behind her. "Ya has hablado con Blas?"

"Mami me dijo que llegó. We haven't connected yet."

"Before you do anything—"

"Before I do anything final, I will talk with my brother. This, tonight, is only a practice. Tomorrow you and I will find Blas and tell him what the plan is. He'll help us. He might even want to come."

Tío Felix looks relieved. She can tell he doesn't think Blas will allow it. She points to the chart.

"What if we go this far tonight?"

*   *   *

It's hard to park at Bayfront so Padre Martín walks the last eight blocks with the rifle held stiffly at his side. Even with the wrapping nobody could mistake it for anything else. This is not a dirt road in autumn. The few people he passes don't seem to notice. It won't happen now, anyway.

When she finds out about Dewey it won't happen. There is destiny and there is common sense and it's a blessing that the old woman wasn't hurt. Moving the plan up a night was bad enough but now with the police and Dewey he can only hope to get them off the boat and hide everything or throw it in the water before the patrol cars arrive.

Padre Martín hurries down the stairs to the docks, a forest of masts draped in blue vinyl bobbing before him. A huge seagull stands calmly at the end of the rail, surveying the area as if he owns it. There is something frightening in the sure stupidity of his eye. Padre Martín walks out onto the floating pier, searching among the tethered boats for the *Nidia*.

Marta is alone on deck waiting for him. The last of the sun oozing past the downtown building casts a romantic honey-colored glow over her skin. She is almost smiling.

"Dónde está Dewey?"

"Tu muchacho está loco. Tomó el fusil de Nuñcz y destruyó su apartamento. Cazando topos. He almost killed his abuela."

Marta nods, thinking. The information doesn't seem to upset her much. Her eyes rest on the hunting rifle in Padre Martín's hands.

"Tienes balas para esto?"

"Dos cajas de cartuchos. But we're not going now."

"Por qué no?"

"The police are with Dewey. He'll tell them everything—"

"He won't talk."

"Cómo lo sabes?"

"Would you?" Her eyes, burning into him. Padre Martín feels the falling sensation again, only this time there is a thrill to it.

"No. I took a vow."

She touches his arm. "We're probably better off. He was very nervous. Load that and then come below."

Padre Martín lays the rifle down on the bench seat. "I don't know how."

Marta shrugs, begins to pull the wrapping off. "Watch me then. You have the cartridges?"

"Sabes cómo?"

"Dewey showed me."

"Dónde está tu tío?"

"Down there. Getting ready."

"Does he know we're going all the way?"

"He will soon enough."

Padre Martín walks to the edge of the boat to look out over the bay. A seaplane is taxiing past the Port of Miami terminals, a blimp hangs overhead. Birds circle. Light is bleeding out of the sky.

He could just say no.

Say no and take the car back to the lot and climb the stairs to his little room and shut the door. Tunafish salad for dinner tomorrow. He realizes how hungry he is.

Beyond the concrete and the last low bars of land was the open sea. He'd never really been out on it at night. Away from people. Out alone with only the sky and the vast ocean and God or whatever it was there at the edge of the world. Signs would be clearer there. Elemental. Signs would be there for the ones willing to make the leap, to give themselves up to the whim of violent action.

The leap of faith.

Padre Martín watches Marta painstakingly slide a cartridge into the hunting rifle. The smell of newness is intoxicating.

"It only takes one," she says.

Padre Martín shrugs. "I told him I wanted it for hunting. He said a real hunter only needs one."

"And you got hollow-point."

"Es un problema?"

"Those are for animals. To make a bigger hole."

"Lo siento. I should have had Dewey with me. Or Nuñez." He looks across the deck. "Viene Nuñez?"

"He's late," she says, not looking up from the rifle. "We give him an hour, then go without him."

Padre Martín sees the cooler the bikers gave them, on the floor under a life vest.

"We won't need him," says Marta softly, lifting the lid of the bench seat up and laying the rifle inside.

"No," says Padre Martín, something like raw fear or adrenaline or grace rushing into his blood. "Not for what we're going to do."

THIRTY-NINE

BLAS IS WATCHING from unit Nine when the convertible screeches into the lot. The streetlights have just come on, and the lurid yellow lights over the doors of the units ring the parking lot. Blas doesn't have the best angle to see. The man is muscular, with dark hair and the face of a hawk. The man slams the car door and hurries into the large unit at the rear of the lot.

Blas gives the windowsill and doorknob a final wipe with a dry washcloth from the bathroom and steps into the evening air. It's going to be a warm night. There are a half-dozen cars parked in front of the other units. As he passes the office Blas can see through the window to the one with the bad skin, watching a small television propped up on a phone book on the counter. He isn't worried about anything from that direction.

The man comes out of the apartment. No problem. Whatever is going to happen might as well be in the open.

The man is in the front seat with the engine started when Blas taps on his window. The vinyl top where he rests his other hand is still warm from the day's heat. The man looks out at him for a long moment. The yellow bulb over the unit entrance is too high to throw much light into the car. Blas can't see the man's hands. The window buzzes down.

"Qué quiere?"

"Está Nuñez?"

"Qué quiere?"

"Conoce a Marta de la Pena?"

The man's eyes are unblinking. His right hand rests on the shift stick. There is supposed to be a skull tattooed on the back of the other one, the hand he can't see.

"Who wants to know?" says the man.

"You're in some business with her. Walk away from it."

"Who says this?"

"Yo."

The man gives a small, chilling smile. "Simón Bolívar?"

"Marta tiene amigos."

"You tell her friends to fuck themselves," says the man, and pulls the stick into reverse.

Blas moves his right hand down to the door handle, opens his jacket with his left to show the gun and somebody kicks him as hard as they can just under the collarbone and then in the face and there is no sound though he knows there must be hanging on somehow to the door handle being dragged on the ground dragged back on the rough parking lot by the car and a searing rush of hatred shoots through him bastard shiteater left hand finding the gun as the car slows to shift forward shooting blind, blind, squeezing the gun empty over his head into the door the open window the car stopping, the horn. Complaining. Shouting to the ones in the units, to the one with the bad skin. The horn. Blas lets go of the door handle and lies on his back staring at the darkening sky. The lights of airplanes cross above him. Through the horn he hears doors slamming and cars revving to life, rats deserting, and it's hard to breathe. Hard to breathe. It's cold on the parking lot blacktop. He manages to roll and prop himself against the car door and the others are gunning out past him and a woman screaming curses at her deserting trick and the horn, wailing like a baby that won't pacified. Blas tries to open the door but his right hand is fucked up and there is a gun in the left so he has to concentrate, think, put the gun on the vinyl roof and pull the door open with the left. The man is slumped forward against the steering wheel with a seeping hole where his eye was and Blas yanks him out to stop the horn, finally, the gun in the man's left hand clattering to the pavement and he hangs half out of the car held by the seat belt. A skull tattoo on the hand. Think. So hard when it's so hard to breathe. Blas pushes himself in, lying across the man's lap, coughing up a throatful of something hot and frothy and it's blood on the velour interior and the seatbelt comes loose. Blas leans away and when the man falls out his foot comes off the brake and the car idles forward, pulling Blas along till he can lunge and push the stick to neutral, the door buzzing now that the seat belt is unfastened and the man still wedged partly in the door Blas kicking the last of him out and crawling behind the wheel. Something. Think. Blas gropes for his own gun on the roof, reaching up through the window, finds it. The lights are off in the office, the one with the bad skin on the floor, on the phone. No matter. Concentrate. It's cold, a cold wind blowing and so hard to breathe. Blas puts the car into gear, back tire bumping over some part of the man as he rolls out onto LeJeune and swings north into a flock of complaining horns.

The safe house is not far, straight up into Hialeah. They'll take care of everything. He should have sent somebody else for this Nuñez, one of the hungry ones, but it was family. A man takes care of family on his own. It's so hard to see.

There are glass chips everywhere from the windshield and it's hard to see out the bullet-cracked section and it's hard to breathe. The steering wheel is sticky with blood, somebody's blood. The rearview mirror is off tilt and Blas can see himself. The right side of his face is discolored and swollen with a small blue hole where his cheekbone should be and every time he breathes there is a wet sucking sound from under his collarbone and the icy wind blowing. A traffic light snaps red in front and he mashes the pedal through more horns, screaming at him that Hialeah is a long way off. Estoy jodido. Estoy totalmente jodido. He can't breathe through his nose and the other way hurts it's like sucking it through a wet sheet he fucking had it in his left hand the whole time, skull hand, why didn't they tell him, why don't they ever tell you what you need and there's a ringing loud and constant not the car warning him about the belt but him, Blas, the whole side of his head ringing and how do I get over out of this fucking exit only puta madre I'm in the fucking airport. Fucking Miami.

More horns as he slows. Coño. Think. Concentrate. Signs appear with parking information, the names of airlines. Think. So hard to see, to breathe, the icy wind. He swings the car to the shoulder, waits for an opening, then makes a sudden wide U across the ramp something smacking hard against the rear fender sending him skidding into a ditch on the far side, facing the wrong way toward the traffic moving into the airport. The wheels spin as he guns the engine. The icy wind. Coño. The fucking air-conditioning. Fucking Miami. He pounds the switches with his broken hand till the wind stops. The lights coming at him burst apart in patterns as they hit the shattered glass. Still so cold. So hard to breathe. The wheels spin.

The car shakes as a jet tears into the night sky.

FORTY

"IF WE KEEP GOING this way we hit Africa," says Tío Felix. "Las Canarias, cerca de la costa de Marruecos."

It is a calm night, clear, with more than a half moon. No lights anywhere now but their own. Marta hears the engine laboring, the thud of hull against each swell sending a fine spray across her face, but in the vast darkness it's hard to believe they are getting anywhere. Padre Martín sits back in the fighting chair, swiveling left and right, with a smile she's never seen before on his face.

"You go straight through Norris Cut," says her uncle, "and head east. Then the Coast Guards are not so interested in you. Is better to get away from the Keys before you turn south."

"How much time does it add?"

"Poco. Good weather like this, una hora más en cada dirección."

Tío Felix is smiling too, the smile he gets when he is out on his boat and the sky is clear and the swells are low and the engine is running smooth. He pulls back on the throttle and turns the wheel to the right.

"Sud-sudoeste ahora," he says. "Hacia la isla."

"We go around the western tip?"

"If we were going all the way. A menudo hace más calma en la otra dirección, entre Cuba y Haití, pero añade seis u ocho horas más al viaje. This way we get there almost the same time tomorrow night. If we were going all the way."

"Hay bastante gasolina?"

"Enough to get there. To get back we have to refuel in the Caymans."

Marta sits on the bench seat behind him. The rifle is loaded, ready, but she won't do that. She won't have to.

"I'm glad Nuñez doesn't come tonight," says Tío Felix. "No tengo confianza en él."

"Ni yo tampoco. We don't need him."

"Maybe Blas will take his place, like you said."

"Blas isn't coming, Tío. You know that."

He turns to look at her, not smiling now. "Qué dices?"

"We're not turning back tonight. Esta es la misión."

She gets up to stand next to him, looking over the bow into the dark ocean. She feels him struggling, emotions breaking forward, sliding back. He has always been this way, her Tío Felix, not the strong constant flood of her father or her brother Blas, but a rider on the tide, giving in to the current then fighting it, then giving in again.

"Solamente nosotros tres?"

"Just the three of us, Tío. You'll have to stay with the boat while we go ashore. Lo siento."

It's good that they are already pointed south. It will take more will for him to turn around now.

"Eres un hombre, Tío. Hombre de nuestra familia. And this is your boat." She can't get him to look in her eyes. "So it's up to you—yes or no?"

Tío Felix looks out into the black mouth of the night, lost in indecision. Marta brushes him with her arm as she reaches across his body to take hold of the throttle.

"Can we go any faster?" she asks.

FORTY-ONE

RIVKIN WANTS THE CONVERTIBLE. Not with the blood and the windshield gone and the dent in the rear of course, or the Playboy bunny head hanging from the mirror and the license plate saying PELIGRO but the car is a classic, a white '57 T-Bird, the year before they bloated into tanks. Pull out the velour, put something like the original upholstery back in, little work on the body, replace the chrome and it's a work of art. If this guy kicks and it comes up at the deadbeat and perpetrator auction, who knows?

The patrolmen have flares out and are moving the airport traffic past in a single lane. Ochoa has bagged the weapon and the contents of the glove compartment. Rivkin climbs up the side of the ditch to find Duckworth sitting on the hood of a patrol car, the flasher strobing blue on his face.

"Registration was in the box, Chief. Got a Guillermo Nuñez, motel address on LeJeune."

Duckworth nods toward the ambulance, the tail still open, the view inside blocked by men in white. "That's not Nuñez."

"They find something on him?"

"Nuñez got whacked in the parking lot at the Cockpit an hour ago. Just came over the radio."

"The Cockpit. Christ, what a place to die." Rivkin recalls the OD they pulled out of one of the units a year ago. Fake red velvet wallpaper. He shudders. "Who's this, then?"

Duckworth slides off the hood and starts across to the ambulance. "Blas de la Pena," he says.

The man is not the right shade. One side of his face is lead-colored while the rest is too white, a waxy, fragile white like skin kept under a plaster cast for months. There is a tube leading into his neck above his sternum hooked to an oxygen regulator and his eyes seem startled and unfocused. Duckworth squeezes in next to the paramedic fixing the blood bottle over his head.

"Blas," says Duckworth, leaning down close to call into the man's ear. "Long time no see."

Rivkin watches as the paramedic unclamps the tube from the bottle and bright red blood falls into the man's arm. Somebody with a sense of drama figured that one out. What if it was clear, or yellowish like urine? Life would be that much duller. But this—red blood, white uniforms—it concentrates everything, very stark, very primal. Very Caribbean. You want a bit of that for your moment on the edge.

"So what's the story, Blas? What happened?"

"Qué pasó?" echoes Rivkin.

The look from Duckworth. He's so touchy lately. "He speaks English."

"He might be in shock, Chief." Rivkin turns back to the wounded man. "Cuál es la historia? Drogas? La guerra contra los colombianos?"

"Is Justo Camejo in on this?" says Duckworth.

"Podemos ganar la revancha para usted," says Rivkin. "Cuál es su conexión con Nuñez?"

The man turns his face away from them.

"Looks like it all caught up to you at once, buddy," says Duckworth. "Am I right?"

The man turns his head back and seems to drift into focus then, looking up at Duckworth with a sneer.

"Pendejos," he says. "Nunca entenderán."

"What's that?"

"We'll never understand," says Rivkin.

"I thought you spoke it."

"No, that's what he said. He said, 'You'll never understand.' "

Duckworth leans down and gives the man a reassuring squeeze on the arm. "You got that one right, buddy," he says. "You hit that sucker on the *head*."

FORTY-TWO

ON HER DAYS OFF she likes to do it in the morning.

Rufo climbs the outside stairs to the second-floor balcony, wondering how he is going to work this. A little boy is rumbling back and forth on a plastic Big Wheels tricycle. Damp laundry hangs over the rail. There is a strong cooking smell, salt cod maybe, and reggae music playing behind one of the doors. He knocks on number five.

"Está abierta," she calls.

Water is running and he hears her singing something. He loves being in her apartment. He loves just the idea of it—something separate from himself, intimate, that he is allowed to enter. He steps carefully inside. Luz is not a tidy woman. There are magazines on the floor, on the little couch, on the table by the kitchenette, magazines open to where she left off reading, piles of pictures torn ragged from their pages. There are clothes, clean clothes considered and rejected in the way he has seen her do deciding what to wear, pulling something on and walking around in it a few minutes before deciding no and peeling it off. Rufo wanders around the room, picking up the clothes, feeling them, thinking about the way she looks in them. There are records and tapes littering the floor around her stereo. The place is never dirty, no food or dishes left out, but there is no mistaking that she lives here. Luz. He likes to think of her alone in here, singing to herself the way she does, doing things, maybe sometimes thinking of him. He checks his watch.

The men are meeting at noon and he should make a report. There will only be time to ask a few things about the woman and then go.

But on her days off Luz likes to do it in the morning. She's never said so, but that's the way it has worked out every time before. Rufo sits on the couch and there is a scent of her. He knows it's weak of him. Thinking about her, planning ways to be with her. Twenty minutes. The woman, Marta, hasn't been at work, hasn't been around her mother's place, no answer on the phone at her apartment. He's let it slip away. The men give him something to do and he lets it slip away.

Rufo shifts to free the lump caught under him on the couch and finds the diary.

Warped with water damage, the pages stained. He flips quickly to the back. There is fresh writing on the last occupied page.

Mi querida Luz—it begins.

Rufo has time only to glance across the shapes before he hears her and has to toss it aside. Luz steps in drying her hair with a towel, wearing shorts and a T-shirt.

"You came," she says, and smiles.

It's so fucking crazy. Seeing this woman with the one he was following and seeing her again and introducing himself and now this. It's like a drug. He knows it's weak of him but it's like a drug and that smile, for him, she's really pleased he came over and he sees himself grinning like a fucking idiot. Brujería. One of the guys at work who knows of her but doesn't know her well says she's supposed to be a witch but where are the candles, the chicken blood, all that? Just the smile and the way her skin smells, damp and warm from the shower, as she leans down to kiss him hello.

"I thought maybe you were Marta."

"She's coming over?"

"She knocks. We work together years now, talk every day, como hermanas, no? Still, when she stays here she knocks like a stranger. Cada vez."

"She's staying here?"

Luz tosses the towel onto a chair across the room. Her hair glistens, dark and curly. Sometimes when he gets his fingers in her hair it is hard to get them out. Like the way she wraps her legs around you, clutching—

Twenty minutes. Twenty minutes and he's gone. There must be some way to get a better look at that diary.

"She came over a couple nights ago," says Luz. "She didn't

come in last night, though. Maybe she went back to her own place."

It's her diary. Marta's. He can see it by the arm of the couch.

"Or maybe she found herself some guy," says Luz and sits in his lap. "Finalmente."

Her color against his isn't the surprise it was at first. Now it's only Luz, *her* color, one of the parts of her that he thinks is so beautiful. Her mouth. He kisses her, Luz sitting on his lap, and he knows it's weak of him but sometimes he thinks about her mouth and just that makes him hard. Crazy. Thinking about her, about her mouth, looking at other women on the street and only able to compare them to her, coming back to her, her skin, her smile, her mouth, the only one he wants. Like a drug.

"Why was she staying here?"

Luz gets up and puts a tape on. Celia Cruz. "Don't worry," says Luz. "If she comes back she'll knock first."

She pulls him to his feet and puts her arms around him and starts to move. It isn't a game with her, a way to something else. He's seen her do it on her own, swaying her hips to the music and half singing along and since he's here she might as well have a partner. Her hips seem to pull him close, though hips can't really do that. Brujería.

"You're taking me dancing tonight," she says.

"I am?"

"Sí. I know this for a fact."

"Y a dónde?"

"No sé exactemente. Pero será un club muy elegante, muy costoso."

She is teasing him a little, her arm around his neck, getting him to move with her.

"I wonder sometimes how you know these things."

"It's because you are so crazy about me," she says. "I can feel it here."

She puts her hand on his chest, inside his shirt, and leaves it there, leaning her head on his shoulder and closing her eyes and swaying, flowing with the music. Rufo sneaks a glance at his watch.

"You have three days off now?"

"Two. I'm covering one for Marta."

"She isn't back to work?"

"Not since her father died. It's hard, going back to where it happened."

"I don't see how you can work there at all. Viejos, cadáveres—"

She looks up at him. "You will be there one day, chico. Todos terminarán allá un día."

"Not me."

She smiles and hugs him, then steps away, looking at him the way she does when it seems she's just met him. Like she doesn't trust him. Not that she should.

The handwriting at the back of the diary was sharp, all hard angles and desperate strokes.

"I'm worried about you," says Luz. "Sometimes I think you're something different, something special. And then sometimes you're just another guy, como todos los otros."

Rufo doesn't like to think about all the others. Luz is not so young, never married, and he can't imagine her being too long without a man. He tries to make it dead in his mind, as if she didn't exist until the night he found her.

"You don't know me that well yet," he says.

"Maybe."

"There are things that a man has to do—"

"Ay de mí!"

"—that he has to do to feel right about himself. Maybe it's different with women."

"Maybe."

"I am not always going to work in a warehouse."

"Nobody says you have to—"

"I am going to do things."

"¿Cómo?"

"No puedes entender."

"Try me."

"I am going back to Cuba."

He has never said it out loud to her before, has never talked about any of it.

"Rufo, you can't go *back* to a place you never been."

"Bueno. But I am going there and I am going to be one of those who charges things."

She smiles, a sad, pitying kind of smile.

"You Americans," she says.

He knows she is half teasing but it always hurts him. "Eres

cubano," his father always said to him as he was growing up. "Nunca lo olvides." His parents came north in the late forties and settled and never quite made it back and then there was the Revolution and the relatives pouring in and the stories and at first it was awful, the jokes at school from the anglo kids who had gotten used to him but now were swamped by this new bunch who hung together and had thick accents and had run away. On the other side was his father who had never become a citizen and the uncles and their friends each with a different story and the games with the new kids playing guerrillas, playing firing squad with clumps of dirt at the site where the new apartments were going up and it began to burn in him, *soy cubano, soy cubano,* the Revolution looming as the one great evil in the world, a personal shame that had to be put to rest. "You refugees," the anglo teachers said, "you exiles," and soon Rufo was including himself though it was not a wholly honorable thing to be, it was the losing side. And Americans, he knew, could have no respect for a loser.

"Soy cubano," he says to Luz.

"Es cierto," she says and smiles and kisses him in a nice way. "When you go down there you will send me lots of postcards and put all the Communists in jail and be at the head of big marches with thousands of people cheering. You will have a big house in La Habana and go to the Hotel Nacional for lunch every day and everyone will point and say, 'Mira, ese es el gran Rufo, héroe del nuevo régimen.' But one day something will be wrong. Something will be missing. And you will think Oh how I long for that Luz, that woman I left behind a los Estados and sent her only cheesy postcards. Why did I ever leave her for this fucking hot sun and these mosquitos and these thousands of noisy cubanos when I could have had all that back in Miami and her as well? But it will be too late, she will be married to some norteamericano, some rico with a very big boat like Bebe Rebozo. It tears my heart to think of this."

He knows it is weak of him but he is laughing and she is back dancing with him again, hips pulling at him, and there is something familiar about it, like something he lost but never missed before.

"It tears my heart," she says. "Because he will be with some hembra dura, some reformed Communist woman with big muscles who secretly still longs to be the bride of Fidel and makes soup from the feet of chickens, every night. He will come home and there will be a pot stewing with the feet of chickens, dozens of them, sticking up from it with their little toes bent and he will think of his Luz, cruising somewhere beautiful on a boat the size of an apartment building."

Celia Cruz is singing faster now but they are moving in the same rhythm as before. He only had time to glance at the end of the writing in the diary.

"Sí que tú eres cubano," says Luz, softer now. "I can feel it here." She does something with her hips and they are glued to his, moving together with the underbeat of the music and the other is starting, his hands sliding down her back to hold her cheeks, feeling them move, kissing her, deep, her mouth. Her mouth. He knows it is weak of him but lately he feels like she is what has been missing all along, Luz, and that if he can make her really his, all the way, that will be the victory he's been longing for.

"I love your mouth," he says, and she smiles and he knows it's because he's never said that out loud to her, never said any of the bullshit that usually goes down and he means it now and it gives him a little shiver of fear.

"It loves you," she says and bites him softly on the shoulder.

Maybe if he just stops going the men will forget about him. They pay almost no attention to him now. He knows they are not to be taken lightly, that they are men of action. But maybe—

"Do you have to go back to work?" she asks and gives him a hot, licking kiss above his collarbone meaning no, you better not have to.

He only had time to glance at the writing on the last page. The final word, written in sharp curves and desperate strokes, was *sword*.

"There's something I have to do," he hears himself say. He wonders vaguely what his watch is up to as she kisses him on the mouth again, biting his lip a little. He has never seen a man die. Luz has, dozens of times at her job, and she knows things, can tell you things she senses about people just from talking with them, and she's funny when she wants to be and when she fights it's out in the open, not moody or underhanded and her eyes, her eyes, her eyes ask him to be good to her but they won't beg, she has her own self like this place that is apart from him and intimate but she'll let him in if he wants.

"You can do it later," she says, almost a question. "Can't you?" It isn't true. The men are coming together at noon and they won't be there later. The men have given him a job to do. But his hands are caught under her T-shirt now, he can't get them free, his hands on her breasts which are alive with her, the blood up in them the way it does when she's excited and he is lost, lost.

"No hay de qué," he says, closing his eyes, breathing her warmth like a drowning man surrendering to water. "It can wait."

FORTY-THREE

Noon. A BOAT in the ocean. Tiny as a single bird in the unbroken sky.

FORTY-FOUR

➤ "IF SOMETHING WAS wrong with Jesús they would tell you," says Diosdado.

"They stayed behind their desks," says the old man.

"Esa es su ocupación, sentando en los bufetes. There is nothing bad about it."

"They had to look his name up on a list."

"Hay muchos soldados en Africa. Muchos nombres."

"They said there was no information."

"If something was wrong they would tell you," says Diosdado. "Te juro."

"I had a dream," says the old man.

The boy walks in front, rifle held away from his body, alert. He takes several steps, then pauses, listening, breathing deeply through his nose. He can tell how far they are from the ocean.

"You have to forget about that. Dreams are not real."

"It has been such a long time," says Salvador.

"The news from Angola is very good," Diosdado tells him. "If you want I can read to you from the newspapers."

"I have a feeling," says the old man. "I had a dream."

They step off the road, ducking through marabú till they find the path through the trees. The old man carries his rifle like a stick of firewood. Several times the boy has to pause, listening, to let Salvador catch up.

"Why would they lie to you?"

"If the war is going badly," says Salvador, "if many boys are killed, they don't like people to know. I don't blame them for this.

But I have only one son, el único que sobrevivió, and I have to know."

They are quiet again, Diosdado stalking, sensing the night, the old man wandering behind. They reach the second road and step out into the open. It is a clear night, half a moon guiding their way.

"If it is the worst I hope they will not leave him there."

"I think they bring the bodies back." Saying it makes the boy feel uneasy.

"No deben abandonar a mi hijo en Africa."

"Nada ha pasado," says Diosdado, weary of the conversation, which has not changed for a week since Salvador went to the authorities. "Cuando hay un muerto hacen una procesión, al muerto se le honra como héroe de la revolución."

"We have enough heroes in Cuba," says the old man. "They are like mosquitos, you can't take a walk without running into a swarm of them."

"Nothing has happened, viejo. To worry is useless."

They have come to the haunted place, the place of the lost battalion. As always Diosdado thinks he smells sulfur in the air. Salvador stops in the middle of the road. Diosdado waits, then moves back to stand by him.

"I can only hope he was not captured by Africans," says Salvador.

"Viejo, there is nothing you can do."

"When the Spaniard finally captured the great chief Hatuey," says the old man, "he was given a choice. 'If you choose to remain a pagan we will burn you at the stake,' they told him. 'You will have a slow and terrible death. But if you agree to be baptized, then, my son, we will give you a swift release at the point of a sword and you will rise directly to Heaven.'

" 'If I go to the Christian heaven, will there be white men there?' he asked.

" 'Of course,' said the Spaniard.

" 'Then I choose to be burned.' "

Diosdado listens to the night. A light breeze with a nip of smoldering charcoal in it. He can hear waves now. He puts his hand reassuringly on the old man's shoulder.

"The Africans are not savages anymore," he says. "They have automatic weapons."

They continue down the road. The barrel of the old man's gun nearly touches the ground.

"In the dream I am a negrero," he says. "We are a tribe ourselves, hunting other tribes to take as slaves, only we are cubanos in the jungles of Africa. Cubanos de todos colores, negro, blanco, moreno, amarillo. We are traveling down a river on a raft, chasing a small band. One of our men is sick with fever and we have to leave him on the bank to die. At another place we pass under a branch hanging across the water. There is a wasps' nest on the branch, weighing it down low toward the water, and as we pass the wasps, huge yellow-and-black insects, shoot out from the nest and all collect on the head of one man, a man who is completely bald sitting in front of me on the raft. He is screaming and waving his arms and his head looks like a round yellow flower, alive with wasps, then they lift away and swarm back into their nest. The man's head looks like a strange fruit then, red and puckering, and he is dead. We put him in the water and see crocodiles slide off the bank to eat him."

"Es un sueño extraño," says Diosdado.

"That is only the beginning. We get off the raft and we cut through jungle. We follow a trail of blood on the leaves, the blood of the band we are following. We catch up with them in a small village, a village of thatched huts. The people who live there all run away as we approach, leaving our band in one hut, too exhausted to keep going. We surround the hut and set fire to it, calling for them to give up. They all come out but one man, who stays inside as the hut burns to the ground. It is a long time before he starts to scream. It smells like pork roasting."

The old man is silent for a moment, staring down the road as if for a sign. He shakes his head and speaks again.

"We put the others in chains, chains around their necks, around their wrists. We march them back through the jungle. We don't see their faces. In the dream they are so ashamed to be slaves that they keep their faces turned away from us.

" 'Vamos a Cuba,' we tell them, 'la isla más linda del mundo.' They don't care where they're going or how beautiful it is. They keep their faces hidden. The chains are heavy and their bodies are slick with sweat as we cut through the jungle. I have a bad feeling about these men. They are slaves, but they are all colors, just like us, como los cubanos. Black, white, brown, yellow, everything in between. The jungle cuts us all. We are all exhausted. When we can hear the river the man in the lead breaks away, his chains making horrible noises as he crashes through the thick vines. When we get to the river we see his head sticking above the water in the deepest part. The current is much too strong for a man in chains to swim across. We can't quite see his face. The man begins to sing, something in African, and the other slaves answer him, singing, and then his head goes under and crocodiles slide from the bank.

"I sit on the ground and I feel very bad. Somehow I know, the way you know things in dreams without seeing or hearing them, that the man in the river and the man who burned in the hut were both my son. My Jesús."

"Both of them?"

"Los dos. Though I never saw the faces I am sure."

Diosdado holds his rifle tight to his body. Something is wrong with this night. "Es solamente un sueño," he says. "Los sueños no son la verdad."

"I have a feeling," says the old man.

They have come to the place where the old man always sings.

"Salvador," says Diosdado, "sing me the one about the mermaid. The funny one."

The old man shakes his head. "Tengo miedo de que está perdido, mi Jesús. Está perdido para siempre."

> *Una noche, luna llena,*
> *Oí la voz de la Sirena—*

sings Diosdado, trying to cheer his friend up—

> *Reposando en su lado*
> *Con su olor de pescado—*

In the distance Roa's dog begins to bark.

FORTY-FIVE

➤ TÍO FELIX THINKS about the turtles.

As soon as the launch disappeared into the darkness he began to worry, began to think about how bad an idea all this was, and so now he concentrates on the turtles.

There are two of them, giant green sea turtles, a male and a female. They swim in calm, warm waters, soaring over coral, one never losing sight of the other. Now and then they bump shells, lightly. They have been swimming in the waters since before there were politics. Columbus sailed over their heads. They are very wise. At night they lie on the beach and there is nothing to hurt them. They make sea-turtle love, which is warm and weighty and very slow. They leave babies in the sand.

Tío Felix lets the *Nidia* drift. The word is that gas is scarce and the patrol boats can't keep up if you give them a good run. The priest has the flare gun if there is trouble. Felix can't see the island but he can sense it out there, can smell it.

The turtles leave babies in the sand and swim away. The babies will hatch on their own. When you have lived for centuries you know that you can't protect them.

Maybe it will be easy. They'll go in, do what they think they have to, come back. The other times, the other missions, he never had to wait. Drop the men off and leave. None of them came back, only the word that they'd been shot or captured. He quit when he started to feel like an executioner. A few times he was close enough to see the island, but never step ashore. Never touch ground.

Tío Felix dreams of giant sea turtles soaring in warm seas as the *Nidia* drifts, rocking him gently.

FORTY-SIX

THEY ARE JUST OFF the beach when they hear the singing. They crouch in the low bushes at the edge of the sand, listening, then the woman starts ahead. A dog is barking. The woman carries a hunting rifle and the priest has an ancient pistol in his hand. The beach looks like a resort in the off season. Empty cabanas, brightly painted, no litter. Tiny crabs scatter in front of them on the sand. They try to angle away from the voice.

There is half a moon out and it isn't hard to find the pressed dirt road. The priest has to hurry to keep up with the woman. He is cut on the back of his arm, raked by thorns as he passes into the woods. The priest carries a Styrofoam cooler by its plastic handle.

The woman steps off the road and moves up a path through the trees for several yards and then stops. The singing is closer. The dog is still barking. The woman and the priest crouch again, waiting, hoping it will pass. They smell charcoal burning. The singing comes closer still, moving up the path toward them.

Something about a mermaid.

They hold their breath when it stops and there are only footsteps. The footsteps stop.

"Quién es?" calls a voice, older than the one that was singing.

The woman hugs the rifle, taut and heavy in her arms, her finger curled, the power held back, muscles clenched at her spine. Everything has been leading to this, pointing to this.

Para mi padre, Scipio de la Pena—

She knew the air would be like this, thick and sweet—

Para mi hermano Blas, héroe del pueblo cubano—

She feels the host of God's avenging angels, straining beneath her finger—

Para mi hermano Ambrosio, mártir de la sagrada lucha—

She feels a twinge, a moment of panic, cold and black, a moment balancing, as if she could lose everything right now, her will, her honor, her soul, balancing, then pulls it back—

Pulls it back.

The priest drops the cooler when the shot explodes next to him. He drops the ancient pistol when the answering shot rips through the branches by his head. Something big and dark flaps away behind him.

Then the woman is gone and there is an old man with a rifle asking the priest who he is and a boy sitting on the ground holding his stomach, blood coming through his fingers.

"Quién eres?" says the old man. "Quién eres?"

"Soy un cura," says the priest, and kneels by the boy.

"Qué pasó?" says the boy.

The priest begins to touch the boy on various parts of the face with his fingertips. "In nomine Patris et Filii et Spiritus Sancti," he begins, "extinguatur in te omnis virtus diaboli per impositionem manuum nostarum—"

The priest understands now why he was meant to be here. It was all pointing to this. He wishes he had oil.

"Qué pasó?" says the boy, weakly.

Only sensation now. Branches. Black water. Air thick and sweet like something about to die. The sound of her own ragged gasp.

At the edge of the great swamp the woman is running, breathless, lost on the dark island.